WEAPONS *of* REMORSE

WEAPONS of REMORSE

CHEVRON ROSS

This book is a work of fiction. Any references to historical events, real people, or real places are used fictitiously. Other names, characters, places, and events are products of the author's imagination, and any resemblance to actual events or organizations or places or persons, living or dead, is entirely coincidental.

Biblical quotations from *The Daily Bible,* Copyright © 1984 by Harvest House Publishers,

Library of Congress catalog number 83-83372. ISBN 978-0-7369-4431-1

The quote from Shira Maguen in Chapter Four was taken from Maggie Puniewska's article, "Healing a Wounded Sense of Morality," *The Atlantic,* July 3, 2015

"Still," Copyright © 2002 Reuben Morgan/Hillsong Publishing (ASCAP)

Green Lantern oath Copyright © by DC Comics

"The Sing," by Joe Raposo, Copyright © by Standard Music Ltd

Sandy Hook quotations from https://www.findagrave.com/virtual-cemetery/345407

ISBN 9-781692-814014

Book design: Authorsupport.com

AUTHOR NOTE

Chevron Ross is a pseudonym for this novel's typist.
Its author is God, the author of love and salvation.

The men seized Jesus and arrested him. When Jesus' followers saw what was going to happen, they said, "Lord, should we strike with our swords?" Then Simon Peter, who had a sword, drew it and struck the high priest's servant, cutting off his right ear. (The servant's name was Malchus.) "Put your sword back in its place," Jesus said to him, "for all who draw the sword will die by the sword. Do you think I cannot call on my Father, and he will at once put at my disposal more than twelve legions of angels? But how then would the Scriptures be fulfilled that say it must happen in this way? No more of this!" And he touched the man's ear and healed him.

Matthew 26:50-54

Mark 14:46, 47

Luke 22:49-51

John 18:10, 11

CNN News crawl, October 30, 9:45 a.m.

Police are converging on the scene of a school shooting in Huntington, West Virginia. Witnesses fleeing the building describe it as "another Sandy Hook." More to follow …

CHAPTER 1

"How do you sleep at night?"

Everyone who worked for Armed and Ready was armed. Few were ready, though. Most were clerical staffers who knew less about guns than their subscribers. But after open carry became a Texas law, Vern Saginaw made it a job requirement. He raided the company's marketing fund to outfit his employees with pistols and shoulder holsters.

Hank Phillips objected to the rule, but Vern was adamant: "We've got to practice what we preach." He even gift-wrapped and proudly presented Hank with a vintage Colt .45, including an expensive leather hip holster. Unwilling to hurt the boss's feelings, Hank yielded.

The gun made his life awkward. People on the street eyed him warily. Passing cops leaped from their patrol cars, demanding to see his permit. "Oh, it's you, Mr. Phillips," they apologized. It seemed the only Texans taking advantage of open carry were A&R employees.

Today, he entered his office to find his assistant packing a .38. "Good morning, Hank. Here's the draft of Vern's speech."

"Thanks, Warren." He plopped into his chair and put four candy bars on the desk. "Happy Halloween tomorrow. The Baby Ruths are for your kids. The Snickers are for you and Brenda."

"Hey, my favorite! Thanks." Warren sat and began unwrapping his. "You got two more speaking invitations. Want me to book them for you?"

"Who are they?"

"Sharpshooters of America and Christians in Unity."

"Now there's a combination. Yeah, check my calendar and see what you can do."

Warren bit into his candy. "So what do you think about Tischner?"

Hank rolled his eyes. "I've been trying not to."

"Did Vern consult you before the announcement? Or is it none of my business?"

"You know Vern. He doesn't consult. He decides." He frowned at the speech. "Warren, did you read this?"

"Just glanced at it. Why?"

Hank sighed and dialed Vern's number.

"Good morning Sarge, how's it going?"

"Vern, you know I'm not a Marine anymore. Can't you make it plain old Hank?"

"Sorry, it's habit. You'll always be Sergeant Phillips to me. Did you read the new draft?"

"That's why I'm calling. Vern, we've talked about this before. You're only making both our jobs harder."

"Boy, are you cranky this morning! What's the matter?"

"Every time you go on a tirade, you get people all stirred up and they start taking sides again. Can't you just restate our official position and leave it at that?"

"Now you sound like a politician. How'd you win that medal, anyway – love the Taliban to death?"

Hank closed his eyes and said nothing.

"Look, we're in a war here, boy! The anti-gun brigade never lets up. Now let's have no more of this. I want you to check that draft for dates and stats before I go onstage tonight."

"All right, I'll send you the revisions in an hour or so. But Vern, please think about what I've said. I've only got your interests at heart."

"I know that, buddy. Gotta go. Good luck with those veterans tonight." He hung up.

"Want me check it for you?" Warren asked.

"Do you mind? My plate's full today and I've got to polish my own speech."

"That's what I'm here for." He took the manuscript and candy bars to his office.

Hank spared a glance at the traffic outside his window. Without Vern's political influence, Sandstone might have been just another hamlet in central Texas. Thanks to Armed and Ready, Vern's home town had acquired Sandstone University, Pierpont Electronics, Jade Packaging, Boone Medical Center, McCullough Utilities, and numerous other businesses responsible for thousands of jobs and their ripple effects – housing, schools, parks, municipal services, even a respectable arts community. Hank had never dreamed he'd become a big-shot executive. But he'd never dreamed he'd become a killer, either.

The boy was dozing when LaRonda tapped on his door. "Hmm?" He stirred slowly, opened bleary eyes. The room spun. "Uh ... who are you?"

"I'm Officer Cage. Are you feeling okay?"

He rubbed his eyes. "I feel terrible. Where am I?"

"Didn't the doctor tell you anything?"

He looked around at the tubes and machines plugged into him. "I'm in the hospital? What happened?"

She pulled up a chair. "You don't remember driving like a maniac? Stumbling out of the car, waving a gun? I had to shoot you. How's your leg?"

The boy pushed the bedsheet aside and examined his bandaged thigh. "You shot me?"

"Yeah, I did."

"I had a gun?" His eyes widened. "I don't have a gun! I've never fired a gun! What is all this? How'd I get here?"

"Hey, take it easy."

"What's going on? Where's Sandy and ... oh."

"Sandy. That was the girl in the back seat."

"Yeah ... yeah, Sandy. Where is she? Where's Mitch?"

"They're in the juvenile detention tank. Where you'd be if you weren't injured."

The boy stared at her, bewildered. "I don't remember any of this!"

"What's the last thing you do remember?"

He massaged his temples. "I was out walking after school and Mitch offered me a lift. And ..."

"What?"

"I remember now. They gave me a drink. Sandy said it'd make me feel better. I guess she saw my face at school." He fingered a large purple bruise on his cheek.

"Want to tell me your name? The paperwork around here calls you No Name Juvenile."

He gasped. "Oh God, my dad! When he hears about this ..." He wept into his hands.

"Okay, okay. Let's take it slow. Give yourself some time." She fetched him a tissue from the bedside table. "Does your leg hurt?"

"No, it's my head that's ... wow!" He gripped it again. "I must have drunk the whole bottle."

"It'll probably start to hurt after the anesthetic wears off."

The hangover gave way to fear. "Are you here to arrest me? Am I going to jail?"

"I'm here to make sure you don't get in any deeper. Tell me about the gun."

"I don't remember it. I guess it was Mitch's. At some point he asked me to drive and got in the back with Sandy." He gaped at her. "Did I shoot at you?"

"You came close."

He started crying again. "I'm sorry! I'm so sorry! I've never done anything like this."

"Why don't you tell me your name now?"

He hesitated. "It's Gil. Gilbert Starnes. But please, please don't tell my dad!"

"Gil, how did you get the bruises on your face?"

The boy stared silently at his lap.

"Did you get into a fight at school?" No response.

"Did your father do this to you?" He nodded.

"Do you want to tell me about it?" He shook his head slowly.

"All right, that's okay. But Gil, listen to me. You're in trouble. You're charged with speeding, evading arrest, drunk driving, and threatening a police officer with a firearm. Those are serious charges. You're going to need some legal help. Will your parents handle it for you?"

"When my dad finds out?" He rolled away from her.

"What about your mom?"

"They're divorced. I don't know where she is."

She placed a hand on his shoulder. "Gil, I'm going to file a report with Child Protective Services. They'll probably come see you today. They'll arrange for a lawyer and make sure you're safe."

"You mean safe from my dad," he muttered.

"Yeah."

"What are you going to do about the gun and all?"

"We'll let the judge worry about that. When your hearing comes up, I'll be there to testify, and I'll make sure he understands what you've been going through. In the meantime, let the medical staff take care of you."

He grimaced as he tried to sit up. "I think the painkiller's starting to wear off."

"Okay, I'll tell them on my way out. And Gil?"

"Yeah?"

"While you're in here mending, think about finding yourself some better friends."

He smiled. "I'll do that. Thank you, officer."

She patted his face. "It's LaRonda to you."

Shelley Phillips and Patti Shore were up to their elbows in pumpkin surgery when the preacher walked by. "Yuck! I'd forgotten how messy those things are. How many more do you have?"

"Six more in the back of my van," Shelley replied. "Hey John, would you mind bringing them in? They're kind of heavy."

"That depends. Is there a pumpkin pie in my future?"

"No, but there's some zucchini bread on the coffee table."

"That'll do." He wandered toward the parking lot.

"Zucchini bread," Patti reflected. "Carrot cake. Spinach muffins. How do you suppose people come up with ideas like that? Making desserts out of vegetables?"

"Maybe they ran out of fruit. Zucchini was all they had left."

"What if all they had was turnips or cabbage?"

"Actually, I think there are recipes for those, too."

"Turnip bread? You must be joking!"

John bumped and backed his way through the door, a large pumpkin dangling by the stem from each hand. "Shelley, 'heavy' doesn't do justice to these things," he panted.

"Need any help?"

"No, I've got it. You two have the hard part." He hoisted them onto the orange-spattered table and headed for the door again.

"I guess we should have bought plastic ones and saved ourselves the mess," Patti said.

"No, this is fun! Like making mud pies. Makes me feel like a kid again."

"Makes me feel like a mortician."

The minister struggled through the door with his second load. "Just set them on the floor, John. We don't have room up here anyway."

"You talked me into it. Whew! Why didn't you get plastic ones?"

The women looked at each other and burst out laughing. "What's so funny?"

"Sorry, John. We already settled the plastic issue. Take a break. Get your snack and come sit with us."

Late October sunlight filtered through the trees surrounding the church, throwing leaf patterns onto the work table. John cleared a space for his plate and coffee cup in the pumpkin clutter. "These look great. Are you going to put candles in them?"

"You bet," Shelley said.

"I can hardly wait for the party Thursday night. Halloween was always my favorite time when I was a kid. Where'd you get the pumpkins?"

"Hank and Bruce helped me gather them last Saturday at Tommy Martin's place. Bruce said it was like hunting Easter eggs."

"Speaking of Hank, how's he doing? I didn't get a chance to visit with him Sunday."

"Doing good." Shelley wiped her hands on a paper towel. "He's speaking at the VFW convention tonight at the Civic Center."

"What about?"

"Guns, what else? They're raising money for a gun rights rally in Austin. Vern's speaking tonight too, in Minneapolis."

"Hank's become quite a celebrity."

"Bruce and I are so proud of him. He's going to be on the cover of *Young Executive* next month."

"Wearing his gun?"

"Yes, well, it comes with the job. At least he doesn't wear it to church."

"Tell John that story you told me," Patti said. "About how you met."

She grinned. "I'd only been waitressing for two weeks when Hank and his mom came into the restaurant. We were so busy I didn't pay him much attention at first. After I brought their order, he kept finding excuses to get me back to their table. 'Oh Miss, may we have some more water? Oh Miss, may I have a fresh napkin?' Then he asked for the dessert menu and made me describe every item on it. I was frantic! I was behind on my other tables and the manager was glaring at me. Finally Hank said, 'I know I'm getting you in trouble. I'll leave you alone if you'll give me your phone number.'"

"And did you?"

"I didn't have much choice. The next day he called me for a date. We were married three months later."

"Nice story."

Patti didn't know the whole story. Hank had returned from Afghanistan with invisible injuries that spilled out on their third date. "I was standing over the bodies," he agonized, "when all the guys surrounded me, whooping it up, pounding my back like I'd scored a touchdown or something. I yelled at them to knock it off and regroup. That just made them admire me even more, like I was so tough that killing six men was all in a day's work."

"Why did you do it?"

He shook his head. "My training. I just ... reacted."

"So now you feel guilty?"

"I'm a Christian, Shelley. Christians aren't supposed to kill."

"Then why did you join the Marines?"

He snorted. "It was a guy thing. 9/11 had just happened. That's all I was thinking about."

Shelley's parents, Charles and Ivy Spurlock, were strident pacifists. She'd never considered war from a soldier's point of view. "I guess even an idealist has to make unpleasant choices."

"Jesus was an idealist. He didn't throw His ideals out the window when things got tough. He gave His life for them."

"Hank, I'm sure God understands."

"Maybe He does. I sure don't."

Shelley had never met anyone so unabashedly religious. Hank spoke as though he and God were best buddies who'd grown up together. Sat side by side in class. Helped each other with homework. Played on the same football team. Shelley's religious training was confined to occasional Sundays at her grandparents' fundamentalist church. Their pastor painted God as a vindictive Zeus, ready to zap her with lightning bolts for the least transgression.

She continued waitressing, with Hank as her best customer. After he proposed, the owner hosted a prenuptial party for the couple and their parents. Marie Phillips embraced Shelley warmly, but Charles Spurlock went on the attack. "Destroying an entire culture to stamp out a few insurgents!" he ranted. "How do you sleep at night?" "I don't, Mr. Spurlock," Hank replied humbly.

"I'm sorry, honey," Shelley apologized afterward. "Mom and Dad are political activists. They get carried away sometimes."

"Don't bother. He didn't say anything I haven't asked myself."

Hank had returned from Afghanistan during the 2008 recession, job-hunting with nothing on his résumé but a high school diploma and his Marine Corps tour. The newlyweds were barely surviving on his reservist pay and Shelley's waitressing.

Then came the Medal of Honor. Hank refused to attend the Presidential ceremony in Washington. Later, after two Marines brought it to their apartment, he stuck it in a drawer and lay awake all night. A VA doctor diagnosed Hank with "moral injury." He second-guessed himself into brooding funks that lasted for hours. His platoon had outnumbered the six guerrillas. Why didn't he just wound them? Or pin them down with gunfire until his men could take them prisoner? It took counseling sessions with VA psychiatrists, hours of prayer, and lots of TLC from Shelley before Hank was able to put Afghanistan, if not behind him, at least in the background.

Vern Saginaw's job offer was a great opportunity for Hank and great PR for Armed and Ready: a war hero for the gun lobby. The young family moved to Sandstone and quickly rose from poverty to prosperity. Hank had a natural talent for public speaking. His forthright aura endeared him to audiences, his popularity rivaling even Vern's. Speaking invitations poured in. Politicians sought him for their reelection campaigns. Only Shelley knew the personal cost of Hank's success.

Now, after eleven years, she congratulated herself for following her heart instead of her father's rhetoric. She had a happy marriage, a bright young son, good friends, nice neighbors, and two homes: her luxurious house and her church.

She hoisted another pumpkin onto the work table. "How's Matt's team doing this year?" she asked Patti.

"They're three and two. He thinks they can make it to State if they beat San Angelo."

"Bruce wants to play quarterback for him when he's old enough."

"Good. I hope he doesn't mind getting yelled at."

The preacher gulped the last of his coffee. "Well, thanks for the veggie bread, ladies. Say, how did you come up with an idea like that? Making a dessert out of zucchini?"

Shelley looked at Patti. Patti looked at Shelley. They sputtered and exploded in laughter. "*Now* what'd I say?" John demanded. They sobered up and stared at him solemnly, but his puzzled face set them off again. "A cheerful heart is good medicine," he quoted Proverbs 17:22 as he went to fetch the last two pumpkins.

A "ding" noise interrupted their merriment. Patti checked the news alert on her phone. "Oh no! Not another one!"

CHAPTER 2

Robert Tango 32

By the time LaRonda got home, Alvin had finished his first round of torso exercises and was waiting with mock impatience at the kitchen table.

"Sorry I'm late, Pop."

"I'm not surprised. There's never a cop around when you need one."

She handed him a sack of bagels. "I hope you haven't had break-fast already."

"Celeste tempted me with pancakes, but I was sure you'd come up with something better."

"I heard that," Celeste said, emerging from the hallway. "If you prefer fast food to home cooking, I'll just nuke your meals from now on."

"Touchy, isn't she?" Alvin wheeled his chair around to face her. "I love your cooking, Celeste. I didn't know home health aides were gourmet chefs until you came along."

"Uh-huh. You ought to be a politician. See you tonight. 'Bye, LaRonda."

"'Bye." Celeste hoisted her shoulder bag and headed for the door and a good morning's sleep.

Alvin smeared a bagel with cream cheese. "So what happened?"

LaRonda dropped into a chair. "Oh Pop, I had to shoot a kid last night."

"A kid? Oh, the news had something about that. So that was you?" He listened as she recounted the car chase, Gil's drunken antics and his bruised face. "And from what I was able to drag out of him, his own father did it."

"Did you arrange for CPS and a lawyer?"

"Yeah, I made the calls after I talked to him."

"Then you did all you could, so don't worry about it. Besides, even if he is just a kid, he was dangerous. To you, the kids he was with, Mike Ferguson, and anyone else who might have been around. You handled the whole thing like a professional. I'm proud of you."

LaRonda eyed him suspiciously. "How'd you know Mike was there?"

"Oops!" he grinned meekly.

"Were you listening? Pop, you promised! No scanner while I'm on duty!"

"I can't help it. I worry about you. Anyway, it worked out okay." He chewed the bagel. "I guess you know you'll have to face a CRB hearing."

"Yeah, Captain Vanderbilt mentioned that."

"Well, from what you've told me, I don't think it'll amount to much. You followed correct procedures. You have a fellow officer as a witness. And you just wounded him."

"Did you ever have to go before the CRB?"

"A couple of times. It can get pretty rough. When you use your weapon to take down a citizen, they have to assure the public that they take it seriously."

"I sure hope I don't become a headline. Cop shootings make all cops look bad."

"Honey, these things happen all the time, and the next day people forget about them. You still think you'll try for detective in the next rotation?"

She frowned. "I don't know. It's an awful lot of studying."

"I thought you'd made up your mind."

"Well, it's a great career move, but so what? You were a beat cop for fifteen years, and you loved it."

"Uh-huh. And look where it got me." LaRonda had just entered the police academy when a convenience store robber's bullet damaged Alvin's spinal cord. She volunteered for the overnight shift so she could drive him to physical therapy three mornings a week. It took both of them

– Alvin pulling himself up from the wheelchair with the grab handle, LaRonda swinging his lifeless legs into the car.

"How's your love life?"

She shrugged. "Arrested."

"What happened to Shaker? Did you scare him off?"

"Oh, you know. He's on days, I'm on nights. Anyway, he probably has to beat them away with a stick."

"Don't sell yourself short! You're the prettiest cop on the force. Where was it again he took you last time?"

"Schubert's Ninth Symphony. Fantastic performance!"

Alvin shook his head woefully. "Who'd believe the odds? Two black cops in the same precinct addicted to classical music. Don't you know you're supposed to dig jungle rhythms?"

"Racist. Want some more coffee?"

"Not now." LaRonda put the pot back on the stove. "Well, despite your snobby taste, I'd advise you to give Shaker a little encouragement. Good-looking guys who share your interests don't grow on trees."

"I know." She yawned, stretching her legs under the table.

"Seriously honey, you're in a rut. I want you to get out more. Have dates. Go to a movie. Or throw a party. We've got enough room."

"Okay. I'll think about it."

Alvin scowled. "No, you won't. You'll go right on spending every free minute on me. How do you think that makes me feel, stealing your life away? I'm not so helpless that you can't spare some time for yourself. Now this is an order. You take a night off this weekend, or I'll call old Shaker myself and tell him you've got an itch for him."

"You wouldn't dare!"

"Try me!"

They tried to stare each other down. Then LaRonda smiled. "Okay, I'll make you a deal. I'll invite Vanessa over for dinner Saturday night. We'll watch a movie on Netflix."

"That's fine, *if* you ask Shaker instead."

"I can't. He's got tickets to a concert that night."

"How do you know?"

LaRonda squirmed. "Uh, well, he ... sort of invited me."

Alvin slammed the table. "And you turned him down, didn't you? Because you don't want to shell out extra money for a sitter!"

"Oh, Pop, let's drop this. I'm happy with things the way they are. Don't worry. I'll work up a night on the town one of these days ... nights." She went to the sink and filled a glass with water. "Here, don't forget to take your pills. I'm about ready to crash. Do you want anything else before I go to bed?"

"No. No, you go ahead." He slumped, the sign of imminent gloom. LaRonda turned his face up to hers and kissed him. "You're the best dad a girl could want. I love you." Humming a few bars from Schubert, she headed for her room.

Alvin glared at his pill dispenser. He'd been an athlete in high school and proudly applied his talents to policing. His colleagues shared hilarious stories about watching him run down fleeing criminals like a cornerback chasing a wide receiver. Now he was fifty-one, stuck in a chair and living off his daughter.

When the doctor brought Alvin the bad news, he'd rebelled immediately. No wasting away for him! If he couldn't patrol anymore, he could fight crime at a desk. His captain had even wangled an office and a minor command for him.

Then he'd thought about it. Alvin needed regular therapy on his back and his useless legs, meaning long absences during his shift three days a week. Breathing problems from the injury made him partially dependent on a ventilator. Alvin couldn't let himself take advantage of fellow cops. He knew that as the years passed, their sympathy would wither into resentment. Then, as younger officers replaced his retired colleagues, they would inherit this troublesome dinosaur. Alvin had declined the captain's kind offer and done his best to accept that his policing days were over.

He spent a couple of years working at home as a medical transcriptionist until the doctors began switching to voice-recognition software. Discounting his modest disability pay, that left LaRonda responsible for the bills, including Celeste's services and the ten years remaining on their mortgage.

LaRonda bought him a scanner so he could feel part of things. By then, Sandstone police were following a new trend, discarding the old dispatch codes in favor of plain English. In Alvin's day, "chase in progress" was 10-80. "Domestic disturbance" was 10-16. "Ambulance needed" was

10-52. Alvin missed the codes. They were like passwords to a secret fraternity to which he no longer belonged.

While listening to cop traffic he made toys, using castaway items from the Goodwill store. Hand puppets fashioned from gloves and oven mittens. Wooden spoon dolls with painted faces. Alphabet dolls with a different letter for each. Tiny jigsaw puzzles in old CD cases. He sold most of them at a neighborhood flea market but kept a few around the house, to remind LaRonda of the grandchildren he expected from her.

The worst part of his disability was forcing his twenty-eight-year-old daughter to play nursemaid by day and consort with criminals by night. No one knew better than Alvin that a cop's number could come up at any moment. When Robert Tango 32 walked through his door unharmed each morning, Alvin always sent God a silent thank-you.

He wheeled into the living room and turned on the news. Another preschool shooting, this one in West Virginia. Cops swarming the scene, too late as always.

The large audience of veterans applauded warmly as Hank finished his speech. "Thank you, Sergeant Phillips," the host said. "Now, if we haven't tired you out too much, we'd like to allow our members to ask you a few questions."

"Certainly."

A man to Hank's right accepted a wireless microphone from an usher. "Sergeant Phillips –"

"Just Hank, please."

"Hank, there's been some talk lately that Congress ought to repeal the Second Amendment and create a new one, more specific to the gun problems of our own time. What do you think about that?"

"I believe the Founding Fathers deliberately made the Second Amendment general and simple for the sake of future Americans: 'A well-regulated militia, being necessary to the security of a free state, the right of the people to keep and bear arms, shall not be infringed.' Gun violence springs from personal and social problems that changing our Constitution won't eliminate. We should attack those problems, not our country's foundations."

A woman took the mike. "You make a strong argument for the

Constitution, Hank. But don't you think there are too many guns out there? I've heard that there are more guns in private hands than there are people."

"Yes, I do, because I doubt that most of their owners have had adequate training. That's why Armed and Ready offers free gun safety courses all over the country. It's fear that's driving most gun sales. Fear that our police officers are powerless to protect us from the random violence infecting our nation. Fear that we have to do it ourselves. I hope that people who shop for firearms study their motives first, so they don't take steps they'll regret later. You can't un-pull a trigger. You can't un-kill a person. If you must own a gun, let it be your last resort when all other options have failed."

More people raised their hands. "That's a pretty big gun strapped to your waist, Hank. Do you think open-carry laws can help prevent shootings?"

"No, not at all. This sidearm is just a symbol of what I represent, like a doctor's white coat. It comes with being a spokesman for A&R. It's not loaded, and I have no intention of using it." He grinned. "My wife wonders why I can always remember my gun but keep forgetting my house keys."

They laughed. A man in a combat jacket took the microphone. "Hank, Vern Saginaw also speaks for Armed and Ready, and he's your boss. Do you agree with everything he says? A while back he advocated putting armed guards in every public building in America."

"I think Vern was speaking out of personal frustration. He founded Armed and Ready sixty years ago as a kid, with money he earned delivering newspapers. He loved outdoor life and wanted to share it with everyone. It's Vern's dedication that's made A&R America's most powerful gun rights advocate. Because of that, he gets blamed unfairly for shooting incidents like the one today in West Virginia. To answer your question, I think we can find a practical solution to gun violence without going to extremes. Jesus himself said it best: Blessed are the peacemakers."

A woman took the microphone. "What do you think about David Tischner's appointment, Hank?"

"To be honest, I haven't met him yet. He's certainly got a lot of business experience. He's served three terms on the city council, and he's on six other corporate boards besides ours. I hope he'll be an asset to our organization."

"What about that bunch of Texas radicals he's mixed up with?"

"It's my understanding they're working to preserve Confederate monuments. I'm sure all that secession talk is just a rumor."

A man wearing a Vietnam veteran's cap rose. "Hank, would you mind telling us about the incident that won you the Medal of Honor?"

Hank's face fell. The hall became silent.

"I gather from your headgear that you're a combat veteran yourself." The man nodded. "People like us are the only ones who know what it's like to make a life-or-death decision. Let me just say that it was an honor to receive the medal, but I'm not proud of what I did to earn it."

"You should be, sir! The 9/11 terrorists forced that war on us!" The audience applauded. Hank remained grim.

"In high school, I read a poem called *The Rime of the Ancient Mariner*. It's about a sailor who kills an albatross that led his ship out of danger. As punishment, he has to wear the dead bird around his neck until it rots and falls off." He drew the Colt .45 from its holster. "This pistol represents one of my freedoms as an American citizen. But it's also my albatross. It reminds me every day of what I did in Afghanistan."

He searched their eyes. "It's one thing to read about killing, or watch movie actors pretend to kill, or even join the Marines and be trained to kill. To actually do it is something else. Once you kill, you'll never be yourself again. Because you'll never forget it."

His throat tightened. "Six men are dead because of me, and the fact that my platoon survived because I shot those soldiers doesn't make me feel any better. Hardly a day has passed since I got home that I haven't wondered about them. Who they were. What they were like. Whether they had wives and children and hopes for the future. If we hadn't been soldiers, if we'd met some other way, we might have liked each other, maybe even become friends." He choked. "Jesus died like a criminal for the sake of every soul on Earth. His sacrifice made those six men my brothers. God didn't give me any special license to snuff out their lives. Sometimes I wish I could take back those bullets and use them on myself."

The crowd was silent. The host appeared from the wings. "On that note, I think we should say goodnight. On behalf of the VFW, thank you, Mr. Phillips, for your informative and inspiring remarks."

The veterans rose, applauding loudly. Hank smiled through his tears, shook hands with the host, and headed backstage.

"This is so cool," Macy said, watching Bruce glue the wing on a fighter jet. "Is that the kind of plane your dad flew in?"

"No, he was a Marine. A combat soldier."

"Don't they get to fly in airplanes?"

"Sometimes, I guess. Mostly they fight ground battles with machine guns."

"I'd rather be a pilot. Who was your dad fighting, anyway?"

"The bad guys in Afghanistan. Didn't your parents tell you about 9/11?"

"Yeah, but that was a bunch of hijackers. So why did our guys have to go to Afghanistan?"

"The people who sent them here lived there. The President sent our guys to punish them."

"Oh." Macy watched for a moment. "Can I do the other wing?"

"Okay." The fourth-graders were working in Bruce's bedroom. His walls displayed posters of attack planes, helicopters, tanks, and jeeps operated by muscular young men in uniform. Models of the same vehicles crowded his desk and bookcase.

"Did your dad buy all these for you?" Macy asked, running a glue bead over the wing's edge.

"Sort of. He gives me an allowance and I can spend it any way I want. I don't think he likes this stuff very much, but he never says anything."

"What's not to like? I wish my room looked like this."

The door opened and Shelley appeared. "Hi, boys. I baked some cookies and they're still warm. Interested?"

"Yeah, great! As soon as we finish this piece."

"Well, I'm going to take a bath, so listen for the phone in case your dad calls."

"Okay."

"Say hi to your mom and dad for me, Macy."

"Okay, Mrs. Phillips." She closed the door.

"How come everybody calls you Macy? Isn't it really Mason?"

The boy rolled his eyes. "My dad says most of the time I act like Macy.

He says he'll call me Mason when I start acting like Mason. Why? Doesn't your dad call you Brucey?"

"No."

"Wanna trade?"

Bruce laughed.

"So why doesn't your dad like these models?"

"I guess they remind him of the war. He had to kill some enemy soldiers."

"My dad says your dad's a hero. He's glad you and me are friends."

"He *is* a hero." The military decorations couldn't convey the depth to which Bruce idolized his father. "Come on, finish that wing before the cookies get cold."

"I think that's got it. Let's go."

Bruce's room was dark when Hank got home. "Hi Dad."

"Hi Bruce. Did I wake you?"

"No, I just got to bed a little while ago. How was your speech?"

"Okay, I guess. What did you do this evening?"

"Macy came over and we worked on models. Mom made some great cookies."

"Yeah, I can smell them. Did you leave any for me?"

"Sure."

Hank sat on the edge of the bed and turned on the lamp. Bruce squinted. The combat scenes looked ominous in the shadows surrounding the small pool of light. "How was school today?"

"Pretty cool. We got a break to decorate for Halloween."

"Hey, that's right, you get two parties tomorrow. Have you tried on your costume?"

"Everything but the makeup. Mom promised to help me with it."

"Well, don't let her make you as pretty as she is. You might give Dracula a bad reputation." Hank stood and pulled the bedsheet over him.

"Dad, did you like being in the Marines?"

"Some parts of it. I met a lot of great guys. And the people in Afghanistan were interesting. But war's not a very good way to meet people."

"What's it like to kill somebody?"

A shadow passed over Hank's face. Bruce was instantly sorry he'd asked.

"Son, I just hope you grow up in a world where you don't have to make choices like that. Now come on. Let's get you off to dreamland." He embraced the boy. "Good night, Bruce. I love you."

"I love you too, Dad."

In the kitchen, Hank munched cookies and leafed through one of Shelley's magazines, trying to settle his thoughts. When he finally went to bed, he dreamed he was the star of an action movie, slaughtering the guilty and innocent alike.

CHAPTER 3

Truthway@Vigilance

"Good morning, everyone. It sounded almost like a declaration of war last night as Vern Saginaw, president of Armed and Ready, challenged his membership to stand up for gun rights. From Minneapolis, Celia Masters has our report."

Hank sat at the breakfast bar and turned up the TV. Vern stood at a lectern, flanked by American flags. A backdrop displayed the familiar A&R logo with its rifle silhouette. Vern's face was red, his white hair tousled. With his shoulder holster, he looked like an ancient bandito cruising for a shootout.

"Our Constitution is grounded in the assumption that the forces of tyranny will do all in their power to destroy America's freedom. That's why the Founding Fathers gave us the Second Amendment, which proclaims that our right to bear arms is a sacred right, to be cherished and defended at all costs. Instead, our short-sighted enemies are working tirelessly to subvert a privilege the patriots of 1776 gave their lives for. The losers in this treachery are people like you, the most responsible gun owners on Earth. You don't deserve this!"

The camera swept across a cheering audience. Shelley came into the kitchen and placed her hands on Hank's shoulders.

"As founder of Armed and Ready, I make you a solemn pledge tonight. I will defend to my death the right of American citizens to own firearms and to use them for recreational, defensive, and if necessary, patriotic purposes. I pledge to stand up to the mindless conspiracy gathering in this country to deprive you and me of a fundamental right guaranteed by our Constitution. I pledge to you that any politician who votes to undermine this right will have the wrath of Armed and Ready to deal with. And finally, I pledge to you that any gun owner with the courage to defend this right will have the blessing, the financial support, and the legal support of Armed and Ready!"

The crowd roared. Hank groaned.

"Our forefathers were willing to give their lives for the principles of democracy and freedom. They were patriots. And so are the fifteen million members of Armed and Ready across America! They're patriots! And patriots do whatever it takes to defend their flag, their Constitution, and their country!"

Hank buried his face in his hands. "Honey, is that the speech you approved yesterday morning?" Shelley asked.

"No, that one was just bad. This one's a disaster."

"I call on our loyal, patriotic membership to take the initiative in this fight! You don't defend a principle with compromises. You defend it by fighting the forces bent on destroying that principle. So I summon to action all Armed and Ready members and all freedom-loving people across this land. Go after our enemies! Use your God-given voice, your social media voice, your ballot box voice. And if you have to, use your weapons! The patriots of 1776 did it! And so will we!"

As the listeners leaped to their feet in a thunderous ovation, the screen switched back to Celia. "The White House had no immediate comment about Mr. Saginaw's remarks. But with the speech coming only hours after yesterday's preschool shooting in West Virginia, it's likely the President, a card-carrying A&R member, will be forced to make some sort of statement, and very soon. This is Celia Masters in Minneapolis."

Hank turned off the TV and sank back with another groan. Shelley pulled up a stool beside him. "Hank, I'm so sorry. I've never heard him this belligerent."

"I have. Just not in public." He shook his head. "I got such a positive reaction from my speech last night, telling those veterans about our gun safety programs. Our scouting activities. Our land preservation campaign. I really felt I had done some good for the organization. Now people are going to watch this and start taking sides again. Oh, Vern! Why can't you see the whole picture?"

"Honey, this situation has been frustrating you for months. Why don't you try to find something else to do?"

"We've been over this, sweetheart. I owe Vern everything. He gave me an executive job when I came out of the Marines with no college and no business experience. He's given our family a good life and a future. How can I quit on him? And where would I go if I did?"

Shelley grasped his hands. "I can't believe you're the same guy who courted me in that restaurant. Where's that initiative? That self-confidence? That persistence? Hank, people look up to you! When you make a speech, they're spellbound! Everyone in our church thinks you ought to run for something. Honey, Vern Saginaw is just an angry old man with a gun. You're nothing like him."

"Your parents think I'm even worse. Because I'm a killer."

"Forget about them! Do what your heart tells you."

He rose and gazed through the kitchen window, watching leaves re-clutter the lawn he had raked two evenings earlier. "I guess it's the military man still in me. You don't run an army or win a war by fighting your commanders. You follow orders and get the job done."

"And here I am, playing the nagging wife." She gently turned him around to face her. "Well, I'm loyal, too. And no matter what you decide, about your job or anything else, I'll back you up. I know you'll always make the honest choice." She kissed him.

"Look, Vern's supposed to be back in the office this morning. I'll have it out with him and let you know what happens." He lifted his holster from the table and strapped it on. "I'm sorry I can't make the Halloween party, but if I don't get some things caught up today, I'll be working all weekend."

"I'll save you some treats. What's your pleasure? Skittles? Gummy Bears?"

He embraced her. "Just you, my lady. Just you."

Vern's speech had social media buzzing that morning. So did the pre-school massacre in West Virginia. David Tischner, A&R's new board member, sat in his living room leading a Twitter chat.

Truthway@Vigilance

The liberal news media has cooked up another shooting fantasy. I give them an A for acting and an F for facts.

Marla stopped beside him on her way to the car. "Don't tell me you're wallowing in that hoax chatter again."

"Haven't you got some place to go?"

"Yes! I've got a Food Bank committee meeting. I hope they don't know Truthway at Vigilance is actually my lunatic husband!"

He ignored her. She left, exasperated. David sat reading comments on his message.

BillWatson@expoman

I'm with you, Truthway. This is another Sandy Hook con job. We need to expose these phony school shootings & prosecute the perps!

Wendel B@wendelbrown2

WV is just more of the same gun haters trying to drum up support using non-existent moppets!

Theo West@theoscorner

Actors posing as kids, parents & cops! When will people wise up?

David wasn't your typical conspiracy buff. His company, Pierpont Electronics, was sixteenth among the fifty largest corporations in Texas. His friendship with Vern Saginaw opened doors for him in the conservative Texas legislature and in Congress, leading to rich military contracts that provided thousands of manufacturing jobs. Pierpont employed nine percent of Sandstone's workforce.

In most ways, David was an asset to his community. His shrewd business mind made him an indispensable member of the Sandstone City Council, the Municipal Development Board and the Sandstone University Board of Regents. When policy disputes arose, his grasp of facts and keen judgment inevitably proved him right.

But David didn't just argue; he went for the jugular, and he did it in public. "Why should we pay an outside consultant a half-million dollars for a feasibility study?" he demanded of Howard Stone, the city's traffic engineer. "What do you think we're paying *you* for?" His rebuke, rebroadcast on the nightly news, left Stone humiliated and bitter. Similar attacks on the sanitation and parks departments sparked more resentment.

David's membership in the New Texas Confederacy, a right-wing group with secessionist ties, raised cries of hypocrisy because his company thrived on federal contracts. "David Tischner may be Texas' most astute executive," a *Forbes* writer commented. "He may also be the most hated."

David was a long-time firearms enthusiast. He had excellent vision and concentration on the gun range, and he loved the challenge of precision target shooting. His den contained seven first-place trophies from A&R's national target competitions. Vern Saginaw often joined him on the firing line and invited him on deer hunting trips with his corporate allies. Nominating David to fill a vacancy on A&R's corporate board was a natural move for Vern, who had met David at a gun show twenty years earlier.

When the first Sandy Hook conspiracy allegations popped up, both men dismissed the bloggers and tweeters as idiots. Then Paul Sellars, David's executive assistant, began sending him email attachments. "These are garbage!" David mailed back. Paul wouldn't give up. He produced a set of pictures. "Look, here's this kid's father smiling on camera, right after the shooting. Why would he be smiling if his daughter was dead? And the kid and the father don't even look alike!"

"So what? Maybe he was in shock. Maybe it's a sad smile. Maybe the girl took after her mother."

"That's not all. See this woman bawling her head off? The same woman got caught on camera after the movie theatre shoot-up in Aurora, Colorado and the Boston Marathon bombing."

David compared the pictures. "She's got the same expression on her face in all three of them. Somebody copied and pasted it to make it look like she was at all three places."

"No, it looks too natural. And look at this. The lawyer sitting in court beside James Holmes after the Aurora massacre is a dead ringer for one of the Sandy Hook parents. David, they're all a bunch of actors!"

"You need to get a life, Paul." But the notion stuck in his mind like a splinter, leading to his own research and his own questions. Why did Newtown's 2012 crime statistics show zero murders? How could on-line memorials to the dead children have timestamps earlier than December 14, the day of the massacre? What about contradictory police reports of other shooters at the scene? Who was responsible for suppressing crime scene photos and autopsy reports on the victims? Why was Newtown so quick to demolish the school building? He began monitoring Twitter chats among people who thought Adam Lanza sounded like a badly-scripted villain from a cheap action movie. Their conclusion: Sandy Hook was a drama staged by anti-gun forces.

And who was behind those forces? The news media, of course. David had a long-standing grudge against them, always looking for dirty deals behind Pierpont's military contracts. Bad press was inevitable for successful businessmen like David and Vern. Just read Ayn Rand. Come up with an innovative idea like Pierpont's combat mini-drone, and everybody wanted a piece of you.

Once, a *Newsweek* reporter spent a month investigating how Pierpont always managed to underbid its rivals. He found nothing illegal, but the article itself amounted to guilt by implication. David's refusal to grant the reporter an interview didn't help. "Nobody ever accused me of anything until you came along," he barked into the phone. "Where were you while I was working eighteen hours a day to get this company off the ground?" The reporter responded by quoting unfounded allegations from rival contractors, ending with "Tischner refused to comment," like he was hiding something.

Vern Saginaw was too smart to sanction conspiracy theories. He had enough targets on his back already. But history had taught David that new enemies could pop up anywhere. Paul was right. The leftist anti-gun army was up to something new and sinister. Registering under a fake Twitter name, David asked anyone with additional proof about the conspiracy to speak up. Unfortunately, the responses were usually more opinion than fact.

EyesOfTheNation@LauraSwan

Everybody with the courage to question Sandy Hook is being threat-ened & harassed. Some even get fired. What happened to free speech?

JordanB@JordanBranch

Why would the New York Times, Washington Post, etc., spend so much time trying to whitewash Sandy Hook if they weren't behind it themselves?

HWatchdog@HWatts

Ask any New York journalist about his stand on gun rights. You'll get a 99.9% vote against them!

David's son Jason scorned the hoax theorists, but that was the least of their differences. Successful as he was in professional life, David had failed as a parent. His domineering nature alienated his children who, repressed and resentful, fled the nest as quickly as maturity allowed, Veronica to Seattle with her husband and two children, Lesley to Harvard Medical School. Jason remained in Sandstone with his wife and son, but they might as well have lived on the moon for all David saw of them. Jason was still furious about the day he caught David showing Andy his gun collection. "You have no business corrupting my son with your murderous toys!" he shouted.

"I didn't let him touch them," David protested as Jason scooped up Andy and carried him out to the car. "I was just letting him look. You know I'd never let a four-year-old handle a gun." Jason backed out of the driveway and roared off. That was two months ago. Jason had refused to let Andy visit ever since. It was the most effective punishment he could inflict on David, who yearned for a better relationship with his grandson than he had with his own kids.

It's the duck, he thought. Fifteen years, and he still hasn't forgiven me for the duck.

A Twitter alert returned David's attention to his phone.

PaulRevere@WadeStevens

The gun haters in Congress are helping the media fund this conspiracy. I know which ones they are. Let's launch a campaign right now to vote them out in November!

David logged off and headed into a full day of business decisions. But as he left the house, he phoned Vern to congratulate him on his speech.

Warren DeVries was worried about Hank. Despite his lofty status at A&R, his door was always open. Staffers usually stopped by to chat and joke with him. Today he was preoccupied and snappish. Every time Warren peeked in, Hank still seemed to be on the first page of the budget outline he'd started yesterday. Warren wasn't getting much done himself. People kept poking their heads in to whisper, "What's wrong with Hank?" It wasn't hard to guess. Vern's speech was all over the news.

About mid-morning, Vern broke the tension by bounding into the reception area with a cloudburst of enthusiasm, roaring greetings and shaking hands. He zipped through the suite like a tornado, grabbing a couple of secretaries and waltzing them around before finally landing in his own office. Warren noticed that Hank stayed put during the disturbance.

Eventually, Vern noticed it too. He marched into Hank's office and plopped into a chair. "Happy Halloween, Sarge! You going trick-or-treating with Bruce tonight?"

Hank managed a weak smile. "I'm afraid not. I've got to finish this budget proposal before I can get out of here, and it's going to take some juggling to make everything balance."

"Not to worry." Vern dismissed the budget with a wave of his hand. "You'll nail it like you always do. Did you see me on the news?"

"Yeah, I saw some, uh, highlights."

"So what did you think?"

Hank seemed at a loss for words. "I thought you got a very positive response."

"Positive? They ate it up! I haven't felt this great about a speech in twenty years!"

Hank smiled. "I'm glad you had a good night, Vern."

"What's wrong with you today? You seem a little down. The budget can't be that rough."

"I'm okay."

"Come on, open up. You can tell old Vern anything, you know that."

Hank put down his pen, strode to the door and closed it.

"Vern, what happened to the speech I corrected for you yesterday morning?"

"Oh, that. Well, it was okay, but it didn't quite get the message across. At the last minute, I decided to wing it. Why? You think I didn't appreciate your work on it? Sure I did. I just made it a little stronger."

Hank sat on the edge of the desk. "Vern, don't you realize how much damage you did last night?"

"What are you talking about? It was great! I had them eating out of my hand."

"You were preaching to the choir. But what about the millions more out there who are worried about guns? Worried for their children's safety? Terrified that they might be the next target of some maniac? What about police officers, who have to defend us against people who take the law into their own hands? What did you give them last night, Vern? You declared war on them!"

"That's nonsense, I –"

"You told people to do whatever it takes to defend the Second Amendment, even if they have to do it with bullets. You wrote a blank check to every frustrated gun owner in America. You gave them our blessing to commit murder in the name of democracy! Vern, you even violated the law with that speech. It was incitement to riot!"

"Now hold on here!" Vern rose from his chair, his face florid. "Did you hear what I said right from the start? I was speaking on *behalf* of those worried people. I told them we're here to support their right to *protect* their children, *and* themselves. Hank, that speech gave people hope! Hope that there's somebody here at A&R who understands their fears and is ready to back them up. You should know that's what I meant, Hank. You've been my VP for nine years."

Hank drew a breath to calm himself. "Vern, please, just step back and look at this from another point of view. You know there are people in anti-gun groups who will use what you said last night as a weapon against A&R. These people are just as smart as you are, and they can make speeches too. And what they'll say is that we're a bunch of rednecks so determined to protect our rights that we'll kill anybody who gets in our way!"

"You think I'm a redneck?"

"Of course not! But that's what they'll say about every person with an A&R sticker on his car bumper, and every hunter with a gun rack in his truck. They'll paint all gun enthusiasts with the same brush, and before you know it, you'll have a whole new set of enemies. We won't have just the anti-gun crowd to worry about. We'll have all the people in the middle of this issue against us, too. We won't have any friends at all except our membership, and as big as that is, it's tiny compared to the vast majority of people who just want to live in safety."

Vern turned and kicked his chair across the room, followed it, kicked it again.

"I don't think I'll ever understand you, Hank. I thought you took this job because you believed in what we're working for here. Yet lately, every time we talk, you sound like one of *them*. How do you think we're going to protect our rights if we cave in to criticism? I told you yesterday and I'll tell you again today. We're in a war, mister! You of all people should know you can't win a war by surrendering. We've got to stand our ground. And if you aren't ready to do that, you're a traitor!"

"Vern!" Hank was shocked.

"That's right, a traitor! And you know what happens to traitors in war, don't you?" He advanced on Hank until their noses were inches apart. "You'd better make up your mind which side you're on right now, Sarge. Medal of Honor or no Medal of Honor, you either fall into ranks or I'll mow you down with the rest of our enemies!"

He stomped out of the office and slammed the door.

CHAPTER 4

The disappointed face of Jesus

Hank decided to spend his lunch hour in the park across the street. The office atmosphere was tense following Vern's tirade. Even with the door shut, nobody within fifty feet could have missed it, so everyone was carefully avoiding both men.

He sat on a bench, watching toddlers frolic in the mild sunshine and chase geese along the edge of the pond. Tonight's trick-or-treat weather looked promising.

Afghanistan wasn't what Hank expected when he arrived in 2002 following his training. Nineteen years old and pumped up, he was on a crusade. But the Taliban was largely scattered by then, and he found the Afghan people, discounting their culture and religion, to be pretty much like himself. They went about the business of getting married, raising kids and struggling to get by. Nobody shook a fist at Hank or yelled "Death to America!" Most took his presence in stride, having bigger things to worry about. Living conditions were primitive, food was starchy and scarce, health care almost non-existent. Land mines were buried everywhere, one reason why a quarter of the nation's children died before age five. It wasn't long before Hank was sneaking his MRE rations to street urchins so he could sleep peacefully.

Taliban units were still active around the countryside, fighting a guerilla war against the invading forces. One day, Hank's platoon was searching a bombed-out village when an RPG exploded among them. As his men took cover, Hank ignored shrapnel pains in his limbs to drag two badly injured Marines into an abandoned house. Then, hearing boots crunch through the sand, he limped outside to kneel behind a crumbling stone wall as six Taliban soldiers closed in.

He stood, aimed quickly and riddled the surprised party with steely jolts, the four closest men ripped to pieces. The other two quickly dropped to the ground, firing blindly at the source. But Hank had already crouched and scrambled to a new vantage point. Now he rose and shredded a fifth attacker who had leaped to his feet.

Seeing his companion drop, the last soldier stared frozen into the dark aperture of Hank's M16. Hank had time to register the terror in the boy's eyes before blasting him backward into the dust.

Afterward, he was too busy evacuating his injured men and organizing a counterattack to think about what he'd done, or to notice the blood seeping through his uniform from the RPG fragments. His captain praised him for swift action that saved his platoon and drove the Taliban from a district it had occupied for weeks. But that night, as he lay stitched and bandaged in his hospital bed, "Thou shalt not kill" echoed in his skull like a movie sound track. The video was the disappointed face of Jesus.

Hank sometimes thought he'd been three different people: the teenager shocked into action by 9/11; the valiant Marine sergeant; and the wreck he'd been since the day he came home and peeled off the military façade. With his utilities crumpled on the floor, his mirrored body dressed in civvies, Hank finally felt the full, crushing weight of the six souls he'd sent to oblivion.

"You were a soldier," his mother consoled him. "You did what they would have done to you." But that last Taliban kid was alone. Whipped. Paralyzed. *Why didn't I take him prisoner? Or scare him away? Vern's right. I* am *a traitor. I betrayed God, I betrayed Jesus, and I got a medal for it.*

The many men, so beautiful!
And they all dead did lie:
And a thousand thousand slimy things
Lived on; and so did I.

Not only had Hank returned home a killer; he didn't have a job.

But he wasn't too ashamed to flirt with a pretty waitress the night his mother finally persuaded him to get out of the house and stop brooding. Not too ashamed to share his bride's shabby apartment while he looked for work. Not too ashamed to capitalize on the Medal of Honor by accepting Vern's offer of a dream job, plus a tuition-paid tour through business school. God had given him a devoted wife, an adorable son, a fancy home, money, fame and admiration. Everything, except a clear conscience.

> *An orphan's curse would drag to hell*
> *A spirit from on high;*
> *But oh! more horrible than that*
> *Is the curse in a dead man's eye!*

Like Coleridge's poem, Afghanistan seemed to follow Hank home like a virus, infecting the whole country. Massacres at a Virginia college, a Texas military post, a Colorado movie theatre, a Connecticut grade school, a California disabilities center, a Florida nightclub. Charleston, Las Vegas, Sutherland Springs, Parkland, Dayton, El Paso, on and on. Another school shooting only yesterday. It was a domestic war. And America was losing.

After every major incident, politicians started talking gun control again. When they talked, more people bought guns and donated more money to A&R, which paid Vern and Hank to remind congressmen that you don't get re-elected by alienating fifteen million gun owners and snubbing millions more in campaign dollars. A&R won the lobbying battle every time. The dead and bereaved were forgotten.

Hank and Warren were lunching at a restaurant one day, trying to ignore the boisterous conversation at a nearby table.

"I keep a .45 next to the front door, a shotgun by the back door, and a .38 under my pillow."

"Why your pillow?"

"If anybody breaks in, I can shoot him without having to get up!" They all laughed.

"My wife keeps a SIG Sauer in the glove compartment for street punks, and an extra clip for gangbangers."

"What about you?"

"I drive, she rides shotgun. She's a better shot than I am." More laughter.

"Our constituency," Warren remarked wryly.

"Aw, they're just kidding around," Hank replied. But he had lost his appetite.

Opponents in the gun debate spoke of rights versus safety. People like Hank who had actually shot someone had their own grim perspective. "Nothing really prepares you for killing in war, even with the training," said Shira Maguen, a pioneer in the study of moral injuries. Hank had survived Afghanistan, but with a scarred body and an ailing spirit.

He leaned forward on the bench, bowing his head and squeezing his hands together. "God, please help me. I feel so lost and confused. I've tried to be a good Christian since Afghanistan, but something's wrong. Please God, forgive my past and light the path you want me to follow."

He straightened up to find a small boy staring at him. "Hi there."

"Whatcha doin', mister?"

"I was praying. Praying to God."

"How come you're wearin' a gun?"

Hank frowned at his pistol. "Good question." He rose and drew his phone from his pocket as he trudged back to the office.

Standing outside the church in gathering darkness, Shelley and Patti admired the results of their pumpkin artistry. Bright rows of grinning jack-o-lanterns flanked the entryway. Inside each was a candle, radiating a sinister orange cheer upon the parents and children arriving for the party.

"I think it's gorgeous," Patti said. "We make a great team, don't we? Maybe we ought to go into business."

"I'm with you. Too bad Halloween only comes once a year."

"We can't let that stop us. If we can do this well with pumpkins, there are plenty of other holidays we can exploit."

Before she met Hank, Shelley had never been to a Halloween party. Not once in her activist youth had she gone trick-or-treating, stuffed herself on Thanksgiving Day, decorated a Christmas tree or attended an Easter church service. Her parents dragged her cross-country in a prime-val hippie van, marching against genocide, global warming and gender inequality. Secretly, she prayed for a stable home life, but God didn't seem to hear. She might have become an atheist if not for Hank, who was never embarrassed to talk about God and needed Him more than ever after Afghanistan. When they moved to Sandstone for his new job, they spent a few Sundays church shopping. That was how they met Matt and Patti Shore, whose congregation was warm and nurturing.

When she lost their first child in her third month, Shelley blamed herself. Maybe an ex-hippie wasn't good enough for Hank. "Don't do that to yourself!" he scolded. They tried again, and the result was Bruce. "Didn't I tell you?" he beamed as they watched the sleeping infant his first night home. "You just needed a little practice."

"So Matt couldn't make the party?" she asked Patti.

"No, the coaches are having a strategy meeting for the San Angelo game. He's afraid they're going to get stomped."

The two mothers followed the Halloween crowd inside. The shadowy lobby sported orange and black streamers, dried corn stalks, bat silhouettes, skeleton cutouts and more pumpkins. Moaning voices from the sound system broadcast a good-natured eeriness. Costumed children with colorful bags dashed excitedly from one trick-or-treat station to another. The dining room across from the auditorium was a haunted house, where young monsters and superheroes nervously awaited their tours.

The pastor, disguised as Frankenstein's creature, appeared with cups of hot apple cider. "Hi, I'm FrankenJohn! Welcome to the party! This ought to warm you up a little. Love your costumes!"

"I love yours," Patti laughed. "You ought to wear it when you preach about Lazarus." John wore tattered grave garments, plus the obligatory skin stitches, neck electrodes and greenish complexion. Patti's bonnet bore the title Little Bo Creep. Large plastic spiders infested her ragged pastoral frock. Her shepherd's crook was a bloody scythe. Shelley was a witch, complete with black cape and pointed hat. Her broomstick hung crossways on her back like an itinerant musician's banjo.

They sipped their drinks. "Nice turnout," Shelley observed.

"Yes, I think it's the biggest in years. I want to thank you both for all your hard work. It's a shame it all has to come down tomorrow so we can get the church back in shape for Sunday."

"Don't worry, I'll be glad to help. What time do you – yipe!" Shelley squealed as a miniature Dracula jumped her from behind. "I vant to bite your throat!" Bruce boomed into her ear.

"Forget it, Count, I'm already a pint low from the blood drive yesterday."

"How about some cider instead?" John asked the vampire. "I'll bet it tastes better."

Patti seized Bruce's shoulders and spun him around. "You look great, kiddo! I love your makeup."

"Mom did it. I gotta go find Macy and Wally." He dashed away, his cape flapping behind him. Shelley watched him happily. "This is so much better than letting them roam the neighborhood in the dark, ringing doorbells."

"Safer anyway. Excuse me, I'd better go check on my own little monsters." Patti drifted away.

"John, I meant to tell you how much I liked your sermon last Sunday. This series you're doing on Jesus' parables has meant a lot to me and Hank."

"Thanks, Shelley. The parables were my favorite part of ministerial training. Say, where *is* Hank? Couldn't he make it tonight?"

"No, he had to work late." She declined to mention his disturbing phone call.

"Well, please tell him we missed him. Excuse me, will you? I'd better do some mixing with the other ghouls." He headed toward a group of parents at the snack table.

Left to herself, Shelley resumed worrying. When Hank called earlier this afternoon, she was standing on a ladder. "Honey, I'm all tangled up in party decorations. Can I call you back?"

"No, don't let me interrupt. I just wanted to hear your voice."

"Is something wrong?"

"I've been thinking about what you said this morning. But it'll keep. We'll talk some more tonight. 'Bye, sweetheart." He hung up.

Despite her vow of support this morning, Shelley had wished for a long time that Hank would find another job. Though Vern Saginaw had been to their house many times, taken them to dinner, lavished birthday and Christmas gifts on them, Shelley had always quietly disliked the man. His single-minded intensity about firearms disturbed her, especially when he ranted around Bruce. Vern tended to overwhelm introspective people like Hank. Growing up with crusading parents like hers, she knew exactly how he felt.

A tap on the shoulder interrupted her reverie. She turned to face another vampire, this one fully grown. "Why Roger, how you've changed since last Sunday!" Grateful for the distraction, Shelley let herself merge with the spirit of the evening.

Hank kept his door closed all afternoon to avoid talking to anyone, especially Vern. He stared moodily at the computer, where CNN was updating the West Virginia preschool shooting. Eleven dead, fourteen wounded, perpetrator a suicide, motive unknown. The same old refrain. By now, benumbed parents would be planning funerals. Strangers would be stopping by the school to place bouquets and stuffed animals on the lawn. Others would skim through the details, click off their phones and get back to work. Another day of life in America.

I know you'll always make the honest choice, Shelley had said.

Abruptly, he drew a sheet of paper from the printer and wrote a long, passionate note. Sealing it in an envelope, he wrote "Shelley" on the outside and stuck it in a drawer. Maybe now he could concentrate.

It was after dark when he finally finished the budget. Everyone else was gone, the lights dimmed, the hallways shadowy. Hank printed the revision and left it on Vern's desk. He thought about driving over to the church party, then decided he wasn't in the mood. Tonight, he just wanted to go home and wait for his family. Maybe some popcorn or hot chocolate would take the edge off a bad day. He drove through the night, past homes with porch lights blazing, cheerful invitations to goblins in search of sugar.

A small figure darted into his path. Startled, he whipped the wheel to the right, bounced over the curb and smashed into a large oak tree. The airbag deployed in time to protect his face from the shattered windshield. He unbuckled and dragged himself out to find a tiny, astonished Wonder Woman staring at him.

"Are you all right, little lady?" he asked, bending to face her. "Are you hurt?" She shook her head. "What are you doing in the street?" She looked around and began picking up candy packets, peppermints and cookies, spilled from a small plastic pumpkin in her hand. Hank helped her gather them. "You should be more careful. I almost hit you."

"Katrina!" A woman rushed out of the darkness and kneeled beside the girl. "Is she all right? What happened?"

"She ran in front of my car. She's okay."

"Oh, sweetie!" The woman grabbed the child and clutched her tightly. "Katrina, what are you doing here? The rest of us were halfway down the block before I noticed you were gone."

"I dropped my pumpkin." She held it up to the woman's face.

"Oh, baby, you scared me half to death!" Hank looked around. Two boys in X-Men outfits stood on the sidewalk, gawking at the ruined Prius. The woman turned to Hank. "I'm sorry, sir. Are you all right?"

"I'm fine. The airbag saved me."

"Oh, this is terrible!" She surveyed the wreckage. "I'm sorry about your car. Do you have a way home? We're all on foot or I'd give you a ride."

"It's okay, I can walk home from here." He faced Katrina. "I'm sorry if I scared you. You scared me, too." He introduced himself to the woman. "Of course, Mr. Phillips, I've seen you on TV. I'm Donna Malone. This is my daughter and my neighbor's two boys." She gestured at the pair on the sidewalk. "Are you sure you're okay? What are you going to do about your car?"

"Don't worry about it. I'll call my insurance company. I'm just glad your daughter wasn't hurt." He turned to Katrina. "I guess you'll stay out of the street from now on, won't you? There's a big shortage of superheroes your size." The girl smiled shyly and hid behind her mother's legs.

Mrs. Malone drew a pen and an old grocery receipt from her jacket pocket. "Here's my phone number in case you need me for an accident report."

"Thanks. You'd better get these little guys home. It's chilly out here."

"You're right. Again, I'm so sorry about this. Please call if you need me for anything."

"I will. Good night, Wonder Woman." The girl waved bye-bye as her mother led her to the sidewalk. "Let's go, boys. Halloween's history for this year."

Hank watched until they disappeared, trembling as the accident's impact began to settle on him. *Dear God. I killed six men, and now I almost killed a child.* He turned up his jacket collar to warm his neck as he headed home.

"Robert Tango 32, we have a prowler report at 6343 West Dartmouth. See the woman at 6342, across the street."

"Copy, on my way." LaRonda checked her GPS and discovered she was only a few blocks from the site. So far it had been a quiet night, for Halloween. It gave her time to think ahead to her CRB hearing. Captain Vanderbilt had assured her she had nothing to worry about.

An elderly woman answered the door. "I was treating some children when I saw someone circling the Phillips house, trying the windows."

"Was it just one person, or did you see more?"

"Just one, I think."

"Do you know if the people who live there are at home?"

"I don't think so. Mrs. Phillips told me they were going to a Halloween party tonight at their church."

"Could it have been a trick-or-treater?"

"No, this was somebody tall, and he was definitely trying to get in."

"Was he carrying anything, like a weapon or tools?"

"I didn't see anything, but it's pretty dark."

"All right. Thank you, ma'am."

Crossing the street, LaRonda peered intently through the gloom. She saw no sign of activity. Nevertheless, she drew her pistol, aiming it aloft as she crept up the driveway.

CHAPTER 5

What have I turned into?

By the time Dracula and the witch left the party, Shelley was exhausted. She drove swiftly through the darkness, anxious to get home and hear Hank's news, whatever it was.

"Mom, look!" Bruce exclaimed as they approached their neighborhood. Shelley slowed to examine the silver Prius, its crumpled hood nuzzling a tree trunk. "That looks like Dad's car."

"Yes, it does." She peered through the window. "Do you see Dad, or anybody?"

"No."

"Must be somebody else's." She weaved her way through the subdivision and turned the corner onto West Dartmouth. A swarm of vehicles with flashing emergency lights convened three blocks ahead.

"What's all that, Mom?"

"I don't know." Their minivan crept forward. There were so many police cars, ambulances and TV news vans that she had to stop three houses away.

She pulled over to the curb. "Bruce, stay in the car and keep the door locked."

"But Mom –"

"Do you hear me? Stay in the car!" She jumped out and ran toward the scene, her black costume blending quickly with the night.

Bruce squinted at the flashing lights. A lot of people in bathrobes and warmups stood in his yard. Every few minutes, an EMT or a policeman appeared, got something out of his vehicle and trotted back to the house. Bruce began to fidget.

At last he climbed out and ran, his Dracula cape snapping in the breeze. He followed a policeman around the side of the house, past groups of neighbors chatting in subdued tones. In the back yard, pools of TV lights swirled over a crowd of reporters and cops. Three officers surrounded a policewoman, taking notes. Nearby, two EMTs squatted beside a dark shape on the lawn. Bruce crept closer. It was his mother.

"Mom!"

Mrs. Valdez from next door seized him as he started toward Shelley. "You'd better come with me, Bruce. Your mom's not feeling well."

"Let me go, that's my mom, let me go!" He threw himself at Shelley. "Mom, wake up!" He shook her.

"She's okay, Bruce. She's all right, she just fainted. She'll be okay."

"What happened?"

Mrs. Valdez and the EMTs looked at each other. "Bruce, there's been an accident involving your dad."

"My dad? What? Where is he?"

She hesitated and glanced at the flower bed. He followed her eyes to a dark shape lying among the autumn blossoms.

Bruce tore loose from Mrs. Valdez. He raced back through the front yard, down the sidewalk, past the minivan, desperately pursuing the Bruce of fifteen minutes ago. He thought if he ran fast enough, he might be able to catch up to him.

Matt Shore met Patti at the door. "Send the kids to their rooms," he whispered. "I've got something to tell you." She could hear the TV news blaring from the den.

Two minutes later she was speeding along Janus Boulevard, past Hank's car. As she turned the corner she saw a small vampire running past her. "Bruce! Bruce wait, it's Patti!"

She parked haphazardly and raced after him. Twelve years and three kids ago, Patti had been a high school sprinter. Now it took all she had to catch up and bring him down in a flying tackle, the two of them landing on someone's front lawn. "Bruce! Bruce, it's me, Patti." The boy scrambled to rise. "Bruce, stop it, I'm here to help you."

Gasping, he rolled over to face her. At the sight of a friend he began to cry. "Patti, my dad ... my mom ..."

"I know, baby, I know. Come here." They held each other and wept. Patti drew back, gently gripping his shoulders. "Bruce, where's your mom?"

"She's back at the house. She fainted or something when ... when ... the flower bed ... Dad was ..." He began to sob again.

"Oh, Bruce! Come on, let's get you some place safe. We'll go to my house." She gathered him up and carried him to the car.

Most of the police and EMTs were gone by the time Patti returned. The rest were discussing what to do with Shelley, who had revived but was sitting, stuporous, in a lawn chair. Patti pushed her way through them and kneeled beside her friend. "Shelley, it's Patti. I'm here, honey. I'm here to take care of you."

Shelley began to focus. She looked around. "Patti ... Hank's gone."

"I know. Come on, let's get out of here."

"Ma'am, will you be taking responsibility for this lady?" an officer asked.

"Yes." Patti gave the man her name, address and phone number. "She'll be all right at our house. I've already got her son over there."

Shelley was staring at the flower bed. "Patti, where's Hank?"

An EMT spoke up. "He's been taken to ... uh, a place where they can take care of him properly."

"I want to be with him."

Patti gently helped her stand. "Come on, Shelley. Let's go home. We'll visit Hank later." She walked her friend out of the nightmare.

LaRonda collapsed on Alvin's lap and poured her anguish into the soft sweater he liked to drape around his neck against the autumn chill.

"Do you feel like telling me about it?"

"I can't explain it," she gulped. "When I told him to freeze, he jerked around so fast, and then there was the gun and my finger just pulled the trigger. Oh, Pop, the poor guy never had a chance!" Alvin held her while she cried it out. After a few minutes, she collected herself and moved to the sofa. "I shouldn't be sitting on your lap."

"Do you have any idea why he drew on you?"

"No! I mean, why was he out there in the first place? I thought about it on my way back to the station, and I figured maybe he was taking out the trash or something and got locked out. So he decided to use his gun to break the back doorglass."

"Yeah, that makes sense."

"Pop, that's not a high crime neighborhood. I shouldn't have drawn my pistol. I should have just blinded him with my flashlight and ordered him to stop. Then he'd be alive, and he'd be safe and happy in his home with his wife and son, and ..." She choked and wept again. "Oh, Pop, how can I ever make it up to them? That poor little boy doesn't have a daddy anymore!"

Alvin tried to rise and sit beside her. Then he remembered he couldn't. Blasted paralysis!

"While the guys were debriefing me, Mrs. Phillips showed up in a witch costume. She passed out cold. Then her son showed up dressed like Dracula and went into hysterics. I thought I must be having a nightmare. I wanted to reach out and comfort them. But I'm the one who hurt them!"

"LaRonda, stop this. You did just what you were trained to do."

"No, no, I ..."

"Yes, you did! You were working in the dark, in uncertain, possibly dangerous circumstances. Yes, it went horribly wrong, but you were doing your job."

She slumped. "My job. My job is 'to protect and to serve.' I sure violated that one last night."

"You were there to protect the neighborhood. You're a soldier, as much a soldier as Mr. Phillips was. Soldiers get put into tough spots all the time, forced to make life-or-death decisions that nobody else has to make. You made the best decision you could." He took her hand. "I know that doesn't make you feel any better. You wouldn't be the daughter I love if it did. Yesterday I told you I was proud of you. I still am."

"Thanks, Pop," she murmured, unconvinced. I shot two people, two nights in a row. What have I turned into?

"Shaker called earlier, worried about you. Why don't you call him back?"

"Not now."

"Do you think you could eat something? Celeste had to go home, but I can still work my way around a stove when I have to."

"No. Maybe I'll try to sleep for a while." She smiled sadly. "Anyway, it doesn't matter what kind of schedule I keep. I'm on indefinite suspension."

"Paid suspension?"

"I don't know. Captain Vanderbilt promised to call me when he finds out."

"I know Don. He's a good cop. And he'll defend a good cop if it means sticking his own neck out. You get some rest. Take a hot shower, put on your PJs and sleep all you want."

"Pop ... Mr. Phillips took a firing position on me."

"What?"

"You know, where you drop to one knee and aim with both hands."

"Why would he do that?"

"It was like he expected an attack. But his ammo chamber was empty."

They were silent for a moment, picturing the scene. "Pop, no matter what happens, I'm supposed to be looking after you, not vice-versa. I haven't forgotten that you need help with the bathroom and your exercises. Don't you dare sacrifice your needs to give me a few winks of sleep. I'll set the alarm and be up in time for therapy."

"We'll skip therapy today."

"No, we won't! And in the meantime, you call me if you get the urge. I'll make you regret it if you don't."

"All right. Now go take care of yourself. I'll holler if I need you. I promise."

She stood, and they stared at each other. She bent for one more embrace, then trudged silently to her room.

At the mirror, LaRonda watched her reflection remove its uniform. It seemed to be stripping away her identity. By the time she was dressed for bed, the tears were back. She kneeled and prayed for Hank Phillips, for his family, and for forgiveness.

There were numerous other shootings around the country that night. In Phoenix, the manager of a pizza store emerged from his office to find a frightened employee emptying the cash register. The gunman grabbed the money, shot both of them and fled. He got thirty-seven dollars for his trouble.

Four teenagers cruised around Santa Monica looking for a Chinese boy who'd gotten too friendly with a white girl at their school. One of the boys turned out to be a crack shot. He nailed the offender right through his forehead as he exited a drugstore with a prescription for his grandmother.

An eighty-five-year-old man in Coral Gables kneeled beside his wife, shaking her and wondering why she was sleeping on the floor. Two hours earlier, his .38 had gone off while he was cleaning it. Before dementia set in, he'd been a deputy sheriff and gun safety instructor.

In Huntington, West Virginia, twenty-five families sat weeping in homes or worrying in hospital rooms, depending on whether their children were dead or struggling to survive the latest massacre.

Gunfire erupted in other communities, large and small. Each story got a sentence or two in the local newscasts. Such things happened all the time in America. None of the people involved were famous.

CHAPTER 6

Hankering

Marie Phillips flew into town early Friday afternoon with her surviving sons Gerald and Sam, their wives and children. As rental cars carried the family along Janus, the puzzling sight of Hank's Prius nose-deep in a tree gave way to another concern: yellow police tape surrounding his house. An officer obtained permission for the family to go in but cautioned them to avoid the back yard. Still, they had to wait until Patti arrived with Shelley's keys. The officer entered first and sealed the back door from inside. While the children played, the adults sat in the living room watching CNN updates, wishing Hank would appear and announce that it was all a misunderstanding.

Vern Saginaw appeared on the screen and delivered a statement to reporters. "Every single staff member here at A&R loved Hank Phillips like a brother, and I loved him like a son. Our hearts go out to his wife Shelley, their son Bruce, all his family, and the countless Americans who admired him. Replacing Hank will be impossible, because there was no one like him. But the entire A&R team and I are determined to carry on our defense of Second Amendment rights in the same spirit that Hank did throughout his nine years with us."

Sam stormed out the door and marched around the block, muttering and kicking an orphaned Batman mask down the street. "I don't understand this," he said on his return. "How could anybody mistake Hank for a burglar?" He sat beside his mother and let her weep on his shoulder. News commentators were packaging Hank's death with the West Virginia shooting and A&R's open-carry rule. The rusty firearms debate raged for hours.

As darkness fell, the family moved into the kitchen and made sandwiches for the kids. Later, Gerald and Sam slouched around the table with Marie while their wives, Christine and Lynette, put the children to bed on makeshift floor pallets.

"What's going to happen to Shelley and Bruce now?" Marie wondered.

"I don't know," Sam sighed. "They're welcome to come stay with us. I suppose she'll have to find some sort of job."

Gerald frowned. "I thought Hank left her pretty well fixed. He had an executive's benefits."

"Those can't last forever. I guess we can discuss it later, when she's up to it."

Everyone was worried about Shelley and even more worried about Bruce. On Halloween night, his parents had suddenly vanished in a chaos of cops and paramedics. When Patti drove him home the next day, Mom's body sat beside him, but Mom was absent. Dad was an indistinct flower bed memory that Bruce fiercely pushed away. Patti escorted the boy into the house, where unfamiliar relatives wandered around in confusion.

"Can I come stay with you?" he asked Patti.

"No honey, your Mom needs you."

But Mom closed her door and went to bed. Bruce hid in his own room, aimlessly rearranging his military models, indifferent to the grownups trying to break through his fugue. "Let him handle it his own way," Christine suggested. "We're here for him when he's ready."

The adults slept in the spare bedrooms or on sofas. Sam woke early Saturday morning, made coffee and stared through the back window at the ruined flower bed. By the time he remembered to take a sip, it was cold. He dumped it in the sink and roused the other adults. "Let's get this over with."

They set the service for Tuesday at Hank and Shelley's church, with John Daniels officiating. Vern phoned and asked permission to speak, as did several church elders. Gene Sanders, a member of Hank's Marine Corps unit, was flying in to tell about their military days together. Shelley drifted through the preparations in a fog, emerging from the bedroom only when the family needed her to approve details. Marie broke into fresh tears when they discussed whether to have the coffin open or closed. "I don't think I can bear to see my son like that," she told Gerald and Sam. "We had an open coffin for your father's funeral, and I've never forgotten how awful it was. It didn't look like him."

The brothers approached Shelley, who said she wanted it open. "Let them see what they've stolen from me." She closed the bedroom door without explaining who "they" were.

Across the street, Abigail Morton suffered alone. After talking to LaRonda, then hearing gunshots and watching police cars converge on the house, she had hurried across the street, collapsing at the horror in the flower bed. An officer escorted her back home, where she watched the turmoil unfold beyond her front window. "It wasn't a prowler, it was Hank!" she wailed to her late husband's portrait. She paced the floor, kneeled and cried out to God. She fretted all night, unable to sleep, sick with guilt, powerless to fix what she'd broken.

On Friday, she watched Hank's relatives arrive and disappear into the house. She wanted to confess her crime to them but lacked the courage. She got out her vacuum cleaner and attacked the carpet until exhaustion forced her to lie down.

The next morning, she stood by the window as neighbors, church friends and A&R employees arrived with covered dishes and fast food bags. She sneaked across the street and blended in with them. The doorbell rang and a woman entered with a casserole dish. "Are you family?" she asked Abigail.

"No, I'm a neighbor."

"Hello, I'm Hank's brother," Gerald said.

"I'm Donna Malone. The other night, my daughter ... you won't believe what happened." She tearfully described the encounter in the street. "He was the sweetest man. His car was wrecked, but all he cared about was my daughter's safety."

"Oh, we wondered about the car. That explains a lot. Will you join us, Mrs. Malone?" Gerald ushered her into the kitchen.

The others stood around in groups. "How could this have happened to a great guy like Hank?" a neighbor asked. "What could that cop have been thinking?"

"What was she doing here, anyway?"

"The news said the police got a prowler report. Apparently, some neighbor saw him walking around the house and called 911."

"Should have minded their own business."

Abigail drifted back home. All her life she had been a Christian and had tried to live as one. Now she knelt and begged God to forgive her. She was still praying when she finally fell asleep, in the middle of her living room floor.

On Sunday, Shelley's parents arrived, their ancient van coughing smoke and covered with faded bumper stickers. Decades of activism showed in their lined faces, graying hair and frumpy clothes. Shelley sat in the living room with them while Sam was on the phone, trying to get a police update. When he hung up, unable to reach any investigators, she excused herself and escaped to the bedroom.

"I was afraid something like this would happen," Ivy said as the family dined on the mountain of sympathy food. "Those poor GIs always come home with their heads full of war, hanging around target ranges, drinking beer and bragging about their exploits with other Army nuts."

"And wearing gun belts like Old West outlaws!" Charles added.

The Phillipses exchanged glances. "I'm sure that's not the case with Hank, Mr. Spurlock," Marie said. "Hank worked for an organization that promotes gun owners' rights and gun safety. Wearing the pistol was part of his job."

"And my brother wasn't any kind of nut!" Sam added, his face flushed.

"Well, if anybody told me I had to wear a gun to keep my job, I'd tell him to take a hike! It's the gun-crazy mentality in this country that's got people at each other's throats."

Gerald tried to change the subject. "Mrs. Spurlock, I understand Shelley and Hank met in a restaurant after he came home from the service."

"And now look at her, a widow with a son to support all by herself, all because of guns! I hope you folks can help her. Charles and I have to get back to the glass factory after the funeral."

"How long have you worked there?"

"Three weeks. Just until we save enough money for a human rights march in Saudi Arabia next month."

On Tuesday, the church doors opened with a small volunteer choir, as TV crews set up their equipment.

Hide me now
Under Your wings
Cover me
Within Your mighty hand

For those not already crushed by the news, the sight of Hank lying in a box amidst floral arrangements did the trick. The hymn could not drown out the sobs that echoed through the auditorium.

When the oceans rise and thunders roar
I will soar with you above the storm
Father, You are King over the flood
I will be still and know you are God

Not all the mourners were family or church members. Vern Saginaw and Warren DeVries led a large contingent of red-eyed A&R staffers. Dozens of ex-soldiers had dug their service uniforms out of trunks and closets to add a military formality to the proceedings. A troop of uniformed Boy Scouts filled two rows of pews. They had wangled their parents' permission to say goodbye to the man who took them on hikes and camping trips.

In the lobby two Marines, Bart Fisher and Devlin McAlister, clutched each other desperately, reunited for the first time since they lay bleeding in a shattered house, while Hank dispatched the six enemies bent on executing them. They entered the anteroom where the family waited, only to choke on the words of comfort they'd rehearsed during their airline flights. Stumbling into the auditorium, they took their seats and stared miserably at their savior's remains.

There was one other mourner who could have been in uniform but had come as a civilian. LaRonda Cage hid in the back pew alone, hoping no one recognized her. She was in agony.

Macy Shore rose with his parents as Hank's family entered and took their seats. He whispered to Patti, who nodded. She and Matt watched proudly as the boy walked down the aisle to sit beside Bruce.

The last hymn faded away and John Daniels took the stage. "Hank and Shelley Phillips came to our church about nine years ago looking, as Hank put it, for a place to get well. Hank said he had spent six years surrounded by war, suffering and death. He asked me if I thought God would forgive his part in it. I assured him that God is always ready to forgive anyone who is repentant, and that healing hurt souls is one of His specialties. Hank and Shelley were committed from that day, and they quickly became an integral part of our ministry.

"War does terrible things to people. I know from my conversations with Hank that he never got over what he was forced to do in Afghanistan. He tried to make up for it by committing himself to God, his family, his community, and his country. I believe with all my heart that God loves Hank and is holding him now in His comforting arms."

Gene Sanders reminded the audience that a soldier's life isn't all about combat. "In his off-duty hours, Hank used to organize kids in the villages we entered into soccer teams. He couldn't speak their language, but he had a way of making them understand him. By the time we moved on, the kids had stopped calling it soccer and were calling it Hankering."

The crowd chuckled. Several church elders told anecdotes about Hank's work with teenagers. One described how Hank made peace between his rebellious granddaughter and her parents. Now the girl sat in the audience, crying. She'd had a crush on Hank ever since.

The last speaker was Vern, minus his pistol. John had taken him aside and persuaded him to leave it in the car. Still, he clearly had an agenda in mind.

"I recruited Hank as my second in command because I thought his unique military experiences qualified him to help our cause. Since the day I started Armed and Ready, I've always insisted that with proper training, anyone can own and use firearms safely. Hank agreed, and he was all I hoped for. He spoke frequently and eloquently at civic gatherings around the country, convincing people that they have nothing to fear from protectors of the Second Amendment. Like everyone on our staff, Hank wore a handgun in public to assure people that A&R members are solid, responsible citizens. Hank was a patriot in the Marines and a patriot here at home. And ladies and gentlemen, Hank Phillips gave his life for the Second Amendment! His gun was with him when he was shot, and he was defending our rights at the very moment –"

"That's a lie!" Shelley screamed, leaping to her feet. "That's a dirty, filthy lie, Vern Saginaw! Hank didn't die fighting for your precious gun rights. He died trying to get into his own house! And he was murdered! With one of your precious guns!"

The crowd gasped as she strode to the stage and pointed at Vern. "*You* did this to him! You, with your stupid, stubborn obsessions. Hank spent all his time trying to clean up the hateful things you said, so people wouldn't be afraid. But they *were* afraid, even the police, so when they saw him with that pistol of yours, they shot him dead! *You* killed Hank, just as surely as that cop did!"

She collapsed to her knees, sobbing. Christine and Lynette lifted Shelley and led her back to the anteroom. John Daniels took the stage as Vern slunk away through an opposite door. "I'm sure we all understand that Mrs. Phillips is under a terrible burden today. Let's conclude this service by asking God to comfort her and her family in this time of pain and sorrow. Will you bow your heads with me, please?"

New sobs erupted as John prayed. The choir sang "Beyond the Sunset" as pallbearers approached the casket. LaRonda wasn't there to hear it. She had fled following Shelley's outburst.

At the graveside ceremony Shelley, quiet but still wild-eyed, sat with Bruce and the family as John read scriptures over Hank's coffin. Other mourners huddled in the chilly air.

Standing apart from them were two men in business suits. "We need to get together," one whispered. "Right away." The other nodded.

CHAPTER 7

Groping for fragments

After the funeral, Hank ascended to martyrdom. News commentators painted him as a champion of civility, struck down in his prime by a careless cop, abetted by a boorish gun fanatic. Vern tumbled overnight from patriot to pariah. He cancelled his speaking engagements and waited for the infamy to blow over.

LaRonda attracted a torrent of hate chatter and death threats on social media. Suspended with pay, she hid at home, despairing over Hank and worrying about Alvin's future. The CRB hearing was bound to end in her termination, maybe imprisonment. Even if she eluded jail, how could she start a new career with a high-profile killing on her record? Alvin's pension wasn't nearly enough to support him, let alone both of them. Their house still had a mortgage and needed repairs. His disability benefits covered only his medical bills and therapy.

She spent hours reading on-line tributes to Hank, while her mind's eye watched the hapless man tumble backward, over and over, into his flowerbed. She buried herself in household chores as juries of Alvin's spoon dolls and rag puppets watched in silent judgment.

Alvin silenced the scanner and watched his daughter anxiously. Before his injury, he had comforted several fellow cops who persecuted themselves after killing suspects. Not one of them was ever the same again.

Fearful of drawing their weapons, all eventually quit or applied for desk jobs. Alvin was determined to prevent this disaster from destroying his child.

"Come sit with me a minute, honey," he said one day as she dusted furniture. "Tell me what you're thinking about."

"That's the point of all this drudgery. I'm trying *not* to think."

"Have you talked to God about this?"

"I've been praying since it happened, more than I ever have."

"Does it help?"

"It helps to know God's listening. I'm not praying for myself, though. I'm praying for Hank Phillips' soul, and for his family. I don't know how that woman and her son can stand it." She gazed out the window. "I wonder if they pray."

"I'll pray with you."

LaRonda smiled. "You already pray *for* me. I don't need to see your head bowed to know that."

"I haven't heard any music since you've been hanging around here. Why don't you play your CDs?"

"You don't like classical."

"So give me a chance! Maybe I'll learn something. Or better yet, why don't you go to a concert? You need to get out of here, get your mind on something else. And don't tell me you're too busy taking care of me. How do you think I feel, watching you torture yourself while you wait for the axe to fall? Please, baby, give yourself a break. Give us both a break."

"I don't know, Pop. I don't feel much like getting out. Besides, we're saving money without Celeste."

"Well, I miss her. I want her back when this is over."

LaRonda's phone rang. "Hey Shake, what's happening? ... Uh-huh ... No, I'm all right, I guess ... He's fine too ... Yeah ... yeah, I heard about that." She glared at Alvin. "Well, uh, can I call you back?" She hung up. "Pop, how could you?"

He looked innocent. "How could I what?"

"Don't give me that! What did you do, tell him to call at exactly" – she checked the clock – "10:30 so you could set me up?"

"Oh, was that Shaker? How is he?"

"Ohhhh!" She rose and shook Alvin's shoulders. "Listen, Cupid, I'm perfectly capable of getting my own dates. I'm not some wallflower who needs a pity outing."

"Of course you're not. And if Shaker asked you out, why it's just good timing."

"Oh, please!" She smoldered for a minute. "He said his mother volunteered to stay with you so I can go."

"Great! I get a date too. Where's he taking you?"

"The symphony, of course. The Dvořák cello concerto."

"Never heard of it. But I'm glad you're going."

"Well, it *is* one of my favorites. But you watch out, mister. You pull a stunt like this again, I'll put tabasco sauce in your oatmeal."

Alvin considered this. "Actually, that might be a good idea. Oatmeal needs all the help it can get."

The two men sat facing each other at the rear of a coffee shop. One of them drew a phone from his suit pocket.

"I asked you here to discuss this." He showed his companion a video of Shelley's attack on Vern. "This went viral on the internet within two hours of the funeral. It's been broadcast nationally on every news outlet."

"I know, I saw it again last night. Very disturbing."

"That's not all. The night before Hank was shot, he made a speech to the VFW while Vern was speaking to the A&R convention. Now the VFW is pressuring all its members to cancel their A&R memberships unless Vern steps down immediately."

"Oh, no!"

"The office is being bombarded with phone calls and emails demanding that Vern resign. He's the hottest topic in social media. The President's under pressure to drop his A&R membership. There's even a movement in Congress to hold hearings on A&R's influence on the epidemic of mass shootings around the country."

"What did Hank's speech have to do with all this?"

"I was there. Hank did just what he always did, spoke reasonably about gun rights. Vern's speech in Minneapolis and the funeral incident built a fire under them."

"Whew!" The other man sipped his coffee. "What do you think we ought to do?"

He shrugged. "Vern's got to go."

"We can't do that! Vern started A&R. He's America's gun rights symbol. And despite what happened to Hank, and the funeral and everything, our core membership still believes in him."

"For now, maybe. But if he goes on the way he has, he's going to alienate so many people that our political support and funding will start to dry up. This whole mess is just what the anti-gun crowd's been hoping for. They can crucify us with it."

His companion thought for a moment. "All right. Let's call a board meeting and see what we can do."

"Don't forget, Vern's chairman of the board. He's not going to take this lying down."

"If we can get enough votes, he won't be able to stop us."

"There's one other thing. We're going to have to find someone to replace him. Do you have any ideas?"

The man snorted. "Yeah. Hank. He would have been perfect."

"Obviously, that's no longer an option. We'd better ask for suggestions while we're contacting everyone."

Sam, Gerald and their families went home after the funeral. Marie took a leave of absence from her real estate job, groping for fragments of Hank's spirit as she wandered through his house. Shelley's parents hung around through Wednesday, phoning volunteers for their Saudi Arabia rally.

As weeks passed, Marie found some solace in routine. She cooked, cleaned and did laundry. She deflected calls from the news media. She kept up with the mail and paid the bills. Shelley and Bruce mostly stayed in their rooms.

One of Bruce's responsibilities was to take out the trash after supper each evening. The first time he tried it after the burial, he couldn't turn the back door knob, fearful of what might be lurking in the flowerbed. It haunted him, like the open coffin that he'd shunned, staring doggedly at the floor throughout the funeral. So he carried the trash through the front door, out to the sidewalk, down the street to the next block, and threw it into a neighbor's dumpster. Then he walked back home, trying to think about something else. He repeated the routine each night until it became habit.

Bruce was confused. The grownups said a cop killed his father. "Police officers are our friends," Dad used to say. "They work day and night to protect us from evil." Then there was Mom. The shrieking harridan who'd leaped from his side to denounce Mr. Saginaw had frightened and bewildered him. Mr. Saginaw had always been nice to Bruce. Why was she mad at him? Bruce had never heard Mom scream at anyone, had never even seen her angry. Suddenly, she had fangs and claws.

Now, a washed-out ghost impersonated the Mom who kissed Bruce awake each morning, made him blueberry pancakes, worked jigsaw puzzles with him, tickled and wrestled him to the floor, sang songs with him while they did the supper dishes together, and kissed him to sleep at night. Sometimes he had nightmares in which the funeral Mom, clad in her witch costume, turned her flaming wrath on Bruce and swarmed over him, suffocating him in her black cloak. Other nights she was the zombie Mom, seizing her son in a catatonic hug and plunging both of them headfirst into an icy lake of death. Bruce snapped awake crying out for Dad. Marie came and stroked his hair until he dozed off.

One night, Shelley woke to a silhouette beside her bed. She turned on the lamp to find Bruce watching her solemnly. She smiled and reached out to him. He backed away and crept into his grandmother's room. When Marie woke the next morning, he lay asleep beside her.

The next day while Shelley was napping, Bruce returned and began quietly removing things from a chest containing Hank's military souvenirs. His Marine dress blues and sword. His combat uniform. Framed pictures of himself wearing both. His photos of fellow soldiers and Afghan civilians. His Medal of Honor. Once, Bruce had asked Dad why he didn't frame the medal and display it on the wall. "It's something that came from a war, son. Nothing good ever comes from war."

Nevertheless, Bruce gathered up all the objects and carried them to his room. He decorated the walls and his small desk with these things his father had touched. This way, Bruce could touch them too, and imagine that he and Dad were touching them together. Sometimes Marie came into his room, sat on the bed and told him stories of Hank's boyhood.

When Shelley was awake, she spent hours caressing a framed picture of herself in Hank's arms on their wedding day. She often fell asleep hugging it to her chest. One day she climbed out of bed and stumbled to the dresser, where Hank's keys still lay untouched. She squeezed them until her fingers hurt and sank to her knees, pressing both fists against her temples. Then she crawled back into bed, clutching the keys beneath the pillow.

Matt and Patti Shore invited them over for Thanksgiving dinner. "It'll do you good," Patti insisted. Marie was willing, anything to take her mind off her son. "I want to have Thanksgiving with Hank!" Shelley sobbed and fled to her room. "It wouldn't be the same without Dad," Bruce agreed. Marie cobbled together a take-out meal that she and Bruce consumed, absently watching the Lions thrash the Jaguars, 31-10.

The following Monday, Marie woke Bruce and told him it was time to go back to school. "Your friends Macy and Wally have called several times, asking if they could come over. And I know your teacher misses you. Come on, get up and get ready. I'll fix you some breakfast and you can catch a ride with Macy and his mom."

The thought of his friends seemed to dispel Bruce's inertia. Marie watched as he piled his backpack into the rear seat beside Macy. Behind the wheel, Patti gave her a thumbs-up before driving away.

Marie wandered into the boy's room and pressed her face to the uniform Bruce had hung on his closet door. Though Hank hadn't worn it for eleven years, she thought she could still smell him. Her tears erupted again, and she reclined on Bruce's bed, wishing God would lift this stone from her chest.

Around noon she found Shelley staring out the living room window. She gently guided her daughter-in-law to the sofa. "Shelley, listen to me. You've got to snap out of this and get on with your life."

She didn't seem to hear. "Remember my wedding day, Marie? Hank wasn't allowed to see me until the ceremony that evening. Even with all the preparations and confusion, I didn't think I could wait that long. Now I have to wait forever to be with him again."

"I know how you feel. I wasn't much older than you are now when Carl died. But I still had three boys to raise. I had to put it aside as best I could, for their sake. That's what you have to do. Bruce needs you. He's waiting for you to tell him what happens next."

Shelley stared dully at the floor. "What does happen next, Marie? How can there be a next after what I've done?"

"What do you mean, Shelley? What did you do?"

"Hank was always forgetting his keys. I *knew* that. I was married to him for eleven years. I was supposed to help him remember. If I had, he would have come home, unlocked the door, and waited for us to get back from the party."

"Oh, Shelley, you can't –"

"Hank had something important to tell me. He said we'd talk about it when I got home. Now he can't tell me because I let him down. He was miserable because of that awful Vern Saginaw, but he stuck with the job because he wanted Bruce and me to have a comfortable life. Well, Hank did his part. We've got a comfortable life. The trouble is, it's not worth living." She headed for the bedroom.

Marie grabbed her and spun her around. "Stop it, Shelley! Don't you dare blame yourself for what happened to Hank. It wasn't your fault, and I won't have you using it as an excuse to give up!" She pulled her close. "Do you have any idea how much you did for Hank? I saw him after Afghanistan before you did, and he was doing the same thing you're doing now. Punishing himself over what soldiers are forced to do in every war. Then one night he saw you waiting tables in that restaurant. It was the first time he seemed like his old self. Shelley, you saved my son. You gave him a reason to go on, and I've always loved you for it, and I always will."

The two women held each other. "Did I really save Hank?"

"You did, Shelley. You saved him."

She wiped her face. "I must look awful. Maybe I'll take a bath. Where's Bruce? Maybe we can all take a walk together. Get out of this place for a while."

"Bruce is at school. I thought he should get back to his normal routine."

"That's good. You're right, I've been neglecting him." She patted Marie's cheek. "Poor Marie. You've been crying too, haven't you? I'm sorry for being so selfish."

"Never mind. Now, how about that walk?"

"Give me twenty minutes." She disappeared into the bedroom.

As they strolled along the sidewalk, Marie's heart lightened. Though it was late November, the sun was out and the air was warm. Leaving that gloomy house was like a resurrection.

They circled the block. On their second lap Shelley waved at Abigail

Morton, watching from her front porch. Abigail scampered into the house and closed the door. What's with her, Shelley wondered.

A police car drifted slowly down the street in their direction. Shelley stopped, watching it cruise past.

"What's the matter?"

Shelley's eyes followed the car until it disappeared. "Nothing. Let's walk."

Across town at Sandstone Preschool, two teachers sat on an old wooden bench, watching children romp in the dusty playground.

"I used to think recess was for the kids," Janine said. "Now I realize it's for us. Don't they just wear you out?"

"Recess wears me out, too. It's harder to keep track of them out here."

The bell rang. The women counted the children as they filed back into the building. "Somebody's missing," Janine said. "I'll go look around." Hannah led the others back to their rooms.

Five minutes later Janine burst into the office. "Alexis, call 911! It's Andy!"

CHAPTER 8

A stuffed balloon

Gil Starnes watched nervously as Cora Mitchell showed some documents to the judge.

"Your honor, these photographs were taken shortly after Mr. Starnes' arrest. They clearly show deep bruises on his face and torso. I also offer these five affidavits from neighbors regarding other violent outbursts at the Starnes home."

She gave copies to the city attorney. As the judge scanned the pictures, Cora turned to the witness chair. "Officer Cage, what else happened during your hospital visit with Mr. Starnes?"

"Gil seemed more worried about what his father might do to him than his legal problems. I promised him I would notify CPS of his situation, and that they would make sure he was safe."

"What was his response?"

"He thanked me. He seemed relieved that he didn't have to go home."

"Did you take any other action on his behalf?"

"I spoke to the two kids he was with that night. The other boy admitted stealing the gun and whiskey from his parents. I also phoned Gil's high school counselor to report his arrest and his physical condition. She said Gil has some emotional problems but no disciplinary issues. She knew about his home life."

"Why did you go to so much trouble with this boy, Officer Cage?"

"I felt badly that I had to shoot him. I wanted to see if I could help."

"Thank you, officer. I have no more questions."

"Ms. Mitchell, what is the defendant's domestic status?" the judge asked.

"Mr. Starnes lives in a foster home. CPS determined that it would not be safe for the boy to return to his own residence. The restraining order against the father is still in force."

"Thank you. Mr. Starnes, will you stand please?" Gil rose. "Has your attorney explained to you that in juvenile court, we don't empanel a jury? That the judge has the power to determine your guilt or innocence in this matter?"

"Yes sir."

"And do you also understand that if you are found guilty of the charges brought before me today, I have the power to sentence you to juvenile detention?"

His voice trembled. "Yes sir."

"Do you have anything to say in your own defense?"

"No sir."

"Very well. It is the decision of this court that Mr. Gilbert Starnes be sentenced to no more than two years and not less than six months in custody for the crimes of reckless and drunken driving, evading arrest, and threatening an officer of the law with a firearm."

Gil cried out and buried his face in his hands.

"At the same time, the court recognizes extenuating circumstances in this case, particularly the defendant's youth and his obviously perilous domestic situation. Accordingly, I order that the sentence be suspended, and that Mr. Starnes be placed on probation for a period of six months. If, after that time, Mr. Starnes has shown himself to be rehabilitated, the charges will be dismissed. Mr. Starnes, do you understand what this means?"

"Yes, your honor."

"I hope you do, young man. As much as I can sympathize with you, we cannot have people, teenagers or adults, endangering our citizens and our police officers. I am giving you a very big break, Gil Starnes. If you were eighteen I'd throw the book at you. Take advantage of this break, of CPS, your foster family, and this kind police officer who has tried to help you. Go back to school, learn to be a proper citizen, and grow up to be somebody we can all be proud of."

"Yes, your honor. Thank you. Thank you."

Cora smiled and hugged her client. Gil looked over her shoulder at LaRonda, who was leaving the courtroom.

"Officer Cage, wait, please!" He ran to her, hesitated, then embraced her fiercely. "Thank you Off – I mean LaRonda. Thank you for all you did for me."

"Hey, I'm the one who filed the charges on you!"

"You did, and you were right. I'm so sorry for what happened. I'm so glad I didn't hurt you." He hugged her again.

"Okay, Gil. I can see you're going to be all right. Call me some time and let me know how you're doing." She gave him her phone number and watched Gil's lawyer escort him to the probation office.

Stanley Baxter, Gil's prosecutor, was waiting for LaRonda in the courthouse lobby. "Nice job, Officer Cage. You're going to give hard-nosed cops a bad name."

She grinned. "I sure hope so."

"I'm sorry about your predicament. Is there anything I can do for you?"

"Nothing legal I can think of. But if you're a praying man, I'd appreciate it if you said one for me."

He smiled. "I am, and I will. Have a nice day, and God bless you."

Before she became a drug addict, Amy French was Pechora High School's best student and everyone's nominee for next year's valedictorian. Then Cody Sewell transferred over from Simmons and immediately asked her for a date. By the time Halloween rolled around, Amy had deteriorated into something her own parents wouldn't have recognized.

In fact, Steve and Barbara didn't know where she was. The last time they saw her in April, Amy was in police custody for breaking into a neighbor's house. They learned this from the booking officer's two a.m. phone call. By the time they got to the jail, Amy had been transferred to a rehab facility nearby. They rushed over there, only to learn that she had collapsed and was lying unconscious in a secured room.

They stared through the window at their daughter and wept. A counselor appeared and suggested they go home. "She's bottomed out and she'll probably sleep for hours. I'll have someone call you when she's awake and stable."

The call came late that afternoon from an embarrassed administrator, who reported that Amy had escaped. The man asked Steve if he had any idea where she might have gone. He didn't. "The police caught her breaking into the Lunsfords' house three streets over from ours. Why would she do that?"

"Unfortunately, people in Amy's condition often resort to burglary for things they can sell to buy drugs."

"Oh, Lord!" Steve's legs weakened and he sank to the floor. The Lunsfords were family friends.

"I'm sorry about this, Mr. French. We're working with the police to trace Amy's movements. If you hear from her, please call me immediately. I can be reached at this number twenty-four hours a day."

Amy's initiation into the drug culture began with a line of white heroin powder on a hand mirror one January night. "If you feel sick later," Cody had advised, "use this. You'll feel great in no time." He placed a stuffed balloon in her hand.

"Cody, I don't do drugs. I shouldn't have done what I did tonight."

"Keep it anyway. Just in case you need it."

The next morning, she woke nauseous and aching all over. She climbed out of bed, rummaged through the bathroom drawers for a mirror, and carefully spread the powder over it. Soon she was flying high again. Her Saturday morning jaunt to the mall with friends felt like a trip to Disneyland.

But the next day she was hurting again, badly. After church she hid in her room, trying to study. She took some aspirin, then Advil. They didn't help.

At school Monday, Cody led her into an empty classroom. "This is the last free one," he warned as she snorted another line. "I have to pay for this stuff, you know."

"It's okay. I just need to clear my head a little." She gathered up her books and rushed out the door as the first period bell rang.

By the end of that week all Amy's old priorities – Student Council, Thespians, church ministry, and tutoring – had vanished in a cycle of ecstasy and pain. She was making excuses to her friends and spending every free moment – and every dollar – with Cody, who seemed to have an inexhaustible supply of balloons.

Amy's parents didn't catch on until much too late. They'd had no reason to suspect anything was wrong with their daughter, who had always been a model of maturity. By the time they did, the girl had graduated from balloons to needles and was beginning her master's studies in cocaine.

When Cody wasn't around, Amy could always depend on his "consultant," Giselle Hoover, who tutored her through the various wonders of Uppers, Vitamin R and Blue Ice. When her allowance didn't stretch far enough, she borrowed cash on her credit card and loaded up on Crack.

Shortly after the card maxed out, Barbara went into Amy's room to discover that her laptop was missing. She claimed she had left it in her locker at school. But Barbara never saw it again, nor the other things Amy sold to pay for drugs – her bicycle, TV, Bluetooth headphones, Smart Watch and jewelry. Finally, Amy abandoned all pretense and disappeared – except for the nights when she sneaked into the house while her parents were asleep to steal more collateral, including her car title.

Desperate, Steve called the police, who issued an alert with Amy's description and found her Civic in a used car lot. The dealer had paid her $2,500 in cash – a steal for him. Amy didn't call home or attend classes. Her only friend now was Giselle Hoover.

As for Cody, he had transferred out of Pechora the same way he transferred in: by snowing a girl in the administrative office into revealing the password to the school system's database. He left with a profit of $8,300 and a new alias enrolling him at another school. Amy and a dozen other brand-new junkies were on their own.

Now it was November. Pechora High School's brightest star lived in an abandoned warehouse downtown with other addicts who pooled their begged and stolen resources to get by. Amy had lost twenty-seven pounds and looked like a model for a famine poster. She rarely thought about her happy life of nine months earlier. These days, she had more immediate concerns.

Warren DeVries watched from his office as twelve grim-faced men marched down the hallway toward the conference room. He hadn't seen the Armed and Ready board members gathering for months. It could mean only one thing. They were here to discuss The Crisis.

Since Hank's funeral, A&R had been inundated with hate texts and membership cancellations. Demonstrators picketed outside headquarters, and at this very moment, workmen were cleaning anti-gun slogans and slurs off the walls. Vern's defenders countered with a tirade of conspiracy claims: that Shelley's outburst at the funeral was scripted; that Hank was an imposter, his Afghanistan adventure a lie that he used to infiltrate A&R; that Hank, Shelley and LaRonda were actors in a plot to pressure Congress into a firearms ban.

These days, Vern spent most of his time away from the office. Shelley's denunciation seemed to take the spark out of him. His brisk morning return from the A&R convention, when he went around high-fiving everyone, seemed years ago.

Warren hoped the directors were up to something good. Vern's domineering enthusiasm and Hank's kindly spirit had been the core of daily life at A&R. Now the atmosphere was morgue-like. Clerks and secretaries worked in morose silence, their phones forwarded to voicemail against the daily tide of crank calls. Still, they loyally wore their pistols to work, obeying Vern's open-carry edict. Sometimes Warren thought Vern was begging for trouble. In the high-pressure atmosphere of corporate America, all it took was one personality clash to ignite a shootout. Imagine the consequences of such a catastrophe at America's biggest gun lobby.

Warren felt torn. He had come to work for Vern because he was an outdoorsman himself. Though most people thought of A&R in terms of guns, it also had branches devoted to fishing, camping, exploring, skiing, mountain climbing, boating, river rafting and wildlife preservation. Warren had grown up in a part of Wisconsin where boys learned about game hunting early. His father wouldn't let him even touch a gun until Warren could recite all the safety rules. Dad never approved of hunting for sport. You cooked and ate what you killed, and you thanked The Good Lord before you did.

Then there was Hank. Warren hadn't known much about him when he arrived at A&R, aside from his military legend. Hank had surprised him. This wasn't your standard-issue macho Marine. He once told Warren in strict confidence that after Afghanistan, he'd sworn never to touch a gun again. He wore Vern's gift pistol out of obligation. Warren thought he missed Hank more than anyone else. He missed their morning chats over coffee, their lunch outings, even their rare disagreements. Most of all, he missed the man. Hank was the most decent guy Warren had ever met.

Some of the office staff suggested that Warren might be chosen to replace him. The thought was loathsome. Building a career on the corpse of a friend. Still, he was anxious to know what the board was going to do. With Vern gone so much, Warren was handling Hank's old duties plus his own. This woolgathering wasn't getting any of it done.

"I read the A&R bylaws before I agreed to join this board," David Tischner declared, "and this meeting is illegal! Vern Saginaw is chairman. Any decisions you make in his absence are invalid."

"It's not a formal meeting, David," Wesley Hawkins replied. "We just want to discuss the situation and get a show of hands."

"We can't address this problem with Vern present anyway," Marcus Thorne added. "Vern himself is the issue. Besides, the bylaws provide for removing the CEO under extraordinary circumstances."

David glared around the table. Staring back at him were the president of Northgate Pharmaceuticals, the founder and CEO of Gamma Microsystems, the chancellor of Sandstone University, and eight other elites.

"I'll tell you what the issue is," he retorted. "It's what Vern said in his speech that you guys are so anxious to bury. Nothing that happened to Hank Phillips changes the fact that our country's very foundations are under attack! Vern's working to protect them. We've got to stand behind him."

"If you're so concerned about our Constitution, how come you're mixed up with that bunch of secessionists?"

"They're not secessionists! Sam Leopard and Joe Brunnel are fighting to protect our state's heritage from all these politically correct judges tearing down Confederate monuments."

"David, we're all trying to do what's best for America," Hawkins said. "But some of us feel the organization would be better served if we replaced Vern with someone more moderate. Any thoughts?"

"Depends on who you'd replace him with, Wes," Harvey Wexler said. "Regardless of what happened with Hank and the funeral, gun owners trust Vern because he's always defended the Second Amendment. I won't agree to a change that's going to weaken A&R's support."

"Harv, there are plenty of executives in the smaller gun lobbies who could step in," George Masters argued. "Who wouldn't jump at the chance to replace a media star like Vern? Let's worry about succession after we take a test vote."

"Any objections to that?" Hawkins asked. "All right, let's see your hands. All in favor of removing Vern." Eight hands rose. "All against." Three hands. "Sid, what about you?"

"Undecided."

"All right, that's eight out of twelve in favor of removal. It takes nine to pass, so unless one of you wants to change his mind, we can't call a formal meeting on this issue anyway. What about it? Anybody want to change his vote?"

Silence.

"So what do we do now?" Marvin Hayes asked.

"I don't care about the rest of you, I'm washing my hands of this," David said. "Vern Saginaw built this company and this entire city. He's been my friend for twenty years. I'm not going to sit here and watch you Judases make him a scapegoat." He rose and left the room.

The parents were grateful to see a black-and-white parked in silent vigil by the curb after school. Some of them waved cheerful thanks at the cruiser as they packed their children into minivans. But LaRonda wasn't watching for speeders or pedophiles. She was watching for Bruce Phillips.

Captain Vanderbilt had pulled a few strings to let her keep her patrol car. He knew she couldn't afford her own wheels. Alvin Cage had been Don's probation partner during his rookie year, before a petty thief sentenced his mentor to life in a wheelchair. If you had to break a rule, the captain thought, you ought to break it for a good reason.

LaRonda was breaking one now, stalking her victim's son. She didn't see it that way. She just wanted to get a sense of what the boy's life was like.

The school door swung open, producing Bruce and two other boys. One of them had gone to sit with him at the funeral. She watched as they ambled along the sidewalk, Bruce listening as his friends chattered about something. They climbed into a family van that carried them away.

LaRonda yearned to follow, knowing she couldn't, not in a police car, not being who she was.

"What are you doing here?" she muttered. "How is this helping him, or you, or anybody?" She couldn't resist. She felt she ought to do something for the boy.

More children exited the building, laughing, talking, horsing around. LaRonda wished she were nine years old again, backpack on her shoulders, playmates or homework waiting, running to catch the bus, running back to the days when Pop was still whole and working. More than anything, she wished she could relive Halloween night.

A Twitter alert pinged her phone. "Trick or Treat!" it said. "Killer Cage calling!" Her tormenters never ran out of witticisms. Some of them were pretty clever. "Sandstone Police motto: shoot twice and ask questions later." Or "You can have my gun when you can pry LaRonda's from her cold, dead fingers." One rewrote an old Beach Boys tune: "Help LaRonda learn to shoot the bad guys instead." Alvin urged her to close the Twitter account. She refused, deliberately absorbing the abuse like a medieval penitent.

The kids were all gone. Just a few teachers heading for the parking lot. There was nothing more to see. LaRonda rested her head on the steering wheel and prayed silently. Then she picked up her phone and typed in a number.

CHAPTER 9

Doctor Luke

Jason and Alexis Tischner sat on their second-hand sofa, clutching each other tightly.

"Think hard," the officer urged. "A relative? Somebody at work maybe?"

Alexis shook her head. "I work part time at Andy's preschool, bookkeeping. It's just me, the boss and two teachers. We're all friends."

"It can't be anybody at Special Olympics," Jason added.

"What about your father, Mr. Tischner? The note was directed specifically at him. Do you know who his enemies might be?"

"Take your pick. My father's not known for his congeniality."

"Could it be somebody who has a grudge against your family, maybe from something that happened years ago? Any sort of incident, no matter how minor, could be important."

The parents looked at each other and burst into tears. "I'm sorry," Jason wept. "It's so hard to think straight!"

"Let's give them a minute, Rex," Wendy Cruz suggested. The two cops retreated to the kitchen, where a forensics officer studied the evidence. "I've never worked a kidnapping before, have you?"

"I know the drill. The family's our best hope for figuring out who took him."

"What about a Facebook or Twitter search? The guy might have spilled his guts about kidnapping somebody before he got up the nerve to do it."

"That's worth a try, I guess." They stared at the note on the table.

Andy Tischner will come home when David Tischner does the right thing.

Doctor Luke

That was all. Typed and printed on an ink jet printer. Folded in a plain white business envelope. Sealed with water, not saliva. No prints, except those of the cop who found it in the playground's jungle gym.

"Wendy, what do you think that signature means?"

"Doctor Luke? Sounds like a rock star."

"Could be a clue. Look, I'll notify Cap. He may want to contact the feds. Why don't you stay here and see what else you can get out of the parents?" She returned to the distraught couple in the living room.

Tears crept slowly over LaRonda's cheeks as she sat beside Shaker, the sweet melody washing over her. Onstage, a young woman played cello as the conductor waved gently at the orchestra.

"Are you all right?" Shaker whispered.

She nodded and dabbed her eyes. Dvořák's poignant second movement seemed to express everything she'd been feeling lately. She thought she'd never be able to hear it again without thinking of Hank Phillips. Shaker watched her from the corner of his eye, a mixture of admiration and concern distracting him from the music. He had never seen LaRonda looking this beautiful.

Shaker had dated almost every single female on the day shift – cops, clerks, dispatchers, even the watch commander's daughter. The other cops called him Officer Fickle, but he meant no harm; he just wasn't ready to settle down. Then one night he met LaRonda while covering for a fellow cop. He couldn't decide which enchanted him more: her looks or her personality. She had a way with people, charming even the suspects she cuffed and piled into the police van. He watched as she sat on the curb beside a violently trembling junkie, speaking softly until he agreed to let her drive him to a treatment center. "Thank you, officer," the man wept. "It's LaRonda to you," she smiled.

Shaker gave up tomcatting and pursued LaRonda like a lovesick teenager. Getting a date with her required patience. They worked different shifts, and Alvin absorbed most of her free time. Determined to corral her, he began plotting a transfer to night duty. Then the Hank Phillips disaster struck.

Police officers who shot citizens sometimes lost their jobs, then got rehired, either through the appeals process or because other communities short of manpower gave them a second chance. But LaRonda had shot two people within twenty-four hours, killing one of them, a nationally-admired figure. Shaker couldn't imagine a darker scenario. He hoped he was wrong. Alvin's future depended on LaRonda's. After only two dates with her, Shaker decided his did, too.

The performance ended, the soloist bowing to cheers and applause. The magic was over. Shaker escorted his date to the parking lot. LaRonda was glad he'd brought his own car. This wasn't the night for a police cruiser.

"Did you like the soloist?" he asked, the music still echoing in his head.

"I was wishing I could trade places with her. Don't you wish you had a job like that? Wouldn't you love to spend your whole life lifting people's spirits?"

"With a standing ovation at the end of your shift?"

"Exactly!"

"I was just thinking how much time I wasted in my teens, listening to pop songs."

"What changed your taste?"

"Well, there was this gorgeous music teacher in my junior year ..."

"What a surprise."

Shaker laughed. "My reputation is worse than I thought."

"You wouldn't have appreciated classical otherwise. I sure didn't."

"Really? I thought you were a born highbrow."

"Not me. My mother liked Gospel music, and my father likes jazz. He thought I was a heathen because I spent my allowance on Michael Jackson CDs."

"So what changed *your* taste?"

"That old movie, 'Amadeus.' When I was a senior, I rented it one Sunday afternoon. When it was over, I couldn't believe I'd been sitting there for three hours. I went on line and ordered a handful of Mozart CDs. I was hooked."

"I guess there's hope for everyone, then. Even hip-hoppers."

They arrived at a small coffee shop. Through the window, they could see several couples chatting at tables. The place looked warm and inviting.

"It was nice of your mother to stay with Pop tonight," LaRonda said over hot chocolate. "He doesn't get much company outside of me and Celeste, and she's got another assignment right now."

"She was glad to do it. Mom gets lonely sometimes."

"You haven't told me much about your family. Was your dad a cop, too?"

"No, he worked at Pierpont, on the assembly line. When I decided to enter the police academy, he said he wished he could have a job like that, outdoors, not having to do the same thing all day."

"What happened to him?"

"Cancer, three years ago. He was only forty-eight. Mom and my sisters took it awfully hard. So did I."

LaRonda became pensive. "I wonder which is worse. Losing someone you knew and loved, or not ever knowing that person. I barely remember my mother. I still ask Pop to tell me stories about her."

"I admire your devotion to him. It must be hard for you."

"Oh, no, I'm used to it. Besides, we're very close. Being a cop, you see so many dysfunctional families. It must be awful to hate your own kids, or your own parents."

"You must be thinking about that Starnes kid. Are you worried about the CRB hearing next week?" She frowned. "Oh, what's the matter with me? I asked you out to get your mind off it. I'm sorry."

"Don't apologize. It's never far from my thoughts anyway." She sighed. "I've done a lot of on-line research about Hank Phillips. The more I've read about him, the worse I've felt. Then tonight, the music was ... I can't explain it. His face was in my head, and it was like Dvořák was telling his story. I thought I could feel his personality, his love for his wife and son, his pain from the war, all in that second movement. I guess that sounds crazy."

"Not at all. That's what I like about classical. It's so full of things you can't express in words."

"Dvořák spent his life making music. Cops spend theirs cleaning up people's messes. Now I've got my own mess to clean up." She was quiet for a moment, watching cars whiz past the window. "Shake, you've handled prowler calls, haven't you?"

"Yeah. Quite a few."

"Did you ever draw on any of them?"

"Sometimes, if I thought it was necessary."

"You've never shot anybody, though. Why not?"

Shaker put his hand over hers. "LaRonda, it was a judgement call. If I'd been in your place, I might have done the same thing."

Her eyes filled again. "I don't understand why I drew my pistol. I could have waited. Then, even when I saw his gun, there would have been a few seconds ... time for both of us to –"

"Hey! It's done. You made the best decision you could. Stop beating yourself up." He paused. "Listen LaRonda, I can rearrange my days off so I can go to the hearing with you. What do you think?"

"That's sweet of you, Shake, but they won't let you in. It's supposed to be very confidential."

"So I'll sit with you in the hallway until they call you, and I'll be there when you get out."

"No, you stick to your schedule. Keep your mind on your job."

Shaker frowned at something behind LaRonda. She turned to see several customers whispering and gesturing toward her. It was a reaction she'd begun to notice when she went anywhere. "We'd better go," she said. "Pop needs the ventilator sometimes. Your mother's never handled one."

A chilly breeze followed them to the car. As he started the engine, Shaker decided to go for broke. "LaRonda, I know this isn't the best time to bring it up, but what would you think about marrying me?"

"What?" she asked, startled.

"I've been in love with you since that drug bust we worked together."

She laughed. "I'm not sure how to take that."

He took her hand. "There's something about you that feels like ... coming home."

She hesitated. "Well, since you're putting your heart on your sleeve, I'll be honest. I think about you a lot more than you realize. But Shake, my father needs me. I can't promise you anything, the way things are now."

"How long are you going to carry this load by yourself? You know Alvin wants you to have your own life. And it's not like you have to choose me over him. He could live with us. I don't know anybody I'd rather have for a substitute dad than Alvin Cage."

"You sure make it sound cozy. All right, I'll think about it. Seriously. But Shake, the review board is probably going to sacrifice me to get the pressure off the department. You're courting a doomed woman."

"Come on, your chances are better than that. The CRB knows what cops face, and the decisions they have to make. You'll come out all right." Silently, Shaker cursed himself. He didn't think she had a prayer.

"Still, I won't marry you and have you wind up supporting all three of us."

"I know. Your integrity is one of the things I like best about you. That and the way you look tonight." He kissed her.

"Mmmm." She closed her eyes, then broke away gently. "It's been a lovely evening, Shake. Thank you."

He put the car in gear. "Come on. Let's go break up the old folks' orgy."

CHAPTER 10

Remnants

The doorbell was ringing, but Shelley's attention was on the gun. It lay before her on the kitchen table, a spiteful remnant of Hank. Remnants were all she had left. His wedding ring. His wallet. His watch. His clothes. His reproachful house keys. A scrap of paper with Donna Malone's phone number.

A police officer had returned the Colt a few days after the funeral, Marie locking it in the file cabinet. Shelley had forgotten all about it until this morning, when she went looking for Hank's financial portfolio. And there it was, hiding in its leather holster.

She'd been trying to get an idea of where she and Bruce stood money-wise. Hank's investments were solid, but his portfolio was only nine years old, and the house had a hefty mortgage. There were insurance premiums, car payments, taxes and other expenses. Shelley's résumé listed only two qualifications: ex-activist and ex-waitress.

Since the day Marie forced her out of lethargy, Shelley had tried to build some momentum toward recovery. Each morning, she made herself rise and get Bruce off to school. She drew strength from Marie, who helped her cook, clean house and run errands. Now Marie was gone, back to her job in Cincinnati. When she woke without Hank beside her, Shelley felt as though an iron blanket held her in the bed. What was the point of getting up to another day of grief? Wait for the day to be over so she could sleep it off and wake to another one? Hank didn't come home last night. He wouldn't be coming home tonight. Where was the incentive?

The doorbell rang again. Shelley ran her fingers slowly over the gun, feeling the cold, hard texture of the barrel, the grip, the trigger guard. The rational part of her could understand why the officer had shot Hank, but Shelley didn't want to be rational. It felt better to blame the cop, the pistol, Vern Saginaw, and everyone who thought guns could solve problems. She'd like to show LaRonda Cage a few of hers.

Every TV talk show in America kept phoning her for interviews about Hank, Vern Saginaw, mass shootings and gun rights, forcing her to screen her calls. She supposed she could milk them for a pile of cash, but she didn't want the spotlight. Her light had been Hank. Now he was with God, who wouldn't share him anymore.

Last week, Shelley called Donna Malone and made her describe her encounter with Hank, desperate to salvage any last scrap of him. She called again the next day, repeating her questions until she could picture the entire episode. "Call any time you want, Mrs. Phillips," Donna said. "Your husband's quick thinking saved my daughter's life."

Hank's family and Shelley's mother phoned regularly to check on her. Actually, Ivy's calls devoted about thirty seconds to Shelley, then thirty minutes of griping about Charles. Their marriage was beginning to fray after thirty-five years on the road. "He never asks my opinion," she fretted. "He just says we're going to New York, to Caracas, to New Delhi, like I'm his travel secretary or something. Now his blood pressure's out of control. He won't see a doctor, and we're both wearing ourselves out doing piecework between trips. The van needs a new transmission and we're broke. Can you wire us $700?"

The doorbell persisted. After Marie left, Shelley began surfing the internet for fresh news on the investigation. She studied Officer Cage's police photo, searching for the murderous soul behind the cheerful smile. The DA had declined to indict her, pending the CRB hearing. Although Hank's life insurance would pay double if the shooting was ruled an accident, it would be worth the loss to see that cop behind bars.

Yesterday, she decided to check her voicemail. There were dozens of messages, mostly from reporters, sympathetic friends and Hank's A&R colleagues. Then this one.

"Mrs. Phillips, this is LaRonda Cage. I guess you know who I am." There was a short pause. "If you don't mind, I'd like to come visit you and try to explain about what happened that night. I don't mean to make excuses, just help you understand why I ... why I did what I did." Another pause. "I want to explain. I want to apologize. I want to help. Anything I can do for you. Please, if you don't mind talking to me for a little while, please call me."

Shelley had stared at the phone as LaRonda left her number, then hurled the monster violently against the bedroom wall, caught it on the rebound and bashed the wall repeatedly with it, hating it, punishing it, finally collapsing to the floor in a cloud of Sheetrock dust. Her fury spent, she sat there, possibly for hours, thinking about nothing, finally touching the cracked screen out of curiosity. Amazingly, it still lit up. Steve Jobs had done himself proud.

The doorbell rang again, followed by aggressive knocking. Shelley sighed and rose to answer it. Probably more reporters. "Who is it?"

"Shelley, it's John and Patti. May we talk to you, please?"

She hesitated. "John, I'm not in very good shape for company today. Can you come back another time?"

"Shelley, please let us in."

"Well ... okay. Give me a minute to freshen up."

She slogged to the bathroom. Her mirrored image with its rumpled bathrobe, disheveled hair, bloodshot eyes and ghostly pallor might have won the best costume prize at the church Halloween party. So much for the cute little waitress who captured the heart of Hank Phillips. She began to weep.

The knocking resumed. "Shelley? Are you all right?"

She returned and opened to worried faces. "I'm sorry to keep you out there in the cold. Some hostess I am. Please, come in."

She led them to the kitchen. "Would you like some coffee? I was just about to make some."

Their silence made her turn around. Both visitors were gazing in horror at the gun on the table. "Oh, that's Hank's. The one he was wearing that night. I was just looking at it before you got here."

John and Patti exchanged glances. "Why don't you let me take this, Shelley?" he suggested. "This isn't a good thing to have around."

"That's what I used to tell Hank," she smiled wanly. "I was right, wasn't I?" The anguish surged up and she sank into a chair. "I'm sorry," she choked. "I didn't want anyone to see this anymore. Just a thought, or a memory, or even the sight of good friends like you is enough to make me fall apart." They sat as she yanked a tissue from the box on the table. "What did you want to see me about?"

"Shelley, I realize you probably haven't felt like attending services," John said, "but Church is more than a building with rituals. We can come to you just as easily. People are concerned about you."

"I don't know what anyone could do. Hank's mom and his brothers keep calling, but after a while they run out of things to say. They're hurting, too. We all just have to get over it."

"What about your parents?"

She smiled wryly. "They called me from Guatemala last week. Got arrested during a human rights demonstration. The State Department's trying to get them out."

"Honey, you don't have to bear this alone," Patti insisted. "That's what the Church is for, to give you strength."

"We had an elders' meeting last night," John added. "We went around the table, and each one said a special prayer for you and Bruce. There's comfort in God's arms, if you'll open your heart to Him. What do you say? Can we schedule a prayer meeting, either here or at the building?"

Shelley's face darkened. "I'm in no condition to be in God's presence. I'm too angry. I don't want to be comforted, I want my husband back, and if I can't have him back, I want that cop to get what's coming to her!"

She leaped to her feet, her voice shrill. "How could she do it? He was just locked out of the house, he was just trying to break a window or something! People lock themselves out of their houses and their cars and their offices all the time. It's just a little mistake. None of them get killed for it. Why did Hank have to be the one?"

She paced the floor, fresh tears streaming down her cheeks. "He had something he wanted to tell me. He called me early in the afternoon and said he had something to say, something about his job, something important. I know it was! I waited and wondered all afternoon, all through the Halloween party, right up to the moment I saw him lying there dead in my flower bed! He had something to tell me, and now I'll never know what it was!" She collapsed into her chair, sobbing.

Patti kneeled and wrapped her arms around her friend. "I know, Shelley, I know. He was such a wonderful man."

"Hank was one of my best friends," John added. "He was an inspiration to me, as he was to everyone who knew him."

Shelley wiped her eyes. "I know. I was so proud of the way people looked up to him. Oh John, I miss him so much, I can't stand it."

He took her hand. "You're right. You can't. Not by yourself. As long as you hide within yourself, you'll never get better. Pain and bitterness feed on each other until you can't see or feel anything else. So let us help you. Let God help you. He's right here, He knows exactly how you feel, and He's ready to heal you. All you have to do is ask."

She released a long, exhausted sigh. "Oh, what a bore I am. You must hear this all the time, John. And Patti, you've got your own family to worry about. I'm sorry. This is the reason I stay home. I hate myself like this." She dabbed her eyes. "All the elders prayed for me? Max and Scotty and Terry Williams and funny old Arthur Hackett?"

John nodded. "Every one of them."

"They ganged up on me, huh? All right. You win. Will you and Patti pray for me John? Now?"

"I thought you'd never ask." As they bowed their heads, John discreetly slipped the Colt into his overcoat pocket.

"When's Mommy coming to pick me up?"

"Not for a while."

"I don't like this place. I'm supposed to be in school."

"We can have school right here. Let's work on your story books some more."

"I'm tired. I wanna see Grandpa."

"Grandpa's busy. But he's thinking about you."

"Why do I have to be here?"

"I need you to keep me company. Will you stay? Please? So I won't be lonely?"

"Okay. But just for a little while."

Two FBI agents watched David and Jason Tischner trade stares across the table, each waiting for the other to look away or flinch.

"I'm sorry you two are having to meet under these circumstances," Gary Rivers said. "Does this note mean anything to either of you?"

"No. Nothing." David replied. Jason shook his head.

"Do you have any idea what this person's talking about? This 'right thing' he wants?"

"No. No idea."

"What about the signature? Do either of you know anyone named Luke or Lucas?"

"I've got a question of my own," David said. "How did this scumbag abduct my grandson in broad daylight with two teachers watching?"

"We've questioned both of them. There were thirty-five kids on the playground at the time, hard to monitor when they're all running around. Also, there was a jungle gym with a playhouse. We think the perp hid there before recess, lured Andy into it and kept him there until the playground was clear. Then he just walked away with the boy."

"So now it's up to me to get him back. This Doctor Luke expects me to do the 'right thing,' whatever that is, although this situation can't possibly be my fault, because I'm not allowed to see my own grandson!"

"Nothing's ever your fault, Dad!" Jason retorted. "The buck stops at the bottom with you!"

"You don't put this off on me, you hear? I offered to pay for a private school. Instead, you put him in a cheap public preschool so that he gets snatched right from under the noses of two incompetent –"

"You don't run my life anymore! You don't run my son's life! You're not going to screw him up the way you did me! My son's going to grow up happy and normal, not like the miserable –"

"Gentlemen, this isn't –"

"You screwed up your own life, boy! I gave you everything you needed –"

"STOP IT! Both of you!"

The two men sat back and looked away from each other.

"This isn't helping us find your boy. Please, put your differences aside and concentrate on that one thing. Please."

Agent Steve Sanders was leafing through some documents. "Mr. Tischner, you're CEO of Pierpont Electronics, and you're on the boards of several other organizations, including Armed and Ready. Your business connections indicate wealth, which suggests the kidnapper may be after money. But the note doesn't demand money. Can you think of someone who might have approached you for a business deal that you refused?"

David concentrated for a moment, shook his head. "No. No one."

"Could someone else have a grudge against you, as this note seems to suggest?"

"Only about a million people," Jason muttered.

David glared at him. "It's possible, I suppose. Pierpont's been on a roll since I restructured management and cleared out all the redundant staff positions. Making enemies comes with authority."

"What about these New Texas Confederacy friends of yours? Sam Leopard and Joe Brunnel have posted some pretty radical remarks on their website."

"That's just Sam blowing off a little steam. They couldn't have anything to do with this."

"Sir, I'd like you to go home and make a list of every person you laid off, and anyone else who might be at the bottom of this."

"Yes, I can do that."

Agent Rivers spoke up. "Mr. Tischner, do you have a good relationship with Andy?"

"I did have, when I was allowed to see him."

"And when was the last time?"

"About two months ago."

"Why haven't you seen him since then?"

He looked at Jason. "You want to hear my version or his?"

"Both, please."

"We –" he paused. "Jason, I just wanted to do better with Andy than I did with you. I was showing him my gun collection to help him get to know me." He swallowed. "I love that boy."

Jason tried to speak, then slumped in his chair.

"Mr. Tischner – Jason – why is your, uh, financial status so far below your father's? You and your wife are both college graduates."

"I didn't want to be like my father. Career ladders, board rooms and stock options. Special Olympics doesn't pay much, but helping disabled children sets a good example for my son. Alexis has an accounting degree, but she wanted to stay close to Andy. So she works mornings at his school."

"Still, even with both your jobs, it must be hard to make ends meet."

"We manage."

"Jason, did you write this note?"

He blinked. "What?"

"Are you trying to extort money from your father?"

He gaped at the agent. "That's the most ridiculous ... how could you ... I couldn't possibly do such a thing!"

"I'm sorry, sir. I had to ask. We have to take all possibilities into account, and the animosity between you and your father is quite obvious."

Jason rolled up his sleeve. "Give me a polygraph exam. Right now."

"That won't be necessary, sir. We just –"

"No, let's get this out of the way. I don't want you guys distracting yourselves with unwarranted suspicions, picking through my personal life, upsetting me and my wife, instead of tracking down the monster who's got my son!"

"All right, I'll arrange it. I'm sorry I had to bring it up. Please believe me, we want to recover the boy as much as you do."

"What about the AMBER alert?"

"We're postponing it, for now. Your father's a prominent man. If the public finds out who Andy is, we'll get a lot of publicity clutter and phony ransom demands that will only complicate the investigation."

"But everybody at the preschool and Special Olympics knows about the abduction."

"We've already spoken to them. Everyone's promised to keep quiet."

"How can I help?" David asked. "I'll do anything. Pay a ransom. Talk to the guy. Whatever it takes."

"Just make that list I asked you for. Tonight. The sooner we start eliminating suspects, the better chance we have."

CHAPTER 11

"I just had a feeling"

SANDSTONE CITIZENS REVIEW BOARD
Wyman Lopez, Executive Director

LAW ENFORCEMENT PROCEDURAL HEARING
JANUARY 14, 10:00 A.M.

AGENDA ITEM ONE
Police officer LaRonda Cage, firearm discharge, October 31, 12:28 a.m.

AGENDA ITEM TWO
Police officer LaRonda Cage, firearm discharge, October 31, 9:20 p.m.

PANEL CHAIRMAN: FELIX SCOTT

PANELISTS: SHARON BASS, ARNOLD WILSON, MELISSA
                    STANFIELD, BUFORD MCCANDLESS, SADIE
                    GREGORY, HAROLD SMITH

TRANSCRIPTIONIST: SALLY DUVAL

SCOTT: Let the record show that the subject of this hearing, Police Officer LaRonda Cage, Badge Number RT32, has been advised of her right to have an attorney present during this panel's interrogation, and that she has waived that right. Is that correct, officer?

CAGE: Yes sir.

SCOTT: Do you understand that you are under investigation for discharging your firearm while on duty? That your actions have resulted in the injury of one person, and the death of another?

CAGE: I understand.

SCOTT: Do you also understand that unless you are able to justify your actions in these incidents, you are subject to disciplinary proceedings that can lead to termination of your employment and criminal prosecution?

CAGE: Yes sir, I do.

SCOTT: Very well. Has everyone read the shift reports regarding item one, the shooting of Gilbert Starnes?

(ALL INDICATE AFFIRMATIVE)

In that case, I'll open the questioning to the panel.

GREGORY: Officer Cage, your report on the Starnes incident indicates that the subject appeared disoriented. How do you justify discharging your firearm at him?

CAGE: Mr. Starnes didn't respond to my order to drop his weapon. Officer Ferguson repeated the order, and I repeated it two more times. Then he pointed it at me.

GREGORY: Did he threaten you or anyone?

CAGE: No ma'am.

GREGORY: Did he point the weapon at his fellow passengers or Officer Ferguson?

CAGE: Not directly, no.

GREGORY: Did he say anything to indicate that you were in danger?

CAGE: He didn't speak at all. It was only when he raised his gun in my direction that I felt compelled to fire at him.

GREGORY: Did you feel you were in danger?

CAGE: At the time, I didn't think about it. He pointed the gun at me, and I just reacted.

GREGORY: But your report says you didn't go for a fatal shot. It says you "fired at his lower extremities, striking him in the right leg." So you must have had time to choose the direction of your shot.

CAGE: Well, not exactly. I thought about it afterward, and I guess I just fired at his leg instinctively. Officer Ferguson was about ten yards behind him and would have been in my line of fire if I'd aimed higher and missed.

GREGORY: When Mr. Starnes pointed the gun at you, how long did you wait before shooting?

CAGE: About a second, I think.

STANFIELD: Officer Cage, I'm intrigued by the part of your report in which you refer to a "pistol-like object" in the suspect's hand. This morning, you're calling it a gun and a weapon. Does the phrase "pistol-like object" mean you weren't sure the object was a gun?

CAGE: That's correct. I wasn't sure until he pointed it at me.

STANFIELD: So until that moment, it could have been anything, from a cell phone to a whiskey bottle.

CAGE: I suppose so.

STANFIELD: But a moment ago you were calling it a weapon, then a gun, not a "pistol-like object." It sounds as though you'd made up your mind that it was a gun before he pointed it at you. Was that the case?

CAGE: As soon as I saw he had something in his hand, I had to assume it was a gun until I knew otherwise. There were people in the area, myself included, who were in danger if it did turn out to be a gun.

STANFIELD: When you seized the pistol, was it loaded?

CAGE: Yes, the ammo chamber was full. The safety was off.

STANFIELD: You say you fired instinctively at the subject's leg to avoid hitting Officer Ferguson. At any time during the incident, did you consider aiming higher?

CAGE: I don't recall thinking one way or the other. It was just a reaction.

SCOTT: For the record, Officer Ferguson's testimony states that he would have shot the suspect himself when he raised the weapon if Officer Cage hadn't.

STANFIELD: Did you attempt to interrogate Mr. Starnes after you disarmed him?

CAGE: I read him his rights. He didn't seem to hear me. I wrapped his wound to stop the bleeding and turned him over to the EMTs when they arrived.

MCCANDLESS: Officer Cage, our investigation revealed that you visited the suspect in the hospital later that morning. Didn't you know this was a breach of department policy?

CAGE: Yes sir. I wouldn't have done it except for his age, and for the facial bruises I noticed after I shot him. I had the feeling that something bad had happened to him that led to this incident. I thought I should find out what it was.

MCCANDLESS: That's commendable, Officer Cage, but didn't you realize how it would look? You shot somebody, then went to visit him. It looks like an attempt to influence the boy's testimony about the shooting in your favor.

CAGE: Sir, I was worried about him. And it turned out that his bruises were inflicted by his father, who has a history of abusing his son. I wanted CPS to get involved before the father found out about his arrest.

MCCANDLESS: How did Mr. Starnes react to your visit?

CAGE: At first, he was disoriented and seemed to have no memory of what happened. After a few minutes, he remembered some of it. He cried and expressed remorse.

SCOTT: Let the record show that Mr. Starnes is now living with a temporary guardian, under a suspended juvenile court sentence. Does anyone have any more questions regarding this incident?

(NO RESPONSES)

All right. Let's turn to item two, the fatal shooting of Hank Phillips. Once again, has everyone read the reports?

(ALL INDICATE AFFIRMATIVE)

If no one objects, I'd like to get to the heart of the matter. Officer Cage, this case has some very disturbing elements. I hope you can clear them up.

CAGE: Yes sir, I'll try.

SCOTT: You wrote that when you saw the suspect at his back door and ordered him to freeze, that he spun around with a gun in his hand, took a firing position and aimed it directly at you. Is this correct?

CAGE: Yes sir.

SCOTT: And that when he did, you fired twice, striking him in the chest.

CAGE: That's right.

SCOTT: And that you subsequently discovered that the gun was empty, and that the subject was Hank Phillips, an executive with Armed and Ready.

CAGE: Yes sir.

SCOTT: Officer Cage, how can you justify merely wounding a drunk teenager guilty of reckless driving and threatening an officer with a gun, and then, less than twenty-four hours later, fatally shooting a respected citizen in his own back yard?

(WITNESS INDICATES EMOTIONAL DISTRESS)

Officer Cage, do you understand the question?

CAGE: Mr. Phillips' reaction to my order took me by surprise. It was dark, there was no moon, and at the time I thought he was a burglar. I had no idea he was armed.

WILSON: I don't understand, Officer Cage. Your report stated that he was holding a pistol.

CAGE: I didn't see that at first. It was only when I told him to freeze that he displayed the gun.

WILSON: At what point did you draw your sidearm? When you saw him, or before that?

CAGE: Before. As I approached the house.

WILSON: Why?

CAGE: I'm not sure.

WILSON: You're not sure? Officer Cage, you've been on the force for ten years. Haven't you investigated prowler reports before?

CAGE: Yes, I have.

WILSON: Do you normally draw your firearm on such occasions?

CAGE: Not usually, no.

WILSON: What made this occasion different from the others?

CAGE: I can't answer that. I just had a feeling. Drawing the gun seemed the safe thing to do.

WILSON: Your report says Abigail Morton across the street believed the family was out of the house. Did you try to verify her story before drawing your pistol?

CAGE: I thought about ringing the doorbell. But the windows were dark. It seemed prudent to check on the prowler first.

WILSON: The prowler might have been a child out trick-or-treating. Did you think of that?

CAGE: Yes. Mrs. Morton insisted it was an adult trying to break in.

SMITH: Officer Cage, will you describe your impressions when you approached Mr. Phillips? What did you think was going on before you saw the gun?

CAGE: I thought he was trying to break the backdoor glass. He was tapping it with something that turned out to be his gun.

SMITH: How far away were you from Mr. Phillips when you ordered him to freeze?

CAGE: Seven or eight feet, I think.

SMITH: You shot Mr. Phillips twice in the chest. With the teenager, only hours earlier, you aimed low and fired only once. He was pointing a gun at you, too. Why the difference?

CAGE: I didn't know Mr. Phillips had a gun.

SMITH: But you said he was holding something. You also said that the previous night, Gil Starnes was holding something. Yet, with Mr. Phillips you went for a fatal shot.

CAGE: He assumed a firing position. I didn't have time to think.

SMITH: What position was that?

CAGE: He dropped to one knee and aimed the pistol at me with both hands.

SMITH: Why didn't you order him to drop it?

CAGE: I never got a chance. I was still saying "freeze" when he turned on me, like he was ready to shoot.

SMITH: You said earlier that it was dark, and there was no moon. How could you tell he was holding a gun?

CAGE: I couldn't, actually. It was his reaction, his aiming posture that convinced me he had a gun.

SMITH: So we're back to the Starnes case. You assumed it was a gun.

CAGE: Yes sir.

SMITH: As far as you knew, the object Mr. Phillips was holding could have been a gardening tool, couldn't it?

CAGE: If it had been a gardening tool, I don't think he'd have reacted the way he did. But I admit that I couldn't really be sure it was a gun.

SMITH: The coroner's report stated that Mr. Phillips was wearing a business suit and a hip holster. Didn't you think it peculiar that a prowler would be dressed that way?

CAGE: I couldn't tell how he was dressed. It was too dark.

STANFIELD: Officer Cage, when you ordered Mr. Phillips to freeze, did you shout or speak?

CAGE: I spoke firmly, not loudly.

STANFIELD: Do you think your voice startled him?

CAGE: Yes, it seemed that way.

STANFIELD: Your report says the words you spoke to Mr. Phillips were "Police! Freeze! Don't move!" Is that correct?

CAGE: Yes.

STANFIELD: He pointed the gun at you before you said "Don't move," is that right?

CAGE: Yes.

STANFIELD: Did you fire while you were still speaking, or after all the words were out of your mouth?

CAGE: I think I was still speaking.

STANFIELD: I ask because you said earlier that you waited about a second before firing at Mr. Starnes after he pointed his gun at you. Now I get the impression that you fired at Mr. Phillips immediately, before he had a chance to obey your order. Do you see what I mean?

CAGE: You're right. I ... I didn't give him a chance.

STANFIELD: You fired twice. Why twice?

CAGE: He ... Mr. Phillips ... I don't know. I've asked myself that over and over.

GREGORY: Officer Cage, your first action before you even saw Mr. Phillips was to draw your pistol. What was this feeling you had that made you do that?

CAGE: Again, I just don't know. It was just a feeling. I can't describe it.

GREGORY: Did you feel you were in danger?

CAGE: No ma'am. I mean, not exactly.

GREGORY: Can you be more specific?

CAGE: No, I can't. I'm sorry.

GREGORY: Did you feel you were in danger with the Starnes boy?

CAGE: I didn't feel anything. Later, though, I did. Feel I had been in danger.

GREGORY: You said earlier, and I'm quoting, that on the Phillips property you drew your gun because it "seemed the safe thing to do." Doesn't that suggest that you felt endangered?

CAGE: I ... It means ... Ma'am, it was just a feeling. I'm sorry I can't give you a better answer.

BASS: Officer Cage, only one night earlier, you discharged your firearm and wounded a teenage boy. Can you describe your state of mind the following evening when you were summoned to investigate the prowler report?

CAGE: I was kind of upset when I arrived for my shift. I'd never shot anyone before.

BASS: Do you mean you regretted shooting the boy?

CAGE: Yes and no. I hated doing it, but it was necessary to stop him from waving his gun around.

BASS: If you felt so badly about it, why were you so quick to draw your gun the following night?

CAGE: I can't explain that. It was that feeling I had.

BASS: You said a moment ago that you believe you startled Mr. Phillips when you ordered him to freeze. Wasn't he justified in reacting instinctively, just as you did?

CAGE: Yes, I believe he was.

BASS: So this again calls into question your decision to draw your pistol before approaching him. Do you think you were right in doing so?

CAGE: No. Now I wish I hadn't.

BASS: Officer Cage, if you had it to do over again, under the same circumstances, would you shoot Mr. Starnes?

CAGE: Yes ma'am. He was out of control and he disobeyed my repeated orders to drop the weapon. He was a danger to me, to his fellow passengers and to Officer Ferguson.

BASS: Officer Cage, if you had it to do over again, under the same circumstances, would you shoot Mr. Phillips?

(WITNESS INDICATES EMOTIONAL DISTRESS)

Please answer the question, Officer Cage.

CAGE: Mrs. Bass, if I had it to do over again, I'd shoot myself instead. I've done a lot of research on Mr. Phillips since that night. He was a decorated soldier, a nationally-admired citizen, and a devout Christian. He had a wife and child whose hearts are broken because of me. I know you have the power to end my career and help the district attorney put me in prison. I'll understand if you do.

SCOTT: Does anyone have any further questions?

(NO RESPONSES)

Officer Cage, do you have any further statement to make?

CAGE: No sir.

SCOTT: This hearing is concluded. Officer Cage, this panel will deliberate and let you know our conclusions within the next ten days. Thank you for your testimony. You're dismissed.

CHAPTER 12

An accomplice

"What was it like?" Macy asked. "Seeing your dad – you know. You don't have to tell me if you don't want to." It was Saturday morning. Macy was helping Bruce catch up on school work.

"I didn't really look. When I saw what was going on, I ran away."

"Were there a lot of cops and ambulance guys and stuff?"

"Yeah, and TV people with mikes and cameras. Did you see any of it on the news? I didn't."

"Mom and Dad wouldn't let me watch it. What about that cop who did it? Did you see her that night?"

"I don't remember. There was so much going on. It's all kind of blurry now."

"What do you think they'll do to her?"

"I don't know. Do they put cops in jail when they shoot the wrong people?"

"Well, on TV everybody who kills somebody gets a trial, even cops."

Matt entered the room. "Macy, your mom needs you for a minute." He closed the door as his son left. "How's the math work going, Bruce?"

"Okay. I'd be caught up already if Mrs. Crandall would quit giving us homework."

Matt chuckled. "I don't know how I wound up with a son who's a math whiz. Most of it was over my head. How'd you like the game last night?"

"I thought we were going to lose until that interception. Bobby Kretzler did great."

"You still want to play for me when you get to high school?"

"Yes sir, if I'm good enough."

"There's always room for boys who try hard." Matt took a seat. He'd coached boys for fourteen years now. The ones without fathers required special handling. "How's your mom?"

"Okay, I guess. She doesn't talk much."

"I'm glad you're back in school. Is it helping you feel better?"

"Sort of. I sure miss Dad, though."

"What do you miss about him?"

"Everything. Talking to him. Playing games. Doing Cub Scout projects. And stuff like sports. Dad coached our Little League team last summer. He showed me how to play shortstop. I didn't understand what it was until he did. I just thought there was a guy for every base."

"Yeah, the shortstop's a handy guy to have around. What else did you do?"

"On Friday nights, Mom and Dad had a date, except they took me along with them. We'd go to a different restaurant every week and order something none of us had ever tried before. That was the rule. No steak, no fried chicken, none of the usual stuff. It was fun." He paused. "Mr. Shore, why do you think that cop lady did it?"

"I wish I knew, Bruce. She's under investigation for it right now."

"You mean like a criminal?"

"Well, sort of. If they find her guilty of something like negligent homicide –"

"What's that?"

"Killing someone out of carelessness. Not following the rules. Anyway, if they convict her of that, she could face a prison term."

"Do they really throw cops in jail? I thought only criminals went to jail."

"You're right, that's true most of the time. But cops have authority over the rest of us, so we have to hold them to a higher standard of behavior."

Bruce thought about that. "What if they find her innocent? Will she go back to work?"

"Probably, if she wants to. She may decide she doesn't want to be a cop anymore."

"Why would she think that? It's her job, isn't it?"

"Well, sometimes people become unhappy in their jobs. They want to try something different. I don't think Officer Cage is going to be happy again for a long time. Can't you imagine how she feels, shooting somebody's father? Somebody's husband?"

"Gee, I never thought about that. Do you think she's as sad as Mom?"

"I wouldn't be surprised. Have you been sad, too?"

"Yeah, sure, but with Mom ... she doesn't want to do anything anymore except cry about Dad."

"Have you tried talking to her?"

He stared at the floor. "I don't know how."

Matt scooted over and put his arm around the boy. "Bruce, if you ever need somebody to talk to, I'm right here." The warmth brought fresh tears to the surface. Matt held him quietly for a while.

"Mr. Shore, do you think they'd let me meet her?"

"Who?"

"That police officer."

Matt was surprised. "I hadn't thought about that, to tell you the truth. You know, Bruce, she may not want to meet you. It might make her feel worse."

"I want to meet her anyway."

"Why?"

"To see what she's like."

"Hmm ... I'll tell you what. Let's give the officer some time to get through her hearing and see how that turns out. If she's cleared of the charges and goes back to work, I'll put in a good word for you. I have some friends on the police force."

"Okay."

"In the meantime, why don't you and your mom join Macy, Patti and me for dinner out next Friday night? You can help us pick out the dishes we've never tried."

"That sounds great. I'll ask her."

"Good. I'll go find Macy so you two can get back to work."

Matt returned to the kitchen, where his son waited patiently. "He's all yours ... Mason."

That same morning, Shelley realized she had never thanked all the friends and neighbors who sent flowers and brought food to the house after Hank's death. She decided doing so now would be therapeutic. She made a list and drove to the store for thank-you notes.

On her way back, she happened to glance across the street at Abigail Morton's house. She realized she hadn't seen her neighbor in weeks. She walked over and rang the bell. Opening the door was a shock for both women. Shelley was the last person Abigail wanted to see. And to Shelley, Abby looked like a corpse. In the middle of the day she wore pajamas and a bathrobe. Her hair was scraggly and she wore no makeup.

Shelley recovered first. "Abby, I'm sorry I haven't visited you in so long. Are you all right?"

Abigail hid behind the door as best she could. "Hello, Shelley. I'm ... I'm not dressed for company."

"That's okay. I just want you to know that Hank and I always considered you our favorite neighbor, and to me you still are."

Abigail crumbled to the floor, weeping.

"Abby, what is it? Are you sick?" She dropped her manners and stepped inside, raising the lady to her feet and leading her to a chair. Shelley didn't know what to think. Despite her age, Abigail had always been outgoing and energetic. This shell of a woman was weak and fragile. She seemed to have lost weight. Shelley wondered if she had cancer.

She kneeled and held her friend until the crying subsided. "Shelley, how can you stand to talk to me? How can you stand to be around me?"

"What a thing to say! Abby, you look like you're sick or something. Have you seen a doctor? Should I call someone for you? Someone in your family?"

The kind words just set her off again. "Abby, please tell me what's wrong. What can I do for you?"

She pulled away, drying her tears with her sleeve. "I thought you knew. I thought you hated me. You must. How could you not?"

"Hate you? Why should I hate you? Abby, what is all this?"

"It was my fault. I'm the one who called the police. The night Hank ..."

Shelley stared at her, beginning to understand. "You called the police? Why?"

"I saw someone prowling around your house and I thought it was a burglar. The house was dark, I didn't think anybody was home, so I called 911. And that officer came to my door, then she went across the street, and ..." She turned away, unable to bear what was dawning in Shelley's eyes.

"So it was you. This all happened because of you."

"Because of me!" Abigail had been a recluse since that night. Too ashamed to attend the funeral, she had dropped out of her bridge club, abandoned church, silenced her phone and now left the house only to buy food, which she could scarcely taste. She spent most of her days in front of the TV, hardly conscious of what she was watching. Her children, unable to reach her, came to the house to find her as Shelley had and could not comfort her.

"I wanted to tell you," Abigail moaned. "But when I saw all your relatives hurting and saw they were hurting because of what I'd done ... I didn't know what to say. I don't know what to say now. I don't know how to make this right. All I know is, I'm sorry. I'd give anything, do anything to make it right, Shelley. Anything at all."

Shelley stood. "You can't. You can't make this right. Nobody can make this right." She marched out of the house, back across the street to the scene of the crime. Only now, LaRonda Cage had an accomplice.

Vern's normally ruddy complexion was almost purple. "Out? What do you mean, I'm out? Who do you think you're talking to?"

He stood at the head of the conference table, twelve men squirming under the imperial glare that had shriveled opponents for decades. "You don't vote me out. You don't do anything without my say-so. I'm the only reason you guys are even sitting in this room. What do you mean, I'm out?"

They exchanged furtive glances. Wesley Hawkins finally spoke up. "Vern, what happened to Hank ...what happened to you at the funeral ... we can't overcome that. New A&R subscriptions have taken a nosedive in the past two months, and so have contributions to the Second Amendment Fund. Our ad revenue is down. The President's resigned his membership. People don't feel comfortable with us anymore. And the reason is you."

Vern snorted. "What are you guys, born yesterday? When has gun rights not been an emotional issue? Do you know how many of these battles I fought when you pansies were still in diapers? The Kennedy brothers, Charles Whitman, Martin Luther King, John Lennon, Jim Brady, and all those other nut cases? Every one of them was an excuse to torpedo the Second Amendment. Without me, this organization would have sunk back in the Sixties."

"But this is different. This is one of our own men, shot by a police-woman with a spotless record because he was packing a gun, on your orders. How do we come off looking like the good guys after you made that ... that challenging speech the night before? Medal of Honor winners are almost deities in this country, Vern, and this one made a conciliatory speech the same night you made yours."

"Vern, that widow's attack on you at the funeral made us all look like monsters," Marcus Thorne added. "If we don't change something, and quickly, we won't have any influence in Congress."

"He's right Vern," Ethan Preston said. "I met with Senator Maxwell just last week. The West Virginia attack put Congress back on the hot seat. There's going to be tough new gun legislation in the spring. He thinks it's got a good chance to pass."

Vern's scowl remained. "You people make me sick. None of you has ever stood up for America like I've been doing all my life. Even Hank was more patriotic than any of you."

"That's just the point, Vern! He was a war hero. Now he's a martyr to your open-carry policy!"

Vern placed his hands flat on the conference table. "What's the vote here? How many on my side?"

"It's nine to three."

He nodded. "Three-quarters majority, just barely enough to wreck the organization you should be thanking me for. I want a show of hands. Who's on my side?"

Sid Barnes, Calvin Butcher and Marvin Hayes raised their hands. Vern scanned the other faces. "David ... you voted against me?"

He cleared his throat. "Yes, Vern. I'm sorry."

"I don't believe it. I hand-picked you as Galloway's replacement. We've been friends for two decades. How could you do it?"

"Vern, it had nothing to do with our relationship. It ... I had a per-sonal reason."

Vern's face fell. "Stabbed in the back, like Caesar." David hung his head. "All right, you've had your vote. But you mark my words, there's not a man in this room with the spunk to build A&R back up the way I have after every crisis. So go ahead. Fight over the scraps like a pack of dogs and see which one of you winds up on top. And when you finally get it through your heads that scraps are all you've got, you'll be begging me to come back and clean up your mess."

He glared around the room. "I didn't spend sixty years in this business resting on my laurels. When Americans think of Armed and Ready, they think of me. I *am* A&R! Without me, you're going to have nothing!" He stormed to the door and spun around. "Have a nice day!" He exited with a slam.

Hawkins broke the ensuing silence. "Okay, the worst part's over. Let's hear some discussion about a replacement."

"I have a question first," Arthur Hudson said. "David, last time we met, you were with Vern all the way. Why'd you change your vote?"

"I have nothing more to say." He stared stonily out the window.

The day after Vern's ouster swept through the news, an email message appeared on Jason Tischner's computer:

Andy Tischner will come home when David Tischner does the right thing.

Doctor Luke

During lucid moments, Amy French briefly escaped from Drug Amy. Lying on the dirty floor of a fellow junkie's apartment, she relived Christmas mornings with her parents, volunteering at Make-A-Wish, tutoring fellow students and hanging out with friends. Her teachers' faces floated into view, and she basked in their warm smiles as they returned her A-plus papers.

She recalled her acceptance into the National Honor Society and the ensuing flood of scholarship letters. She remembered laughing, the kind of laugh that came with being young, full of the future, and so happy to be alive that you *have* to laugh to relieve the pressure.

At such times, Real Amy stepped out of herself and saw what Drug Amy had wrought. She'd never dreamed she could be suckered into drugs. But she'd also never had a boyfriend. Popular as she was, Amy was only average-looking, so she was thrilled when the new guy with the dark hair, magnetic eyes and easy stride asked her out. By the time her cravings took over, Amy realized that to Cody Sewell, she was just another customer.

The pain drove her further into chemistry. Then, as each hit wore off, she envisioned Jesus sadly looking down on her from Heaven. She curled up to hide from Him, seized her oily, matted hair in both scrawny hands and pulled until it hurt. Each time, she vowed that it was over, that she was done with this junk, finished, quits, never again, never, never.

Rising from the floor, she would stumble into someone's dingy shower stall. She ignored the hunger rising through the cascade of warm water, tried to scrub away Drug Amy, seed and grow a Repentant Amy, reconciled with her parents, reinstated in school, graduating, enrolling in college and letting God lead her wherever He wanted her to go.

Then as she toweled off, her bones and joints would start to hurt, the chills would come, and the nausea. She fought to drive it underground so she could organize her thoughts. It was no good. The craving crushed and scattered her spirit. She needed something to help her focus.

And that was when Drug Amy would pull on her dirty clothes, scrape together whatever cash she could borrow or steal, or whatever junk she could sell, and stagger to the nearest dealer, buying just enough relief to help Real Amy think. And she *would* think ... until the cycle began again.

"I'm not like this!" she sobbed one night to a nameless street source. "I don't do drugs. Please, help me!" Whoever it was laughed harshly, snatched her money and drifted away as Drug Amy's mind blinded her, pulled her into herself and devoured her.

This was what happened when you threw God's precious gifts back in His face. You stumbled from some junkie hotel, crawled out of some alleyway, or crept from behind some dumpster, begged a few dollars from a pitying stranger and started over. Drug Amy had checked her into Hell, and the best she could do was pay the rent.

CHAPTER 13

Two laughing cops

The dinner outing for Shelley, Bruce and the Shore family did not go well. Maybe if the CRB verdict had come in later. The news broke that very morning, when Felix Scott stood before a crowd of reporters.

"After a careful review of the facts and circumstances surrounding these incidents, and after carefully questioning everyone involved, the Citizens Review Board has concluded that Officer LaRonda Cage should not be held responsible for the death of Hank Phillips, or the wounding of Gilbert Starnes on October 31 of last year. The Starnes shooting was a clear case of self-defense. Although there was evidence that the officer might have handled the Phillips situation better than she did, we found nothing to indicate that she was in any way willful, negligent, or careless in her approach to what she thought to be an attempted burglary. In each instance, Officer Cage was suddenly faced with a gun pointed directly at her. The Starnes gun was fully loaded. The fact that Mr. Phillips' gun turned out to be empty had no bearing on the board's recommendation, because there was no way the officer could have been aware of that fact. She reacted as anyone else might have done in similar circumstances. We also took into account the officer's excellent service record. Before the unfortunate date of October 31, she had never fired her weapon at anyone and had helped persuade several armed subjects to drop their weapons."

An anchorman appeared. "The CRB did reprimand Officer Cage for visiting Gilbert Starnes while her case was pending. However, it seems now that an indictment is unlikely, and that Officer Cage will be reinstated."

In Cincinnati, Marie Phillips was showing a house to some newlyweds when her phone began vibrating like an angry rattlesnake. She excused herself and stepped outside. The screen showed missed calls from Sam, Gerald and a barrage of numbers she didn't recognize. There was also a news alert about the CRB verdict. She leaned against the door, trying to hold back tears. Somehow, it was like losing Hank all over again.

The phone buzzed. "Sam, I'm showing a house. Try to calm down and I'll call you later." She put on her realtor's face and went back inside. After the couple left, she sat in her car, deflecting calls from reporters and trying to sort out her feelings. She started to call Sam when the phone buzzed again.

"Did you hear? Did you *hear?*" Shelley shrieked. "She got away with murder! How dare they? How *dare* they!"

"Shelley –"

"She's back on duty like nothing happened. My husband's lying in the dirt, and that woman's out writing parking tickets and – and – shooting *more* people, for all I know! What kind of country is this?"

"Shelley, please stop shouting. I know what you're saying. You feel cheated. I guess I do, too. But Shelley, even if they'd thrown her in jail, Hank would still be gone."

"Marie, how can you say that? That's your son she killed!"

"Shelley, you've got to get past this. Bruce needs you. Are you going to let this poison eat away at you until there's nothing left for him?"

"There's nothing left for me, either!" She wept wrenchingly into the phone.

"Shelley, when my husband died, I had nothing to blame but leukemia. Maybe you could try thinking of it that way."

"This wasn't some disease, Marie! This didn't have to happen."

"You and Hank were so devoted to God and your church. Have you reached out to God? What about that nice man who preached Hank's funeral? Have you talked to him?"

Shelley exhaled raggedly. "They came over here one day, John and my friend Patti Shore. We did pray, and I felt better for a while. But Marie, it never goes away. No matter how hard I try, I can't erase that picture of Hank lying in my flower bed." She was crying again. "How do you get rid of this? How do you stop hurting?"

"That's what I'm trying to tell you. God is there for you. He's waiting to help you, if you'll only have faith."

"I did have faith, Marie. When God brought Hank into my life, I committed myself to His Church. But then He stole him away. Why would He do that?"

"It's not just you, Shelley! We all loved Hank. Maybe He's testing us. Testing our faith."

"Why?"

"To see if we love God as much as we loved Hank. Love Him enough to give Hank up."

"If that's what you believe, then I've been wrong to worship a God that cruel!"

"Oh, Shelley. I don't know what else to say."

"You've already said it. 'Think of it as a disease.' Well, that's not good enough for me. God owes me an explanation, and if you really loved your son, you should demand one, too!" She hung up.

Marie checked her calendar. Three more showings and two angry sons. Shelley had a point. Forgiving LaRonda Cage felt like betraying Hank. Why did God give people such awful choices? She dialed Sam's number and drove toward her next appointment.

For the rest of the day, Shelley channel-surfed from one newscast to another, stoking her fury. Meanwhile, reporters kept calling. She ignored them, paced around the house and fumed. By the time Bruce returned from school, she was a wreck.

"Mom? What's wrong?"

She shifted her scowl from the TV to her son. "That woman who killed your dad got off. They didn't even make her pay a fine."

Bruce put down his backpack and sat beside her, listening to the details. "What's 'acquitted'?"

"It means found not guilty. How do you like that?"

He thought about it. "I'm glad. I didn't want her to go to jail."

Shelley rolled her eyes. "That's what your grandma said! Bruce, you and your dad were so close. Don't you have any feelings for him anymore?"

"Yeah, sure. I think about him all the time. But it's like they said on the news. She didn't mean to do it."

Shelley threw up her hands. "I give up. Everybody's on the cop's side, even my own son!"

"Mom, the Bible says we're supposed to love each other and forgive each other's trespasses."

"I know that, Bruce. But some things just can't be forgiven."

"Then why does the Bible say that?"

"Oh, who cares what –" His open, honest face stifled her. "You'd better get cleaned up and change your clothes. Macy and his parents will be here in a little while."

He stood hesitantly. "Mom, I really do miss Dad. But I miss you, too. You're like somebody different. When are we going to be happy again?"

Shelley covered her face. "I don't know! I don't know!"

The Shores arrived without the twins, whom they had left with a sitter, and the little party headed for a popular seafood restaurant. Shelley noticed they were all avoiding the subject. She concentrated on a story Patti was telling about the day's carpool. They arrived and scampered in quickly to get out of the cold.

"What kind of seafood do you like, Bruce?" Matt asked as they took their seats and opened menus.

"Anything that doesn't taste fishy." He wrinkled his nose. "But the rule is, we have to order something we've never tried before."

Bruce and Macy decided on crab cakes with fries. Patti chose clam chowder and salad. Matt got stuck with raw oysters, having tried everything else over the years. "I hope they taste better than they look. What about you, Shelley?"

She scanned the selections. "I don't know, what's good here?"

"Everything. I'd get the deep-fried shrimp again, but Bruce won't let me." Matt elbowed the boy, who giggled.

As a girl took their orders, Shelley suddenly found herself back in her own waitressing days. She was finally grown and independent, free of her parents and their chaotic lives, barely able to pay her rent, but happy. She was young and starting a new life. Anything seemed possible. Then she was back to the night Hank and Marie came into her restaurant. Hank was giving her the eye every time she passed. He was ordering fresh napkins, more breadsticks, water refills, finding excuses to keep her at his table, teasing her, charming her, making her laugh, Marie watching the impromptu courtship with great amusement. It was one of the happiest nights of her life, and her fondest memory of Hank.

"Ma'am, what can I bring for you?"

Shelley started, suddenly yanked back to the present. "Oh, I'm sorry, uh ..." She lifted the menu again, and that was when she saw two blue uniforms at a table across the room. They were young officers, two women, smiling and laughing over something. Some joke perhaps, or a funny story from their police experiences. Both wore gun belts.

"Ma'am, do you need a few more minutes to decide?"

She looked around. Matt, Patti and the boys wore guarded expressions.

"I'm sorry, you know, I don't think I'm very hungry. Why don't you just bring me ... uh ... some hot tea?" She offered the menu to the girl.

"Mom! Hot tea?"

"Yes, please Shelley, order something. This is a great place. And you don't have to eat all of it if you can't."

She lowered her eyes to her lap. "Thanks, Matt. I think I'd ..." she trailed off. The silence grew awkward.

"I guess that's all, Miss. Hot tea for the lady, please."

"Yes sir, thank you." The girl left.

Bruce put a hand on his mother's arm. "Mom?"

She tried to avoid looking at the two officers. "Maybe it's too soon. I'm sorry, everyone. Will you excuse me for a minute?" She rose, marched briskly to the ladies' room and burst into tears, whether in anger or grief, she didn't know.

"Shelley, are you all right?" Patti asked from outside.

"I'm ... I'm okay." She stifled the sobs and emerged, blotting her eyes with a tissue. "I'm sorry, I'm ruining everything. Will you call me a taxi? Then you and the others can enjoy yourselves, and I'll try to do better next time."

Patti grasped her hands. "Shelley, stop apologizing. Nobody expects this to be easy for you. We're all your friends. Come on back to the table."

"It wouldn't be so bad if everything didn't remind me of Hank."

"That's right, you met in a restaurant, didn't you? But that's a happy memory. Come on back and let's see if we can't make a new one."

"All right." Patti led her to her seat. "I'm sorry, everyone. Please ignore me. And please enjoy your dinners." She smiled as best she could.

The waitress brought their orders, and everyone carried on with surface gaiety. Everyone except Shelley. Her attention was on the two laughing cops. Yes, this sure was a nice place. When the law was on your side, everything was just dandy.

LaRonda sat at the kitchen table, studying the checkbook and trying to ignore the newscast blaring from the living room.

"What does it take for a cop to get convicted of murder? Who's next, if even the most respected citizens aren't safe?"

"It just shows how all the cops stick together. The whole system's rigged in their favor."

"I saw her in a coffee shop one night with some big, tall stud. I'll bet Hank Phillips' widow doesn't have anybody to waltz her all over town."

"Two shootings in less than twenty-four hours? Whoever heard of a cop like that getting off with a reprimand? Something stinks. The federal government should move in and clean house!"

"Idiots!" Alvin turned off the TV and wheeled into the kitchen. "LaRonda, why are you messing with this? Paying the bills and balancing the checkbook is my territory."

"I know. I just wanted to get a feel for where we are. Even though we didn't lose my base pay during the suspension, I missed some great bonus chances around Thanksgiving, Christmas and New Year's."

Alvin rummaged through his toy-making materials. "The flea market's closed until spring. Maybe there's some kind of phone or internet job I could do at home."

LaRonda frowned. "I wouldn't let you work for one of those sleazy outfits. Trying to scam old people into crooked deals. Everybody hanging up on you all day. Stop worrying! We're doing okay."

"Hmph! How's Shaker? You talked to him since the news?"

"He called me as soon as he heard. He wants to take all three of us out to celebrate. What do you think?"

"I'll pass. I'm not the one he wants to marry, and I certainly don't want to be your chaperone."

"Come on, you know how much he likes you. Anyway, we don't

talk about anything we wouldn't want you to hear." She returned to the checkbook. "So, what do you think about me and Shaker? Do you think I ought to tell him yes?"

"You should have said yes already."

"What you said isn't true, you know. He really does want to marry us both. He thinks with one house and three incomes, it'll make life easier for all of us."

"Oh no! Ohhh no! I'm not part of the deal. This is your chance for happiness, LaRonda. I will not be a drag on your marriage."

"Oh, Pop! You know I wouldn't get married without considering you."

"You'll just have to. I'd never do a thing like that to my daughter. You've done too much as it is."

"What do you think I'm going to do, stick you in an invalid's home and forget about you? You know me better than that."

Alvin gave her the same glare he'd once used to humble foul-mouthed criminals. "What you're going to do is make your plans and let me make mine. There are plenty of options for people like me in a country like this, and best of all, I've got Almighty God to ask for help whenever I need Him."

Somehow, her father's brave posture reminded LaRonda of Hank Phillips falling backward into his flower bed. She collapsed over the checkbook.

"What's the matter?"

She cried so hard that Alvin wheeled himself close and put his arms around her. "Hey, what is all this? I'm sorry, I don't know what I said to bring this on."

LaRonda struggled to speak. "It's ... you're being so noble, and Hank Phillips is still ..." The sobs broke forth anew. "I tried to phone her. I wanted to explain how it happened. I wanted to give her something, anything ..."

"Oh, baby, you're still carrying that cross, aren't you?" He held and patted her. "Never mind, let's forget about this for now. Shh. Shh. Don't fret, we'll figure something out."

CHAPTER 14

A whiskey sour without pleasure

Warren DeVries sat at the conference table in shock. Eleven faces beamed at him.

"I'm sorry, did I hear you right?"

"You heard right. Effective immediately."

His head swam. Five minutes earlier Warren had been at his desk, smothered in paperwork. He'd had no idea how much Vern and Hank had to handle, and he had been Hank's right-hand man. There were six corporate divisions to direct, payrolls to approve, federal reports to file, conferences to plan, congressmen to woo, A&R publications to oversee, meetings to attend, membership campaigns, on and on. Desperately, he had borrowed a couple of assistants from other executives. It was like spitting on a roaring campfire. How could anyone run an organization this big?

He'd been irritated at the knock on his door. Somebody else wanting something. That somebody turned out to be Wes Hawkins, the acting chairman. Could he come to the conference room for a few minutes?

"Let me get this straight. You're not offering me Hank's job. You're offering me Vern's?"

"That's right."

"Well ... I don't know what to say. I mean, why me? I'm just a cog in the machine here. I thought you'd be looking for some corporate super-star to replace Vern. He was a celebrity. Nobody's ever heard of me."

Hawkins smiled. "Warren, you know the organization better than anyone. You helped Vern and Hank with every lobbying campaign on the Hill. Our membership reached an all-time high before the shoot-ing, thanks mostly to you. You're intelligent, you speak well, you already know the job, and you know the issues we face. Why should we look outside A&R for Vern's replacement, when we've got a natural choice right here in this room?"

Warren scanned the men's faces for signs of doubt. He saw only smiling confidence.

"Well, I'm … I'm very, very flattered. Thank you."

"So does that mean you'll take it?"

He hesitated. "You're right about one thing. I do know what the job entails. I've hardly seen my wife and kids this week. I'll have to know some details before I can accept. Pay, of course. Contractual terms. Hiring an assistant or two. I'll certainly have to talk it over with my wife. How soon were you thinking of announcing it?"

"The sooner the better. Our members and donors need to know who's in charge, or we'll suffer more attrition."

"Yes, of course." Warren frowned. "How much leeway would I have? Are you wanting some sort of rubber stamp figurehead to carry out the board's wishes? Or would I have the kind of power Vern had?"

Hawkins tossed him a thick folder. "This is your CEO contract. It's what Vern had, with minor modifications. Essentially, you would have complete authority, subject to board approval in cases of major policy change." He smiled. "We wouldn't be offering you carte blanche if we weren't pretty confident of what to expect."

Warren flipped through the documents, then laid the folder aside.

"You know, Vern started A&R and kept it going and growing for six decades. He made it what it is today. Yet, you folks gave him the boot. What's to prevent you from doing the same thing to me?"

Gavin Taylor spoke up. "Vern had to go, Warren. He was practi-cally talking anarchy in his speech the night before Hank's death. Even our biggest donors were uneasy. We know that's not going to happen with you. We're counting on you to take a more moderate approach to gun rights."

Warren nodded. "Gentlemen, you do me a great honor. I will most certainly consider your offer and get back to you. Thank you. Thank you very much." He rose to accept their handshakes. And even though he still hadn't recovered from the shock, Warren knew he would take the job. It was an opportunity to do something he'd dreamed of for a long time.

David Tischner had signed Warren's contract offer but skipped the meeting. He sat in the den with Marla, sipping a whiskey sour without pleasure.

"If you feel so lousy about cutting Vern loose, why'd you do it?" she asked.

"I thought it might satisfy this Doctor Luke character. Maybe he knows I'm one of Vern's best friends." He sighed. "Or was."

"Then it's got to be something else."

"Well if you're so smart, you tell me!" He saw the pain in her eyes. "I'm sorry."

"David, I'm so scared. What if this guy's some kind of pervert or child murderer?" She lay on the sofa and wept. He watched her, feeling helpless and angry. Abruptly, he went to the kitchen, poured his whiskey down the sink and dialed Vern's number. The phone rang and rang.

A soft knock on his door woke John Daniels from a contemplative fog. A haggard face peeked in timidly. "Well hello, Shelley." He rose and took her hand. "My, it's good to see you back in church. How are you?"

"That's why I'm here. I hope I'm not interrupting anything."

"Just another of my tedious sermons in the making. Please, sit down." Secretly, John was appalled. Her cheeks were hollowed, her eyes haunted. John was used to counseling widows and widowers. They usually improved over time. Shelley looked worse than ever.

"I guess I should have called first, but I've been trying to build up the nerve to do this, and I always put it off. So today I just decided to show up and take whatever comes."

"Shelley, you know you can talk to me about anything. Please, go ahead."

She took a deep breath. "John, I feel like a hypocrite, coming here in my state of mind. When LaRonda Cage was acquitted, I said some terrible things against God. Then that night, Patti and Matt took Bruce and me out to dinner. I ruined the whole evening.

"The next day, Hank and LaRonda Cage were all I thought about. And the day after that. I can't go on like this, John. I've got to start living a normal life. It's hard enough to job-hunt with my puny résumé, without wallowing in self-pity all day. And poor Bruce. He comes home every afternoon, shuts himself in his room and only comes out for supper. He's so miserable." Her eyes dropped shyly to her lap. "So I was wondering if there was something I could do around here. Maybe some secretarial work, or help with daycare, or just clean up the kitchen. I need to busy myself in some way. Be around people. Be useful. Do you have any ideas?"

John's expression softened from concern to relief as she spoke. "Shelley, I've been praying for this since that awful Halloween night, and now God has answered me. This is a definite sign of healing." He leaned back in his chair. "So let me see. Were you wanting a paying job? We don't have any openings on the staff right now."

"No. I just need to get myself into a working frame of mind. Otherwise, no one will want to hire me."

"Well, regrettably, we won't need any more pumpkins carved for about eight months." She laughed. "However, I do know of something that might interest you. Al Jefferson has been trying to recruit some help for his Senior Outreach ministry. Do you know about that?"

"A little."

"Al and his group visit elderly people and ... oh, they sort of provide what's needed. A lot of seniors are in retirement homes, or in their own homes, with few visitors. Some have poor vision, so Al's people read to them. Others need help with simple errands, like grocery shopping. Many are just lonely. They want to go for a drive, or lunch at a restaurant, or a movie. Al works full time, so he can only do this on weekends, and he has his own family to consider. He needs a lot more help, especially on weekdays. What would you think about joining his team?"

Shelley's eyes were shining. "Actually, that sounds better than my ideas. Being out and about and thinking of other people's troubles. I like it. Yes, please, sign me up."

"Good! Al's going to be thrilled. I think he's only got three or four helpers, and they're not always available."

"He'll be able to count on me."

"I have no doubt of that. You were always one of our most dependable volunteers. We've missed you around here."

"I miss being here." She looked around his office at the shelves of books, the stacks of lesson plans. "John, do you think God took Hank away to punish me?"

"Punish you for what?"

"For worshipping my husband instead of Him."

"Is that what you've been doing?"

"Well, I only joined the Church because of Hank. At first, I mean. Then I started feeling at home here. But last week, I said something awful things about God to Hank's mother. Maybe I deserved to lose him. As a punishment. What do you think?"

"What do *you* think?"

"I don't know. I'm so confused!" Tears welled in her eyes.

"What are you doing to cope with your anger?"

"Not much, I'm afraid. Hank's mother, and even Bruce, tell me I have to forgive. I know Hank would want me to, and that God wants me to. But knowing it and feeling it are two very different things."

"Feelings have their own lives, don't they? Have you prayed about it?"

"I'm not sure I know how to pray anymore. That's another reason I came here today. Will you pray for me, John?"

"Of course." He took her hands.

Denver, Colorado had many sporting goods stores, but Monday was usually a slow business day. So Forest Kirk was surprised when a customer walked in right after he opened. The timing wasn't so good either. Forest was in the back, fiddling with the heating unit.

He came out to greet the man. "Can I help you?"

"Do you have any semiautomatic rifles?"

"Not for sale. Denver's city ordinance outlaws the ones I've got in stock."

"Then why do you stock them?"

"For out-of-town gun shows." Forest saw the man's disappointment. "You can order them on-line, you know."

"Can I look at the ones you've got?"

"Yeah, sure." He led the man to a storage closet. "I'm sorry it's so cold in here. There's something wrong with my heating unit. The pilot light won't work."

"Want me to take a look at it?"

"You a mechanic?"

"Sort of." He followed Forest to the utility room and sniffed the air. "I don't smell any gas." He tried lighting the pilot himself. "No dice. I'll bet it's the thermocouple."

"The what?"

"This thing." He pointed to an assembly near the pilot. "It looks shot. I can replace it for you."

"That'd be great! Are you a repairman?"

"No, I just know how to fix things. I can run over to Denver P&E for a new one. Have you warmed up in a few minutes."

"Well, that's a nice offer. Thanks." He extended his hand. "I'm Forest Kirk. I own this place."

"Jerry Richards."

"Nice to meet you, Jerry, especially now." He laughed. "But before you go rescuing me, come on back inside and let's see what I can do for you."

They returned to the counter, where Forest placed two semiautomatics. Jerry hefted each one. "You can probably tell I'm new to these things. Which one's best?"

"Depends on what you want it for. Are you a hunter?"

"No, I just want to buy one while I still can."

"I hear that a lot. Well, they're both reliable, just different in some ways. See, the AR-15's a little lighter than the AK-47. It's longer, more accurate, and gives you more rounds per minute. Changing magazines is quicker, and it's easy to modify. On the other hand, the AK-47 packs more of a punch. Most popular semis in the world. And there are accessories for both, depending on what you want and what you can afford." Forest gestured at Jerry's hat. "You an A&R member?"

"Yeah."

"Me too, for many years. Although I don't like what's happening with them right now."

"What do you mean?"

"Seems like there's some change in the wind, with Vern Saginaw gone. I'm afraid they might cave in to the anti-gun crowd." He watched as Jerry examined the AK-47 closely. "If you want my advice, go on-line and do some research on the various brands. Or, if you don't mind a long drive, there's a gun show up in Casper, Wyoming two weeks from now. I'll be there, and I'll have these with me. You'll probably get a better deal at a gun show anyway. In fact, if you save me a service call on my heater, I'll give you a special discount on these babies."

Jerry thought about it. "Can you give me the location and directions?"

"Sure, right here." Forest handed him a flyer from the stack on the counter. "When you get there, just ask for Forest Kirk's table. Everybody in the business knows me."

"Do I have to get a gun permit?"

"No, just a background check. I can run that now if you like, and you'll be all set for the gun show."

"Great!" Jerry handed over his driver's license.

"Your enemies list came up dry, Mr. Tischner," Gary Rivers said. "They can all account for their actions the day Andy disappeared."

"What about this message to Jason's computer? Can you trace it?"

"We were able to identify the computer it came from. It's a laptop originally registered to Amy French, a student at Pechora High School."

"Originally?"

"Yes, then it gets complicated. Amy disappeared about nine months ago after getting involved in drugs. She pawned her laptop to support her habit, so we traced the serial number to Shubert's Pawn Shop on Westbury Street. Somebody bought it, but pawn shops don't keep sales records very long. We tried tracking the kidnapper through its IP registration, but that's been changed from Amy French to a Hobart Loggins of Green Bay, Wisconsin. Loggins died about eight years ago. He was ninety-five, didn't own a computer and had never used one. Looks like somebody hacked into the ARIN database and falsified the records."

"So the kidnapper's a hacker? Somebody who bought the laptop and used its email account to throw you off?"

"Apparently."

"What about this Amy French? You said she's an addict. Could the kidnapping be drug related?"

"Unlikely, since there's been no ransom demand. I've checked out her parents. They're solid citizens with no financial problems. The Frenches have no more idea where their daughter is than we do about Andy."

David scowled. "So we're right back where we started. I sold out my best friend to get my grandson back. Now I have no grandson and no friend. Any other leads?"

"Well, your son passed the polygraph, as we expected. He and his wife don't seem to have any enemies we can investigate."

"They just haven't lived long enough. What do we do next?"

"All we've got now is this 'right thing' the perp's talking about. He obviously expects you to know what that is."

"Well, I don't! Why can't he just tell me?" David rose and paced his office. "I thought he was mad at Vern Saginaw, so I helped vote Vern out. I even leaked my vote to the news media. Obviously, that wasn't 'the right thing.' If he wants money, I'll give him money. Just tell me how much."

"You could go public and make him an offer. I wouldn't advise it, though. You'd get a ton of fake responses and we'd have to waste time checking them out."

"What if I go on TV and ask the guy what the right thing is? Maybe he'll tell us."

"Same thing. Every crank in the country will bombard you with suggestions. No, this is something he believes you already know. The answer's somewhere in your own mind. You'll just have to puzzle it out."

David stared out the window. "I've spent my whole life doing what I thought was right. Served my community, ran my business, provided jobs for people. I've never killed anybody, or cheated anybody, or broken any laws. I built a home for my kids and raised them to be good citizens. Not that any of them appreciated it."

Rivers came over to stand beside him. "Mr. Tischner, you may have some enemies you've never met."

"What do you mean?"

"I'm talking about your Truthway at Vigilance account."

He blinked. "How do you know about that?"

"I'm FBI. It's my business to know."

David flushed angrily. "Who do you think you are, invading my privacy? You're supposed to be tracking down my grandson!"

"Your private life may have something to do with this. Mr. Tischner, what's the problem between you and your son?"

"Why?"

"The more I know about you, the better chance I have of finding your grandson."

David turned his back to the agent. "When Jason turned ten, I took him on a hunting trip one Saturday. There was this ... this duck ..." A long silence. "I'd rather not talk about it. Anyway, it has nothing to do with Andy's disappearance."

"All right. What about your Twitter chats? Has it occurred to you that this hoax talk of yours doesn't sit well with most people? It could have something to do with the abduction."

"In what way?"

"A hacker can find out who you are as easily as I did. Maybe he doesn't like what you've been saying about fake school shootings."

"Do you have any evidence of that?"

"No, but think about it. Who's most likely to be upset about your opinions?"

"The victims' families, I suppose. Except there aren't any victims, like I've been saying."

"What if you're wrong?"

David glared at the agent. "Mr. Rivers, I don't make wild assumptions. The facts just don't add up when it comes to this so-called massacre epidemic. Adam Lanza's death certificate is dated December 13, the day *before* the Sandy Hook shooting. His mental diagnosis was Asperger's disorder, which isn't associated with violence. After the so-called attack, the Connecticut legislature secretly drafted and rushed into law a bill barring release of murder victims' death photos. That's because there *aren't* any victims! These school dramas are part of a conspiracy against the Second Amendment. There are no angry parents kidnapping my grandson to get back at me, if that's what you're implying."

"If you feel so strongly about this, why are you hiding behind a false Twitter identity?"

"Who says I'm hiding? Whoever took my grandson has some other motive than trying to shut me up about Sandy Hook and those other charades. Stop wasting your time on wild-goose chases about undead kids and follow the leads you've got! That's what the U.S. government pays you to do!"

Rivers headed for the door, then hesitated. "Mr. Tischner, let me give you some personal advice. Don't get too cozy with those New Texas Confederacy friends of yours."

"Meaning?"

"That's all I can tell you. I'll be in touch." He left. David snatched up his phone and logged onto Twitter.

Truthway@Vigilance

I'll pay $10,000 to anyone who can provide proof that the West Virginia school shooting was staged, just like Sandy Hook, Parkland and all the other bogus massacres. Wake up, America! Our Constitution is under attack!

CHAPTER 15

Thinking about Gandhi

"All units, be on lookout for a blue Camaro, license number GHT 4746. Occupants wanted in connection with burglary of Granger Appliance Center earlier this evening. Vehicle has deep dent in driver's side door."

LaRonda made a mental note of the bulletin as she cruised her precinct. She was preoccupied with something Captain Vanderbilt said when she came on duty.

"Hank Phillips' son wants to see you."

Her stomach knotted. "What for?"

"I'm not sure. A friend of the family called. I got the impression the kid needs some kind of closure. Here's the phone number. I'll leave it up to you."

And that was all. LaRonda gassed up her vehicle and drove into the darkness of a late winter evening, her head spinning. First Shaker, then her father, now this.

The CRB's verdict had intensified Shaker's courtship. And she had to admit, he made a very good case. With two incomes they could buy a van with a wheelchair lift, so Alvin could go places without struggling into and out of a car. They could renovate his house, maybe even trade for a new one. Shaker and LaRonda could start an investment portfolio to accompany their pension plans.

LaRonda had always steeled herself against falling in love, for Alvin's sake. Shaker was wearing her down. He'd been to the house several times, bringing pizza, hamburgers, chicken and, on Valentine's evening, a Mexican food buffet. He fixed leaky faucets, repaired the fence, mulched the flower beds, even sold his married friends some of Alvin's dolls and puppets. The most eligible bachelor on the police force was courting both daughter and father.

Alvin nagged her constantly. "You've done enough for me to qualify for sainthood," he said one night after Shaker left. "Now you marry that hunk and make me some grandchildren. In the meantime, I'll learn how to manage on my own." This time, LaRonda's tears did no good. Alvin would not budge.

Her stomach clenched again at the thought of facing Bruce Phillips. Maybe the boy wanted to condemn her face to face. Or maybe he just wanted an explanation of how it happened. He certainly deserved one.

"All units, be advised suspect vehicle GHT 4746 last seen in the vicinity of Pecos and Alamo Drive."

LaRonda still brooded about Hank. The relentless CRB questions had shaken her confidence. *Do you normally draw your firearm on such occasions? ... Wasn't he justified in reacting instinctively? ... What was this feeling you had?*

Lately, she found herself thinking about "Gandhi," the scene in which a Hindu rioter confesses that he has killed a Muslim child. To atone, Gandhi replies, the man must find an orphaned boy and raise him as a Muslim. But how could LaRonda atone for a murdered husband and father? She had finally gone to her pastor. "I can't find what I want in the Bible," she told Reverend Thornton. "Can you tell me where it is?"

"If you can't find a remedy in the scriptures, go to God directly and ask Him."

"I have asked! I've been pleading with Him for months!"

"Then keep praying. He'll answer you in His own good time."

LaRonda whispered another prayer as she checked car tags and watched for blue Camaros. Passing an alleyway, she braked to a halt.

In the dim light of a street lamp, she could barely make out the shape of someone slumped against a picket fence. She rolled down the window, winced at the frigid breeze and aimed her flashlight beam at the figure, too far away to see clearly.

"This is Robert Tango 32, exiting vehicle at the alleyway between Brinkley and Snow, 300 block. Possible vagrancy."

"Copy, Robert Tango 32."

LaRonda activated the car's LEDs and walked slowly toward the alley. Her flashlight exposed a young woman shivering, head resting on her knees, arms hugging her legs.

"Hello there. Are you all right?"

The girl raised her tear-streaked face. Drugs, LaRonda thought. She kneeled beside the whimpering figure and shined the light directly into her eyes. "Well, now. At least your pupils contract. That's a good sign. What are you doing out here?"

"No place else to go."

"No home? A pretty girl like you? I don't believe it. How long have you been sitting here?"

"I don't know. I ... I don't know."

"You want to tell me your name?"

The girl shook her head.

"It's awfully cold. Why don't you come sit in the car with me for a minute? Get warmed up."

The girl glanced at the patrol car. "Am I under arrest?"

"Have you broken any laws?"

"Well ... not lately."

LaRonda smiled. "Then you're not under arrest. But I'm starting to freeze my ears off. You'd better take me up on my offer, or I'm gonna go warm up by myself."

The girl wiped her eyes. "Okay. Thanks." She rose and followed LaRonda to the car.

"This is Robert Tango 32, back in the vehicle, with passenger, same location, resuming patrol."

"Copy, Robert Tango 32."

LaRonda drew a small box of tissues from the door pocket and offered it to the trembling girl. "When's the last time you had something to eat?"

"I don't know. I'm not hungry."

"You sure could have fooled me. You look like you haven't eaten in six months. Are you on some kind of crash diet?"

"Officer, you don't have to coddle me. You know I'm on drugs."

LaRonda nodded. "You're right, I do. Are you hurting?"

"I will be soon."

She checked the surroundings. Most of the houses in this part of her beat were dilapidated and abandoned. "Did your source stand you up?"

"I guess so. Doesn't matter. I'm broke anyway." The girl shivered and hugged herself.

"Listen, I've got to return to my patrol. You want to join me? Maybe we can stop for a bite to eat along the way."

The girl looked doubtful. "Are you allowed to do that?"

"I won't tell if you won't."

Her companion smiled. The gesture took ten years off her appearance.

LaRonda put the car in gear and drove into the night. "You want to tell me your name now?"

"It's ... Amy."

"Amy what?"

"Just ... just Amy."

"Okay. At least I know what to call you. How'd you get yourself in this fix, Amy?"

The years poured back into the girl's face. "It's been so long I can't remember."

"You know, contrary to what you may think, I don't have an arrest quota to fill. Unless you've done something worse than get high, you're safe in telling me your name. Don't you want your parents to know where you are? They must be worried about you."

Amy slumped. "Too ashamed to go home."

"Well, I can understand that. I'll bet you weren't always like this, were you? I'll bet you went to school. Made good grades. Had lots of friends. And then you got curious and made one mistake. And now, here you are."

Amy covered her face. LaRonda drove quietly until she was back to sniffles. "You know, a while back, I had to arrest a boy about your age. Actually, I had to shoot him in the leg because he was drunk and waving a gun. You know what he said to me?"

"What?"

"He said he didn't want to tell me his name because he was afraid of what his dad would do to him when he found out. Imagine that! Sixteen years old, and he was more afraid of his father than the police. I had to arrange protective custody for him. I'll bet you're better off than he is. I'll bet you've got parents who don't care what you've done. They just want you back."

Amy hung on every word. Then she looked down at her lap. "Amy French."

"Amy French. That's a nice name. Is your parents' last name French?"

"Yes."

"You can't be sure these days. Families have more last names than they know what to do with."

"Officer, I –"

"Call me LaRonda."

"LaRonda, I'm not really like this. I used to be the most popular girl in my class. Now I'm a wreck. I've got to get myself cleaned up. I can't face my parents until I do. But every time I try ..." She began to cry again.

"Reminds me of when I was fifteen," LaRonda smiled. "A couple of girls and I got drunk on a bottle of bourbon. I'd never tasted the stuff before and didn't know anything about pacing yourself. Boy, I got sick. My dad found out about it, and was he mad! So he took me to an AA meeting and made me listen to the horror stories. You'd never have thought it. People with important jobs. Pillars of the community. Every one of them a slave to the bottle. Wrecked marriages, ruined careers, bankruptcy, the whole roll call of disasters. I was already ashamed of what I'd done, but after listening to them for an hour, I never drank anything stronger than soda pop again."

She glanced at Amy. "I understand. That old demon's been running the show a long time, and you think he owns you. But Amy, if you had enough moxie to become the most popular girl in school, you've got the edge on him. You're stronger than he is. You just have to believe it. And you have to make getting home more important than what he has to offer." Amy began to shiver again. "Reach in the back seat. There's a nice, warm overcoat you can borrow."

The girl bundled up and tucked her feet under her. "You sure don't seem like a cop. More like somebody's mom."

"Thanks."

She snuggled deeper into the coat. "This is the way it used to be. Hanging out with friends, talking about anything. I miss it. I miss my mom and dad."

"How long's it been since you've seen them?"

"Seems like years. Just one year, I guess. I was supposed to graduate this coming May. Now ..."

"Do you ever think what this is like for them? Not knowing where you are or what's happening to you?"

Amy nodded. "That's why I can't go home. You couldn't ask for better parents. They don't deserve this. Even if I did go home, I'd still have this thing on my back. I can't do that to them."

The radio crackled. "All units, suspect vehicle GHT 4746 reported exiting eastbound Morris freeway at Albany Avenue."

LaRonda made a U-turn. "Help me look for this car. It's a blue Camaro with a dented door."

"Okay." Amy watched the passing scenery. "What kind of car do you drive when you're not patrolling?"

"This is it. The department lets some of us use our units off-duty. It helps discourage crime to have a police car in the neighborhood."

"How about you? Do you feel safe?"

"Sure I do. There's always a cop car in my driveway."

Amy laughed. "How can you be so cheerful? I mean, you spend all your time with criminals. Losers like me. Isn't your job sort of depressing?"

"The Bible teaches us that all people are God's children. Just because someone's taken a wrong turn doesn't mean He's given up on them. Quite the contrary. Jesus lived among sinners and outcasts. Sick people, poor people. He showed us that every life and every soul is important, and that if we stumble, God is willing to lift us back up and give us another chance. You aren't the world's first drug addict, you know. And you're what, seventeen, eighteen? So you did something wrong and you're ashamed of it. That's good. Some people don't know the meaning of remorse." She patted Amy's knee. "You're going to be all right, girl. I promise."

"LaRonda, do you think – hey, there's that car!"

It was parked by the curb, opposite the direction they were traveling. The headlights were off, the interior dark. LaRonda made another U-turn and headed back. Her headlights illuminated the license plate: GHT 4746.

She stopped behind it and turned on her flashers. Amy could make out two figures in the front seat.

"This is Robert Tango 32, I've got suspect vehicle GHT 4746, blue Camaro, parked curbside, 7200 block of Norris."

"Copy, Robert Tango 32. Do you require backup?"

She hesitated and glanced at Amy. "Negative at this time. Will advise." She switched to the PA speaker. "Occupants of blue Camaro, this is the police. Open the door and step slowly from the vehicle. Put your hands above your heads."

The two dim figures in the car were motionless.

"I repeat, open the door and get slowly out of the car, hands in the air." There was no response.

LaRonda switched off the PA. "Amy, listen very carefully. I have to check out this car. You stay right where you are. Lock the door on your side, and on mine after I leave. Understand?"

"Yes ma'am."

"I mean it. Stay put." She nailed Amy with a solemn stare, put on her cap and climbed out. Amy locked the doors and watched LaRonda walk slowly toward the Camaro, aiming her flashlight at the interior. She stopped a few feet behind it, the LEDs flashing off her patrol jacket.

Amy squinted at the two figures, both still immobile. Through the closed windows, she could hear LaRonda ordering them to get out. There was no response.

LaRonda unsnapped the cover on her sidearm. She drew it from the holster and started forward, holding it in front of her with both hands. Then she hesitated. She stood still for a few seconds, lowered the pistol, and re-holstered it. She looked around and smiled at Amy. Then she walked to the driver's door and rapped on the window.

The driver lowered the glass. LaRonda leaned toward him and spoke words Amy couldn't hear.

A flash of fire and a loud bang erupted from the window. LaRonda fell backward, hard, onto the asphalt. The Camaro roared to life and sped away, tires screeching.

"Oh my God!" Amy cried. She yanked the door handle, jumped out and ran to kneel beside the fallen officer. "LaRonda! LaRonda!"

Her eyes fluttered open. Her dark shirt grew darker in the center of her chest. "Oh God, you're shot! What do I do? What do I do?"

LaRonda spoke weakly. "Radio. Radio."

Amy nodded. "The radio. Yes. Hang on, I'll be right back."

She raced back to the car and grabbed the mike. "Police? Police dispatcher? Help! There's been a shooting! She's down, Officer LaRonda is down, she's been shot! Answer me, please!"

"Caller, identify yourself."

"This is Amy French and I'm with the officer, LaRonda, I don't know her last name, she's shot, the car she stopped, they shot her and drove away, she's shot, get somebody here, quick!"

"Amy, where are you? Where are you and the officer?"

"We're at –" Amy looked around wildly. "Oh God, it's dark, I don't see any signs!"

"Amy, listen to me. Are you at the same location the officer gave a few minutes ago?"

"Yes! Yes! Just before she left the car!"

"That's good, we've got it. Ambulance is on the way. Now look under the dashboard. There should be a first aid kit, and inside there'll be a bandage you can use to cover the wound."

Amy pulled the kit out and yanked it open. "I've got the bandage."

"Good. Go put the bandage over the wound and keep pressure on it with both hands until the ambulance arrives. Are you sure the gunman has left the scene?"

"Yes, they drove away. I've gotta go, she's bleeding!"

Amy raced back to LaRonda, whimpering, praying and ripping the plastic cover. She tore open the uniform blouse, gasping at the amount of blood pumping forth. The bandage was soaked instantly.

"LaRonda, can you hear me? The ambulance is on its way."

Her eyes were closed. Amy put her ear to the woman's chest. She thought she heard a heartbeat. "LaRonda, it's me, Amy. Say something, please."

The eyes opened, rolled around. Then they focused on Amy. A brief smile crossed her face before they closed again.

"LaRonda, stay with me! They're coming. Please, stay with me!" A siren began to wail and grow in the distance. Other joined it, LaRonda's fellow officers hurrying to her rescue. But as fast as they drove, they could not outrace the hand of God.

CHAPTER 16

Some desolate cosmic landfill

In a headscarf and dark glasses, Shelley sneaked Bruce through a crowd of reporters and camera crews. She hoped they could escape as easily when the funeral was over. She was afraid of the questions they would shout, and how she might answer.

Now it was her turn to hide in the back of a church as a squad of police officers escorted a middle-aged black man to the front, wheeling him around to face the casket. Shelley thought she'd never seen so many cops in one place. She'd certainly never seen so many of them crying.

Her son was also crying. Shelley was baffled by the grief Bruce had displayed since the news. This was the cop who killed his father! Yet it might as well have been Shelley herself, for the way Bruce wept and clutched his mother fiercely. She thought she had known her son. Now she realized she'd had no clue to his depth of character.

When Bruce insisted on attending the funeral, Shelley didn't know what to say. Her own feelings had not changed, despite her newfound solace in the church's outreach ministry. Her hours with the elderly pushed the bitterness into the background during the day. At night, it came roaring back.

She went to John Daniels for help. "John, I know Christians are supposed to love and forgive and all that. But it's not that easy. How can Bruce be doing what I can't do?"

"Shelley, God has given you a heavy burden. He's also given you a son to help you bear it. Could it be that Bruce is stronger than you are? That the loving, nurturing home you and Hank built for him has given him a strength you never got from your own parents? And that he's sharing that strength with you now, when you need it most?"

"LaRonda was more than a cop," Reverend Thornton was telling the mourners. "Her fellow officers have told me many stories of how she would collar suspects, throw them in the clink, then launch a crusade to save them. LaRonda cared about more than the people she was sworn to protect. She wanted to help the ones who had lost their way."

Shaker nodded, tears running down his cheeks. He'd once seen her subdue a belligerent drunk driver by yanking his arm behind him and using his own off-balance weight to send him crashing to the pavement. She cuffed him, stuffed him into the back of her car and hauled him away. The next morning, she appeared at the jail with coffee and the drunk's wife. The incident sprang from a marital spat over money. LaRonda put the couple in a private room, where they ironed things out. "Thank you, Officer Cage," the repentant husband said. "It's LaRonda to you," she smiled.

Shaker got the bad news from a friend on the night shift. Devastated, he raced to Alvin's home, but Amy's frantic cries over the police scanner got there first, plunging Alvin into such convulsive wailing that Celeste phoned his doctor for a sedative. When the pill dragged him into a restless doze, she showed Shaker how to operate the ventilator, then went home to her family. Shaker sat at Alvin's bedside all day, listening for signs of respiratory distress. LaRonda smiled cheerfully at him from a framed picture on the wall.

Late that evening, Alvin woke to ask for details of his daughter's murder. Leaving him with Celeste, Shaker went to headquarters to meet Captain Vanderbilt.

"There they are," he said, staring through the interrogation room's one-way glass. "Don't look good enough to cause this much misery, do they?" The gunman was a puny guy with a wimpy attempt at a mustache. His pal was tall, slouchy, with an incomprehensible mass of tattoos running down both arms. With a dented door, their license number broadcast through the ether, and every cop in town looking for them, they'd never had a chance. Mustache was a two-time loser who specialized in burglary. Tattoo was just along for the ride, or so he said. Surrounded by squad cars and angry officers, they had meekly surrendered to await the special fate reserved for cop killers.

"The little guy panicked when LaRonda approached," Vanderbilt explained. "He was terrified at the thought of going back to prison. That was the excuse he gave, anyway."

Both men studied the pair silently. Abruptly, they turned and headed toward Vanderbilt's office. "How's Alvin taking it?"

"As badly as you can imagine. I kind of hate to leave Celeste alone with him. This is more than she's responsible for handling."

"Doesn't he have any relatives who can help?"

"LaRonda said it was just the two of them." Speaking her name was a knife through Shaker's heart.

"Why don't you take a few days off? You're in no shape for duty." Actually, Vanderbilt couldn't imagine worse duty than trying to comfort Alvin.

"I guess you're right. Tomorrow I'll see what long-term arrangements I can make."

Vanderbilt clapped him on the back. "Do what you think best, Shake. Let us know if you need anything."

"See if you can get some of the guys to help plan the funeral." He turned to leave.

"Shake?"

"Yeah?"

Vanderbilt looked troubled. "LaRonda called off the backup. We had units all over town looking for that car. Backup is SOP in a situation like that."

"Yeah. Yeah, sure it is."

The captain hesitated. "Maybe I shouldn't tell you this, but that druggie in LaRonda's unit? The one who saw the whole thing? She said LaRonda drew her sidearm, then re-holstered it and walked right up to the driver's window."

Shaker was shocked. Even a rookie knew to stop a few paces behind the driver, so he couldn't get an easy shot at you. "Why would she do that?"

"I wish I knew. The warrant on them didn't indicate they might be armed, but still. When they ignore an officer's command to exit the vehicle ... she knew better than that."

"Yeah, she did. I don't know, Cap. I just don't know." He wandered out of the office, more disturbed than ever.

The captain had come through for him. Rows and rows of cops filled the pews, listening to a eulogy all of them agreed with, and none of them had wanted to hear.

Barbara and Steve French didn't want to be here either, but they'd have attended a thousand funerals to have what they had now: Amy beside them.

The past year had been a living death for both parents. Steve spent hours on line, reading about addicts. The recovery statistics were very discouraging. One night, he and Barbara watched a movie called "Traffic." It was a mistake. The girl in the story might have been their daughter.

Then three nights ago, the doorbell rang and their hearts leaped. No words, just the two parents sweeping Amy into their arms, into the house, the quiet police officer on the porch almost forgotten, smiling at the scene. Then Steve turning to the man, inviting him in, the cop declining and trying to escape, Barbara throwing her arms around him in incoherent gratitude.

Amy had dreaded that moment, the shame of it. What they must think of her. How wretched she must look. None of it seemed to matter. Her parents shepherded her into the living room, where they talked until long after dawn.

There was one thing Amy had to tell up front. "Mom. Dad. I'm not clean. Not yet. I didn't want to come home until I was. That's why I've been gone so long. It's very hard. I can't make you any promises. But I'll try. I'll try my best."

Steve's pain was etched all over his face. "Sweetie, how did this happen to you?"

She told them how Cody lured her into the life, omitting details she didn't want to tell and that they surely didn't want to hear, the things she had done for money. That was Drug Amy. "I was at bottom. I had given up. Then last night, this nice police officer ..." She couldn't go on.

"You mean the one who brought you home?" She shook her head. "Who then?"

Amy gasped through her pain. "She was so wonderful! She put me in her car and drove me around. She told me about herself, made me feel better about myself. Talked about Jesus, how God sent Him here for people just like me. And then ..." She choked out the story of the shooting.

"Oh, honey! And she's the reason you came home?" Amy nodded.

"Thank God for ... what was her name, Amy?"

"LaRonda. LaRonda Cage."

Stunned, the parents looked at each other. LaRonda Cage, the most hated cop in America. Barbara shook her head at Steve. Not now.

He took Barbara's hand and Amy's, still smeared with LaRonda's dried blood. "Let's pray. Let's thank God for LaRonda, and for bringing our girl home."

More talk, and finally they had put Amy to bed, where she slept for thirteen hours. It was Drug Amy who woke her, the dream of a needle, loaded and ready, inviting her to sweet relief. She jumped out of bed and into the shower, under water as hot as she could stand, fighting the hunger. She dried herself and dressed in clothes untouched in her closet for more than a year. They hung limply on her depleted body as she knelt at the foot of the bed. "God, please give me strength to beat this. Please, don't let me fail LaRonda. Don't let me hurt my parents anymore. Please, make me what I was before."

Then, like a champion wrestler, Repentant Amy climbed on top and pressed Drug Amy face down in a hammerlock.

Warren DeVries didn't know why he was here. He had too many CEO problems to attend a funeral, especially one for Hank's killer. "At first, I thought she had it coming," he told his wife. "But now I feel worse."

"In what way?"

"Hank was just trying to get into his house. The cop was just doing her job. Now, they're both dead. What does it all mean?" So he cancelled his afternoon appointments and took a seat in the back row. As the service ended and six uniformed policemen marched the casket slowly up the aisle, Warren felt they were hauling away life itself, to be dumped in some desolate cosmic landfill. He returned to A&R and sat in Hank's empty office, wishing his friend were there to comfort him.

At the graveside service, Shaker tore his eyes from the coffin for a look at the other mourners. A woman in dark glasses and a young boy stood shivering at a distance from the crowd, holding hands. Shaker approached them as the minister concluded his prayer and people gathered around Alvin.

"Excuse me, ma'am. My name is Shaker Patterson. You look sort of familiar to me. Do I know you?"

The woman glanced around like a trapped fugitive. "I'm ... Shelley Phillips. This is my son, Bruce."

"How do you do? LaRonda was my – well, not exactly my fiancée, but we were headed in that direction."

"Oh, I'm sorry!" Shelley gasped, her hand flying to her throat. "What a terrible day this is for you, Officer Patterson!" She removed the glasses, nervously eyeing the camera crews around the gravesite.

"Did you know LaRonda?"

Shelley's confusion grew worse. "I'm sorry, I can't talk about this just now. Please accept my condolences. Bruce, let's go."

The boy didn't budge. "My dad was Hank Phillips. Officer Cage is the one who shot him."

"Bruce!" Shelley tugged at his hand. "I'm sorry, we really have to be going."

"Wait, please!" Images of Shelley and the boy emerged from TV newscasts four months earlier. "Of course, Hank Phillips." He looked from face to face. "I don't quite know how to say this, but why are you here?"

"We, uh ... well ... It's hard to explain. Bruce wanted to come," she finished lamely.

Shaker didn't know what to think. Were they here to gloat? The boy saved him. "She didn't do it on purpose, Officer Patterson. I tried to meet her and tell her that. But then ..." His chin began to quiver.

Shaker looked at Shelley, who was looking at Bruce. This was news to her.

"So you came to pay your respects, Bruce. Is that right?" The boy nodded, tears brimming in his eyes.

"I think that's very big of you, Bruce. I wish you could have met LaRonda and told her what you just told me. It would have meant a lot to her."

He turned to Shelley. "Mrs. Phillips, I'm honored to meet both of you. May I call you later? I think we have something to talk about."

She dodged Shaker's question and gestured toward the crowd. "Is that her father?"

"Yes, that's Alvin Cage. LaRonda was all he had in the world."

"What's going to happen to him? He's disabled, isn't he?"

"Yes. Many years ago, in the line of duty. We're all trying to figure out what to do. LaRonda and a home health aide looked after him. There's no way his pension will cover full-time care."

"I see." She put the dark glasses back on. "Bruce, we'd better be going. It's nice to meet you, Officer Patterson. I'm sorry it had to be like this."

"Mrs. Phillips. Your phone number?"

She gave it to him. "My schedule's sort of erratic. If I don't answer, just leave a message."

"You can count on it. I mean it. I think it's important." He shook the boy's hand. "Bruce, I'm pleased to meet you. I hope to see you again."

He turned and went to join the throng of officers around Alvin. Shelley took one last look at the scene. The coffin. The flowers. The open, waiting grave. She decided she'd had enough of funerals to last the rest of her life.

CHAPTER 17

Sad hands of poker

"What did you do?" Shelley asked as they drove home. "Call the police station and ask for her?"

"Not exactly."

"What, then? ... Bruce?" He just stared sadly out the window.

The next day he came home from school, fetched some cardboard boxes from the garage and packed up all his model planes, jeeps, tanks and military posters. He asked his mother to give them "to somebody who needs them more than I do."

Shelley was surprised. Bruce had been obsessed with military toys since he was six. "Honey, are you sure about this? You put an awful lot of work into those models, and the posters look nice with your dad's Marine Corps mementos."

"I think the models bothered Dad a lot. They're just ways of killing people. I figure this way I'll have more room for Dad's stuff, and some other kid can use the models to decorate his room."

She hugged him. "I think that's very nice of you, Bruce. I'll take them over to foster care tomorrow. Maybe they'll make a nice birthday present for somebody who doesn't have a family."

"Thanks Mom."

Shaker phoned that evening, asking her to meet him for coffee. Shelley put him off, suspecting he wanted to explain LaRonda's side of things. She didn't want to hear it.

Now reporters pursued her in earnest for comments on LaRonda's death. She went back to screening her phone calls and ignoring the doorbell. She parked her minivan two blocks from the house to avoid camera crews and sneaked out the back door each morning to do her outreach work. Bruce stayed with Matt and Patti until the media frenzy abated. If the Colt .45 was Hank's albatross, LaRonda Cage was Shelley's. Would she ever be free of that woman?

Even so, the memory of Alvin Cage slumped in his wheelchair haunted her.

For a while, LaRonda's comrades and their spouses took turns staying with Alvin when Celeste was off duty. But they had their own lives. Eventually their support waned, leaving Shaker in charge.

Alvin seemed to disappear after the funeral. He spent every waking hour staring at nothing, loss ravaging his face, apathy distorting his posture. He didn't seem to know Shaker or Celeste, wouldn't eat, neglected the torso exercises and water therapy necessary to prevent muscle atrophy. His doctor diagnosed severe depression and offered to write a prescription. Shaker declined, hating the thought of more pills.

Shaker wondered if people knew what grief was like for police families. How many employees could say they went to work every day knowing their duties might kill them? How many loved ones had to accept their loss as part of the job? Knowing it could happen didn't make the calamity any easier to bear.

Social media didn't help either, as Shaker learned when he idly typed "LaRonda Cage" into his search window one day:

GLittle@3WayTie

Cage was a criminal who got criminal justice!

CopShop@HandyAndy

Too bad Hank's family didn't get to watch her go down!

ArnieCates@BaddBuoy

LaRonda Cage burns in Hell!

and the inevitable:

ConspiracySpan@JFK

Cage kills Phillips. Assassin kills Cage. It's Oswald and Ruby all over again!

Shaker didn't realize how deep his anger went until he answered an "officer down" call one day. Three other cops surrounded a back-yard fence, aiming their pistols at a large bearded man crouched over Monica Everett, jamming her own pistol against her head. She lay in the grass, bleeding from a gash in her cheek. Monica and Shaker had been rookies together.

"Don't shoot him, don't shoot him!" the gunman's wife cried from the porch. "He needs his medicine, he doesn't know what he's doing!" She waved a prescription bottle at the cops.

"Get in the house lady, now!" Phil Taggert yelled.

The woman leaped from the porch and ran toward her husband, who spun and fired wildly, missing her and blowing a hole in the fence six inches to Shaker's right. Quickly the man pressed the gun to Monica's head again. The wife scrambled backwards. "Tony, it's me! Everything's okay, there's nobody out there!"

"Get back in the house, lady!" the cops chorused. "Drop that weapon, mister!" Tony scanned the yard as though looking for something. He didn't seem to see or hear the cops. His eyes were full of terror. "Please don't shoot him! He's just sick. He quit taking his medication and he sees things."

The sight of Monica with a gun to her head pushed a button in Shaker. He tapped Phil's shoulder, pointed to a ladder nearby, then to the roof. Phil nodded. "Hold off a minute, guys!" he shouted.

Shaker ran the ladder to the front of the house, scrambled up and crept rapidly over the roof to find the gunman directly below him. He waved at Phil and pointed upward. Phil fired his pistol into the air. As Tony whirled toward him in response, Shaker leaped from the roof. "Whoof!" Tony gasped, as all six-three, one-eighty of Shaker flattened him and knocked the gun away. Monica scrambled up and snatched it from the grass.

That wasn't enough for Shaker. He yanked out his own pistol, jammed it against Tony's head and cocked it. Monica's eyes widened. "Shaker, back off!" she cried. The wife started screaming again. "Shaker! He's down!" the others shouted, surrounding them. "We've got him! Holster your weapon!" Panting and sweating, Shaker rose to his feet and backed away. Never had he wanted so badly to shoot someone.

Later, Monica crawled into the patrol car beside him as he typed his report. "What got into you?"

"I don't know. Seeing you lying there, helpless, I thought about LaRonda and those two punks ... How'd he get your gun away from you?"

"I was trying to get between him and the woman. He grabbed it from my belt and swatted me. The wife said he's schizophrenic."

"No kidding. Hey, that's a nasty cut." Shaker opened his first-aid kit and applied antiseptic to Monica's cheek. "Are you going to tell Cap what I ... I almost did?

"No. But I think you should."

"Okay, I will. You go get some stitches." He taped a bandage over the gash.

Monica patted his arm. "Thanks, Shaker. Thank you for myself, and for my family."

Celeste and Shaker sought a remedy for Alvin in his photo album. It was thick with LaRonda pictures, from the first hospital snapshot in her mother's arms to her eighth Citation of Merit ceremony. One morning they placed it on the kitchen table, wheeled Alvin into position and sat on either side of him.

"I don't think I've seen any of these," Celeste said. LaRonda was skipping rope. Pedaling a tricycle. Cuddling a cat. Climbing a tree. "How old was she when these were made?" They glanced at Alvin, hoping he would take the bait.

"I don't know," Shaker replied. "She looks like she might be four or five, I guess." Alvin stared out the window. Shaker tried again. "I wonder what the cat's name was?" No reaction.

Celeste turned the page. "Oh, isn't this one good!" LaRonda wore a plaid dress and shiny shoes. Her hair was decorated with two small ribbons, and she held a child's New Testament. "She looks like she's on her way to Sunday School."

"Yeah, that figures. I'll bet Alvin and her mother took her to church every Sunday."

Alvin was still elsewhere. The next page showed eight-year-old LaRonda embracing him, her cheek pressed to his, her bright smile shining at the camera. Alvin wore his police blues. "Wasn't Alvin handsome?" Celeste marveled. "I can see where LaRonda got her looks."

Shaker squinted at the photograph. "Alvin's got a ring on his right pinkie. I can't make out what it says. Some kind of inscription."

"Neither can I. Looks like Greek Liquor or Goose Liver, or something."

"Green Lantern." Alvin was smiling at the picture. "It says Green Lantern. She got that ring from a cereal box. Green Lantern was her favorite comic book hero."

Shaker glanced hopefully at Celeste. "Green Lantern. I remember him. I used to read those comics, too."

"She made me recite the Green Lantern oath before I went to work every day:

In brightest day, in blackest night,
No evil shall escape my sight
Let those who worship evil's might
Beware my power – Green Lantern's light.

"She made me wear that ring to work. She said it was Green Lantern's magic ring, and it would protect me from the bad guys. It was too small, so I had to wear it on my pinkie."

Celeste dried her eyes with a corner of the tablecloth. "Who took the picture, Alvin?"

"Her mother. That was the last picture Ruby took of me and LaRonda together before she died." His smile turned nostalgic. "Ruby always said LaRonda was Daddy's girl. It wasn't true. She loved her mother. She just thought I was a superhero because I was a cop."

Shaker and Celeste held their breath, afraid to break the spell.

"Ruby predicted LaRonda would become a cop, too. I said no, she'll grow out of it, find something else interesting. Ruby was right, though. She did become a cop. Then she became a cop's nanny. And then ..."

Alvin's dam burst, his grief washing away the apathy. Shaker and Celeste cried too, with relief.

Celeste switched her shift to days and stayed with Alvin while Shaker was on duty. The two men spent their evenings dealing sad hands of Poker, with one player missing. The police scanner gathered dust. Alvin didn't want to listen anymore. Ever.

"I was so happy when LaRonda finally caved in and let you take her to that concert," he said as they sorted their cards. "I was afraid she'd turn into an old maid taking care of me. Now I'd welcome her back on any terms."

"Me too. I never would have stopped courting her, though. She just lit up something in me. I can't explain it."

"She filled a need you didn't know you had. That's why I married her mother. It was like I'd found a missing piece of myself."

Alvin laid down his hand, a full house. Shaker sighed. "Good thing we aren't playing for money. I'd be broke."

"Speaking of which." Alvin looked sternly into Shaker's eyes. "Don't you think it's time we talked about liberating you from this trap you've put yourself in?"

"Trap? What trap?"

"Don't play innocent. You're doing exactly what LaRonda did. Sacrificing your life to take care of me. I won't have it, Shaker."

"Alvin –"

"Just because I'm in a wheelchair doesn't mean my mind is crippled. I know what's going on. When LaRonda was working, we had enough to pay for Celeste, the mortgage, the taxes and the monthly bills. I know what you've been doing. You've been depositing part of your pay in my account. That's very generous of you. Now knock it off."

Shaker held up his hands. "Wait a minute, Alvin. I'm not sacrificing anything. Remember, I'm living here now. Celeste cooks my meals. I take showers in your water. It's your roof over my head. If anything, you're taking care of me. All I'm doing is paying my fair share."

"And still paying the rent and utilities on your own place."

"It's just temporary! Just until we can work something out for you. Besides, you're all I've got left of LaRonda."

"Shaker, you know this can only go one way. Her life insurance won't support me for long. My disability income won't pay for Celeste and everything else. And there are no decent jobs for anyone in my condition. My only option is to apply for Social Security disability. Maybe sell this house and move into a nursing home. The cheaper, the better."

Shaker stood and paced. "Alvin, I can't let you wind up in one of those places. Even the best ones have trouble getting good help. You can't afford the best ones." He stared at LaRonda's photograph on the wall. "You think I'm being generous. The truth is, I'm selfish. Living in her house, surrounded by her pictures, is the next closest thing to having her with me." He turned back to Alvin. "If I left you to fend for yourself, I'd be ashamed. So why can't we just leave things as they are, at least for now? Maybe something will turn up. Something we haven't thought of."

"You think God's going to intervene? He's got worse problems to deal with than mine." He sighed. "What a mess! Still, I have to admit I like having you around. I just wish you were a son-in-law, not a nursemaid."

"Me too." He took his seat. "Deal the cards."

Three men in camouflage jackets surrounded Forest Kirk at the Casper Gun Show, discussing a letter from Armed and Ready.

"They're asking for delegates in all fifty states to attend conventions on the Second Amendment. Looks like this guy who replaced Vern Saginaw's trying to stir up something."

"And they invited you?"

"Yeah." He passed the letter around. "I'm supposed to give them an answer within ten days."

"How come they picked you?"

"Apparently, they want all kinds of people. Retailers like me, gun lovers, gun haters, politicians, and so forth. Get 'em all in one room and hash out their differences."

"And then what?"

"Hang on, I've got a customer." He glanced at the man's A&R hat. "Oh, hi there! Jerry ... Jerry something, isn't it?"

"Richards. Glad you remember me."

"Sure I do. You saved me from freezing to death in my own store." They shook hands. "Let's see, you were interested in semiautomatics, right?"

Forest turned to the display rack behind him. Jerry looked around. The gun show was packed with visitors, wandering among acres of booths and tables.

Forest waited while Jerry compared the two rifles. "You said they're both good weapons. How much are they?"

"This particular AK-47 is $750. The AR-15 will run you about $1,100."

"Whew! What about ammo?"

"I'll tell you, my friend. I make it a rule never to sell ammo at gun shows. With all these massacres in the news, I don't want to be the first one to get blamed for a shooting at my own table."

"I see."

"I'm sure some of the other guys around here will be glad to fix you up. In fact, if you wait around, you might find a bargain on ammo mags. Just watch for someone packing up and getting ready to close. Then you can make them an offer."

"That's good advice. How about you?" Jerry grinned. "Any chance of dropping the AR-15 below $1,100? That way I've got a fighting chance at affording the ammo."

Forest laughed. "Look, I promised you a deal for fixing my heater. Let's call it $900 and it's yours."

"Great, thanks!" Jerry dug through his wallet.

"Jerry, how'd you know about that thermo-what's-it? If you're not in the heating and air business?"

"Oh, I do a lot of tinkering at home. Figuring out how things work. Any machine is just an arrangement of parts. You put them together to make what you want."

Forest zipped Jerry's credit card through the reader and let him sign it. "Okay, buddy, she's all yours. And here's the instruction booklet."

"Thanks." He shook Forest's hand and turned to leave.

"Jerry? Keep it pointed straight up. You don't want to scare anybody."

"Will do." He melted into the crowd. Forest turned back to his visitors. They were still discussing the A&R letter.

Shaker looked around the cozy room. A blaze crackled in the fireplace. Most of the pictures on the mantel seemed to be family photographs, including a studio portrait of Amy. She looked like the last person in the world to become a druggie.

He'd decided to make this visit after his crisis with the schizophrenic husband. "Do you want some time off to pull yourself together?" Captain Vanderbilt asked.

"You mean to see a psychiatrist?"

"Might not be a bad idea."

"I'm not crazy, Cap. I'm just angry. You'd be mad too, if it happened to you."

"Sure. Still, you shouldn't be on patrol duty if you can't control it."

"You gonna bench me, coach?"

The captain smiled. "I know you too well for that, Shake. Just don't let me down."

He rose as Steve returned with Amy and her mother. "I want to offer you the same apology I gave Mr. French. I'd have called first if I'd had your number."

"It's all right. Please, sit down." Barbara placed Amy between herself and Steve. Shaker's heart swelled with pity. The girl in the pictures and the girl on the sofa were like Jekyll and Hyde. How could someone so young age so much in only a year?

"Amy, did your father explain why I'm here?"

"Yes sir."

"If you don't mind, I'd like to hear about your experience with LaRonda. If it's too hard to talk about, just say so."

Amy swallowed. She stared at her hands. She brushed her hair back from her face. She fidgeted constantly as she talked. Obviously, the battle within her wasn't over yet.

"LaRonda found me in an alley that night and invited me into her car. We rode around for a while, a half hour, I guess. She was nice. She didn't act much like a cop, except when she talked on her radio. It was more like she wanted to be my friend."

Tears formed in Amy's eyes. "She'd almost talked me into going home when I spotted a car she'd been looking for. She pulled up behind it and ordered them to come out. When they didn't, she got out and drew her gun. Then she put it back. I've always wondered why she did that."

"Me too. Did she say anything to indicate why?"

"No sir. She just told me to lock the door behind her and stay inside.

I could hear her telling them to come out with their hands up. And ..." a gasp of misery burst from her. "And then she turned and smiled at me. The sweetest smile, like ... like she was *loving* me with that smile. Oh God, I'll never forget that look!"

The parents held her while she cried it out. Shaker felt like joining her. Not now. Later, on the way home.

"Amy, you told the duty officers that LaRonda spoke to the killer after he rolled down the window. Could you hear what she said?"

She shook her head. "I just saw her lips moving. Officer Patterson, she saved me from what I was doing to myself. I didn't think I could ever break out of it. The craving. It was eating me up. Well, actually, it still is. Except now I'm fighting it. For LaRonda. And for my parents."

"Are you getting some help?"

Barbara spoke up. "Amy's seeing a drug counselor and attending those Addicts Anonymous meetings every week. We wanted to go with her, but the counselor said we should give her some time first."

"The people at the meetings are nice," Amy added. "They all have different stories, some worse than mine. It feels good to talk to somebody who's been there."

Shaker studied their faces. Without the comfortable room and their nice clothes, they could have passed for war refugees.

He stood and offered his hand to each of them. "I'm glad I came here. Knowing that LaRonda spent her last hour saving someone from drugs makes me feel better. Amy, I hope talking about this hasn't been too unpleasant for you. You're right. You beat this thing. Do it, and it'll make her death easier for me to handle. Easier for her father, too."

"Was he the man in the wheelchair at the funeral?"

"You were there?"

"Yes sir. We all were."

He smiled. "Alvin was a cop himself before he got disabled. He'll be glad to hear about you. Amy, you've done us both more good than you know. Thank you."

Steve escorted him to the door. "I'm sorry about your loss, Officer Patterson. What are your plans for the future?"

"Right now, I don't have any. I guess I'm like you and your family. We're all recovering, aren't we?"

"Yes, we are. Please stay in touch and let us know how you're doing. It's been a pleasure to meet you."

Shaker headed home, to Alvin. Cops mostly saw only the ugly side of humanity. He wished he could have more encounters like this, if only the price wasn't so steep.

Bruce sat at the dinner table, eating meatloaf. When he was quiet like this, he reminded Shelley of Hank in one of his Afghanistan moods.

"What are you thinking about, Bruce?"

"Nothing."

"Are you upset about me taking that volunteer job at the church?"

He shook his head. But his fork began stirring his mashed potatoes, aimlessly.

"Honey, I know I haven't been much of a mom to you the past few months. Losing your dad has taken a lot out of me. But I'm trying to get better. That's why I'm doing volunteer work. I thought it might help me get well."

He was silent.

"Bruce, you and I were so happy before all this. I want us to be happy again. What can I do to help you?"

He stopped stirring, his eyes still on his plate. "I wish everything could be the way it was before."

"So do I." She watched him for a moment. "Do you remember our fishing trip to the lake two summers ago? We sat in the boat for three hours and nobody caught anything but you."

Bruce grinned. "Yeah. Dad made me trade places with him. He said I got the good side of the boat and was hogging all the fish."

"And as soon as you put your hook back in the water, you caught another one, right where he'd been sitting."

Bruce chuckled.

"What's your best memory?"

He thought about it. "Last Christmas, when you and Dad sang 'O Holy Night' at the church party."

"You liked that? I thought I sounded terrible!"

"No, it was nice. You looked so happy together."

"We were." Tentatively, she reached out to stroke Bruce's hair. It felt so much like Hank's. "You and I used to sing too, doing the dishes. What was that song you liked so much?"

He smiled. " '*Sing ... sing a song ...*'"

"Oh, yeah. '*Sing out loud ... sing out strong.*'"

" '*Sing of good things, not bad ... Sing of happy, not sad.*'"

They sang together.

Sing ... sing a song
Make it simple to last your whole life long.
Don't worry that it's not good enough for anyone else to hear,
Just sing ... sing a song.

They continued as they rose and began to clear the table.

CHAPTER 18

An email to Heaven

Alexis was crying so hard when Jason got home that she couldn't speak. "What is it, honey?"

She showed him the Twitter alert on her phone:

Andy@DoctorLuke

Andy Tischner will come home when David Tischner does the right thing.

"Oh, God!" He held her tight, squeezing the phone between them.

Jason had to give his dad credit. He'd publicly announced large personal donations to charity; launched a fundraising campaign for homeless people; committed Pierpont Electronics to a college scholarship endowment. All of it high-profile, anything to get his name on TV or the internet, a scattershot approach, so the kidnapper would see that David Tischner was doing *some* right things, even if they weren't *the* right thing. Doctor Luke's response was always the same.

When the kidnapper began communicating via Twitter, the FBI got a warrant to probe his registration profile. But they ran into a firewall that even the company's software technicians couldn't penetrate. "This guy is definitely a hacker," Agent Rivers said.

Meanwhile, other Twitter users pounced on David's $10,000 reward offer for conspiracy proof in the West Virginia shooting:

Hoaxwatch@MandyG

Listen closely to the 911 caller's voice. She sounds exactly like one of the callers in the Parkland hoax!

Torrie@TorrieLake

The news video shows the EMTs fumbling around with gurneys like they've never used one before. Obviously actors!

JustTheFacts@Dragnet

The only news guy who got into the WV school building was arrested, and the police confiscated his camera!

None of the tweets came from Doctor Luke. "See?" David said to Agent Rivers. "I told you my Twitter talk wasn't his motive."

"All that proves is that he doesn't want your money. We already know that."

The one positive result of the ordeal was a shaky peace between Jason and David. Months of agony and frustration had forced them to put aside their differences for Andy's sake. Jason dialed his father's number. "Dad, we got another one."

"Good Lord, what does he want? Why doesn't he tell us?"

"Dad, it's got to be something you know about. Don't you have any ideas?"

"Maybe it's time we went public. I'll go on TV tomorrow."

"But the FBI guys said –"

"What good have they done us? I'm sick of dancing around this thing! Aren't you?"

"All right. Do you want us with you?"

"Yes, all of us, on camera. Maybe he just wants me to beg. If he does, I'll get down on my knees."

"Five months ago my grandson, Andy Tischner, was kidnapped from his school's playground," David announced to reporters outside Pierpont headquarters. "Until now, we've kept this crime quiet for Andy's safety. Since all our attempts to locate him or to satisfy his abductor have failed, I am making a direct plea to you, whoever you are. Please bring Andy home, unharmed and unscarred by all this. Remember, he's only four years old. He can't possibly understand why you've taken him away from his family. He must be very frightened. You were a small child once yourself. Think how you would feel in his place. Tell us what you want. We have no desire to punish you, and I promise we won't. We just want Andy back. Please bring him home."

The reporters pressed forward. "Mr. Tischner, how do you know it's a kidnapping? Have you received any ransom demands?"

"We've received a series of messages indicating that it's a kidnap situation. I can't reveal the contents."

"How did the kidnapper contact you?"

"In order to avoid copycat messages, I can't answer that."

"Have you issued an AMBER alert?"

"Yes, and we have pictures for you." Jason and Alexis distributed photos of Andy to the reporters.

"Sir, why are you representing the family instead of his parents?"

"The messages were directed at me, not at them."

"Why you?"

"I can't answer that either."

The reporters clamored. "Does this have anything to do with your vote to fire Vern Saginaw?"

"Is this the reason for all your charitable work lately?"

"Is the FBI involved?"

"Has the kidnapper offered any proof that he has the boy?"

David held up his hands. "Please, please. None of this has anything to do with why I'm here today. My only purpose is to speak directly to the kidnapper. I repeat: I will do anything to get my grandson home safely. You know how to contact me. I'll be waiting to hear from you."

Under a hail of questions, he escorted Jason and Alexis into the building, just as an alert sounded on Jason's cell phone.

Andy@DoctorLuke

Andy Tischner will come home when David Tischner does the right thing.

The tweet was dated one minute earlier.

Speagle Beagles was an enormous indoor fast-food playground. Decorated with bright colors, giant stuffed animals and streamers, it featured a merry-go-round, slides, see-saws, a playhouse, and playpens for toddlers. A row of game consoles lined one wall. Cartoons ran on large video screens. Employees dressed as clowns and jugglers prowled the dining area.

"I thought the kids would enjoy this place," Shelley told Patti. "Besides, I want to prove I'm not the world's worst dinner companion."

"You were nothing of the sort!" Patti cried. "It was just too soon for you, that's all. Besides, we're friends. What can be wrong between friends?"

"Just the same, it's my treat."

Matt turned in their lunch orders while the Shore twins, Diane and Dana, watched a clown create balloon animals. Bruce and Macy played video games.

Patti sneaked another glance at Shelley. Lately, her friend had begun to shed the pallor and scrawny physique of mourning. She almost looked beautiful again. Maybe she was finally moving on.

Matt and the boys returned with the food and the twins, who wore balloon hats. Everyone held hands, bowed their heads and gave thanks for the meal.

"Bruce, I understand your tenth birthday's coming up soon," Patti said. "How are you going to celebrate?"

"I don't know." He looked at his mother.

"What would you like for your birthday, honey?"

"Oh, I don't need anything." He bit into his pizza.

"You're not worried about how much it'll cost are you?"

Bruce shook his head and chewed.

"Good, you shouldn't be." She turned to Matt and Patti. "He's been such a trouper lately. Gets himself up every day, washes his own break-fast dishes, works hard in school, comes home and helps me with the chores." She returned to Bruce. "So tell me, what's your birthday wish? Just name it."

"Anything I want?"

"Anything."

He hesitated. "I want you to call Officer Patterson."

She stared back at him blankly. "What?"

"I want you to call Officer Patterson."

Shelley was speechless. "Who's Officer Patterson?" Matt asked.

She dragged her eyes away from Bruce. "He's ... a policeman we met at LaRonda Cage's funeral."

Patti was agog. "You went to her funeral? I didn't know that. Why didn't you say something?"

"Bruce insisted. He's been ... well, it's sort of been an issue between us."

Matt was puzzled. "What's this guy got to do with you and Bruce?"

"He was dating LaRonda Cage, or they were engaged, or something. He said we needed to talk. He's called me several times. I ... I just can't." Her eyes begged Bruce for a reprieve.

"Mom, please call him. It won't hurt to listen to him, will it?"

Shelley studied his face. "This is that important to you? This is really your only birthday wish?" He nodded.

"All right, son. A promise is a promise. I'll call him when we get home." Bruce threw himself at his mother and hugged her.

The following night she sat across from Shaker at Starbucks. "Please don't be offended. I'm only meeting you because my son wanted me to."

"I'm not offended, Mrs. Phillips. I have an idea what you're going through. I'm in pretty rough shape myself. Where's your son?"

"He's at his friend's house. I thought it best to make this just the two of us."

"So Bruce is your only child, is that right?"

"Yes."

"From what little I've seen, he seems pretty bright."

"He is. His teacher brags on him all the time."

"You must be very proud."

"I am." She smiled, with reserve. The ball was in his court.

"Mrs. Phillips, you probably know why I asked for this meeting. I wanted you to hear LaRonda's side of things."

"I already know her side. I've read the news reports."

"But you don't know the whole story. Mrs. Phillips, police officers who discharge their weapons in the line of duty undergo a grueling investigation. In LaRonda's case, it was as bad as it could be. She had to answer for your husband's death, plus the wounding of a teenager who drew a gun on her."

"Yes, I heard about that."

"Neither of those incidents was typical of LaRonda. One night, she caught another kid driving about sixty in a residential area. Instead of citing him, she put him and his buddies in her patrol car and played them a police video of a little girl killed by a speeding car. It showed every gory detail, including the hysterical mother crying over the body. LaRonda let the kid off with a warning if he promised to write an essay about it for his English teacher. Two weeks later, his teacher sent her a copy of it. He got an A.

"Another time she got a noise complaint about a loud party. The caller's mother was a neighbor under hospice care who wasn't expected to live through the night. LaRonda took the party animals next door to see her plugged into IV tubes and oxygen. They apologized and left quietly. Later, the caller said they brought flowers to the funeral."

Shelley's face remained inscrutable.

"The night of her death, LaRonda picked up a teenage drug addict. The girl was still with her when she got shot. This kid didn't know anything about LaRonda and your husband. But despite being strung out on heroin, she insisted on riding in the ambulance, and later to the morgue. And that same night, for the first time in over a year, she let a policeman take her home to her parents. Now she's in rehab."

"Well, I'm glad *somebody's* life had a happy ending." She sighed. "I'm sorry, that was ugly. What's your point?"

"I'm just saying that LaRonda wasn't some trigger-happy cop. She always looked for a peaceful way to enforce the law." He snorted in exasperation. "You wouldn't believe how much trouble I had getting dates with her. She was either taking care of Alvin or visiting somebody she'd thrown in jail."

"I heard she was out on a date during her suspension."

"That's true. I took her to a concert to get her mind off things. Before it was over, there were tears in her eyes. She said the music reminded her of Hank Phillips."

"In what way?"

"Have you ever heard the Dvořák Cello Concerto?"

"No."

"If you did, you'd understand. I have just one more thing to say. I went to see this druggie and her parents. She said it was LaRonda who convinced her to go home. She said LaRonda treated her like a friend."

"So now her father's all alone. And I gather you've taken responsibility for his care."

"Well, not just me. He has a home health aide when I'm on duty. My mother volunteered to stay with him this evening so you and I could meet."

"Still, you must be quite a special man to take on so much, especially since he's not even a relative."

"Mrs. Phillips, before I met LaRonda, I was the Don Juan of Sandstone police. She changed all that."

Shelley smiled a little. "Officer Patterson, what did you expect to gain by telling me this?"

"The internet's full of lies about LaRonda. I wanted you to hear the truth."

"I see." She sipped her coffee. "Was there anything else you wanted to say?"

"No ma'am. That was it."

She stood and offered him her hand. "I'm sorry for your loss. Thank you for telling me about her."

"Has it done any good?"

"I don't know. You've given me a lot to think about." Then she had an impulse. "Would you come to the house sometime and have dinner with Bruce and me? If you can get away, that is. I know you have a lot on your shoulders."

"I'd be delighted."

"Good. I'll give you a call."

Shaker watched until she was out the door. I'm a cop, not a lawyer, he thought. Is this what it's like to argue a case?

Macy and Bruce were playing a video game when Patti opened the door. "Sorry to break this up. I need Macy for a minute."

"What for?"

"You remember I asked you to teach the girls how to make their own beds? How come I'm still having to do it?"

"Aw, Mom, I can do that later."

"That's what you said yesterday. Later is now. Get to it, Mister!"

Macy started to protest, then caught the look in his mother's eyes that had nothing to do with bedmaking. "I'll be back in a minute, Bruce."

"No problem."

Matt squeezed in behind Patti, who left and closed the door. "What kind of game are you playing, Bruce?"

"It's Minecraft." He showed Matt the screen. "You start with this bare landscape and have to figure out how to build a fire and make a shelter before it gets dark and monsters come after you. Then you can go on to build a house, and a whole town, and do other cool stuff."

"Who's winning?"

"It's not like that. You work together to figure things out."

"Well, I'm sorry we had to interrupt. Anyway, I wanted to ask you something."

Bruce's face turned somber. "Is it about Officer Cage?"

Matt smiled. "You don't need help figuring things out. You read my mind." He sat on the bed. "I think you had a special reason for asking your mom to call that policeman. Something only you and I know about. Am I right?"

Bruce nodded, staring at his shoes.

"I did what you asked. I got a message to Officer Cage saying you wanted to meet her."

Bruce was silent.

"That was okay, wasn't it? You really did want to talk to her?"

He nodded.

Matt's voice softened. "I guess our timing wasn't so good, Bruce. She died before you got a chance. Is that what this birthday wish is about?"

A teardrop darkened the boy's jeans.

"I'm sorry you didn't get to talk to her. You wanted to hear her side of what happened, didn't you?"

"It's not that."

"It isn't?"

Bruce was crying openly now. "Mr. Shore, I think she got my message the night she got shot. So what happened to her was my fault."

"How do figure that, Bruce?"

"It *has* to be my fault! It has to be! She thought I was going to curse at her for killing my dad. So she let those bad guys shoot her to make up for it!"

"Oh, Bruce –"

"I wanted to tell her I didn't blame her for what happened to dad. It was just an accident! I don't hate her, and I don't want Mom to hate her. I thought maybe if Mom talked to Officer Patterson, he could make her understand."

Matt moved to sit beside him.

"Bruce, you and your mom have been through a lot the past few months. And I think you've had it worse, because you've had to bear your mom's grief, as well as your own. Now you want to take on a new challenge and blame yourself for something that is *not your fault*."

He let it sink in. "Bruce, Officer Cage was killed doing her job. It happens to police officers sometimes. If you have to blame somebody, blame the guy who shot her. Blame a sad world full of sad people who take their problems out on each other. But Bruce, don't blame yourself. God does not put responsibility for someone's death on the shoulders of nine-year-old boys."

Bruce wiped his eyes. "Her pictures on TV, she looked so nice. I knew she didn't mean to do it. I wanted to tell her that. So she wouldn't feel bad anymore. But I was too late."

"Maybe not. Maybe you can still help her."

"How?"

Matt thought about it. "Do you believe good people go to Heaven when they die?"

"Yes."

"Do you believe your dad and Officer Cage are in Heaven now?"

He nodded.

"Then they're in Heaven together, with God and Jesus. So why don't you write to Officer Cage and tell her how you feel?"

"Write to her? You mean like a letter?"

"Sure. A letter. Or better yet." Matt grabbed Macy's laptop. "Why not send her an email?"

"But ... how can she get it in Heaven?"

"You say prayers, don't you? Isn't an email to Heaven just another kind of prayer?"

"I guess so."

"Tell you what. I'll leave you here by yourself. You type what you want to say to Officer Cage, and when you're finished, you can send it."

"How do I address it?"

"Hmm, that's right, we don't know her email address. Why don't you use your dad's address, and ask him to deliver it to Officer Cage?"

Bruce eyed him skeptically. "Mr. Shore, do you really believe this email's going to Heaven?"

"Sure I do. It's not the way you pray, but what you say that counts." He patted Bruce's back and left the room.

CHAPTER 19

Every snort, every jolt

Amy threw off the covers and swung her legs over the edge of the bed. Drug Amy loved to creep up in the middle of the night and yell Surprise! Her back and knees ached. Sitting up made her stomach queasy. She looked at the clock. 3:05 a.m.

She feared she was weakening. Between the counseling and group therapy sessions stood huge chunks of empty time. Drug Amy capered, tantalizingly, at the threshold of every chunk.

Her counselor had recommended a program of behavior modification to accompany her treatment. She started every morning with prayers and exercises. She read the Bible. She ran errands with her mother and did spring cleaning chores. She caught up on her junior year reading list. *Don Quixote. The Diary of Anne Frank. Lord Jim.* Pechora High School's best student was now a year and a half behind her class. Amy French, ex-future valedictorian.

She filled the remainder of each day with long walks, unaware that her mother waited anxiously by the window. She had good reason to worry. Walking didn't prevent Amy from remembering places where she could score a hit. Yesterday, she found herself outside a familiar doorway, three miles from home. The bogus clinic was a pill mill that doubled as a heroin outlet. If you couldn't afford painkillers, there was always a bargain day sale on Smack.

She peered through the window. It looked abandoned, most likely in a police raid. Someone had hastily scratched an address on the glass: 312 Morrow. Probably the quack's new shop. Amy had already walked three miles. She could handle a few more blocks.

Then LaRonda's final smile glowed through Amy's reflection. *You're going to be all right, girl. I promise.* Tearing herself loose, she trudged homeward. "Sometimes I wish I'd never met you, LaRonda. But thank God I did."

Everyone at church welcomed her back with hugs and encouragement, making the past year seem like a dark novel about someone else. One Saturday, Jodie and Sherrell took her shopping at the mall. The girls asked cautiously about Cody Sewell and her year on the street. Amy was too ashamed to say much. After that, the girls phoned occasionally, but they were mostly busy with school and other obligations. Besides, did their parents really want them hanging around with a drug addict?

Amy's parents were wonderful. As she readjusted to home life, she remembered all the things she had stolen to feed Drug Amy. "Mom. Dad. I promise I'll pay you back someday. I'll get a job and pay for everything I took."

"Don't worry about it, sweetheart. You just get back on your feet. That'll be payment enough."

3:17 a.m. She'd never get back to sleep, and even when her parents woke, there would be another cavernous day to fill. In the old days there was too much to do. Classes. Student Council. Church charity drives. Tutoring. Make-A-Wish. Expectations to meet, a person to be. Amy didn't feel like that person anymore. Drug Amy had reduced her to a brooding, fidgety ghost.

Through the darkness she could see the outline of her desk, where her pawned laptop used to sit. She was shocked to learn that it had briefly made her a suspect in the Tischner kidnapping. One more thing to feel guilty about. She declined Dad's offer to buy her another one. "It's my responsibility. If I want a computer, I'll have to earn it."

It sure would come in handy now, though. Sometimes, Amy felt a restlessness unrelated to drugs. Her eloquence had won her top honors at the National Speech and Debate Tournament. The missing laptop contained some of her best work. She hoped whoever took the Tischner boy appreciated oratory.

Abruptly, she went to the desk, switched on the lamp and pulled out a yellow legal pad. Suddenly, everything that had happened in the past year began to pour out of her. She wrote line after line, page after page, until the pen ran dry. She rummaged through the drawer, found another one, and continued jotting down every step in her downfall, every snort, every jolt, every coke party, every dark alley, every abandoned building, every sleazeball who had sold her a ride on the snowmobile. It was a world of predators. Amy didn't realize until now how many there had been. The more she wrote, the more ashamed she felt, and the more her tears stained the paper. She kept going. The pen seemed to have a life of its own.

She was still writing when her mother knocked on the door. "Amy? Are you going to church with us?" Seven-thirty already! It didn't seem possible. "I'm sorry, Mom. Let me jump in the shower and get dressed. I'll be right there."

She leaned back, her shoulders aching from her prolonged posture over this ugly chronicle. She'd filled forty-three pages, margin to margin. Although she'd never want anyone to read it, she felt cleansed. And nothing felt so welcome right now as the prospect of going to God's house and thanking Him for this breakthrough.

"And thank you, too, LaRonda," she whispered. But as refreshing water flowed over her, she realized her handwritten confession wasn't enough.

Shelley the hostess was a pleasant contrast to the other Shelleys Shaker had met: the flustered mother at LaRonda's gravesite, and the iceberg at the coffee shop.

"How did you know lasagna is one of my favorite dishes?"

"I didn't. It's one of ours, too." She served him another portion. "Don't be shy about asking for more. There's plenty."

"Don't tempt me. I spend too much time fighting calories, sitting in that patrol car."

"How come you're not wearing your uniform?" Bruce asked. Shaker was the biggest man he'd ever met. In a sports shirt and slacks, he looked like a pro football player in disguise.

"Two good reasons. One, I'm off duty. Two, it's a bad idea to show up on somebody's doorstep in uniform unless you're on business. It worries the neighbors."

"They might think you've come to arrest us?"

"Well, rumors get started. People tend to think a cop in the neighborhood means trouble."

"My dad wouldn't wear his Marine uniform. He won the Medal of Honor in Afghanistan."

"I heard about that. You should be proud. They don't give that medal to just anybody."

"Bruce, when we're finished, why don't you take Officer Patterson –"

"Shaker. Please, call me Shaker."

"All right. Why don't you show Shaker your room? He's got it decorated with Hank's Marine Corps stuff."

"Okay." He hustled to finish his meal.

"Why are you called Shaker?" Shelley asked.

He smiled. "My dad was a very energetic guy. He could hardly sit still, so he got very impatient with lazy people. He said the ones who make a difference in this world are the movers and shakers."

"So it's not a nickname? That's your real name?"

"Right there on my birth certificate. I'm just glad he picked Shaker instead of Mover." They laughed. Shelley collected their empty plates. "You fellows go visit Bruce's room while I clean up."

"Excuse me, sir," Bruce said. "I have to take out the trash first." Shaker watched him tie up the bag and exit through the front door.

"I thought all city pickup was in the alleys."

"It is." Shelley watched through the window as Bruce marched along the sidewalk, his flashlight cutting through the darkness. "He won't go in the back yard anymore. That's where ... uh ..." She turned to the sink.

Shaker covered the awkward moment by helping her clear the table. "I hope you'll share your lasagna recipe with me. I'm not much of a cook, but I'm good at following instructions."

"Certainly. Actually, I got it from a restaurant where I worked years ago. It was the house specialty."

His eyes roamed the kitchen. It had such a warm, family feeling. But you could tell someone was missing.

Bruce returned and led Shaker into his room. "Wow!" The boy's display was impressive. He'd refined his arrangements, filling one wall with the dress blues, white cap, gloves and sword, plus framed photos of Hank wearing them. The other walls displayed pictures he had taken in Afghanistan. Small American flags filled the empty spaces. "This is great!"

Bruce opened a box on his desk, revealing the Medal of Honor. "I thought about hanging this up there, but I was afraid it would get dirty or tarnished. So I just keep it in the box."

"It's beautiful." Shaker ran his finger gently around the inverted star, admiring the symbol of Minerva with her shield. "Did you know there's a website for Medal of Honor winners?"

"Oh, yeah. I've read some of their stories. Dad said those guys did things much braver than he did."

"They were all brave, if you ask me."

"After the war, Dad went to work for Armed and Ready. He went around the country making speeches about gun rights."

"Yeah, I saw him on the news a couple of times. He sounded very reasonable."

Bruce carefully replaced the medal. "Did Officer Cage say anything to you about the night she – about what happened – you know. That night?"

"Do you mean why she did it?"

"No sir. How she felt afterward."

He marshaled his thoughts. "It made her sick, Bruce. She wanted to make it up to you, but she didn't know how."

"Mom hates her."

"Yes, I know."

"I guess I should, too. But I don't."

"I'm glad you don't."

Bruce sat on the bed. "I saw her picture on TV. She looked nice."

"She was. As nice a person as you can imagine."

"I think my Dad understood. I'll bet he forgives her."

Thankfully, Shelley appeared at that moment. Shaker's throat was too tight for any more words. "Bruce, I think you'd better finish your homework and get ready for bed. It's getting late."

"Okay."

Shaker offered his hand. "Good night, Bruce," he croaked. "Thanks for a pleasant evening."

"Good night, Offic – I mean, Shaker. I hope I get to see you again."

"Me too." He followed Shelley out of the room and closed the door.

"How about some more coffee?" She fetched two cups and sat opposite him in the living room.

"That's quite a young man you've got there."

"I don't think I could have gotten through this without him. He's handled the whole thing much better than I have."

Shaker sipped his coffee. "So tell me, Mrs. –"

"Shelley."

"Shelley. Why did you invite me here?"

"I'm not sure. Maybe because you seem like a nice guy. Maybe because we both lost someone we loved, and I wanted to talk to someone who knows how it feels. Hank and I were married for eleven years. You don't lose somebody you've been that close to without losing a big part of yourself. How long did you know LaRonda?"

"We worked different shifts, so it was only last year that we started dating. I know what you mean, though. I had all these dreams about our life together. It's been hard to let them go."

"I miss the things Hank and I did together. In fact, I recently started volunteering for one of our church ministries. Doing various things for senior citizens. It makes me feel close to what's left of him."

"What do you do for them?"

"There's one lady who's partially blind. I read to her. There are several outpatients I take meals to. Sometimes Al Jefferson, the outreach minister, calls and asks me to go shopping for people. And there are others who just want someone to talk to."

"If you don't mind my asking, what's your financial situation? It's been several months now. Are you going to have to get a job?"

"Absolutely, at some point. Unfortunately, my only experience is waitressing. And I haven't even done that since we moved here from Cincinnati."

"You could go back to school. Get a degree."

She smiled regretfully. "I didn't even finish high school. My parents are drifters. But that's another story. How about you? Last time, you indicated you've taken responsibility for LaRonda's father."

"Pretty much. He's not happy about it. He nags me like he did LaRonda, wanting her to get out and enjoy life."

"If she was so busy, how did you get her to date you?"

"The first time was actually a working date. I had to go on nights for a week to cover for another cop and talked LaRonda into joining me for our lunch break. It was just burgers in my patrol car at two o'clock in the morning. We sat and talked for an hour, then went back on duty."

"And the next time?"

"That was a classical music concert at the Civic Center. We didn't go out again until she was suspended – the other concert I told you about. Later, we spent some time at Alvin's house. Her devotion to her father was one of the things I liked best about her."

Shelley was silent for a moment. "I guess you can tell how I feel about her. Or felt. I don't know anymore. It's hard to hear someone talk nice about the woman who killed my husband."

"You wouldn't have any feelings at all if you could overcome it that easily. Sometimes I wouldn't mind a few minutes alone with those goons who shot LaRonda." He sighed. "But if she had lived, she probably would have shown up at the jail and tried to straighten them out. So I have to play it her way. Try my best to forgive." He glanced at his watch. "I should be going. One of my off-duty friends is staying with Alvin. I don't want to wear out his good will."

"Just one more thing. What was that music you told me about, that made LaRonda think of Hank?"

"Oh. The Dvořák Cello Concerto."

"Classical music, right? How do you spell that?" Shaker jotted it down on his coffee napkin. "Pay special attention to the second movement."

"All right." She walked him to the door. "It's been nice having you here, Shaker. Please give my best wishes to Alvin. Oh, and give him this." She dashed into the kitchen and returned with the remaining lasagna.

"Thanks. We'll try not to fight over it. Good night."

She closed the door and leaned against it, reflectively. Her first house guest since Hank died was mourning for his killer.

CHAPTER 20

Great pep talks

Warren DeVries was driving to work when a sign outside Castle High School caught his eye.

LaRonda Cage Memorial Fund Drive
Saturday, April 17
Sweets Booths Games Prizes
Everyone Welcome

LaRonda Cage. Why was that school doing a memorial for her? Warren drove on, his head full of CEO problems.

Nineteen thousand A&R supporters had reacted furiously to Vern's dismissal by cancelling their memberships. When Warren stopped requiring A&R staffers to wear sidearms, an internet rumor spread that he was soft on gun rights. More desertions followed.

The Andy Tischner case made things worse. Online chatter speculated that Vern's ouster was the kidnapper's price for the boy's return, even though Andy was still missing. Or the abduction was a hoax to build sympathy for A&R, and David Tischner didn't even have a grandson. Or the liberals killed LaRonda Cage to cover up her role in Hank's fake murder. Has everyone gone crazy? Warren wondered.

He wished people were as concerned about the First Amendment as they were about the Second. Since the advent of social media, freedom of the press had degenerated to the level of tabloid journalism. People didn't seem to know the difference between facts and allegations anymore. If the Second Amendment gave Americans power to kill each other, the First gave them power to kill truth.

It was half-truths that killed Lock and Load, the new gun rights agency Vern created shortly after his firing. His legend was enough to attract startup funds, which he used to launch a national speaking tour. "The subversives want to tear down this country!" he shouted in convention halls around the nation. "They want to destroy the Bill of Rights, starting with the Second Amendment. When nobody listens to them, they resort to outright lies about me and lawful gun owners. I built and ran A&R by the Constitution for sixty years. Now I'm forced to start over. Well, so be it! I've spent my whole life defending America, and I'll defend it to my dying day! Are you with me?"

What killed Lock and Load was newscasts of Vern delivering this speech to roaring mobs of angry musclemen with shaved heads, scruffy beards, fiery tattoos and swastika-covered shirts. Their gun posters mingled with sinister banners calling for the deportation of Jews, Hispanics, Asians and Islamists. In states with open-carry laws, many of these fanatics wore pistols and looked ready to use them. There wasn't a corporation in the country that wanted its logo linked to this Hitleresque spectacle. Vern's financing quickly collapsed and his new company disintegrated. Warren felt sorry for his old boss. Vern was opinionated, but he'd never been a racist.

His loyalists aimed their frustration at A&R headquarters. The anti-gun crowd surrounding the building after Hank's death had dwindled away, replaced by armed pro-gun pickets. They hung around day after day, chanting "We Want Vern!" to the TV cameras. On weekends the crowds grew large and threatening. Warren left the office late one night to find the word "traitor" scratched on his car door. After that, he enlisted twenty-four-hour security to patrol the grounds and escort the employees, an irony that wasn't lost on headline writers: "Gun Nuts Use Hired Guns to Fend Off Gun Nuts."

Warren gradually restored confidence in A&R by venturing outside the building each day to chat with demonstrators. "Armed and Ready is still your Second Amendment champion," he assured them. "What we're doing now is seeking ways to protect your rights while protecting all of us from gun violence." His staff served soft drinks and snacks while Warren answered questions. Despite some grumbling, the crowds eventually thinned out, then disappeared altogether.

Meanwhile, he persuaded Congress to postpone all firearms legislation while he organized his Second Amendment conference. Warren was determined to assemble all the gun factions in one room and get them talking, face to face. Tearing down ideological walls was the most important step in his crusade.

He found himself apologizing to Brenda and their two small daughters for his brief appearances at home and promised to delegate some of his duties to Barney Atherton, Hank's replacement. This morning, Barney handed him an envelope he'd found while cleaning out Hank's desk. "Shelley" was scrawled across it.

Warren held it up to the light. "Why would he write her a note, or whatever this is, and just leave it in a drawer?"

"I don't know. Maybe you should mail it to her."

Warren decided to phone her instead. "It just has my name on it? What kind of envelope? Like a greeting card envelope?"

"No, just the plain business letter kind. It feels like it has an ordinary piece of copier paper inside. Want me to bring it over?"

"Well ..." A fear of the unknown seized her. "Yes, do you mind? Do you have time?"

"I'll make time. I'm sorry I haven't called or visited you. It's just been crazy around here."

"So I've heard. Congratulations on your promotion, by the way! You deserve it. Hank thought a lot of you, Warren."

"That was mutual. Suppose I come by this evening around 7:00?"

Shelley sent Bruce to Macy's house before he arrived. Whatever the envelope contained, she wanted to see it first. Bruce had been through enough.

"Here it is," Warren said. "I'll leave so you can read it in private."

"No, please. Do you mind?" Shelley suddenly decided she didn't want to be *that* alone. "Just until I know what's in it."

"Of course. Take your time." He sat on the sofa and waited.

She examined the envelope, gently caressing her name. Hank had written it with his fingers. Folded the page with his hands. Moistened the flap with his tongue. A last remnant of him. She drew a breath, slit the envelope and opened the single sheet of paper inside.

October 31

My Darling Shelley,

Things went badly with Vern this morning. You were right. I don't belong here. I keep telling myself I'm sticking with A&R to provide for my family. The truth is, I've become addicted to fame and success. It's easy to become prideful when you get so much praise from audiences. I wanted to believe the nice things they said about me. I guess I thought believing them would make them true.

Shelley, I've been raising a son, teaching Sunday School classes, mentoring Boy Scouts, and promoting gun rights, all with blood on my hands. I've lost the intimate relationship I had with God before I took the lives of six men, when I knew killing was an abomination to Him. I will never find peace until I've healed the breach between us. As you said, God has given me the power of speech. Maybe I should use it to work against war and weapons. I don't know how else to atone for what I've done.

However, this should be a family decision. Whatever opportunities come our way, we'll all pray about them first. I'm so blessed to have such a wonderful wife and son. I want us to travel every path of this life together.

Afghanistan was an awful place, full of misery and death. Even after I got home it was still in me, and it's never left. You know that, of course. I hope you also know that it was you, God's precious gift of you, who made it bearable. I'd have been lost without you.

I haven't given Vern my notice yet. You get to hear this first, tonight. But I feel better already.

All my love,

Hank

Tears flowed over Shelley's free hand, which covered her mouth as she read.

"Is it bad?"

"It's beautiful!" She offered Warren the letter.

"No, no, this is obviously something very personal. If it has nothing to do with me or A&R, I don't want to know."

She dabbed her eyes. "He called me that last day. He had something important to tell me when we got home. He never got to say it." She shook the letter at him. "This is it. He was leaving A&R. He and Vern had a falling out."

"I guess I should have known. You could hear them arguing, even with the door shut."

Shelley rose and hugged him. "Thank you for bringing me this. I've been fretting about that call since Halloween, wondering what he wanted to say. I thought I'd never know. Thank you, thank you!"

"I wonder why he wrote you a letter, then sealed it up in his desk?"

"I don't know. Oh, Warren, you don't know what this means to me. This thing with Vern was tearing him up. I'm so glad to know he made a decision he could be happy about."

She was still re-reading the letter when Bruce got home. "Come over here, son. I've got something to show you."

The next morning Warren again passed the fundraiser sign. He barged into Barney's office. "Do something for me, will you? Call Castle High School and find out why they're doing a memorial for that cop who killed Hank."

It was Gil Starnes who approached Castle's principal with the idea. "I can appreciate your feelings, Gil," Wade Carson said, "but LaRonda Cage is still a controversial figure. We'd have to submit your request to the school board, and I'm sure they'd turn you down flat."

"They didn't know her, Mr. Carson. She wasn't a killer, not like people say she was. I want everyone to know that."

Carson hesitated. Gil's escape from a violent, drunken father to a stable foster home had transformed the boy. His grades and attendance had improved, and he'd made new friends.

"What sort of memorial did you have in mind, Gil?"

"A statue outside the building, so people could see her every day when they're driving by."

"Statues are expensive. We're struggling just to buy classroom supplies."

"I'll raise the money myself."

"How?"

"I'll wash cars. Mow lawns. I'll get a job after school and work weekends."

The principal was touched. He approached the school board and won a compromise: a plaque in the school lobby, describing how LaRonda saved an endangered student. The wording must contain no references to Hank Phillips. "I also got permission to host a fundraiser, so you won't have to do it all yourself."

"A plaque?" Gil moped. "She deserves more than that."

"I'm sorry, son. We're lucky they cut us this much slack."

Three Saturdays later, the Castle High School lobby was full of parents and kids shopping at tables of home-baked sweets. Signs pointed to classrooms offering various games. In the gymnasium, boys and girls took turns at the foul line, hoping to win a prize for the most consecutive free throws. Several large headshots of LaRonda adorned the walls. She wore her police blues and smiled brilliantly at the camera.

Warren approached a teacher. "Excuse me, can you tell me where I can find Gilbert Starnes?"

"Yes, that's him." She pointed at a slender teenager talking to two men, one of them in a wheelchair. Warren drifted over to eavesdrop.

"I'm sure glad I saw your sign," the standing man was saying. "I would have missed this. I'm Shaker Patterson. This is LaRonda's father, Alvin."

Gil's face lit up. "You're her dad?" He shook their hands. "This is great! I mean – gee, I'm sorry. You must feel terrible, Mr. Cage."

"I do, but all this makes me feel better. How's your leg now?"

"It healed pretty fast, and in the meantime, LaRonda fixed me up with these people who got me a lawyer and arranged a foster home for me. Those are my foster parents, over there." He pointed to a couple chatting with some teachers. "LaRonda changed my whole life. Then I heard about her getting killed, and I wanted to do something for her."

Alvin watched the children running around and people of all ages munching home-baked cookies and brownies. "Did you organize all this by yourself, Gil?"

"My foster parents and my teachers did most of it. And Mr. Carson, our principal, was great. He had an assembly and let me talk to the rest of the kids about drinking."

"Where'd you get these pictures of her?"

"Mr. Carson contacted the police department. Somebody there made prints from their employee records."

"Well Gil, this is the nicest thing you could have done for my daughter. Something that'll make sure she's remembered. Thank you."

"It's her I want to thank, Mr. Cage. She was the nicest lady I've ever met."

Warren stepped forward. "Pardon the interruption. I'm Warren DeVries. I heard about your project, and I've got an idea I want to try on you." He gave Gil his business card.

"Armed and Ready? They're all about guns, aren't they?"

"Well, not entirely. If you'll call me tonight at that number, I'll explain."

Gil looked puzzled. "Okay, I will. Thank you."

"Excuse me," Warren grinned. "My wife and kids are around here somewhere, and I want to get a bite of those chocolate chip cookies before they're all gone." He headed toward the refreshment tables.

Alvin looked up at Shaker. "What was that all about?"

"Beats me." Shaker seized Gil's hand. The hand came away holding a $20 bill. "I hope this helps. I wish it could be more."

"Thanks, Mr. Patterson." Shaker wheeled Alvin away. "This is the best I've felt since it happened, Shake. It's nice to know somebody cares about us cops, especially my cop."

"*Our* cop, my friend."

Shelley was reading to Alma Peters from Second Corinthians when her phone rang. "I'm sorry, Alma, I'd better answer this." She stepped outside, fumbling with the new device. Her old phone had finally expired from the beating she'd given it. "Hello, John."

"Shelley, I'm sorry to interrupt you. Something important has come up. Can you come by the church today?"

"Yes, but it'll be a while. I have three more outreach errands. How about 3:00 o'clock?"

"That'll be fine." Shelley went back inside. "Now, where were we?"

" 'Whoever sows sparingly.' "

"Oh, yes."

Remember this: Whoever sows sparingly will also reap sparingly, and whoever sows generously will also reap generously. Each of you should give what you have decided in your heart to give, not reluctantly or under compulsion, for God loves a cheerful giver. And God is able to bless you abundantly so that in all things at all times, having all that you need, you will abound in every good work.

"That's you, Shelley."

"Hm?"

"A cheerful giver. Giving so much of your time to an old gal like me."

Shelley blushed. "Alma, I get as much out of these readings as you do. Especially Paul's letters. They're great pep talks, aren't they?"

"They certainly are. Now, I know your time is about up. Before you go, how are things with you and Bruce?"

"He's doing well in school. We're coping."

"If I'm not being too nosy, I hope you'll consider remarrying. I can sense that you're lonely."

Shelley patted her hand. "You're not nosy. You're just a sweet lady trying to help." She checked her watch. "I've got to go. Is there anything you need for next time?"

"Just you, dear. You and the Bible."

Shelley drove home and fetched a casserole she'd made for the Dickersons. She chatted with them in their kitchen while heating the food and setting the table. The husband was a Vietnam veteran who had lost both legs in the war. His wife was recovering from knee surgery.

Next, she ran a grocery errand for a housebound widow, then drove two elderly sisters to Target. They dawdled and argued over every purchase, so that she barely had time to meet John at 3:00. "You look a little flustered," he remarked as she plopped into a chair. "Are these folks wearing you out?"

"No, it's just time consuming. I never realized how many people need help with the simplest things."

John smiled. "Jesus found Himself in a similar predicament when word got around."

"Yeah, and He didn't even have a car! So, what's up?"

He turned serious. "Shelley, Al Jefferson is leaving. The company he works for is transferring him to the West Coast."

"Oh, that's too bad. What are you going to do?"

"What would you think about taking his place?"

"Me? I don't have any experience running things. What about Marge or Kathy? They've been doing this longer than I have."

"But Marge also teaches our preschoolers, and Kathy's only available on weekends. Besides, Al and I have been talking to the elders. There's more demand for outreach services than we can meet. So they've agreed to fund a full-time staff position. With you in charge, if you'll take it."

Shelley eyes widened. "You're offering me a job? A paying job?"

"That's right."

"Wow!" Her mind whirled with visions of money and responsibilities.

"It makes sense. You're the only volunteer we've got who has no other commitments, except your son. And he seems pretty self-reliant for his age."

"But John, I've never been in charge of anything before. In fact, my only job was waitressing, and that was eleven years ago."

"You served people. You took their orders and gave them what they wanted. You're doing that now. What's the difference?"

"Well … is there a budget, for expenses and so forth?"

"Not much, I'm afraid. We'll be doing well to pay your salary, and that'll be just minimum wage. But it's full time, and it includes health insurance, the same the church staff has." He leaned forward. "I should warn you about what you'd be getting into. You'd be working with volunteers. They don't get paid anything. And you're going to need more of them to do this properly. You'll have to launch some sort of campaign to find people you can depend on. And even good ones are going to bail out on you from time to time. You'll have to be ready to find substitutes on short notice or fill in yourself. Al's not leaving for another month. He can give you some good advice. And you'll have me and the office staff to help you get organized."

Shelley hesitated. "I knew I'd have to get a job some time. Now I'm worried about neglecting Bruce to take care of other people. Do you have someone else in mind in case I say no?"

John spread his hands. "Most of our members have all they can handle, or they're just not up to this kind of responsibility. If you can't do it, we'll have to advertise for someone."

"Only this morning I was reading to Alma Peters from Corinthians, about how God rewards people who abound in good works. I guess I'm getting a chance to put my faith to the test."

"You do abound in good works, Shelley. I've heard a lot of praise about your outreach activities. The job's yours, if you want it. Oh, and by the way, so is this." He opened a drawer and produced Hank's pistol.

"How did that get here?"

John smiled gently. "I took it away the day Patti and I came to your house. You were in pretty sad shape, and ... well, you get the idea."

Shelley frowned at the Colt. It was the one thing about Hank she didn't want to remember. "Will you keep it, or give it away, or something? I don't ever want to see a gun again."

"I don't blame you. But it's not something a preacher ought to have around, don't you agree?"

"I guess you're right." She lifted the pistol with two fingers, like it was unsanitary. "I'll see if I can find someone who wants it. As for your job offer, I'll talk it over with Bruce tonight and let you know in the morning."

"Fair enough. And Shelley? Talk it over with God, too."

CHAPTER 21

A ballet duet

A "ding" noise woke David Tischner from a bad dream. Andy had found the key to his gun cabinet and was peering into the barrel of a heavy pistol. It wobbled in his chubby little hands, so that in his struggle to hold it steady, he accidentally squeezed the trigger. There was no bang, though. Just a "ding!"

The ding was David's phone. He grabbed it from the lamp table.

JustTheFacts@Dragnet
Where's the $10,000 you promised? I gave you a solid lead to expose that West Virginia farce!

David flopped back on the pillow. His reward offer had harvested a truckload of groundless theories. The school shooting was a conspiracy against West Virginia's gun laws. Pharmaceutical companies had staged it to divert attention from the state's opioid crisis. Central American immigrants were plotting to disarm Americans as a prelude to invasion.

West Virginia police had learned from the Sandy Hook incident. Once the crime scene was secure and the investigation completed, authorities allowed journalists to tour the school, take pictures and interview surviving teachers. With families' permission, they had even given reporters access to autopsy reports and photos. It made no difference to the hoaxers.

"If it wasn't a conspiracy, the cops would never share evidence that freely," a popular radio host declared. "Besides, it was two weeks before they did so, plenty of time to fake all the pictures and reports they needed."

David wandered into the kitchen. Lately, he'd adopted the habit of drinking two glasses of wine when he couldn't sleep. Each morning, he woke with a headache.

He poured the wine and sat at the table. Sometimes, David felt uncomfortable with his Twitter friends. They reminded him of the Flat Earth Society, Holocaust deniers, JFK assassination junkies and faked moon landing freaks. But surely, something sinister was going on. West Virginia, Vern's incendiary speech and Hank Phillips' death had all occurred within two days of each other, leading to the biggest gun control crisis in American history. Hank had died before they had a chance to meet, but David knew enough about the man to know he couldn't be involved in a hoax. That left LaRonda Cage, who had her own shining reputation prior to Halloween night. Were both their deaths directed by the same liberals at the heart of the war on guns? David had privately called in favors from every government official he knew. None of them had any hint of a plot.

The conspirators, whoever they might be, were effective. Though America had a legacy of gun violence as old as the nation itself, this was the first time the Second Amendment seemed truly endangered. Even Armed and Ready, with its huge membership, vast wealth and solid organization couldn't stand up forever against the persistent shootings pervading the nightly news. If a picture was worth a thousand words, the cascade of victim photos and weeping survivors was more effective than all the lobbying money A&R could raise in a century. Some dark force, David believed, was turning public opinion against firearms. Could that force also be at the heart of Andy's abduction?

"Who are you to pass judgement on me?" he asked the quiet kitchen. "What's 'the right thing'? Who are you, Doctor Luke?"

Another "ding" drew his attention to the phone. It was a Fox News alert.

FBI agents arrested leaders of the New Texas Confederacy early this morning in a raid on a large abandoned aircraft hangar outside Waco, Texas. Sam Leopard and Joe Brunnel, founders of the organization, were led away in handcuffs. According to an FBI source, the warehouse contained two M1 tanks, half a dozen jeeps, plus numerous crates of M4 carbines, M16 rifles, rocket launchers and ammunition. The men are believed to have been preparing for an overthrow of the state government. More to follow.

David was astounded. He'd known both men since grade school. Sam was general manager of Shale Searchlight, an oil drilling company. He was an outspoken critic of left-wing politicians, but he was also a family man and a grandfather. Joe owned a photography studio. He'd taken the pictures at David's wedding. Actually, David knew little about their organization. He'd joined the NTC out of longstanding friendship.

He polished off the wine and decided against a second helping. A whole case of Bordeaux couldn't ease his mind. He washed the glass, turned out the light and went back to bed.

Shelley lay propped up in bed, exhausted from a hectic day of errands. A dental appointment for Della Crowley. A new light bulb for Joyce Thomas's closet. Companionship for Jesse Prosser's widow. Two prescription refills for Ronnie Blair. Three bags of groceries for Mavis Turner. And when she got home, a son to mother. It was exhilarating! Life was full again.

She reread Hank's letter, then opened her Bible to Hebrews.

Therefore, since we are surrounded by such a great cloud of witnesses, let us throw off everything that hinders and the sin that so easily entangles. And let us run with perseverance the race marked out for us, fixing our eyes on Jesus, the pioneer and perfecter of faith. For the joy set before him he endured the cross, scorning its shame, and sat down at the right hand of the throne of God. Consider him who endured such opposition from sinners, so that you will not grow weary and lose heart.

Tired as she was, Shelley felt a happiness she thought she'd buried forever with Hank. His letter was something he had touched on his last day, words he had written just for her. *It was you, God's precious gift of you, who made it bearable.* She kept it in her shoulder bag as she went about her daily business, tucked in a separate pocket with his wedding ring.

Shelley was excited. Tomorrow she would confer with Al Jefferson. Next week, she would officially become Senior Outreach Minister.

Returning the letter to the bag, she noticed a folded napkin inside. It was the note Shaker had written: "Dvořák Cello Concerto." Curious, she reached for her phone and typed the words into the search window. The first popup was a YouTube video. As she struggled to pronounce the soloist's name – Mstislav Rostropovich – the man himself appeared, walking onto a concert stage to applause, cello in hand. He bowed and took his seat. The conductor started the orchestra.

"How about that? A free concert!" Shelley knew very little about classical music. She liked dance music, had loved it since the night Hank took her to a ballroom dancing contest. But this wasn't something you could dance to. She listened, wondering how LaRonda had connected the concerto to Hank. The soloist seemed enraptured by it.

Then, as woodwinds introduced the second movement, Shelley began to get the idea. Tinny as it sounded on her phone, the tender melody drew her most intimate memories of Hank into a bittersweet collage. She closed her eyes, floating on the music's rising and ebbing waves of passion. This *was* something you could dance to, a ballet duet. And late in the movement, as the cello intertwined with a flute, she felt Hank lifting her in his arms and carrying her away to a private place.

She closed the video, turned out the light and fell asleep, dancing with Hank to the cello's magic.

While dressing the next morning, she remembered the gun. She thought back to that dismal day at the kitchen table, touching the Colt because it was something Hank had handled. Now it reminded her of Vern Saginaw and the miserable A&R job. On his last day of life, Hank had committed himself to breaking free of it. Now he *was* free – of guns, of Afghanistan, of guilt.

She dialed Shaker's number and got his voicemail. "Shaker, it's Shelley Phillips. I wonder if I could ask a favor of you. Please call me when you get a chance."

"Mr. DeVries, these are Royce and Janice Porter, Gil's foster parents. And of course, you've met Gil." Warren shook hands all around. Curious eyes regarded him as everyone in Wade Carson's office took a seat.

"Gil, how much money did you raise Saturday?" Warren asked.

"About $235."

"Will that be enough for a plaque?"

"I guess so," he answered glumly, still envisioning something along the lines of Mount Rushmore.

"What if you had enough money for a statue instead?"

"The school board won't let us."

"Maybe I can change their minds."

"Mr. DeVries, what's your interest in this?" Janice asked.

"Gil's given me a great idea. Why don't we build two monuments? One to LaRonda Cage here at your school, another in Washington, D.C., honoring Hank Phillips *and* LaRonda."

Everyone looked at everyone else. "Why Washington?" Royce asked. "Both shootings happened right here."

"I'm planning a national conference on gun violence in Washington. Originally, I intended to use Hank Phillips' death as a platform for it. Then I went to LaRonda's funeral. The eulogy made me realize that Hank and LaRonda are tied together, as symbols of what guns are costing us. I want this conference to start A&R and our entire country down a new path on this issue, so we can bury the Second Amendment controversy and make America a safe place to live again."

"How do your monuments fit into all this?" Carson asked.

"We start with a dedication ceremony here at your school. We'll get the news media interested, tell them it's the first step in our campaign. Then, the day before the Washington conference, we'll unveil the second memorial with a bigger ceremony honoring both Hank and LaRonda. We'll have guest speakers, filmed tributes, the whole works. And Gil, I'd like you to be at both dedications to tell your story."

Carson smiled. "Gil, did you think anything like this could happen to you six months ago?"

"No sir! Six months ago, I thought I was going to jail!"

"So is A&R offering to fund both monuments?" Janice asked.

"That's right. Complete with inscriptions telling the stories of Hank and LaRonda."

Royce frowned. "Warren, how can you tackle gun violence without some sort of radical legislation that'll never get through Congress?"

"That's why we need the conference, to search for an answer acceptable to people on both sides of the issue. So, what do you think?"

"I think it's great!" Gil said.

"Could you make a pitch at the next school board meeting?" Carson asked.

"I'll be there."

Janice and Royce looked at each other. "I think this would do Gil a lot of good," she said.

"Me too."

"In that case, I'll get the ball rolling right away. Gil, I'll want to talk with you some more. You knew LaRonda personally, so you're my touchstone in planning her monument."

"What about her father? Shouldn't he be in on it?"

"Yes, I'll call him and Hank Phillips' widow." Shelley will be the hard part, he told himself.

"I didn't mean to drag you away from your duties," Shelley said, leading Shaker to the filing cabinet.

"No problem, I was in the neighborhood. A couple of cars on Janus had a fender-bender. I was writing it up when I got your message."

She unlocked the cabinet and drew the Colt from a drawer. "This is the gun my husband wore the night he died. I was hoping the police department would destroy it for me."

Shaker checked the empty ammo chamber. "This is a nice piece. Why don't you just sell it, or give it away?"

"There's no such thing as a nice gun as far as I'm concerned. If Hank hadn't been wearing this, he wouldn't have been killed. If I sell it, somebody might get shot with it."

Shaker thought for a moment. "The department doesn't have a gun destruction program. Confiscated guns are usually sold to raise money for crime victims. A friend of mine can probably do it for you. He has a metal saw."

"How much would it cost?"

"He'll do it for nothing. Wow, what happened to your wall?" He walked over and examined the bashed-in Sheetrock.

"Oh. I made that. Stupid of me."

"How'd you do it?"

Shelley wished she could sink into the floor. "Well, if you must know, LaRonda called one day and left me a message. When I played it back I got mad and ... I'm sorry, I shouldn't be telling you this."

"You're very honest. Most people would have made up something. What did she say?"

"She wanted to apologize for Hank. She sounded so ... miserable." Shelley sat on the bed. "I've been on a roller coaster about LaRonda ever since her funeral. You've told me so many nice things about her, and Bruce has been after me to forgive her. Then yesterday, the news had a story about some teenager who's trying to create a memorial to her." Her eyes filled. "This is going to sound hateful, but my first thought was, 'a memorial for the woman who killed my husband.' And then I said Shelley, you can't go on like this. You've got to let it go. But I can't." She broke down. "I'm sorry. This probably hurts you as much as it does me."

"Did you delete LaRonda's message?" She nodded. "I'd give anything to hear her voice again."

Shelley reached for a tissue from the bedside table. "I wish I'd saved it for you. I would have, if I'd known how things were going to turn out. You've been so kind. And last week, I found out that Hank wrote me a letter the day he was killed. It was in his desk at the office. Reading it has meant so much to me. I wish I had something like that to give you."

"So do I. I heard about the memorial, too. Alvin and I went to the fundraiser and met the kid who's doing it. He's the one LaRonda saved from a bad home situation."

"Every time I see you, you've got another heart-warming story about her. Sometimes I feel like I have to choose between Hank and LaRonda."

"Look, I'm probably causing gossip with my patrol car in your driveway. Are you going to be okay?"

She nodded and rose. "I have these crying fits from time to time, but I'm doing better. Oh, I didn't tell you. I got a job! My church has hired me to run the Senior Outreach Ministry, full time."

"That's great! How do you like it?"

"I'm sure I'll love it, once I get organized. It's nice to be useful again."

Shaker wrapped the holster belt around the gun. "Well, don't worry, I'll make sure this thing gets what's coming to it." He headed for the front door, Shelley following. "I'd like to have you over again sometime. Do you think Alvin would like to come?"

Shaker turned, surprised. "You know, I think he might. He doesn't get out much. It takes both of us to get him into the car."

"If it's too much trouble, I can prepare something and bring it to his house."

"That's a good idea, too. He loved your lasagna. Hey, if this keeps up, I'm going to owe you a dinner out. I'm not much of a cook."

"You don't owe me a thing. Thanks for taking care of the gun." He returned to his car and stashed it in his trunk.

Back in the bedroom, Shelley noticed Hank's laptop computer quietly gathering dust on the little desk he had used for working at home. Since his death she had turned it on just once, to check his email. She decided to deactivate the account.

She was deleting junk mail when a name caught her eye: Mason Shore. The message was dated only a few weeks ago. Puzzled, she clicked it open.

Dear Dad,

I miss you. I wish you were still here. Mom and I are sad that you're gone, but Mr. Shore says you're in Heaven with God and Jesus. He says if I write to you, God will see that you get my message.

Dad, will you tell Officer Cage something for me? Tell her I know the shooting was an accident. I know she let herself get killed so God would forgive her. Please tell her that I forgive her, and that Mom is trying hard to forgive her, too.

I am back in school and doing good. I miss you Dad, but I know you're happy in Heaven. I hope I can go to Heaven too someday, so I can see you again.

Your loving son,

Bruce

"Matt, it's Shelley. Have you got a minute?"

"Sure, what's up?"

"I was cleaning out Hank's old email account, and I found a message from Bruce. It looks like it came from Macy's computer."

Matt was silent.

"Matt? He says you told him to write it."

"Yes, Shelley, I did."

Her voice quivered. "Why, Matt? What's Bruce talking about, asking Hank to ..." She couldn't finish.

"Shelley, Bruce was at our house the night you went to meet that officer, what's his name? Patterson?"

"Yes."

"Before LaRonda Cage died, Bruce asked me to arrange a meeting with her. He wanted to get to know her. Now he thinks when she got my message, she deliberately got herself shot to make up for Hank."

"Oh, Matt! How could he think such a thing?"

"That was my reaction, exactly. So to make him feel better, I suggested he use Macy's computer to send LaRonda an email prayer. Since we didn't know her address, we used Hank's." He sighed. "Shelley, I'm sorry you're upset. I thought Hank's account would be inactive after all this time."

"Matt, I don't know how to feel about this. Why did he tell you about it and not me?"

"He thought you hadn't gotten over your anger. And I guess he was right. Are you mad at me?"

"No, no, not at you, Matt. In fact, I'm not mad at anybody, just feeling guilty that Bruce had to ask someone else for help."

"If you ask me, there's been enough guilt. Give yourself a break. Besides, this all happened weeks ago. Things are different now."

"Yes, they are. We had Shaker Patterson over here for dinner one night. He's been going through the same misery we have. We both like him a lot."

"That's good."

"Matt, how do you suppose Bruce got such an idea about LaRonda's shooting?"

"Well, Bruce has feelings for other people. He's very mature for his age."

"Yes, he's a lot like his father."

"Shelley, please don't tell him about our conversation. I want him to feel he can talk to me in confidence. Sometimes a boy needs help only a man can give."

"You're right. Thanks, Matt. I owe you and Patti a lot. I love you both very much."

"We love you, too. Call any time you need us."

CHAPTER 22

"You have to sound sincere"

Amy hid in the tree shadows at stage left, watching her classmates mount the stage as the band played "Pomp and Circumstance." She was glad Pechora had decided to hold graduation outdoors. It was a beautiful evening, light enough for vision, yet close enough to sunset that the moment had a texture the seniors would remember well into middle age. They looked so nice in their blue caps and gowns. In her plain green dress, Amy felt like an intruder.

Twilight approached as Scott Yarbrough's diploma brought the alphabetical ceremony to an end. The principal stepped to the microphone.

"We have one last item that isn't on the program. A young lady who should have been part of this ceremony has asked to speak to you. I'll let her explain why. Pechora graduates and friends, please welcome Amy French."

Cautious applause greeted Amy as she emerged from the shadows and climbed the steps. Her stomach fluttered as she adjusted the microphone and squinted at the footlights.

"Last year, I dreamed of standing on this stage giving my valedictory speech. I don't mean to sound cocky. It's just that I had the grades to qualify, and all my teachers seemed to think it was a sure thing. I was one of the best students in my class. I had friends everywhere I turned. People liked and respected me. Everyone told me I was going places.

"Instead, you have a different valedictorian, Marilyn Keyes, and a salutatorian, Wayne Jenkins, who had the maturity and wisdom to earn for themselves the honor I threw away. Their speeches tonight prove that they're worthy of it.

"You all know what happened. I got involved in drugs. Me, Amy French, the girl most likely to succeed, a junkie. It started one night two winters ago with one little taste, just to see what it was like. That one little taste was a trapdoor to the drug pit. And unless you've fallen in, you have no idea what it's like, trying to climb back out.

"I'm sure you've all seen the movies, heard the lectures, watched the TV commercials, read the slogans about what drugs can do to you. I can guarantee that every single word of those warnings is true, because I'm an expert. I don't have a high school diploma. But I do have a PhD in drugs.

"I asked permission to speak to you tonight because most of you used to be my friends. Maybe some of you still think of me that way. If you do, God bless you, because I don't deserve you. I traded the best things a human being can have – loyal friends, a loving family, my talents, my future, and most important, my God and my savior Jesus – for a fleeting thrill. I turned my back on everything that was right and decent and honorable, all the things that decide whether a person becomes a success or a failure. That's why I'm here. I've apologized to God. I've apologized to my parents. Now, I want to apologize to you."

Her throat tightened. "That pit was a sick, lonely trap. I didn't think I'd ever escape until one night, God's angel came to me in the body of a kind police officer, who pulled me out of a cold, dark alleyway into her heart and convinced me that I still had a chance." She was crying now. "I only knew LaRonda Cage for the final half hour of her life. That was all the time she needed to show that God could love and forgive even me.

"To those of you who think I shouldn't be here tonight, I hope that someday you'll tell your children and grandchildren about the foolish girl who ruined your graduation ceremony. If my intrusion can somehow prevent anyone from making the mistake I made, I'll gladly accept your disapproval and your scorn. Congratulations, graduates of Pechora High. I admire you, and I apologize to you."

Weeping, Amy headed toward the shadows as the band struck up the exit music. A few seniors stood and applauded. A few more joined them. Then a dozen, two dozen, finally the entire class. Dazed, Amy turned back as they rushed the stage, row by row, knocking over the folding chairs, bounding up the steps, grabbing and hugging her, one after another. Jodie, Sherrell, and all the kids she had befriended and tutored mingled the tears on their cheeks with Amy's as they took their turns. Faculty and parents stood and applauded as capped-and-gowned teens passed Amy from friend to friend until she felt dizzy. And in that moment, Amy French was again the most popular girl at Pechora High.

Jason and Alexis were watching the evening news. On the last day of classes, someone had burst into the cafeteria of Kansas City's Shiloh Middle School and shot nine students, four teachers and two food service workers.

"Sometimes I wonder if Andy isn't safer being kidnapped than in school."

"Don't say that, Jason, please don't say that!" She lay her head on his shoulder. On the screen, a police official was reciting the details to the media. It sounded like every post-shooting conference in recent history.

The doorbell rang. Jason rose to admit his father and the two FBI agents. "Gary and Steve have an update on the investigation."

"We decided to dig a little deeper into the perpetrator's computer," Sanders explained, unfolding a sheet of paper. "He managed to change the IP address on Amy French's laptop and used a VPN to hide the new one. But there could be more than one computer involved. So we ran a check and came up with a list of fifty-six other laptops pawned or stolen here in Sandstone over the past three years. This is a list of the owners. Do you recognize any of these names?"

They examined the list, then shook their heads. "Well, it was worth a try."

"You say some were stolen," Alexis said. "Were any of them recovered? Maybe one of the thieves is the kidnapper."

"That was our thought, too. Five have been recovered so far, but the police got those back before Andy disappeared."

"So this is another dead end?"

"Not necessarily. We've added the others to our stolen merchandise database, and we're running the ownership history of each one. That could give us a lead."

"Any more messages, Dad?"

"Not a word. Not since the press conference."

Rivers watched the hope drain out of them. "Folks, please don't let this get you down. The guy hasn't threatened the boy or set any deadlines. I think the fact that he's consistently sent the same message is encouraging."

"Mr. Rivers, what's the FBI's recovery record in kidnap cases?" Jason asked.

"Pretty good, actually. In the United States, most child abductions involve family members or acquaintances. Kidnapping for ransom is pretty rare. It's hard to grab the money without getting caught. My point is this: I don't think the boy's in danger. Doctor Luke just wants your father to do something. I think we still have a good chance of getting Andy back."

"If we can figure out what he wants."

"Exactly. Let us know if you come up with any new ideas." The two agents shook their hands and left.

Jason and Alexis studied the computer list again while David studied their living room. To him, the shabby furniture, faded wallpaper and worn carpet were all symbols of Jason's rebellion. Through the window, he saw derelict houses with junk cars cluttering weed-choked lawns. Motorcycles and trucks roared along the interstate two blocks away. Even if Andy came home, he'd still be living in squalor.

He redirected his displeasure to the TV. "You've got to hand it to the anti-gun crowd. They've got these fake massacres down to an art."

"Oh Dad, don't start that again. I'm not in the mood for another argument."

"I just don't understand how people can be taken in by this. We wouldn't be seeing all this drama if there wasn't some agenda behind it. Mass murderers don't suddenly pop up, one after another, for no reason. It's a conspiracy to undermine the Second Amendment, and that's all there is to it."

"Dad, that's ridiculous! There's no way you could fake hundreds of deaths and injuries all over the country, bribe hundreds of kids, parents, doctors, cops and school officials into a shooting conspiracy without the truth leaking out."

"With enough money and planning, you can fake anything. Just watch any action movie. It sure makes more sense than a sudden epidemic of mass killers on the rampage, willing to give their lives to vent their spleens. It's the gun haters, I tell you! They can't get around the Second Amendment, so they've cooked up a bunch of fake attacks to scare the rest of us into a repeal movement."

"David, wait a minute –"

"Don't interrupt, Alexis. I'm old enough to remember a time when people respected the law and the Constitution because they served everybody's best interest. That's what kept America strong. Now minorities are eroding everything. Legalize marijuana. Make the military pay for transgender surgery. Pardon illegal immigrants. Put every deadbeat on Welfare and Medicaid. People won't take responsibility for themselves anymore. They expect society to do everything for them!"

"David –"

"Dad, that has nothing to do with these shootings!"

"Listen to me, both of you!" They glared at each other, then at Alexis. "David, maybe that's what he wants."

"What who wants?"

"The kidnapper. Maybe he took Andy because of your opinions about shooting hoaxes."

"No, I've already been over that with Gary. It's a dead end."

"What?" Jason asked. "When was this?"

"Oh, the FBI found out I've been doing some Twitter chats and came to the same conclusion Alexis did."

"Dad! You've been spreading this hoax garbage on Twitter?"

"It's not garbage, and don't take that tone with me. I used a fake name. Nobody knows about my Twitter account except your mother and the FBI. Gary was just following a lead. It has nothing to do with Andy's abduction."

"Oh, Dad!" Jason threw the printout at him. "If the FBI can find out who you are, a hacker can too. Why didn't you mention this before?"

"It's not relevant to the investigation, and it's nobody else's business!"

"But David, think about it!" Alexis's eyes filled. "I was scrolling through the internet news this morning, and some guy was claiming Andy's kidnapping was a hoax. Do you know how that made me feel? Well, think of all these parents with dead school children. Can you imagine how they feel when people go around claiming their kids were just crisis actors? Maybe the kidnapper's one of the parents."

"Or not even a parent, just someone else who's mad at you," Jason added.

"Why would anybody kidnap a child and risk prison just to change my mind about this conspiracy? Which I know darned well that's what it is!"

"If Andy had been murdered instead of kidnapped, wouldn't you be upset if people called it a hoax?" Alexis asked.

David sulked. "Yeah. Okay, I see your point."

"So Dad, you could go on TV and take back what you said. Maybe that's what Doctor Luke means about doing the right thing."

Sullenly, David stared at the screen, watching traumatized parents and kids embrace each other.

"All right, I'll do it. Tomorrow morning, while today's incident is hot news. The timing should give us plenty of media attention. But that doesn't mean I've changed my mind. I still think these things are hoaxes, including the one today."

"David, you have to sound sincere," Alexis pleaded. "If this is what he wants, you've got to make him believe you're rejecting this conspiracy idea and the people who go along with it. It may be our only chance to get Andy back."

"Don't worry, honey," Jason said bitterly. "Dad's good at getting his way. He always has been."

"Before my grandson's disappearance, I was involved in a series of Twitter conversations about fake school shootings," David read to the cameras outside Pierpont. "Since then, I have come to understand the agony of families who have lost loved ones, especially children, in these terrible attacks. I regret allowing the notions of a small minority to convince me that these killings were part of a conspiracy against the Second Amendment to our Constitution. I realize now that I was mistaken, that these murders did in fact occur, and I apologize for any harm I may have done with my Twitter statements. I call upon all people who subscribe to the so-called crisis actor theories about Sandy Hook and other gun attacks to renounce them. I urge everyone to search for more constructive ways to address the social issues facing our nation. Thank you."

He turned and entered the building, ignoring shouts from reporters.

The next afternoon, Alexis came home to find a UPS express package on her doorstep. Inside was an unmarked compact disc in a plain cover. When she popped it into her CD player, a child spoke:

"Andy Tischner will come home when David Tischner does the right thing."

She swooned and fell to the floor.

CHAPTER 23

The dreaded flower bed

Shaker backed a van into Shelley's driveway, pulled out the ramp and wheeled Alvin into the house. Shelley took to him immediately. He had the manner of someone who's never met a stranger. "This reminds me of my parents' house. It's so roomy! They don't make roomy houses anymore."

"That's what sold us on it," Shelley said. "We got the space without the eternal mortgage."

Alvin handed Bruce a small gift-wrapped package. Inside was a Ken Doll in Marine dress blues. "Shaker told me about your bedroom," Alvin said. "I thought this might fit with your collection."

"Did you make this?" he marveled.

"A little hobby of mine. I made the uniform from odds and ends of old clothing. The white belt used to be a wristwatch band. The cap's part of a T-shirt stretched over a paperclip. I cut the black visor out of a plastic drinking cup."

"What about the shoes?"

"Those were tough. I did the best I could with some epoxy and paint."

"Cool! Thanks!" He escorted Alvin to his room. Shaker accompanied Shelley to the kitchen, offering to help her prepare dinner. "Actually, I could use some help. How about making the salad? Everything's right there on the countertop."

"You got it." He washed his hands and began chopping vegetables into a large serving bowl as Shelley checked something in the oven that smelled like barbecued chicken.

"I brought some stuff to fix that hole in your wall."

She turned to him. "What?"

He diced a bell pepper. "A cop friend of mine had some drywall, tape and spackling left over from a repair job. He said I could use it."

"Shaker, I can't let you do that!"

"Why not? It's not going to cost anything."

"It costs you time, which you probably don't have, plus labor. Are you good at fixing things?"

"I can do wall repair. It's easy. The only thing is, I can't repaint it until I take a scraping over to the store so I can match the color."

"Well, that's sweet of you, but surely you don't plan on doing it tonight?"

"No, I just thought I'd bring the stuff over while I had use of the van."

"And who loaned you the van? Don't tell me. Another cop."

He grinned. "Yeah."

"Do you have any friends who aren't cops?"

"Just you."

Shelley leaned against the oven, watching him slice a cucumber. "You're right. I guess we are getting to be friends." He flashed her a smile. "Shaker, I'm sorry if I said anything against LaRonda last time. Sometimes I forget I'm not the only person hurting."

"People say things they don't mean when they hurt. I hear them all the time in my line of work."

"That's not good enough. Until I met you, it never occurred to me that LaRonda had a life and problems, just like anyone else. Thank you."

"You're welcome." He started slicing mushrooms. "You sure picked some nice salad ingredients. I never think past lettuce and tomatoes. This is going to be great."

Shelley opened the oven and basted a pan of rolls with garlic butter. "Did you hear about the monument? I mean the one A&R wants to build in Washington."

"Yes, Mr. DeVries called Alvin. What do you think about it?"

"I was wondering what you think. It's a nice gesture, but it feels ... I don't know. Strange."

"Because of how it all happened?"

"Yes. I guess other people find significance in it. I'm too close to it. Besides, Hank wouldn't have liked it."

He was chopping radishes. "I'm okay with it. The monument is for other people, like you said. Alvin and I have our own, private monuments."

"So do I." She thought of the letter in her bag.

Bruce and Alvin invaded the kitchen. "Guess what, Mom? Mr. Cage used to be a policeman, too."

"Yes, I heard about that. Mr. Cage, would you like something to drink?"

"No, thank you, and please call me Alvin. I love your house. How long have you lived here?"

"Let's see, about eight years. Bruce was just ten months old when we bought it."

"Where'd we live before that, Mom?"

"Didn't we ever show you the old apartment from when your dad and I moved to Sandstone? It's 'way on the other side of town. I'll have to take you by there one day." She turned to Alvin. "Hank had just been offered his job with Armed and Ready when Bruce was born. At first, all we could afford was this little old shack behind someone's house. But we sure were happy."

"I know what you mean. LaRonda's still part of my house. I wouldn't trade it for a mansion."

Shelley turned to the oven. "I think this is just about ready. Bruce, will you show our guests to the table?"

"Delicious!" Alvin declared. "This and your lasagna put you right up there with Julia Child."

Shaker was indignant. "What about me? I made the salad."

"And you did a fine job. I've never tasted such well-chopped vegetables." He turned to Shelley. "I heard about your new job. Do you cook for the senior citizens you're helping?"

"Sometimes. The ones using walkers and wheelchairs have a pretty hard time getting around a kitchen."

"I can vouch for that. I'm sure glad I've got Celeste. She's about as good as you are."

Bruce was staring at Alvin. "Does it hurt in the place where you got shot?"

"Bruce!" Shelley was aghast.

Alvin laughed. "That's okay, that's a good question. Actually, I don't feel anything there. The injury that keeps me from walking also keeps me from hurting. So it could be a lot worse, couldn't it?"

"Yes sir."

"You'll have to come watch me in the therapy pool some time. I'm a very good swimmer."

"So am I."

"Then it's a date. I'll race you."

After dinner, Shaker unloaded the drywall materials from the van while Bruce took out the trash. Shelley watched sadly as he carried the bag along the sidewalk.

The adults had coffee while Bruce texted Macy in his room. Alvin smiled as Shelley repeated the story of how she met Hank. "I saw your husband on the news the night before his death. It was good to hear someone speak reasonably about firearms. He sounded very sincere."

"He was. Gun violence was a big issue with Hank. People who admire his war record don't realize how much it hurt him."

"Shelley," Alvin began, hesitantly, "you were very kind to invite me here. I mean, considering what happened." He noted her discomfort. "I'm sorry if this bothers you, but if we don't talk about it, it'll always be between us."

Something dark and bitter crumbled inside her. "To be honest, Alvin, I had mixed feelings about meeting you. But my son recognized long ago what I refused to accept. That it was just a terrible accident." She searched his eyes. "I've been watching you all evening, trying to imagine how you looked before you lost your daughter. I can see by your face what it's done to you."

He swallowed hard. "I thought losing my wife was the worst thing that would ever happen to me. Losing a child is a thousand times worse."

The memory of her unborn daughter rose in Shelley. She stood and put a hand to Alvin's face. She bent to embrace him, the two parents holding one another silently. It was a moment Shaker never forgot.

Shelley dried her eyes with a napkin. Alvin took a deep breath. "Boy, I'm glad that's over." They all laughed with relief. "What do you think about that plan for a memorial in Washington?"

"Shaker and I were talking about that earlier. I guess I'll appreciate it more when I hear the details. How do you feel about it?"

"I'm proud. I was always proud of LaRonda. I'm thrilled that other people realize what a wonderful person she was. And I like knowing that strangers will be stopping to read about her for generations to come."

"Yes. Immortality."

Shaker stood. "Well, tomorrow's a work day. Shelley, thank you for another marvelous dinner, and for sharing Bruce with us."

"Yes, thanks," Alvin added. "And I meant what I said about taking him swimming."

"Sounds like a good idea. School's finished for the year. I'm sure he'll want to join you." She escorted them to the door. "Alvin, here's my outreach card. Please call if you need anything. Or if you just want to talk. And I promise we'll have another dinner soon."

"The next one's on us," Shaker promised. "Except it'll have to be at a restaurant. You're looking at two lousy cooks."

"Speak for yourself. I'm the reason God created microwaves."

The next morning, Shelley phoned Marie in Cincinnati and apologized for what she'd said on the phone about LaRonda's acquittal. Then she walked across the street and rang the doorbell.

Abigail Morton looked better now, but Shelley's presence still disturbed her. She stood in the doorway, cringing a little.

"Abby, I want to apologize to you. The last time I was here, I was still grieving and angry. It didn't occur to me that you called the police because you were being a good neighbor. I hope you can forgive me."

Abigail reached out and drew Shelley into her arms. "Won't you come in and visit with me for a while? I have so much to say to you."

"I'd love to." They stepped inside and closed the door.

The following Saturday she roused Bruce early. "Let's go shopping. Baldwin's has a great sale on spring flowers."

He rubbed the sleep from his eyes. "Where are we going to plant them?"

"We'll make a space. Come on, get dressed."

They returned with a load of colorful blossoms and accent shrubs. Shelley opened the hatch of their minivan and handed Bruce a tray. "Take these to the back yard."

The boy lowered his gaze to the flowers. "Mom, I can't go back there."

"Honey, we're going to plant these in Dad's memory."

"Please, Mom. I can't."

She kneeled before him. "Bruce, you showed me the way back from your father's death. Now you're the one who's lost. It's my turn to help you." She cupped his face in her hands. "Suppose we each carry a tray of flowers and pretend we're bringing them to Dad. I'll walk with you. I'll have my tray in one arm, and you in the other. I won't let go until you're ready, and I won't leave you alone there."

He gulped and nodded. She held him close as they slowly walked around the side of the house. When she stopped, Bruce raised his eyes. The dreaded flower bed was empty.

"I cleared out everything from last year," Shelley said. "The flowers were annuals, so they weren't going to come back anyway. Today we're giving this ground a fresh start. New flowers. A fresh start for them. A fresh start for you and me."

Bruce stared at the bare earth. "I guess I thought I'd see Dad there."

"Dad's in Heaven. And how happy he must be to see his wife and son bringing new life to the place where he fell. Come on. Let's plant some flowers for him."

"Okay, Mom." They slowly approached the site together.

CHAPTER 24

Fighting the establishment

Early in June, LaRonda's killer and his accomplice went on trial. Despite their public defender's clever tactics, the jurors needed only ninety minutes to find them both guilty. They chose death for the gunman and forty years in prison for the hapless passenger, who'd been so drunk he barely remembered the incident.

The verdicts didn't make Alvin feel any better. "How do you do it, Shelley?" he asked. "You found a way to forgive LaRonda. I don't know how to forgive those guys."

"It was you, Alvin. And Bruce. And Shaker. And God." It was the first of many discussions between the bereaved pair. But the miracle that healed Alvin and Shaker was almost two years in the future.

One Sunday morning, Shelley stood before her congregation and made a pitch for Senior Outreach. "I wish everyone could come home at night feeling the way I do. I lie down to sleep remembering the joyful welcome in a lonely man's eyes because I dropped by for a visit. Or the smile of gratitude when I brought a sick lady some homemade soup. Or someone's relief that I could pick up a prescription on short notice. My job is more fun than being President of the United States. The reward I get is greater than money."

After the service, a dozen volunteers approached her, most of them bored retirees. "Shelley, you're as persuasive as Hank was," Weldon Finch grinned. "When do I start?"

"I'll never forget the times Hank taught our Sunday School class," said Jeanette Thatcher. "He made those old Bible stories fresh and meaningful for me. I'd love to help you." Within a couple of weeks, Shelley had all her recruits organized and busy.

She stayed with Alvin one Saturday morning while Shaker repaired the Sheetrock. Bruce was impressed. "I thought you'd have to make a whole new wall." He helped with the job and accompanied Shaker to the paint store. After the paint dried, he couldn't tell where the hole had been.

Sitting at Alvin's kitchen table while he proudly showed her his photo album, Shelley could hardly believe she had ever been bitter toward this sweet-faced woman. Now she wished she had returned LaRonda's phone call.

Deciding Alvin needed to get out of the house more, Shaker traded his car for a repossessed van and persuaded the dealer to deduct the cost of a wheelchair lift from the price. Alvin's first excursion was to a wedding. Shaker gave away his mother Valerie to LeRoy Weaver the last weekend in June, a few months after they'd fallen in love as coworkers at Alamo Bank. Their boss and his wife served as best man and matron of honor. Everyone celebrated by escorting Alvin to the city's July Fourth fireworks display. His last was two months before he was shot.

Sometimes Shaker and Alvin joined Shelley at Bruce's baseball games, cheering as he displayed the shortstop skills he'd learned from Hank. One night, Bruce invited both men to a Cub Scout meeting, where they fascinated the boys with their police stories.

Shelley scolded Shaker for driving Alvin to therapy while on duty. "What if you get an emergency call while he's with you? Let me drive him."

"You've got a heavy load already with your own job. Besides, Alvin isn't your responsibility."

"He isn't yours, either."

"I'm not anybody's anything!" Alvin bristled. "Stop talking about me like I'm the family dog or a demented relative." Shaker finally gave in. The van made it easy, and as head of Senior Outreach, Shelley could draft a volunteer to transport Alvin when she was too busy.

That happened sooner than she expected. "Your father's had a heart attack!" Ivy wailed frantically into the phone one night. "They just took him away in an ambulance."

Shelley stashed Bruce with Matt and Patti while she flew to her father's bedside in Cincinnati. A nurse assured her that Charles was stable and sleeping comfortably. Ivy was so wound up that the nurses banished her to the relatives' waiting room, where she flipped through magazines, stood around, paced and generally wore herself out. She watched visitors exit the elevator, bearing flowers and shushing their children as they headed down the hall.

"Shelley, do you ever wonder if you've done anything worthwhile with your life?"

"What do you mean, Mom?"

"It's just that ... here we are, thirty-five years fighting the Establishment, and your father winds up in an Establishment hospital, under Establishment medical care. Charles would probably be dead now if it weren't for the Establishment. Doesn't that seem hypocritical to you?"

"Are you sorry you became an activist?"

"Not exactly. I'm just ... tired." She looked it, her face jowly, her hair thinning and gray. "You spend your whole life fighting injustice, and you wind up scratching for a living, sorting plastic bottles in a recycling plant all day, stuffing fund-raiser envelopes at night that people throw in the trash without looking at them."

"Not everybody, Mom. A lot of people support what you're doing. Look how much has changed since you were my age. Civil rights laws, environmental regulations, government watchdog agencies. You helped build all that."

"Maybe it would have happened anyway." She studied her left hand in a ray of sunlight streaming through the window. "Have you ever noticed I don't have a wedding ring? Your father said it was a bourgeois custom cooked up by blood diamond miners to get rich off African slaves. The truth was, he didn't have the money for a ring. You'd think I'd at least get a sprig of flowers on our anniversary, or a little box of chocolates on Valentine's Day."

Shelley had never seen her mother like this. "Don't you think Daddy loves you?"

"He loves his work." Ivy's eyes grew dreamy. "I had a chance to marry Dwayne Aldrich before his parents disowned him."

"Dwayne Aldrich? Who was he?"

"Oh, nobody you'd know. I shouldn't have mentioned him."

"Come on, Mom. What was he like?"

She smiled. "Dwayne had this yellow hair and blue eyes that ... when you looked into those eyes, it was like wading in a pool of warm water. You felt drawn to him. He was the smartest boy in our class. When I was sixteen, he asked me to the movies. My mother said no, he's a rebel, he'll never amount to anything." She laughed. "Then *I* became a rebel!"

"What happened to him?"

"It was a Sunday morning. I used to attend church, believe it or not. The preacher was running through a list of countries with non-Christian religions, saying they were all Hell-bound idolaters. Dwayne walked up on the stage and told the preacher, right in front of everyone, that he was as bad as the Pharisees in the Bible. He said Jesus died to save all souls, including the ones the preacher was condemning, and if he couldn't see that, he had no business preaching. Then he walked out. That was the last time I saw him."

"Where did he go after that?"

"Nobody ever talked about Dwayne again. His parents joined some other church to escape the embarrassment. Later, I heard he died during a smallpox epidemic in India while working as a missionary."

"That's sad."

"Yes. Dwayne died for nothing. I guess my life's been nothing, too."

Shelley drew the letter from her bag. "Mom, this is something Hank wrote to me on his last day:

God has given me the power of speech. Maybe I should use it to work against war and weapons. I don't know how else to atone for what I've done.

"Mom, one of the reasons I fell in love with Hank was that his heart was always in the right place. You and Daddy are a lot like him."

Charles woke that afternoon in time for the cardiologist's visit. "I think he just needs to slow down," he told Shelley. "Mr. Spurlock, you're to follow a strict cardiac diet, sleep at least eight hours at night, and nap whenever you can." He turned to Ivy. "That goes for both of you. You're not campus agitators anymore!"

The doctor released Charles the next day. As they escorted him to the car, he turned and put his arms around Shelley. "Thanks for coming, honey." Ivy applied her own hug. Shelley said a silent prayer for them as she headed for the airport.

Warren kept his word and worked closely with Gil Starnes on the LaRonda memorial at Castle High School. Amy French heard about it and contacted the principal, who put her on the speakers' roster. Following Labor Day, the school opened the fall semester with a dedication ceremony on the campus lawn. The date turned out to be a great choice, for the late summer morning was sunny, mild and windless. The statue, covered by a tarp, waited on a grassy spot near the school's main entrance.

Amy took the podium first. Smiling down at her parents, she gave a modified version of her graduation speech, praising LaRonda as "an angel of the Lord who led me out of darkness." Then she introduced Gil.

"I'm the least qualified person to be here," he confessed to the audience of students, teachers and cops, "because I almost killed the woman we're honoring today. The minor wound LaRonda inflicted on me actually saved my life. She risked her job to rescue me from a dangerous home. At the end of our hospital visit I said, 'Thank you, Officer Cage.' She smiled at me and said, 'It's LaRonda to you.' So those words are the theme of our memorial to her."

Alvin got the honor of unveiling the statue. He yanked the heavy cord, drawing delighted gasps and applause from the crowd. A brilliant white marble replica of LaRonda stood atop a granite base with her words etched in black letters:

"IT'S LARONDA TO YOU"

Above the inscription the officer kneeled, her head tilted at a disarming angle, her open palm extended in friendship. The text carved into the base told Gil's story and summarized LaRonda's life and career.

News cameras captured Alvin's tears as he admired his daughter's pristine likeness. "It's beautiful, Mom," Bruce said. "She looks just like Alvin's pictures."

A local reporter recognized Shelley and waved his cameraman over. "Mrs. Phillips, you haven't made any public statements since your husband's funeral. Does your presence at this ceremony mean you've forgiven LaRonda Cage for his death?"

Shaker stepped forward to intervene. "No, it's okay." Shelley collected her thoughts and faced the reporter. "I didn't think I'd ever forgive LaRonda. But when I met the people who loved her, I realized she meant as much to them as Hank meant to me." She posed for pictures with her arms around Alvin and Shaker.

"What about Vern Saginaw? You gave him a pretty rough time at the funeral last year. Have you forgiven him?"

Shelley went blank. She hadn't thought about Vern in months. "That's enough guys," Shaker said. He escorted Shelley and Bruce into the host of cops surrounding the statue. The unveiling, the brilliance of the sun reflecting off the perfect stone, had almost driven him to his knees. "Amy's right," he said to Shelley. "It's like the appearance of an angel. Now I know how the Old Testament prophets must have felt."

As Shaker introduced Shelley and Bruce to Gil and Amy, Warren made his way through the crowd to join them. "The ceremony was wonderful," he beamed. "I hope you approve of the choices we made for the statue."

Amy responded by throwing her arms around him. "I guess that's a yes," he said.

"I'll never forget this day," Alvin said, offering Warren his hand. "God bless you, Mr. DeVries, for this memorial. I can't imagine how you're going to top it with the one in Washington."

"Maybe we can't. But we're sure going to try."

Shelley took Warren aside. "Do you have Vern's phone number?" He jotted it down for her. "I haven't spoken to him myself. I didn't think he'd appreciate hearing from the man who took his job." She tried the number later but got no answer. Despite several other attempts over a period of weeks, she was never able to reach him.

David Tischner peered through his rifle scope and squeezed the trigger. A sharp crack echoed across the range as the bullet nailed his target dead center, five hundred yards away. September was his favorite month for practice, the blistering Texas heat subsiding, the foliage still green and beautiful, butterflies dancing around the late blossoms. Signs of life always meant hope.

He'd clung to hope since the CD. Alexis and Jason had no doubts; they could have picked Andy's voice out of a hundred others. He sounded happy, speaking the ransom message as he might have recited "Jack and Jill went up the hill." Whoever Doctor Luke was, he was taking good care of the boy.

Following David's renunciation of hoax theories, Agent Rivers launched a discreet but fruitless search for Andy among the families of massacre victims. Meanwhile, David went on television again and begged for his grandson's release. He denounced by name several leading conspiracy buffs. He endorsed Warren's plans for a gun violence conference. The only response was a fax message to David's office:

> **Andy Tischner will come home when David Tischner does the right thing.**
>
> **Doctor Luke**

The FBI traced the fax to a disconnected business number in Rapid City, South Dakota. Somehow, the kidnapper had scrambled the call.

David locked another shell into the chamber, sighted carefully and squeezed the trigger. Another great shot, just slightly off center. His membership at this private gun range, landscaped in lush flowers and greenery, was a gift from Vern. The two of them used to meet here regularly, shooting side by side, comparing their targets and discussing ballistics. Now David came alone, at different times on different days, hoping for a chance meeting to heal the breach between them. The last he'd seen of Vern was the crestfallen expression on his face at the A&R board meeting. David tried repeatedly to phone him, but Vern must have been screening his calls. He never answered or called back.

David found it hard to concentrate on Pierpont business these days. The FBI's arrest of Sam Leopard and Joe Brunnel had shocked him badly. The U.S. District Attorney was charging them with multiple counts of illegal weapons trafficking. The Texas Attorney General added another: conspiracy to overthrow the state government.

After their arraignment he went to visit them in Waco, where they awaited trial. A guard escorted the men into the visitors' room, their wrists shackled, their bodies clad in orange jumpsuits. They smiled delightedly as they sat on their side of a plexiglass barrier. "Great to see you, David!" Sam said. "Thanks for coming."

David hardly knew what to say. He'd never visited a prison before. The gauntlet of security doors, weapon scanners and beefy guards was intimidating. "Hi guys. Sorry to meet you under such peculiar circumstances."

"Not your typical high school reunion, is it?" Sam grinned.

"How are they treating you?"

"Okay. It's just kind of boring."

David noticed the TV cameras in the ceiling. "Are we free to talk? I guess they record everything you say here."

"Doesn't matter. We've got nothing to hide, right Joe?"

"Not anymore!" Both men laughed like it was the funniest punchline ever.

"I can't believe you guys! How could you do such a thing!"

Joe shrugged. "Sometimes you have to take risks to do what's right."

David was bewildered. "I joined the NTC to help protect our Confederate heritage, not to start a war. What were you planning to do with all those weapons?"

"Take over the state capital, of course!"

"Just the two of you?"

Joe glanced at the cameras and winked at David. "Let's just say we have sympathizers."

"We were going to let you in on it," Sam added, "but when you voted to fire Vern Saginaw, we weren't sure about you anymore. Why'd you do that, anyway?"

"Never mind. What's your defense strategy?"

"Patriotic Texan!" Sam declared. Joe nodded in agreement.

"You're just going to let them put you away?"

"It won't last. There are plenty of others who feel as we do. The secession's coming, no matter what happens to us. In fact, it should help recruit more allies."

Their cavalier attitude was unnerving. Both men had families. Successful businesses. Hardly the kind of people you'd suspect as seditionists. "What did you hope to gain?"

"Freedom! Freedom from government leftists, property seizures and revisionist judges."

"You know all this, David," Joe insisted. "We've talked many times about standing up for Texas."

"We never talked about a power grab!"

"Not in so many words, maybe. Look, you're a smart businessman. You know how things work. The feds always get their way. The rest of us just lie down and let them run over us. Not anymore. Once Texas is free, other states will jump in to join us. First we'll build a new Texas, then a new America!"

"Time's up," the guard said. The men stood. "Don't take it so hard, David," Joe smiled as they left. "Every revolution in history had its setbacks." The door closed with a clang of finality.

The visit left him in turmoil. What if his vote against Vern hadn't made the news? Sam and Joe would have asked David to commit treason! Of course, he'd have turned them down, but then what? Betray two old friends to the FBI? In a crazy way, Andy's kidnapping had spared him that decision.

Andy's birth four years ago – no, he'd be five now – was like a second chance at fatherhood for David. The boy was so much like Jason at that age: happy, energetic, curious about the world, and delighting in his grandparents. With a child in their lives, David and Marla had something in common again. Their ailing marriage had begun to heal. They'd spent every available moment with him until Jason's blowup over his father's gun collection.

David couldn't understand Jason's hostility. As young as six, he'd begged his father to take him hunting. He had to be satisfied with cap pistols and plastic rifles until his tenth birthday, when David finally took him to the target range. That led to their first and only father-son hunting trip early one Saturday, driving to the lake through darkness, settling themselves in the reeds to watch the sun rise, listening to bird calls and watching ducks gather on the calm water. "Take your time," David whispered. "Be sure you've got a clear shot."

Jason nodded and lifted the rifle carefully, steadying his aim as he peered through the scope. He peered too long. The magnifier put him face-to-face with a young bird innocently scrounging for breakfast. "Hold your breath and squeeze," David coached, but Jason's throat was too constricted at the idea of what he was about to do. The rifle sank to the grass as he gasped in anguish. "I can't, Dad!"

"What's wrong?"

"This is!" He turned his tearful eyes to his father, who scowled, raised his own rifle to his shoulder and blew the duck's head off.

"Where do you think your fried chicken and hamburgers come from?" he barked at his blubbering son as they drove home. "Read your Old Testament. God put the birds and beasts on this Earth for food, and for slaughter in sacrificial worship. There's nothing wrong with it."

"I'm sorry, Dad, I just couldn't!" David plucked the bird, roasted it and served it for dinner that night. "Eat!" he commanded. Jason stared miserably at the greasy flesh on his plate, jumped up and fled to his room. "For Heaven's sake, David, he's just a boy!" Marla rebuked him.

"He's a wimp! I'm ashamed of him!" In rebellion, Jason joined an animal rights crusade at his school. Marla tried to reason with both of them. "Your father's more than a hunter," she insisted. "He's a good provider and a patriotic American." To David she argued, "Give the boy some room to grow." Both remained stubborn. By the time Jason finished high school, they were barely speaking. Even at Jason's wedding, the best either could muster was a polite handshake.

Andy's kidnapping had reunited them in a common purpose. But now, ten months into it, frustration was their only bond. David's scripted renunciation of hoax dogma sounded like what it was: an insincere ploy to get his grandson back. Obviously, it had not satisfied Doctor Luke. Either "the right thing" was something else, or Andy's captor had sensed the truth: that David still believed the massacres were being staged.

The FBI was stymied. Predictably, there were no prints on the CD containing Andy's voice. A trace on the UPS package drew a blank. Whatever Doctor Luke wanted, he was good at covering his tracks. Now he was silent.

With no grandchild as a buffer against their differences, David and Marla grew apart again. Jason and Alexis were emotional wrecks. Agent Rivers could only counsel patience for them and further introspection for David.

Reloading his rifle, he glanced down the firing line. Just a few other shooters today, all of them strangers. Even this pleasant venue was lonely when you had no one to share it with. Soon it would be even emptier, as deer hunters abandoned the range, invading the woods for live targets. By then, the flowers and butterflies would be gone. And worst of all, David feared, so would all hope.

CHAPTER 25

The mark of Cain

A s October 31 approached, the weight of Hank's death descended again on Shelley. The Shores organized another pumpkin harvest for the two families. Reluctantly, she went along for Bruce's sake. Later, she sat with Patti in the church lobby, carving jack-o-lanterns and trying not to cry.

Unable to sleep after the Halloween party, she sought solace in her two bedtime rituals – reading scripture and re-reading Hank's letter.

> *I will never find peace until I've healed the breach between myself and God.*

She wandered into Bruce's room, turned on his lamp and drew the Medal of Honor from its box. She remembered her pride the day two Marines, crisp and ceremonial in their dress blues, came to their modest Cincinnati flop. Hank politely accepted America's highest military award, shook hands with the men, and escorted them to the door. Then he hid the medal in a drawer. The two soldiers might as well have branded him with the mark of Cain.

"Mom, is something wrong?"

"Sorry son, I didn't mean to wake you. I was just looking at your dad's medal."

"Are you okay?"

She went to sit beside him. "Bruce, I know how proud you are of your dad and his military record. What do you think about this plan to build a monument for him and LaRonda in Washington?"

"I think it's great. Everybody in school's talking about it. Why?"

"Well, I've been sitting here thinking. If your dad was still alive, he wouldn't allow it. Do you know why?"

Bruce thought for a moment. "I know he didn't like to talk about the war. He didn't much like my model planes and stuff. That's why I gave them away."

"But you kept Dad's war mementos." Shelley gestured at the wall decorations. "His uniforms. The pictures he took over there."

"Those are different, Mom. Those were his personal things."

"Things he wore? Things he touched?"

"Yeah. So do you think the monument's a bad idea?"

"Why don't we sleep on it?" She kissed him and tucked him in.

"You want to cancel the Washington ceremony?"

"Not all of it. Just the statue part." Shelley sat in Warren's office with Alvin and Shaker. "We've all decided it would be a betrayal of their wishes. Even Bruce agrees."

Warren riffled through some design sketches on his desk. "Shelley, Armed and Ready has invested a lot in this memorial. And I don't mean just money. I've had to do some serious political arm-twisting to establish a site for it. We're building the whole gun violence conference around it. Congress has tabled all its gun legislation to see what our delegates come up with. And I know this conference is something Hank would have wanted."

"Warren, Vern hired Hank to promote gun rights because he got a medal for killing. He didn't feel honorable about the job or the medal. Even his last letter said so."

"Same with LaRonda," Alvin added. "Her acquittal in Hank's death didn't make her feel any better about it. And sharing a memorial with the man she killed? Never!"

"But all of you approved the statue at Castle High School."

"That's different," Shaker replied. "That has nothing to do with what happened between Hank and LaRonda."

Warren looked from face to face. They appeared adamant. "My friends, your loved ones have become valuable weapons in the war on gun violence. Don't you think they'd approve of using their stories to fight that war?"

"Well, when you put it that way, yes," Shelley admitted.

"So what we're arguing about here isn't the use of their names. It's the way we're using them. Can we agree on that?" The others nodded. "Then tell me how we can use them to kick off this conference. I'm sorry if that sounds callous, but I need something to replace the rug you're pulling out from under me."

Everyone was quiet. Then Shaker cleared his throat. "What about remorse?"

"What do you mean?"

"Before they died, Hank and LaRonda were hurting as much as we are now because of guilt. So maybe we could create some sort of memorial about remorse. Something that would be acceptable to them."

"How do you make a memorial about remorse?" Alvin asked.

"People kill other people every day in this world, deliberately, in a moment of anger, or by accident. As a cop, I've seen it happen lots of times. There must be other people like Hank and LaRonda who feel sorry about it. People who wish they could take it back. Maybe that's the kind of memorial we need. A remorse memorial with names, like the ones honoring war veterans. Only these would be names of people saying they're sorry."

"You mean like a confessional?" Warren asked.

"That's right. Instead of statues praising Hank and LaRonda, we make some sort of memorial explaining why they killed, and how it affected them. It would be a place where other people could do the same thing."

Warren drummed his fingers on the statue sketches. "This is an interesting idea. I'll put Barney to work on it."

That night, the letter made Shelley restless again. She phoned Shaker the next day. "Was there anything unusual about LaRonda's death?"

"Unusual how?"

"I've been wondering about Hank's letter. He put it in an envelope, wrote my name on it and stuck it in a drawer. Like I was supposed to read it later. Why would he do that?"

"I don't know. What's that got to do with LaRonda?"

"Remember the phone message I got from her? She said she wanted to apologize, but I never gave her a chance. Then later, I found out that Bruce tried to meet LaRonda. When she got killed, Bruce thought she deliberately let the guy shoot her."

"Bruce told you this?"

"No, he told my friend Matt, who tried to arrange the meeting, and later it got back to me. Shaker, you're the one who brought up the idea of a remorse memorial. Maybe Hank and LaRonda both gave their lives to atone for what they did."

"I don't follow you."

"Maybe she was *supposed* to shoot him."

Shaker was speechless.

"Okay, you're thinking I've gone off the deep end, but I knew Hank. From the time I met him, he begged God to let him make up for Afghanistan. On the day of his death, he wrote a letter about it. Hours later, LaRonda killed him. Soon after LaRonda's acquittal, a criminal killed her."

"You're saying they both asked to die and God said yes?"

"They asked God to let them *atone*."

"Shelley, I believe in God as much as the next person, but I don't think He works that way. LaRonda was my future. Why would God take her from me?"

"He didn't do it to hurt you. Maybe He did it to help her. Shaker, I get the feeling that Hank knew he might not see me again. That's why he wrote the letter."

"But LaRonda didn't write a goodbye letter."

"She prayed though, didn't she? If you begged God to let you atone for something, how do you suppose He'd answer?"

The conversation kept Shaker awake for hours that night. Finally, he sat up in bed and searched "Hank Phillips" on his phone. The results included a video of his final speech. Shaker was struck by the man's contrition. When someone asked him about the Medal of Honor, his agony showed in his voice and on his face. "God didn't give me any special license to snuff out their lives," the suffering veteran said. "Sometimes I wish I could take back those bullets and use them on myself."

A few days later, Shaker sat in Felix Scott's office. Getting an appointment with the CRB chairman had involved a wheedling session with a pessimistic Captain Vanderbilt. "You'll be wasting your time," he warned Shaker. "Those CRB people go by the book. Even the police commissioner wouldn't interfere in a thing like this."

Scott himself was adamant. "CRB proceedings are confidential, just like jury deliberations. Once we complete an inquiry, we announce our findings and make our recommendations to the police commissioner. After that, we're done. We never, ever, publicize the records of our hearings."

"I don't want to publicize it," Shaker replied. "I just want to read the transcript, to find out what Officer Cage said about Hank Phillips' shooting."

"You already know the details and the outcome. They were on the news. She was cleared and put back on duty. Why should the transcript matter to you?"

"This is going to sound crazy, but maybe LaRonda's death was an atonement. Getting off the hook for Hank Phillips didn't take away her feelings for him. Why else was she so careless the night she was shot?"

"You mean ... you think she *let* the guy shoot her?"

"It's possible."

"That's ridiculous! A police officer deliberately letting herself be killed? Besides, for all she knew, the suspects in that car were unarmed. They were just wanted on suspicion of burglary."

"Mr. Scott, she called off backup support, even though they ignored her command to step out of the car. And the witness in LaRonda's unit said she re-holstered her pistol and walked right up to the driver's window."

"Maybe she was afraid to use her sidearm. She'd just been exonerated and didn't want to risk shooting anyone else."

"Maybe. Sir, I'm not asking this to affect the CRB's decision. I just want to know if she said anything to indicate that she was – what's the word? – fatalistic."

"I see." Scott stared at him for a long moment. "Captain Vanderbilt says you were dating Officer Cage, is that right?"

"Yes sir."

"Was it serious?"

"I had almost persuaded her to marry me."

"Why didn't you ask her about the testimony?"

"She was already torturing herself. I wanted to keep her mind off it."

Scott leaned back in his chair. "Officer Patterson, you're asking a great deal of me. CRB hearings are hallowed ground. If word ever got out that I had leaked a transcript, I'd be forced to resign my position here at the bank."

"Yes sir. I'm sorry to put you on the spot. I just need to know. Did she say anything that might explain her actions that night?"

Scott stood and walked to the window. He looked at the city below him for a while, then turned around.

"Officer Patterson, I'll do this much for you. I'll consult with my fellow CRB members. I'll explain to them the personal reasons for your request. If I get a unanimous vote – and I emphasize unanimous – I'll go over the transcript again and see if there's anything that might contribute to your theory. But that's all. You will not be allowed to read it yourself. Whatever it may contain, you'll just have to take my word."

Shaker nodded. "That's fine, sir. I trust you."

"Don't get your hopes up. The others take their responsibilities as seriously as I do."

"I understand." Shaker rose and shook hands with the chairman. "Thank you for your time, sir. I know you're a busy man."

Scott smiled for the first time. "Not so busy that I can't make time for a police officer."

A week went by before Scott called. "Officer Patterson, the other panelists have agreed to let me read you certain parts of the transcript. What you're about to hear stays between the two of us. Do you agree?"

"Yes sir, I promise."

Question: Officer Cage, you've been on the force for ten years. Haven't you investigated prowler reports before?

Answer: Yes, I have.

Question: Do you normally draw your firearm on such occasions?

Answer: Not usually, no.

Question: What made this occasion different from the others?

Answer: I can't answer that. I just had a feeling. Drawing the gun seemed the safe thing to do.

"I'm skipping ahead now.

Question: Officer Cage, your first action before you even saw Mr. Phillips was to draw your pistol. What was this feeling you had that made you do that?

Answer: Again, I just don't know. It was just a feeling. I can't describe it.

Question: Did you feel you were in danger?

Answer: No. I mean, not exactly.

Question: Can you be more specific?

Answer: No, I can't. I'm sorry.

"The panelists then asked Officer Cage about her state of mind when she reported for duty on Halloween night.

Answer: I was still pretty upset when I arrived for my shift. I'd never shot anyone before.

Question: If you felt so badly about it, why were you so quick to draw your gun?

Answer: I can't explain that. It was that feeling I had.

Question: You said a moment ago that you believe you startled Mr. Phillips when you ordered him to freeze. Wasn't he justified in reacting instinctively, just as you did?

Answer: Yes, I believe he was.

Question: So this again calls into question your decision to draw your pistol before approaching him. Do you think you were right in doing so?

Answer: No. Now I wish I hadn't.

Scott paused. "There's one more segment.

Question: Officer Cage, if you had it to do over again, under the same circumstances, would you shoot Mr. Phillips?

Answer: If I had it to do over again, I'd shoot myself instead.

"The hearing ended shortly after that."

And then she turned and smiled at me. The sweetest smile. Like she was loving me with that smile.

"Officer Patterson? Are you still there?"

He swallowed the lump in his throat. "Yes sir. That tells me just what I wanted to know. Thank you, Mr. Scott."

"Do you still think she sacrificed herself?"

"Well, everything I've heard from you and the girl who witnessed it seems to point in that direction."

Scott was silent for a moment. "If you're right, we lost a unique police officer and human being. I'm sorry, Officer Patterson. God bless you."

Shaker kept his word to Scott. But that night, he phoned Shelley and told her about LaRonda's strange behavior with the burglary suspects. "That brings us back to Hank. LaRonda told Alvin that he took a firing position on her. But his gun was empty."

"He was a soldier," Shelley pointed out. "Maybe it was a defensive reaction on his part."

"And LaRonda reacted to his reaction."

"So unwittingly, she was God's answer to Hank's prayer."

"And the punk who shot LaRonda was God's answer to hers." He thought about it. "I don't know, Shelley. Maybe we're both rationalizing too much. Even if LaRonda did provoke her own death, I can't imagine that she'd deliberately leave Alvin alone and helpless."

"Maybe she knew you'd take care of him. It makes you think, doesn't it? We all have different lives now. Hank's death forced me to become a stronger person. Less dependent. What about you?"

"I don't know what to think. I just feel cheated."

On December 14, David Tischner stood shivering in Newtown Village Cemetery, spying on a small group of visitors fifty yards away. He was waiting for them to leave.

Of the twenty children reported killed at the Sandy Hook school, two were cremated. Seven had graves here, in the same section. The rest were in other New England graveyards except for Emilie Alice Parker, buried in Ogden, Utah. This was David's last stop after visiting all the others.

David had begun this odyssey with a troubled spirit. In October, the

FBI had arrested seventeen more men in the New Texas Confederacy plot. One of them was a regular participant in David's Twitter discussions.

His two daughters never phoned anymore, although they did call to comfort Jason and Alexis, who despaired that "the right thing" necessary to rescue their son lay within a man incapable of finding it.

And last month, his wife of thirty-four years had asked him for a divorce.

"You've turned mean, David," Marla declared. "You're mean in private and mean in public. You've alienated our kids, you've humiliated our family with your hoax talk, and you make a spectacle of yourself at city council meetings. You're at war with everybody. And you think of Andy's kidnapping only in terms of how it affects you. You're not the man I married." Marla had packed up and moved in temporarily with her sister.

David had never thought of himself as mean. There were differences between assertiveness and meanness. Assertiveness had built Pierpont Electronics and made him wealthy and influential. Yes, he was opinionated. Yes, he made enemies by sticking to his convictions. But now, with his personal life in tatters, he was reexamining them, particularly the ones about fake shootings.

The Connecticut investigators' reports were detailed, from the killer's bizarre background and lifestyle to survivor accounts of the shooting. Various people who knew the Lanzas painted different pictures of Adam, but the overall impression was that of a very disturbed young man, increasingly withdrawn from people and preoccupied with mass murder. Adam and his mother Nancy hadn't just popped up from nowhere. They'd lived in Newtown since 1998 and were known to be regular visitors at a target range. Nancy, the first victim on December 14, 2012, had purchased six firearms the previous two years, including the Bushmaster XM-15 Adam used at the school. In Classroom Eight, where most of the victims died, investigators found eighty expended 5.56 mm casings. Testing confirmed all the shells came from the XM-15. Hoaxers' suspicions about other shooters at the scene were based largely on the coincidental presence of bystanders, and witness reports of people escaping the attack by climbing through windows.

David listened to the 911 recordings of a woman hiding in the office, a teacher whispering from a classroom, and a custodian reporting gunshots. If they were "crisis actors," as some people claimed, they were certainly good at it. Investigators suppressed autopsy photos out of respect for the families, but the medical examiner told reporters that each child had been shot between three and eleven times.

Were the parents actors? The Fairfield County tax rolls confirmed residency for them. School records verified the children's enrollment dates, the families' names, addresses and contact information.

What about the decision to demolish Sandy Hook? It didn't rise from any coverup. It was the result of many town hall meetings and a people's referendum.

David compiled a list of burial sites for the first-graders from a website. A picture and some memorabilia accompanied each name. Charlotte Helen Bacon's family wrote that she "never met an animal she didn't love and since the age of two wanted to be a veterinarian." Emilie Alice Parker kept drawing materials handy because "I have so many ideas of things to draw and it is hard to remember them all." James Radley Mattioli's family thought he was born four weeks early "because he was hungry. He loved hamburgers with ketchup, his Dad's egg omelets with bacon, and his Mom's French toast."

The memorials reminded David of Andy, who enjoyed storybooks and made Marla read *The Velveteen Rabbit* to him over and over, while he sat beside her drawing pictures of the characters. Marla called him the Cookie Monster because he loved Oreos.

Peering across the cemetery through binoculars, David recognized several Sandy Hook parents from news photos. They sank to their knees, placed flowers on graves and spoke words he was too far away to hear. It struck him that there was no media circus today. Sandy Hook was old news. No TV crews surrounded the mourners. No reporters poked mikes at their faces. No politicians made speeches. Just a small knot of ordinary-looking folks, white puffs of steam issuing from their lips as they chatted in the cold. Some of them hugged each other.

If the massacre was real, the Sandy Hook parents had endured more than grief. Bloggers assaulted Emilie Parker's parents with vile insults. One tirade charged that Emilie's mother used her photography skills to invent a daughter and create fake family pictures. A Florida woman made death threats to Noah Pozner's father. Someone stole memorial signs to two children from a playground, then phoned their families to claim the theft shouldn't bother them, since the kids had never existed. A man personally confronted Victoria Soto's sister with a similar claim at a memorial event for the slain teacher. Others denounced Gene Rosen as a liar for claiming he sheltered six of Victoria's students in his home after they fled the massacre.

The visitors gradually drifted away. David wandered over to the site and checked his list of names against the gravestones. Charlotte Helen Bacon. Chase Michael Anthony Kowalski. Ana Grace Marquez-Greene. Jack Armistead Pinto. Avielle Rose Richman. Benjamin Andrew Wheeler. Allison Noelle Wyatt. All present and accounted for.

Maybe it *was* possible to fake a school massacre. Recruit actors to pose as parents and victims. Fake tax rolls and school records. Bribe cops, state police investigators, EMTs, medical examiners, teachers, witnesses. Tempt multiple funeral homes and cemetery owners into a conspiracy of empty graves. But imagine the huge expense and logistics of so much planning, not to mention the gamble that all participants would keep their mouths shut. Standing among the graves, surrounded by headstones etched with abbreviated lifespans, David had to admit it: he'd believed the conspiracy theories because he wanted to.

"Hi."

He spun toward the voice like a thief caught in the act. A man dressed in a heavy winter jacket stood behind him. "Sorry if I scared you. I hope I'm not intruding?"

"No, I don't have anyone buried here. I was just, uh ..." David's mind went blank.

The man nodded. "I understand. We get a lot of strangers here on the anniversary. Nice people. Sometimes they bring bouquets. Fresh flowers too, not those artificial ones."

"I didn't know that."

"It's the only nice thing about my daughter's death. That it affected other people so deeply that they come here to honor her. It gives me a reason to keep going."

David couldn't remember when he'd been tongue tied. "I'm ... sorry about your loss," he finally managed.

"Thank you." The man's eyes wandered over the new flowers. "I guess I got here late. Looks like the other families have come and gone."

"Which one is your daughter?"

The man kneeled at the grave before him and caressed the stone gently. His eyes began to fill.

"I'm sorry to intrude," David said. "I'll leave you to your ... uh ... goodbye."

He marched quickly to his rental car, his research complete, his mission now clear. Conspirators wouldn't give a fake victim a fake burial two thousand miles from the shooting. Actors wouldn't mourn over empty graves with no reporters watching. And no honest investigator would jump to conclusions based on flimsy notions. Vern had been wrong. The hoaxers weren't idiots. They were just mean.

David folded his list and started the engine. It was time to do the right thing.

CHAPTER 26

Something with teeth

On a Sunday afternoon in April, a large crowd gathered near the Washington Mall to hear the President dedicate Armed and Ready's new Garden of Remorse.

"Anyone with a heart can relate to remorse and regret," the Chief Executive said. "This garden offers people a place to carve their feelings in stone."

He introduced Shelley, Alvin, Gil and Amy, who told their Hank and LaRonda stories to an audience of politicians, gun activists and spring tourists. Then he opened the double gates and invited the crowd to follow him.

"How did you manage to get the President?" Shelley asked Warren.

"How could he resist? It looks like he's doing something about gun violence."

Beyond the garden archway stood the Hank-LaRonda monument at the start of a path meandering through a lush array of cherry trees, shrubs and flowers. Along the path were numerous open spaces reserved for future memorials.

Barney's research had turned up dozens of news stories about people who had killed someone – war veterans, law officers, reformed criminals and others. Their circumstances varied, and so did their reactions, but they had one thing in common: their victims haunted them in some way.

For Hank and LaRonda, Warren's architect built a circular complex of five enclosed cubicles in which visitors could watch a video of their stories. It included commentary by Shelley, Bruce, Alvin, Shaker, Amy and Gil, plus Hank's tearful remarks to the VFW. The alcove walls were transparent, so people could observe each other as they listened. A plexiglass encasement at the center of the cubicles displayed the tools of Hank and LaRonda's confrontation: her service pistol, and his Colt .45. Fortunately, Shaker's friend hadn't gotten around to destroying it.

Website instructions were available at the archway for visitors who wished to submit their own remorse stories. The National Parks Service would be the clearing house for these. Armed and Ready would pay for the design and construction of all future markers.

The garden project and this week's firearms conference got an unexpected boost from a *New York Times* exclusive. David Tischner had spent the past three months quietly visiting families of massacre victims. He had gone to their homes, sat in their living rooms and apologized for the pain he'd caused them with his conspiracy chatter.

The reporter got his tip from a parent touched by the gesture. David had apologized personally to families in Newtown, Connecticut, Parkland, Florida and Huntington, West Virginia. "The public announcement I made against hoax theories last year was an insincere effort to get my grandson back," he confessed to the reporter. "Now I'm acting privately, out of personal conviction."

David's mission got a lot of publicity that put the conspiracy peddlers on the defensive. But Andy remained missing, and Doctor Luke remained silent.

On Monday, the Second Amendment Summit opened to a rowdy media circus of screaming demonstrators. Voices, placards and T-shirts shouted "Protect Our Constitution!" "Stop the Madness!" "Guns Save Lives!" and "Disarm or Die!" District police deployed themselves in two squads, one to separate the opposing factions, the other to protect the delegates inside the hotel.

A vigorous debate had erupted in the weeks leading to the conference.

Gun owners condemned it as a plot to gut the Second Amendment. Their opponents saw hope for tougher gun laws. Warren had talked himself hoarse in TV interviews, trying to satisfy both sides. Now he tried to look composed as he emerged from his taxi for the opening session.

A TV reporter confronted him amidst the pandemonium. "With people so polarized over the gun issue, how do you expect to achieve any kind of consensus at this conference?"

"I think when people understand that we're trying to build a better society, they'll be eager to support us. Excuse me, I'd better get inside." Two cops ran interference for him as he flashed his credentials to the security guards.

A few months before Hank's death, Warren read a book on the Constitutional Convention of 1787. He was struck by the delegates' ability, after arguing daily in the sweltering Philadelphia heat, to gather socially in taverns as though there were no differences between them. By the end of that contentious summer, they were united enough to persuade the colonies to accept the Constitution they had drafted.

This week's summit was the result of fifty state conferences, each electing one delegate to Washington. Warren had arranged for those with opposing views to share hotel rooms, tour the nation's capital, and dine in pairs. He hoped these ice-breakers would help bridge their differences and encourage them to work together. The men of 1787, struggling to create an entire new government, had grappled with numerous complex issues. Warren's group had only one.

To emphasize to the delegates how seriously A&R took their mission, Warren had gone all out, reserving the plush St. Regis Hotel and its beautiful conference rooms. "The two precious citizens whose deaths inspired this gathering are just a fraction of the many lost to gunfire," he declared at the opening session. "You fifty Americans have a tough challenge this week: finding a way to stop this carnage while preserving the right to bear arms. We're all counting on you." With that, he divided them into brainstorming groups.

The couple looked out of place in a fancy restaurant like Fiola. Jim Axelrod, whose idea of eating out was the steak special at Logan's, wished he had bought a new business suit to blend in with the other diners and the lush decor. His companion, Mary Ochoa, felt frumpy in her best Sunday ensemble.

"So how did you end up at this thing?" Jim asked. "You don't strike me as the crusader type."

"I'm not, really. I teach sixth grade history at a public school in Abilene, Kansas. When the rest of the faculty heard about Armed and Ready's project, they recommended me to represent them at the state conference."

"Why'd they pick you?"

"My best friend's daughter lost a child in the Shiloh Middle School shooting. When it happened, I took a week's leave to comfort the family. I came home determined to do something about gun violence and started a petition drive among the teachers in our community. It led to a bill in the state legislature to outlaw all semiautomatic weapons."

"I didn't hear about that one."

"You wouldn't have. It never got out of committee. Too much opposition from gun lobbyists."

"Oh." Jim thought he saw a reproachful glint in her eye.

"What about you? You don't strike me as a gun nut."

"Actually, my only experience with guns was in Vietnam. When my tour ended, I put them behind me. Then two years ago, my best Army buddy got killed in a liquor store robbery. It was one of those nightly news stories people forget about the next day. To me it was personal. So I bought myself a .38, joined Armed and Ready and started my own chapter in Little Rock."

"Has it done any good?"

"I think so. And to answer your question, no, I'm not a gun nut. I just think the honest citizens of this country have the right to protect themselves, and that's all I've ever stood for."

"I see." The waiter brought their orders. Dining filled the awkward silence for a few minutes.

"So you were in Vietnam," Mary commented. "That was a long time ago. You must be retired now."

"I wish I was. Back home in Arkansas, I'm a commercial plumbing contractor. I've got so many jobs going, I'm spending every spare minute running things by phone."

"It's the same with me. I have an extra class this fall because one of our teachers is on maternity leave. I feel sorry for the poor subs covering for me."

Jim chewed a forkful of lobster ravioli. "And yet, here you are. Why? The Shiloh shooting is old news."

"So is the liquor store shooting."

Jim sighed. "I can't let go of it. Dutch was the greatest guy I've ever known. It was worth going through that Vietnam disaster just to meet him. When he got killed, it was like losing a brother."

"I know what you mean. Pictures of those terrified students running from the school building made me furious. Why shouldn't children feel safe in their own school? Maybe I can do something here this week to protect them."

"Like what? Take away my gun and everybody else's?"

"Is it really that important to you? Is your right to own that .38 worth someone's life?"

"It's not my rights I'm worried about, lady. It's about all the maniacs running around loose. From now on, my motto is 'be prepared.' " He patted a bulge on the left side of his jacket.

Mary's eyes widened. "Are you crazy?" she hissed. "Carrying a concealed weapon? You could get arrested!"

"Better arrested than dead." He leaned toward her. "You know, that school lost more than kids in that shooting. It lost teachers like you. Maybe they and all those kids would be alive now if even one teacher had been able to shoot back."

"And what good is that, if we make our country a permanent war zone? What about your friend Dutch? You say he was such a great guy. Why did he go to Vietnam? To fight for people too busy killing each other to notice the war?"

Jim's face flushed. He started to retort, but other diners were staring at them.

"Look, Mrs. Ochoa," he said quietly. "Dutch didn't volunteer for Vietnam. He got drafted, just like I did. We were poor kids, too poor to go to college. When he got home, he borrowed money to go to business school, so he could borrow more to open that liquor store. It took him fifteen years, working day and night, to get out of debt. Then one night, some punk comes in with a pistol and makes him open the cash register.

Dutch gives him the money, and the guy shoots him anyway. Now you tell me, lady. What did he do to deserve that?"

"Nothing, of course. That's not what we're arguing about."

"Sure it is! You love your kids as much as I loved my friend. Don't you want to protect them?"

"I want to give them a world that's safe to live in! Guns don't make things safer. They just make things worse!"

They settled back in their chairs as the waiter approached. "Everything all right here, folks? How's the meal?"

"Fine."

"Excellent." Mary looked around. "I'm sorry for the disturbance. We were having a, uh, discussion."

The waiter smiled. "This is Washington. We get a lot of 'discussions.' They make for some lively dining. May I bring you a dessert menu?"

"Not just yet."

"Fine. Let me know when you're ready."

Jim watched the waiter retreat, then turned back to Mary. "I'm sorry if I got out of line. This is a sore spot with me."

"I guess that's why we're here. It is for both of us."

"For what it's worth, I don't like what's going on any more than you do. Some of the gun people scare me. I think they're using the violence as an excuse to stir up a war right here in our own country."

"All the more reason to fight them, don't you think?"

"But Mary, you can't just take people's guns away. They've got the Constitution on their side. And I think most of them are ordinary folks like me. They have good intentions. Any campaign to disarm honest citizens is just not fair."

She sighed. "You're right. You can't force people to change their minds. About guns or anything."

"So what's the point of this conference? What are we supposed to accomplish if nobody on either side wants to give in?"

"That's what I said when I got nominated for this trip. Back in Kansas, we worked so hard to get that gun bill introduced, and we hit a political brick wall. I don't think a government solution is the answer. We've got to persuade people."

"To do what?"

"For one thing, to care about each other. So we can eliminate the anger and insanity at the root of gun violence."

Jim shook his head. "You're not being realistic. You can't love people out of killing."

"If they can be stirred up to commit violence, they can be stirred up to end it." She drew a pen and a notebook from her bag. "Look, I don't want to fight with you. What do you say we write down some things we agree on? Two people from opposite sides of the argument. Then we set up a meeting with the others in our group and get their input."

"I guess we could. That's why we're here. To share ideas."

"Then let's make our list, go back to the hotel and start calling the others."

"Not yet."

"Why?"

"Let's get that dessert menu," he grinned. "I'll never get another chance for a meal like this." He signaled the waiter.

Jim and Mary's group sat around two tables pulled together in the hotel bar. Though it was late and dark outside, the demonstrators were still shouting, chanting and occasionally fighting. A sudden, loud crack of breaking glass made everyone jump. "I'll be glad when this is over," said Tony Danvers, Arizona's delegate. "I'm afraid somebody's going to get hurt."

"Okay, back to business," said Lloyd Carver, a city councilman from St. Paul. "Legally speaking, the most effective thing we can do is draft a replacement for the Second Amendment. Something with teeth that would preserve the right to bear arms while giving Congress some leeway in regulating them."

"Tampering with the Bill of Rights is political suicide," responded Neal Westwood, a Vermont law professor. "A proposal like that would never make it to the House floor."

"But if we come out of this conference recommending the same old remedies, we'll have wasted our time."

"Maybe not. Let's talk about gun bans," said Dale Wallace, a high school principal from New Orleans. "All the polls nowadays show wide-spread support for an assault weapons ban. Politicians respond to big

numbers like that. A&R could endorse a measure to outlaw semiautomatics and prevent all these high-profile massacres."

"Didn't work in my state," Mary replied, glumly.

"And if the polls are accurate, why is everybody outside this building throwing such a fit?" added Tom Fenton of Fort Lauderdale. "A&R
makes itself look good by hosting this conference, but they wouldn't dare
betray their membership by endorsing any kind of gun ban. If you can
outlaw assault weapons today, you can outlaw handguns tomorrow."

"And speaking for Nevada, I won't go along with any kind of ban," said
Chet Akers, a ranch owner. "The people sent me here to stand up for the
Second Amendment, and I'm going to do it!"

"Even if you did outlaw semiautomatics, there are millions of them
already in private hands," Jim added. "I think we ought to start with the
situation we have and go from there."

"Meaning what?"

"We've made the mistake of combining two separate issues: murder
and the right to bear arms. None of these big-news attacks are the fault
of ordinary citizens. The shootings are random, and they all spring from
each shooter's personal grievances. Our discussion should focus on criminals and psychotics. Leave innocent gun owners out of it."

"So let's look at the people doing the shooting," said Sarah Williams, a
TV reporter from San Bernardino. "Who are they? Why do they become
killers? After the attack by that Islamic couple in my city, our station did
a series on domestic shootings, and it was amazing how many killers sent
signals before they acted. You can't stop people like these from killing
just by denying them guns. There are plenty of other weapons. I think
any campaign we launch has to include a program to identify and help
disturbed people."

Chet was frowning. "Say, what is it with you news guys, anyway? Why
do you always take the side of the criminals?"

Sarah reddened. "Why do people like you lump other people
into categories?"

"Come on, let's stick to the subject," Mary said. "How about a federal
mandate requiring background checks on all gun customers? Some states
already have those."

"Federal law does require them for licensed dealers like me," replied

Forest Kirk of Denver. "It's hard to enforce, though. ATF doesn't have the manpower to make sure everyone complies with it."

"There are ways around the law anyway," Neal added. "That's why gun shows are so popular. A lot of those sales are private deals between individuals."

"So let's close the loophole. Require background checks on all gun sales."

"Same enforcement problem," Forest said. "I ought to know. I attend lots of gun shows."

"Why?"

Forest shrugged. "That's where the customers are."

"Doesn't it bother you?" Mary asked. "One of your customers might be the next school shooter."

"I can tell you've never attended a gun show. My customers are collectors, sport shooters, and others worried about self-defense. Some are even school teachers."

"What about defensive measures?" asked Darnell Adams, a Detroit physician. "Vern Saginaw wanted to put security guards in public places like schools. We could also get behind a resolution for arming teachers."

"Now you're talking," Chet agreed.

Dale snorted. "I'd love to see a show of teachers' hands on that one. 'Kids, turn to page ten while I go shoot it out with that maniac in the hallway.' " A ringtone emerged from his jacket pocket. He wandered away to answer his phone.

"I hate the idea of armed guards in my school," Mary said. "It's like some kind of surrender."

"What about a national registration program?" Tony asked. "If we had a list of all gun owners, we could single out the dangerous ones."

"It's been tried before," Neal replied. "Registration is the first step toward giving the government a database to confiscate weapons. I can't imagine Congress supporting it."

"You make Congress sound like the enemy," Mary said. "Where do they stand on this conference? Why don't they give us some leadership?"

"Because they want to get reelected." Everyone laughed.

Dale returned to the table. "Sorry, I've got to go. That was the police. Someone broke into my rental car. I'd better go see if anything's missing. See you in the morning." He marched briskly away.

"Look, it's getting late," Darnell said. "Why don't we pick up this discussion with the other delegates tomorrow?"

Jim watched as they gathered up their notes. Gun bans. Background checks. Security guards. The same old tired ideas.

The next morning, the delegates entered the main conference room to find tables arranged in a large oval so all fifty could see each other. Outside, the noisy demonstrations continued.

Warren chaired today's session from a podium. "I'm pleased to hear that everyone has been working hard on our campaign, many of you staying up late last night to prepare for this meeting. Did you make any progress?"

"I feel like we're off to a bad start," said Phyllis Thornton of New Hampshire. "Nobody's got any fresh solutions."

"Well, it's only the second day. Let's hear what you've come up with so far." He noticed an empty chair. "Wait, I think somebody's missing."

They looked around. "Where's Dale Wallace?" someone asked.

"He was with us last night," Mary said. "He had some sort of problem with his car."

Warren nodded. "Let's give him a few minutes."

As the delegates resumed their impromptu conversations, he wandered among them, eavesdropping. After ten minutes, Dale still hadn't appeared. Warren decided to phone him.

He stood in the middle of the room, listening to the fourth ring, when the doors burst open. "Sorry, Dale won't be able to make it!" the intruder shouted. "This is for Vern, you traitors!" He was able to pick off Warren, Mary Ochoa and four others before someone yelled, "everybody down!" as a hail of bullets splintered the furniture. Three of them slammed into Darnell Adams, driving her against the wall. Neal Westwood felt something nick his wrist. Tony Danvers collapsed, screaming, on shattered knees. By the time the others dived for cover, the guy had shot up most of the room.

He stopped, reloaded and began overturning tables to expose the crouching delegates. Forest Kirk looked up at his executioner. His eyes widened. "You!"

"You!" the killer echoed. That was when a .38 caliber missile smashed through his right temple and hurled him into Forest's lap.

The episode had lasted only forty-three seconds.

The uninjured fled for the door, screaming and stumbling over each other. Jim Axelrod dropped his pistol and ran to kneel over Mary's body. Shaking, he felt in vain for her pulse. "Oh, Mary, you poor thing!" he cried.

Jim's gesture was the last thing Warren's fading eyesight recorded as he lay, bleeding and numb, on the plush carpet. He tried to make the most of his diminishing thoughts. His wife Brenda. Their two daughters. This project to which he'd devoted his heart the past year. As weakness closed Warren's eyes, his family and his campaign became one cherished image amidst the chaos of screams and rescue sirens. Finally, all thoughts and sounds faded away, until Warren heard nothing and hoped for nothing.

"Police have identified the assailant as Jerry Richards, an unemployed factory mechanic from Denver." Reed Fletcher, seated at his anchor desk, spoke to a camera behind his guest. "His Twitter records show he was upset by the ouster of Vern Saginaw, the founder of Armed and Ready. His gun was an AR-15 rifle. Somehow, he cannibalized parts from other weapons to modify it into a rapid-fire automatic."

He turned to Jim. "Mr. Axelrod, people here in Washington are calling you a hero. Although the toll is six dead and seventeen wounded, it might have been much worse if you hadn't acted as you did. Do you find it ironic that you were forced to use your pistol to stop gun violence, during a conference on gun violence?"

Jim squirmed, miserable under the bright studio lights. He was already sorry he'd agreed to this interview. He could hardly wait to get home to his wife.

"Mr. Axelrod?"

Jim shook himself back to the moment. "I don't know about ironic. All I can say is, we were trying to make things safer in our country, and a bunch of decent people got shot because of it."

"And yet, a lot of them might be dead now if you hadn't been armed. Do you think you've proved your point about self-defense?"

Jim stared forlornly at his host. "I'll put it this way. I came here to protect gun owners' rights. Then I met a really nice lady named Mary Ochoa. We were on opposite sides of the argument, but she meant well. Now Mary's dead, and I ..." He choked on the words.

Fletcher covered for him. "Police who found the body of delegate Dale Wallace in his rental car also found the word 'traitor' spray-painted on the door. They believe Richards lured Wallace there the night before the shooting, stole his security pass, and used it to gain entrance to the conference. He apparently hid the weapon in the lining of his fatigue jacket."

He turned back to Jim. "Speaking of which, the conference members who survived admit they have you to thank because you were carrying a concealed weapon, in violation of the law I might add. Do you think everyone should be allowed to carry guns?"

"Well, I don't know about that. You're right, Mr. Fletcher. Maybe I saved some lives by breaking the law. But I had to kill somebody to do it. I don't want to live in a world where I have to make decisions like that."

"Are you still carrying that .38?"

"Only until I get home. Then I'm going to destroy it."

CHAPTER 27

Trash on a basketball court

For the third time, Shelley found herself sitting in a church, listening to a eulogy. Brenda DeVries was bearing up better than Shelley had. Determined to protect her daughters from emotional damage, she kept them away from Warren's funeral and hid her grief in their presence. She told Christine, the six-year-old, that Daddy was watching over her and counting on her to take care of her sister Jenna. After the relatives left, Shelley devoted several evenings to Brenda, helping around the house and keeping her company. Bruce played games with the girls in their room.

Brenda almost wore out her cell phone, sitting in the living room, feet tucked under her, scanning sadly through family pictures. Then a popup bulletin would announce yet another shooting somewhere, and Brenda would blurt out curses on the perpetrator, Shelley holding her until the anger melted into tears.

"How can I help her get over this?" she asked John Daniels.

"People have to want to get well before God can heal them. That's how you did it. Keep doing what you're doing and give her time."

Those who loved Hank and LaRonda bore a different kind of sorrow. The new monument in the Garden of Remorse got lost in the debate following Jerry Richards' attack. Polls showed that Americans were as divided as ever. Fresh open-carry and gun-ban bills sprouted in state legislatures around the nation. Domestic gun sales soared again. Jim Axelrod's admirers went on social media, announced they were carrying concealed weapons, and dared the cops to arrest them. It seemed that Hank, LaRonda and the conference victims had died for nothing.

Sarah Williams, the reporter delegate, interviewed witnesses for a TV documentary about the massacre. "I used to think that if someone important enough got killed, people would finally wake up," said a demonstrator who'd been outside the St. Regis that day. "But all they do is take sides, like football fans. Meanwhile, politicians make empty speeches and the body count just keeps rising."

"Things like this happen because people have a crazy faith that killing will solve something," said a St. Regis employee who had assisted the wounded delegates. "God will help us find our way if we ask Him to lead us."

"Prayer won't help if you're in somebody's crosshairs," an A&R stalwart told Sarah. "That plumber saved your life, lady!"

Sarah's documentary, which included her eyewitness account of the conference room horror, earned her a Peabody award. By the time she mounted the stage to accept it, five more mass shootings had claimed thirty-seven lives and injured ninety-three others, six of them disabled permanently. Other Americans died daily by the hundreds in smaller incidents beneath the media radar.

Jim Axelrod returned to Little Rock and his contracting business. He kept his promise and used a welding torch to mangle his .38 so badly that it would never fire again. That night, his wife woke to find him sobbing over an internet video of Hank's VFW remarks. Little Rock's civic leaders voted to honor Jim with a monument at city hall. He refused it. "I don't want to be remembered for killing somebody," he told Sarah in her documentary.

Forest Kirk survived the massacre, only to find himself a target again. "Summit Delegate Sold Murder Weapon to Richards," the headlines screamed when a reporter learned that Jerry bought his gun from Forest at a Wyoming gun show. Critics charged that he'd deliberately sneaked out of Colorado to sell the AR-15. The notoriety forced him to close his sporting goods store until the furor abated.

In Washington, several congressmen introduced gun control bills that died in committee hearings, which was fine with their sponsors, who were merely trying to please their constituents without actually voting. Meanwhile, the conspiracy buffs launched a new assault. They alleged that Warren was a stooge for anti-gun forces because of his moderate stance, declared Jerry Richards imaginary because he had no criminal history, dismissed the dead delegates as actors, and harassed Mary Ochoa's family at her funeral.

The Second Amendment Massacre, as it became known, was a disaster for Armed and Ready. Warren's dream of a compromise in the gun debate died with him, as the opposing factions retreated to their old positions. Hard-line subscribers insisted the shooting proved the validity of the Second Amendment and demanded Vern Saginaw's reinstatement as CEO. Gun opponents pounced on the revelation that Jerry Richards had been an Armed and Ready member. The hat he wore during his attack on the delegates was a free gift from his enrollment. It was the only known murder by an A&R member since Vern started the organization, but that didn't stop critics from branding it as a haven for psychopaths.

The result was a chaotic A&R board meeting that mirrored America's polarization. With its founder exiled and two brilliant spokesman dead, Armed and Ready was rudderless, and staff morale was worse than ever.

"The bottom line," Wes Hawkins concluded, "is that we've got fifteen million members out there waiting for us to tell them what we stand for. Whatever we decide, they have to know that we still support the right to bear arms. If we don't, we lose our base and our whole organization."

"What about the moderates?" Arthur Hudson responded. "Hank and Warren worked so hard to get the rhetoric toned down. If we go back to a hardline stance, we'll lose *them*."

"I don't think there are any moderates," Doug Yates said. "The Washington demonstrations and the shooting proved that. Our job is to keep A&R alive and thriving. We can talk about being reasonable later, when things calm down."

The board was so fragmented that they decided to postpone further discussion until they hired a new CEO. "What if we take the politics out of this?" Wes suggested. "Look for a leader with no public record on the gun issue. Somebody who's just good at running things. That's what Warren was." So they drew up a list of successful entrepreneurs, college presidents, business executives and civic leaders.

The one who impressed the directors most was Virginia Echols, the

CEO of an innovative software firm that had recently gone public with its stock, producing fat profits for its investors. Her business reputation was stellar.

"How would you suggest that Armed and Ready move forward from what happened in Washington?" Wes asked Virginia.

"Stick to your guns," she replied.

The directors laughed uncertainly. "What do you mean?"

"I'd like to remind you that only a few weeks ago, the President of the United States dedicated a memorial garden to Hank Phillips, LaRonda Cage, *and* what they represented, right in the heart of our nation's capital. That monument also represents Armed and Ready, because you sponsored it, and Warren DeVries died on behalf of it. If you don't follow through on what he started, your Garden of Remorse will remain a lonely park with a single monument, and Armed and Ready won't really stand for anything."

"So you think we should pick up where Warren left off?"

"I don't think you have any choice."

A heavy silence followed. "If you were our CEO," David Tischner asked, "what would you do now?"

"As flattered as I am that you would consider me, I don't want the job. I already have a business to run. But I care a great deal about this issue. So I'll take a sabbatical to help you out of this mess, if you'll give me the authority."

Virginia's idea was to convene a second summit in August. She deliberately chose the St. Regis Hotel – its conference room refurbished following the attack – as the meeting site, to show that violence could not discourage Armed and Ready from finishing what Warren had started. She also persuaded Jim Axelrod and the other survivors to represent their states again.

Even the injured delegates showed up. Newscasts showed Darnell Adams arriving despite a punctured lung and three shattered vertebrae. Phyllis Thornton entered the hotel in a wheelchair, Tony Danvers on crutches, Lloyd Carver in a neck brace. All were jittery but brave about reuniting in the room Jerry Richards had shot up. The states whose delegates died in the attack sent new ones. The resulting publicity won them respect and refocused the gun debate on their leadership. "What happened here last April is history," Virginia told reporters. "There aren't enough guns or bullets in the world to prevent us from bringing this country together."

Forest Kirk was reluctant when Virginia asked him to represent Colorado again. "Everybody's blaming me for selling Jerry Richards the gun. You'd think I pulled the trigger myself. I could have been killed too, but try telling that to the media. How could I know this was going to happen?"

"All the more reason for you to come back to Washington. You represent both Colorado and the gun retailers caught in the middle of this issue. You didn't do anything illegal, did you Forest?"

"No! I've never made an illegal sale in my life."

"Then join the gang and tell everybody that."

It was easier said than done. "Gun Foes Demand Kirk Step Aside," headlines announced when he agreed to attend. "See what I mean?" he complained to his customers and anyone else who would listen. "I've got the whole country on my back!" Virginia stood up for him. "This issue is bigger than one gun salesman or one killer," she told reporters. "This is everybody's problem."

But when they got down to business, the delegates found themselves debating the same proposals from the first conference. After three days of discussion, they were demoralized.

That evening, Jim Axelrod went for a walk. He still felt sick at the memory of blood spouting from Jerry Richards' head. Now he replayed his restaurant argument with Mary Ochoa and found himself trying to rewrite the scene, wishing he'd been nicer to the idealistic teacher shot dead before his eyes the following morning. In fact, he wished he'd stayed in Little Rock and let someone else fight over guns. "God, I've never been much for praying," he muttered, "but I sure wish you'd tell me how to make sense of all this."

As he crossed the street, a thumping noise interrupted his gloom. He looked up to see a bunch of kids playing basketball on a neighborhood court. Watching them reminded him of an incident he hadn't thought about in years. He spun on his heel and began phoning delegates as he walked briskly back to the St. Regis.

"When I was in high school, I went to a basketball game one night," Jim told his discussion group. "Our fans got very upset by a referee's call and started throwing stuff on the court – paper cups, food wrappers, popcorn boxes, all kinds of trash. We sat there waiting for the janitors to clean up the floor.

"But our coach didn't wait for that. He ordered his own players off the bench, and they went all over the court, picking up the trash their fans had thrown. The sight of their own team cleaning up their mess stopped the riot. It made them ashamed. The players finished the job, and the game went on."

"So what's your point?" asked Barry Washburn, Tennessee's delegate.

"If you want to play basketball, you've got to have a clean court. If you want to preserve the right to bear arms, you've got to clean up the mess that goes with it. That includes being responsible for people who *abuse* gun rights; mass murderers, petty criminals, and all the rest."

"And how would you do that?"

"By setting an example. The basketball players cleaned up the court to set an example of good sportsmanship. When it comes to gun rights, Armed and Ready is the leading player in this country. What if A&R *took* the lead? What if it started some kind of program to help gunfire victims? What if it refused to advertise military-style weapons, even published articles opposing them? What if it launched a private campaign to destroy them? No government bans. No revised Second Amendment. No new laws. No politics. Just a private business taking the bull by the horns."

Lloyd Carver was incredulous. "Are you kidding? They'd be cutting their own throats! Betraying their supporters!"

"Not if they still supported the right to bear arms. They'd just be taking responsibility for the consequences."

"Jim, they'd never go for it."

"A lot of people, like Forest Kirk here, make their living selling guns," Barry added. "They're not going to take an attack on their livelihood lying down."

"That's a good point." Jim replied. "Forest, how long have you been in this business?"

"Thirty-five years."

"And thirty-five years ago, did you open a sporting goods store to make money from gun violence?"

"No, of course not!"

"I'm glad to hear that. I'd hate to think you could sleep at night, selling murder weapons."

Forest's scowl turned red. "Look, I've had enough of this! I didn't shoot anybody! I just sold the guy a gun, like I would to any customer, and he passed the background check. Anyway, I don't just sell guns. I sell lots of other stuff. Camping equipment. Fishing gear. Skiing –"

"I understand, and I'm not attacking you, Forest. I'm saying that if we're going to clean up the gun problem in this country, those who have a stake in the firearms business have to lead the way. Gun owners. Gun sellers like you. Gun manufacturers. And especially, gun rights lobbyists like Armed and Ready."

Jim looked around at everyone. "Warren DeVries brought us all here last April to deal with gun violence. His effort failed, not just because of Jerry Richards, but because innocent citizens thought we wanted to take something away from them. It's not the Second Amendment that's at fault. It's how people abuse it. The killers are the ones throwing trash on the court. But like it or not, those of us who support the right to bear arms can't preserve it unless we're willing to clean up their mess. Armed and Ready sent us here to find a solution. I say Armed and Ready has to *be* the solution."

Darnell Adams had been listening intently. "I think Jim's onto something. So many people think of gun owners, and even gun sellers like Forest, as selfish, insensitive rednecks. This could change the way people see A&R and its members. Especially if they offer to help gunfire victims."

"You mean help them financially?"

"That's one way."

Damon Thomas from Illinois was unconvinced. "Darnell, do you know how many shootings there are in this country? Why, in Chicago alone, there were more than five thousand the past two years. They result in funeral expenses, medical bills and property damage. Are you saying A&R should have to pay for all that?"

"I'm saying there's no difference between responding to a shooting or a hurricane. People always pitch in to help when there's a natural disaster, even though we know there'll always be another one. A&R could be the leading relief agency for gunfire victims."

"And they could encourage A&R members to adopt victims in

their own communities," Sarah Williams added. "Raise funds locally to help them."

Everyone thought for a moment. "Jim, I like your basketball story," Barry said. "But gun violence is ingrained in this country. Even if you had a trillion dollars, you couldn't buy your way out of the social and psychological issues at the root of it."

"You're right. But Barry, things will never get better until somebody is willing to give up something. Look, there's no political solution to this problem. We know we can't get rid of the Second Amendment. We know gun laws are ineffective. We know we can't confiscate the guns. We know we can't lock up all the potential killers, even if we knew who they were. Like Darnell says, there will always be hurricanes, and maybe there will always be shootings. But hurricanes are acts of nature. Shootings are acts of humanity we can do something about."

" 'We' being Armed and Ready."

"That's right."

When Jim presented his argument to the conference at large, it got the delegates excited. "People are afraid and angry, and they're looking for leadership," said Horace Thurber, a Presbyterian minister from Kentucky. "I think Jim's approach could change society's whole attitude about firearms."

"A&R could help a lot with its magazine and website by talking down guns instead of glamorizing them," said Jennifer Marco from Trenton. "And with their large membership, they could persuade other gun organizations to do the same thing."

"I think folks back home would like the idea of reaching out to gun victims," added Chet Akers.

Virginia Echols interrupted. "Before you go down this road, I'd like to point out something. The A&R board sent you back to Washington to bail them out of a public relations disaster. If you vote for this basketball parable, you'll be telling them they have to stick their necks out. *Way* out. They may not swallow it. Shall we vote now and see where everyone stands?"

To Virginia's surprise and secret relief, all fifty delegates voted to draft a resolution in support of Jim's proposal. "I have my doubts," Barry admitted, "but nobody's come up with a better idea."

With the news media awaiting the outcome of the summit, Virginia set up a conference call with the A&R board and read the resolution to them. "Now it's your turn to vote," she said.

"We spent a fortune on fifty state conferences, two Washington conferences, plus the Garden of Remorse," Calvin Butcher fumed, "and you respond by throwing the problem back in our laps!"

"This notion undercuts everything A&R has always stood for," added Marvin Hayes. "If we opposed any sort of firearm, we'd be picking our own pockets. Most of our capital comes from gun manufacturers and private donors. The advertising revenue alone pays for all the A&R publications and our website."

"Wait a minute," Jim interrupted. "You don't have to oppose all guns or refuse all gun ads. But I'll bet the political support you'd earn in fighting the worst guns is worth a lot more than the annual revenue A&R gets from advertising them."

"But our membership will look at this as a betrayal!"

"Not if you show them you still support their rights. You're not endorsing any anti-gun legislation or attacking the Second Amendment. People can still throw trash on a basketball court or sell an assault weapon. You just make them ashamed to do it."

There was silence for a moment. "That would sure take the heat off Congress," George Masters admitted. "It would take the heat off us, too."

"We've always claimed that A&R represents responsible gun owners," said Harvey Wexler. "That's one thing Vern, Hank and Warren agreed on. I can't think of a more effective way to prove it."

"I'll tell you something else," Wes Hawkins said. "Public pressure's been building against guns, in the wake of all these mass shootings. If we don't take the initiative now, we may have to fight some legislation that's worse than what Jim's proposing."

It was a tough sell. The board members slept on it and returned for a shouting match the next morning. Finally, most conceded that Jim's idea was a way out. It passed by a nine to three vote. David Tischner joined the majority.

So it was that on the final day of the summit, the delegates and the A&R board rallied behind the resolution that Virginia read at a news conference.

Because the right to bear arms is a cherished cornerstone of American democracy, Armed and Ready vows to support the Second Amendment just as the Founding Fathers wrote it. We will oppose with all our resources any effort to repeal it, reword it, amend it, or to deprive American citizens of this Constitutional privilege.

Nevertheless, Armed and Ready repudiates any philosophy that advocates firearms as a means to solve social problems. Furthermore, this organization condemns the domestic sale and glorification of military and semiautomatic weapons, and henceforth refuses to accept paid or editorial promotion of such weapons in its publications and on its website.

Finally, We the People who support the Second Amendment commit ourselves to fighting gun violence and to helping its victims, and we hereby establish the A&R Gun Victims Foundation for that purpose.

Sixty years ago, Vern Saginaw created Armed and Ready to promote outdoor sports. He never intended it as a battleground over the right to bear arms. It was gun violence and its aftermath that led A&R away from its origins. Now we, the A&R directors, resolve to return to our founding principles. Henceforth, our organization will support only harmless and benevolent activities.

Neither the Second Amendment nor any other element of our Constitution can survive unless American citizens ground themselves in a philosophy of mutual respect and common purpose. It is unity, not weaponry, that makes a country strong. That is why the Founding Fathers named us the United States of America.

Reporters asked numerous questions, mostly about how A&R members might react to the resolution. Before the news conference ended, Forest Kirk asked to make a statement. "I've always prided myself on being an honest businessman," he told the cameras. "And ever since the summit massacre, I've been insisting that I complied with the law when I sold Jerry Richards that AR-15. Just the same, I didn't have to sell it to him. The fact that I did makes me partly responsible for what happened. So the only way I can make up for it is to refuse to sell a military-style weapon, its accessories, or its ammunition to anyone ever again. That's my pledge, and I urge all gun retailers everywhere to join me."

After the summit broke up, Virginia invited Jim for a drink in the St. Regis bar.

"I suppose you realize," he remarked, "that our resolution may not make any difference. The guns are already out there, and people angry enough to use them don't care about the consequences. When you think about that, our summit was actually a failure, wasn't it?"

"Rhetoric and resolutions won't end violence," she agreed. "But America's most powerful gun lobby is leading us in a new direction, and they're doing it without politics or laws. Now let's see where they take us."

"So what do you plan to do next?"

"Jim, my work with A&R is finished. But the company still doesn't have a CEO. You've done more than any single person to make this conference a success. What would you think about taking the job?"

He laughed. "Are you kidding? I'm just a plumber."

"You're a plumbing *contractor*. I've done some research on you while all this has been going on. Like Vern Saginaw, you started your own company from scratch, and you've run it for over forty years. You're used to giving orders and making sure they're carried out. You're innovative, as you demonstrated with that basketball story. And you're a public figure now, thanks to your heroism at the first summit. Jim, you're a natural-born leader. I believe you can do this job."

"Virginia, I'm not a hero. I just happened to have a gun handy at the right time. Being forced to use it changed my way of thinking. Now I hate guns, and I hate what people are doing with them."

"Hank Phillips hated guns, too. What happened to him in Afghanistan set him on the road to doing something constructive about them. You've given us a chance to finish what he started."

He squirmed. "Virginia, I'm sixty-three years old. I'm grooming my son to take over my business. My wife and I have been talking about retiring and spoiling our grandchildren."

"This is a pivotal moment in our country's history, Jim. America's leading gun rights organization is blazing a new trail, based on your inspiration. You're a leader. Your country needs you. Don't let us down."

He grinned wryly. "I can see how you got where you are. You can talk anybody into anything, can't you?"

"Well, I've got a pretty good track record so far."

"Even if I accept your offer, what makes you think the A&R board will accept me?"

She smiled. "They already have."

Two weeks later, the board and its new CEO gathered at Armed and Ready headquarters to ratify the document. The conference room could barely contain the crush of reporters and camera crews, so no one noticed when the door opened briefly, then closed again. All attention was on Jim Axelrod, passing out pens to the twelve directors preparing to endorse the most dramatic attack on gun violence in American history.

David Tischner was stepping forward to sign his name when a small boy wandered into view. His face lit up. "Andy!" he cried. "Andy, Andy!" He fell to his knees and seized his grandson in a YouTube scene that surpassed ten million views before midnight.

CHAPTER 28

The right thing

Andy Tischner wasn't much help to the FBI. His memories were random: daily homeschool lessons with Doctor Luke; playing with other children at a neighborhood park; helping Doctor Luke plant flowers; decorating a Christmas tree. After almost two years, Andy and Doctor Luke had become a family.

At first, Andy didn't remember David, Marla or his parents and found his reunion with them bewildering. But playing with his old toys in his old room seemed to comfort him. Jason and Alexis, afraid to let him out of sight, took turns watching over him as he slept.

Doctor Luke hadn't neglected his education. Andy could sing the ABC song, "The Star Spangled Banner," count up to one hundred and recite the Pledge of Allegiance. Marla was thrilled when he read *The Velveteen Rabbit* aloud without help.

Agent Rivers gave him time to get adjusted, then gently tried to pry out a description of his captor.

"He looked sort of like Daddy."

"How did he look like Daddy? In what way?"

Andy thought hard. "He was tall."

Rivers tried another approach. "Did Doctor Luke have a job? Did he leave you alone sometimes?"

"He stayed home and used the computer a lot. One day it was snowing and he said he was glad he didn't have to drive to work every day."

Rivers checked weather records for the past two years. Snow was a rarity around Sandstone. The boy's captivity had occurred somewhere else. The only landmarks he recalled were chain stores and restaurants found everywhere. Doctor Luke had a blue pickup truck, but Andy didn't know the make, model or license number. He offered a hazy account of an airplane ride and a flight attendant bringing him a carton of milk, but he wasn't sure whether that happened at the beginning or end of his captivity. He didn't remember his abduction from the playground.

A&R security cameras captured a hooded figure escorting Andy into the building with the news crews, then departing after sneaking him into the conference room. The figure strolled through the halls, out of the building and beyond camera range.

"Andy, did Doctor Luke tell you anything about himself?"

"He had a little girl who died, and he was lonely."

"Did he tell you how she died?"

"He said God took her away."

"Did he tell you her name?" The boy shook his head.

"Andy, did Doctor Luke do anything to hurt you?"

"No. When's he coming back?"

Because Andy's return coincided with A&R's signing ceremony, Agent Sanders speculated that Doctor Luke was an anti-gun activist. "Doctor Luke figured he could use David to manipulate the A&R board into a policy change, in order to get his grandson back. Sure enough, they fired Vern Saginaw and replaced him with Warren DeVries, a moderate. When Warren announced his plans for a gun conference, everything was going Doctor Luke's way. He probably planned to return Andy if the conference was successful. The shooting forced him to wait for the second one."

Agent Rivers disagreed. He still believed David's Twitter activity was the motive, and his apology mission was "the right thing." But the FBI found no massacre survivors or family members named Luke or Lucas. The only person who came close was Luke Hoyer, a teenager who died in the Parkland, Florida attack. Andy didn't know Doctor Luke's full name. Despite several weeks re-investigating families of high-profile shootings around the country, the FBI drew a blank.

Soon after Andy's return, Amy French received a FedEx package containing her pawned laptop. When she opened it, the screen displayed a brief MS Word message:

Dear Miss French,

Sorry for keeping this so long. You're an excellent writer.

Amy's yellow folder titled "Speech Contest Entries" was still there. She contacted the FBI, which dusted the computer for prints and performed a system search for deletions, emails, files, browsing history, and other clues, to no avail. Its memory had been wiped, the operating system reinstalled, the IP address changed again. "He must have bought the laptop here in Sandstone to throw us off," Agent Sanders said. "Make us think the kidnapping was local."

"Well, I wish I knew who he was," Agent Rivers sighed. "We could offer him a job."

By the time Andy came home, David Tischner had reverted to the man Marla married, so she dropped divorce proceedings and returned to him. Though he remained CEO of Pierpont, he resigned from the city council, apologizing personally to its members and publicly to the voters for his abrasive tenure. He also resigned from all his corporate boards except A&R and joined the board of Special Olympics, where he healed the breach with Jason by helping him raise funds and schedule activities for disabled young athletes.

One day, David got a call from Cynthia Turkle, whose daughter Melanie had died in the West Virginia preschool shooting. The Turkles were among the many families David had visited during his apology crusade.

"I was reading the news about your grandson's return," Cynthia explained, "and it reminded me of something. Shortly before Melanie was killed, her teacher asked the children to tell the class about their best friends. Melanie said one of them had a friend named Doctor Luke."

"Do you know which child it was?"

"Yes, it was Aubrey Morgan. She died in the shooting, too."

"That's a very promising lead, Mrs. Turkle. Thank you." Timothy and Cheryl Morgan were the only West Virginia parents David had been unable to contact.

His research turned up four Timothy Morgans in the Huntington area. One was a retired coal miner in a nursing home. Another was in prison for drug trafficking. Pfc. Tim Morgan was in the Army, stationed in Turkey. Timothy Wallace Morgan was in eighth grade.

A search for Cheryl Morgan revealed only one, killed in a car accident three years earlier. Her obituary contained no details about her husband. The funeral home that handled her burial could not find her computer records. County property tax rolls had no listings for Timothy or Cheryl.

"What is this guy, a ghost?" David wondered. He decided to contact Aubrey's school. "I'm sorry, Mr. Tischner," the administrator said. "All of Aubrey's records seem to be missing from our database."

"Somehow, I'm not surprised. May I speak with her teacher?"

"Yes, I'll have her call you."

"I remember Aubrey's story," Darla Lansing told him. "She said Doctor Luke took care of sick people. Aubrey was Doctor Luke's nurse. The two of them had their own hospital where they took people's temperatures and gave them shots and brought new babies into the world. Then one of the babies grew up, and he became a doctor too. All three of them went around healing people."

"Did she say anything that might help us identify him?"

"Mr. Tischner, Doctor Luke was an imaginary playmate."

He laughed. "I should have known."

"I asked Aubrey for the name of the baby who became a doctor. She said his name was Jesus."

"Of course! The Gospel according to Luke. Who was supposedly a physician. Well, at least we know Aubrey went to Sunday School. Did you ever meet her father?"

"Just once. I remember he was a quiet man, very polite. Mr. Tischner, if Tim Morgan did take your grandson, please go easy on him. We're all still trying to get over the shooting. He probably is, too."

"What do you think?" he asked Jason and Alexis. "Tim Morgan, alias Doctor Luke, stole almost two years of Andy's life. I'm sure the FBI can track him down with the information we've got now."

"Dad, you promised the guy that he wouldn't be punished if he returned Andy unharmed. He did what you asked."

"But he kidnapped your son!"

"David, he didn't hurt Andy," Alexis said, "and now he's all alone again.

Why send a man to prison who's already suffering the worst punishment a parent can know?"

David thought of his cemetery visits and the lonely headstones. "Well ... that's very considerate of both of you."

"What do you think 'the right thing' was, Dad? Renouncing the hoax theories? Apologizing to the families? Helping redirect Armed and Ready?"

"Maybe it was all those things. Even if Andy hadn't been kidnapped, I was on the verge of losing everything of value in my life. I like to think 'the right thing' was saving David Tischner."

David and Marla visited their daughters in an effort to mend fences. Veronica and Lesley had their own families by now. Both still harbored old resentments. But they admired their father's contrition and his enthusiasm for the grandchildren he'd never met. In time, he won them over.

David was never able to repair his rift with Vern Saginaw, who had dropped out of public life after the collapse of his new gun rights venture. David phoned occasionally, hoping to explain why he voted to oust his friend from the company he had founded and directed for sixty years. Vern never answered or called back, leaving David with another burden of regret to carry the rest of his life.

"I sure miss him," he confessed to Jason one Saturday as they watched Special Olympics athletes compete at a high school track. "Target shooting by yourself isn't much fun."

"I'm free next Saturday, Dad. Suppose I join you?"

David's face lit up. "I'd like that, Jason. I'd like that very much."

In April of her senior year, Amy French's teachers nominated her for class valedictorian. She refused the honor. "I had my chance with my class. This year belongs to someone else." She graduated with last year's juniors and listened as two classmates she had tutored made the speeches.

"What are you going to do now?" Shelley asked after the ceremony. "You must have had a lot of scholarship offers."

"I've already accepted one, to Redmont Christian Academy. I've been talking with Mr. Daniels about training for the ministry. He thinks I could make a good evangelist."

"That's wonderful! We could use some variety on Sunday mornings."

"I heard that," John said.

"You were supposed to," Shelley teased.

"Don't forget who's signing your paychecks." He gently pinched her arm. "Come see me next week, Amy. We have a lot to talk about."

Gil Starnes stayed with his foster family until he finished high school. In the meantime, he stopped at LaRonda's statue each day and thanked God for her. Gil went to college, majored in chemistry, and became a researcher for a pharmaceutical company. There he married a colleague, fathered three children and founded an organization to aid families of police officers killed or disabled in the line of duty.

Shaker rose to sergeant the year after LaRonda's death. Although he missed street action, he discovered he had a flair for administration. He gave up his apartment to live with Alvin, while Celeste continued as daytime aide. Combining their financial resources, the two men were able to pick up where LaRonda left them and live comfortably. Alvin reluctantly accepted the arrangement on the condition that Shaker bought himself season tickets to the symphony and got out of the house once in a while. Shelley or his mother covered for Shaker on such evenings.

One night, Shaker invited Shelley to a restaurant and a performance of Sibelius' Fifth Symphony. Shelley found the music boring, her classical experience limited to the Dvořák concerto. The evening only reminded Shaker gloomily of his last night out with LaRonda. He wished he'd suggested a movie instead.

Escorting Shelley to her door, he turned her to face him. They smiled into each other's eyes and slowly drew together in a kiss. Breaking apart, both looked away. "How about some coffee?" Shelley suggested.

They sat in the kitchen. "I guess I'm supposed to find someone to replace Hank and give Bruce a father. But if I let someone else take his place, I'll feel I've betrayed him." She took Shaker's hand. "You've been so wonderful to Bruce and me. Do you think we could go on just as we are? As the best of friends?"

"I'm counting on it. Shelley, tell the truth. Do you really believe LaRonda and Hank's deaths were acts of remorse?"

"Remorse? Atonement? Maybe both. They were as close to being pure souls as people ever get. I think that's why God answered their prayers, to remind us of what Jesus did to atone for us all. What do you think?"

He sighed. "It seems like something LaRonda would do. But I'm selfish. If she really did sacrifice herself, she robbed us of a happy life together. I have a hard time forgiving her for that."

After Shaker left, Shelley put on her new Dvořák CD and danced with Hank to the cello's mellow tones.

Charles Spurlock did not survive his second heart attack, so Shelley soon found herself at another funeral. After she got home, her mother phoned so often and sounded so pitiful that she invited Ivy to come live with her. At first, Ivy behaved like Shelley after Hank's death. She went to bed early, slept late, and moped around the empty house while Shelley and Bruce were away.

It was Bruce who saved her. The shrine to his father that he'd made of his room, his stories about his friends and teachers, his curiosity about his grandparents' nomadic lives, and his boyish good manners made Ivy fall in love with him. She could hardly wait for Bruce to return from school each day. She played hours of video games with him, forgetting that Charles had condemned them as "capitalistic pablum for the masses."

One morning, Shelley took Ivy across the street and introduced her to Abigail Morton. The two senior citizens began lunching and shopping together. Ivy helped Shelley with Senior Outreach and even joined her church. Eventually, she began looking for a job, to help Shelley pay the bills. John Daniels told the local director of Goodwill Industries about Ivy's activist history. The agency hired her as a job placement worker for homeless people.

Shelley was washing dishes one evening after putting a cake into the oven when she felt a hand on her shoulder. She turned to find Ivy smiling at her with damp eyes.

"What's wrong, Mom?"

"I'm so proud of you, Shelley. You married well, you've given me a wonderful grandson, and people here look up to you. Can you forgive me and your father?"

"For what?"

"Stealing your childhood."

Shelley embraced her mother. They stood together silently. At last she stepped back, wiped her tears and gripped Ivy's hands. "Want to help me frost this cake when it's done? It's a birthday surprise for Mrs. Pritchard. She'll be eighty-two tomorrow and she lives all alone."

"I'd love to, honey."

After a few months of mourning, Brenda DeVries became curious about Jerry Richards' family. News accounts revealed that he left behind a wife, two small children, and an overdue credit card bill for his travel expenses to Washington. The family was living on the mother's convenience store job and food stamps.

Tavia Richards had read everything she could find about Warren and the other conference victims. When Brenda phoned, Tavia was afraid to talk at first. After the initial awkwardness, she couldn't talk enough. "Jerry wasn't what the TV people made him out to be. He loved me and the kids, and he worked hard for us. He had a gift for fixing machinery, but he could never hold a job. Maybe if he hadn't been so wound up about politics and gun rights and stuff. He kept getting into arguments at work until they fired him from the bottling plant. Then, getting turned down over and over for other jobs made him ashamed. One day he just disappeared." The two widows shared stories about their children and built a long-distance friendship that helped both of them heal.

Following Armed and Ready's transformation, CNN did a follow-up story on the Garden of Remorse, showing that it still contained only one monument. Overnight, the memorial received a flood of applications from ex-soldiers, reformed criminals and others harboring guilty memories.

One of the first monuments came from the family of Pfc. Wendell Hendry, a veteran of World War II. Shortly before his death in 2005, Hendry wrote a letter to his children expressing sixty-one years of anguish over the Battle of Monte Cassino.

I saw so many guys in my outfit, guys I patrolled with and ate with and talked to every day, blown up by German artillery that I started taking it personally. Then one day we came across a bunch of

German soldiers hanging around a tank during a lull in the fighting. There were seven of them, smoking cigarettes, laughing, talking, unaware that we were watching from behind the trees. We charged and emptied our guns into them. At the time, it felt good to get back at the Germans. But it was also the first time I had ever killed anyone. Their eyes were just as shocked and lifeless as the eyes of my dead buddies.

After the war, I read a book about the battle of Stalingrad, how Hitler sacrificed thousands of his men just to avoid a humiliating retreat. Then he had to draft old men and boys to replace them. Hitler, Goering, and all the other Nazi monsters were out of my target range. They're the ones who deserved killing.

Now I feel sorry for those tank soldiers, and all soldiers who die because of evil or just plain incompetent leaders who start wars and don't have to pay the price for them. I pray you kids choose your leaders carefully, so you don't wind up killing somebody just because he's on the wrong side of a military map.

Hendry's children submitted the letter and a picture of their father in uniform, to be enshrined within a granite marker along the garden pathway.

There were other memorials on behalf of servicemen in subsequent wars. A Vietnam bomber pilot confessed that "hardly a day passed in those years that I didn't look down at the rice fields below and think of all the peasant farmers and their families who must be dying at my hands, even though they didn't know what the word communism meant."

Cole Parker was only sixteen when he robbed a pedestrian at gunpoint to earn membership in a gang. "She kept crying while I went through her purse," read the confession on his marker. "She said she'd lost her job, and fifty-two dollars was all she had to support her family for the rest of the month. Then she grabbed at the purse, and while we were fighting over it, my gun went off. Instead of joining the gang, I went to prison. I never did find out what happened to her kids."

Especially poignant were the confessions of people involved in accidental shootings. Robert McPherson submitted a picture of fourteen-year-old Courtney Mosley, along with the weapon that killed her.

My son Lance was showing my deer rifle to his best friend one day when it discharged through the window of my neighbors' house. Their daughter Courtney wanted to compete in the Olympics and was doing gymnastics exercises in her bedroom when it happened. The bullet tore through her heart and shattered the mirror where she was watching herself practice. The Olympics went on without her.

At the time, I blamed Lance for his carelessness. But he was only twelve, and it occurred to me later that I was the one who got him interested in guns. I was also the one who failed to make sure the rifle chamber was empty before I put it away. So even though I wasn't there, I killed Courtney Mosley just as surely as if I'd pulled the trigger myself.

We lost more than Courtney that day. Her parents never forgave us, and even after the jury ruled the shooting an accident, they sued us for wrongful death and drove our family into bankruptcy. Then they moved to another community to escape their memories.

Lance has never recovered. He flunked out of school and eventually became an alcoholic. My wife and I held it together for a while but finally got a divorce.

I haven't been hunting since that day, either. I don't know where I got the idea of hunting as a sport. If it is, it sure is one-sided, especially when you're on defense.

The most intriguing memorial had no text: just an M1 Garand rifle mounted next to pictures of two young men and two young women. Curious visitors who researched their names learned that all four had died in a thirteen-second fusillade of gunfire by Ohio National Guardsmen during a 1970 antiwar demonstration at Kent State University. The rifle was broken into two pieces. The monument had no signature.

CHAPTER 29

Ugly headlines

Andy Tischner's dramatic return at the signing ceremony launched Jim Axelrod's CEO career with a bang, and he took full advantage of it. He began by inviting America's gun retailers and manufacturers to a conference. The retailers came. The manufacturers boycotted.

"As you know, Armed and Ready has committed itself to a new firearms philosophy," he told his guests. "We will always support the right to bear arms. We will always support your right to sell them. But doing what's legal and doing what's ethical aren't always the same thing. Your merchandise is killing and maiming thousands of Americans every year, all in the name of the Second Amendment. That part of our Constitution was drafted in a spirit of patriotism. How can we call ourselves patriots if we turn a blind eye to an armed enemy ravaging our country from within? It's time for us to behave like patriots and fight back."

"What are you getting at, Jim?" asked Julian Welles of Sherrod's, a national sporting goods chain.

"I'm asking you to go along with Armed and Ready's new mission statement. Take responsibility for the danger your weapons pose to your fellow citizens."

The visitors rolled their eyes. "This is the same old dogma the anti-gun crowd's been preaching for years," Welles argued. "Blame the innocent for the actions of the guilty. Everyone knows firearms are deadly, just like smoking, hard drugs or reckless driving. Why should gun merchants be responsible for someone else's actions?"

"For one thing, it's in your own best interest. I don't hear drug makers or food companies complaining about the extra expense of seals on pill bottles and food jars. They're making sure their customers are safe. Why shouldn't gun vendors do the same thing?"

"Safety catches are standard features on firearms, Jim," Wade Moore of Lambert & Moore pointed out," and many of them have trigger locks and bore locks."

"Those devices only prevent accidents, not thousands of murders in the U.S. every year." Jim passed out copies of a document. "Today, I'm asking you to sign this pledge to do just three things: perform voluntary background checks on all your customers; observe a ten-day waiting period before every sale; and join our campaign against military-style weapons. In return, Armed and Ready will defend your Constitutional right to sell all firearms at all levels – local, state and federal."

"You just want us to give our word?"

"That's right."

"How is this pledge going to make people safer?"

"By living up to the pledge, you'll be keeping guns away from danger-ous people. Then, even if a customer does commit murder, you can say you did your best to prevent it."

"And if we refuse to sign?"

"That's up to you. But I'll make my own pledge. If a weapon you sell winds up in the wrong hands, you're going to make ugly headlines."

Jim mailed the document to all gun dealers not in attendance. About half of America's retailers signed it. All the manufacturers ignored it. Jim withheld the results from the news media. "I realize this is asking a lot from gun businesses," he told the A&R board. "We want give those who disapprove of the pledge a chance to think about it."

Meanwhile, Jim rerouted funds from A&R's lobbying budget to the company's new Gun Victims Foundation and appointed his aide, Barney Atherton, as administrator. Barney organized A&R's local chap-ters around the country into volunteer squads to investigate requests for financial assistance.

Soon afterward, a mass shooting took the lives of twenty-three people in Tupelo, Mississippi. Barney acted swiftly. He put Tupelo's A&R chapter to work identifying the dead and injured. A&R paid all funeral expenses, helped the uninsured with medical costs, and offered financial aid to the victims' families.

The killer had purchased his semiautomatic from Harlan's Sporting Goods in Tupelo. "Two weeks ago," Jim announced to the media, "Frank Harlan and Ogletree Manufacturing made a few hundred dollars on the sale of an assault weapon. The killer paid with a credit card. His twenty-three victims paid with their lives. Our Constitution gives us the right to bear arms. It does not give us the right to sacrifice our fellow Americans for profit. Those who do so are traitors to the very Constitution they hide behind."

"The man passed the background check," a harried-looking Frank Harlan told reporters defensively. "He seemed like an ordinary guy. I've sold dozens of semiautomatics, and not one customer has ever gone out and shot somebody with one of them."

"Until now. What if you'd made him wait ten days, like Armed and Ready is encouraging all retailers to do?"

"He'd have bought it somewhere else."

"What do you have to say to the victims and their families?"

"This isn't my fault! I'm a businessman, not a psychiatrist!"

"Harlan's Sporting Goods and its suppliers aren't the first businesses to exploit the Second Amendment," Jim remarked on a TV news show. "Tupelo is just the latest example of how we allow commercial motives to corrupt our Founding Fathers' good intentions. When we value commerce over public safety, we betray the spirit of our Constitution." Such a declaration by a gun rights organization was unprecedented. Frank angrily denounced A&R to the news media and canceled his membership. His customers held a rally outside his store and burned their A&R hats.

A month later, a young man bought a pistol at an Atlanta gun show, went home and murdered his parents and his sixteen-year-old sister. Police records showed the youth had a long record of violent outbursts. He bought the weapon from Clayton Beasley, a private collector.

Beasley was devastated. "I submitted a background check to NICS, just to be safe," he explained to reporters. "They had me on hold for ten minutes. I hated to keep him waiting, so I ran him through one of those independent online background checkers. He turned up clean. Later, I found out there are limits to those online apps." Jim used the incident to bolster his argument for ten-day waiting periods.

Jim kept A&R's pledge to gun dealers, suing three states that passed assault weapon bans and two others that raised the minimum age for purchasing a firearm from eighteen to twenty-one. "We don't need more laws, we need more responsible citizens," he explained at a news conference. "Let's count on people of good will to solve this problem voluntarily. That's the American way."

"Is A&R going to sue every government entity that passes gun control legislation?" a reporter asked. "Don't communities and states have a right to protect their citizens?"

"Sure they do. But laws don't keep people from getting shot. It's up to people to do that."

Two months later, when an Urbana, Illinois high school student shot three of his classmates with his father's Glock, Jim blamed the family. "They failed to store the gun safely, even though they knew he had emotional problems."

"So now you're playing God," Wade Moore remarked at the next teleconference. "Somebody gets shot, and you decide who's guilty."

"We're all guilty," Jim responded. "Armed and Ready is guilty. Gun makers, gun sellers, gun owners, social media, video game vendors, television, the movie industry. The whole American culture is guilty of proliferating and glamorizing firearms."

"What about you? You killed Jerry Richards with your .38. Yet here you are, telling the rest of us that guns don't stop violence."

"But why did Jerry turn to weapons in the first place?" Jim asked. "To express his anger. For years, our response to gun violence has been to defend the Second Amendment. Nobody speaks up for the victims. From now on, we share the blame, and we'll keep sharing it until this insanity stops."

Bowing to pressure, more gun retailers signed the pledge. But the manufacturers still balked. "What am I doing wrong?" Jim asked Barney. "I'm not asking for the moon, am I?"

"The manufacturers are a sort of club, Jim. Sure, they're a multi-billion-dollar industry, but their profits depend on the support of politicians. So they keep the palms greased. That's how they got the PLCAA."

"The what?"

"The Protection of Lawful Commerce in Arms Act. It gives gun makers almost total immunity to lawsuits involving gun violence. Congress passed it in 2005."

"So indirectly, they can get away with murder."

"An anti-gun activist would probably agree with you. But the manufacturers do have their own problems. Their profits are affected by political swings. After Sandy Hook, gun company stocks plummeted briefly. Then sales spiked because consumers feared a firearms ban was coming. There was another sales slump after Trump's election. It got so bad that some gun companies filed for bankruptcy, or retooled to produce other merchandise. Regardless of economic conditions, though, they've always kept a low profile. They never issue public statements about shooting deaths. Gun rights organizations like A&R have always taken the heat for them."

"And now we don't. Got any ideas on how I can get them back on our side?"

"Maybe one. A&R isn't the only gun lobbyist in the country, but we're the biggest. So we have the most influence. What if we could persuade the biggest weapons manufacturer to help us? Maybe then, the others would fall in line."

"How?"

"Talk to them away from the spotlight. One-on-one. With a personal approach, you might make some headway."

Lindsey Satterwhite didn't become CEO of Warner Munitions through business connections. At twenty, he was an assembly worker at the company's small arms plant in Athens, Georgia. The job paid his way through college while he advanced to production assistant, then manager, then supervisor. Before he turned fifty, he was on Warner's Board of Directors. A self-made man.

"Lindsey, you know the firearms industry inside and out," Jim told him over pre-dinner cocktails. "I'm just an old plumber trying to learn a new job. If you were in my position, what would you do?"

"I suppose I'd be schmoozing gun manufacturers," he grinned slyly.

"Did you think you could win me over with a martini and a porterhouse steak?"

"I wouldn't presume to try."

"I know all about your crusade, Jim, and you're wasting your breath. You can't buy me. Even A&R can't match what Warner Munitions spends on congressional reelection campaigns every two years."

"Lindsey, I didn't accept the A&R appointment for money, or because I've got a big ego. I don't even need a job anymore. But I care about what's happening with guns in this country. Don't you?"

"Sure I do. But the violence isn't my fault, or Warner's, or any other manufacturer's."

"Not directly, no. But there are bigger issues than gun rights at stake. You and I are the two people with the best chance to do something about them."

Satterwhite sipped his drink. "I'm listening."

"There's an anti-gun backlash across the country that poses a threat to our Constitution. It started long before I joined A&R. Hank Phillips' death and the conference massacre made it worse. Now, it escalates with every dramatic shooting. Sooner or later, it's going to sweep right over all of us. Before that happens, I want make sure it doesn't swamp our Constitution along the way. If the Second Amendment got repealed in this anti-gun fever, that would open the door to attacks on other elements in the Bill of Rights. Freedom of speech, the judicial system, maybe even the Constitution itself. I'm not just worried about guns, I'm worried about the pillars of our democracy. If you join my crusade, you'll be fighting to preserve the gun industry and your country at the same time."

"I think you're overselling your point, Jim."

"Not at all! Look at the First Amendment. Social media's so full of lies, you can't tell fact from fiction anymore. Sooner or later, Congress will be forced to impose free speech restrictions, and there's another item on the Bill of Rights under siege."

The steaks arrived. Lindsey cut into his and chewed thoughtfully. "All right. For the sake of argument, what are you asking me to do?"

"Warner Munitions is the biggest firearms manufacturer in America. Last year, *Forbes* ranked you fifth in the world. All the other manufacturers admire your business model. If you agree to the three points of A&R's new mission statement, the others might go along."

"The old domino theory?"

"Exactly."

"What do we get out of it? Coming out against assault weapons is like a car manufacturer going on TV and saying 'Driving is dangerous. Please don't buy my product.' You might save a few lives with semiautomatic bans, universal background checks and waiting periods. But attacking the sales process will just create a black market for guns. Legitimate gun businesses will lose money. Why should they cooperate?"

"There's more involved here than business considerations! Armed and Ready is fighting in the courts to protect your right to sell the very weapons used in domestic killings. You manufacturers could help us win this war by declaring, in one voice, that gun proliferation is a public health hazard."

Lindsey smiled indulgently. "Jim, you have a lot to learn about being a CEO. Even a guy like me answers to a board of directors. Those directors answer to their stockholders. Discouraging product sales is like picking the pockets of the people you were elected to serve."

"Stockholders aren't just a collection of investment portfolios. They're people with families and concerns about the world they live in. They can be reasoned with, and they'll respect you for putting the nation's welfare above their own personal gains. Lindsey, I'm not asking you to support any anti-gun legislation. Just voluntary precautions for the sake of your country's welfare. For the sake of its very future."

Lindsey put down his fork and sipped his drink. "You make a compelling argument, Jim. And I'll admit to you that I'm not a cold-blooded businessman, like most people think. I've got a family, too. My own kids harass me every time there's a mass shooting. But I don't own Warner Munitions, I just run it. Even if I wanted to, I couldn't make a unilateral move like this without consequences. The directors would vote me out, then repeal my decision."

"And there you'd be, with your golden parachute gently lowering you into retirement, while your fellow Americans are being slaughtered."

Lindsey scowled. "Now don't get nasty! You can't score points by trying to shame me into become a revolutionary!"

"You're right. I'm sorry." Jim gazed down at his steak. It was cold.

Lindsey studied him for a moment. "I know all about you. The conference massacre and its consequences. Killing Jerry Richards cost you, didn't it?"

"I dream about it almost every night. That's why I took this job."

"What does your wife say? You uprooted her from Little Rock and moved to Sandstone. Took her away from her children. Her grandchildren. Her church. Her friends. How's she handling it?"

"What did you do, hire a private eye?"

Lindsey smiled. "I started checking you out the day of your CEO appointment. I like to know who I'm dealing with, especially a potential enemy. How about answering my question?"

"You're right. Dorothy hated to leave Little Rock. Everything we love is there. But she went along because I needed it. What happened with Jerry Richards ... it was eating me up."

"So you risked everything for this crusade."

"Everything that mattered."

Lindsey dabbed his lips with a napkin. "That was a good steak. You haven't touched yours. Want a doggy bag?"

"No, I'm not hungry."

Lindsey summoned the waiter and asked for a take-out box. "Lunch at the desk tomorrow," he winked. "I hate to waste good food." He stood and shook his host's hand. "I don't have much use for revolutionaries, Jim. History shows they usually cause more problems than they solve. But I'll see what I can do."

As the weeks passed, Jim kept his campaign in the news with announcements and public appearances. He posted a running internet roster of dealers whose guns led to murder, and the amount of profit they made from each death. "Last week, six people died so your store could net $250," he challenged Bill Norris during a talk show. "That's about $41 per life. Is that how much you value your fellow Americans?"

"Who are you to decide who's responsible for someone's death?" Norris fired back. "You can't know what kind of weapon a killer is going to use."

"No, I can't. But this guy used a semiautomatic. If you'd joined A&R's campaign, you could have stopped him."

"If he was determined to kill those people, he'd have found another way."

The debate wore on. Then one morning, Barney burst into Jim's office. "Turn on the TV, quick!"

A reporter appeared on the screen. "In a stunning turnaround for America's firearms industry, Warner Munitions announced today that it is discontinuing domestic sales of its semiautomatic weapons and joining Armed and Ready's crusade against gun violence. Warner CEO Lindsey Satterwhite issued a statement following a board meeting at company headquarters."

Jim and Barney whooped, jumped up and down, hugging each other as Satterwhite appeared before the cameras. "Armed and Ready has taken a bold step forward with its campaign against gun violence. We at Warner Munitions believe it is time to put aside business concerns and join that campaign. Beginning immediately, we are suspending all domestic sales of our Strike Force Repeater assault weapons. To prevent a consumer run on this product, today's action includes an immediate recall of all SFRs currently in retail stores, as well as elimination of all SFR on-line sales. Furthermore, effective today, Warner Munitions is instituting a ten-day waiting period for all our domestic firearm sales, while continuing to comply with the federal mandate requiring criminal background checks."

Later, Jim called Lindsey to thank him. "Don't get too excited," the chairman replied. "We didn't give up much. Domestic sales account for less than one percent of our annual revenue. The military contracts are our bread and butter. Otherwise, I couldn't have gotten away with this."

"Then why did you give me such a hard time about it?"

"Vern Saginaw and I go back a long way. The gun industry had some leverage with A&R until they kicked him out. Now, you've come along and changed the game. Anyway, I've been thinking of dumping assault weapons for quite some time. But I wanted to feel you out first, make sure you were someone I could go to the wall with."

"Well, thanks. I appreciate your confidence."

"Jim, don't think you've won the war. Gun manufacturers are a maverick bunch. Most are legit, but there are some shady characters and a lot of dirty money in the mix. You're not going to win the others over as easily as you did me."

Jim soon realized that Lindsey was playing another angle with his announcement. The Warner brand name became a symbol of integrity in the tarnished world of gun manufacturing. Sales of Warner hunting

gear, handguns and accessories increased twenty-eight percent in the following quarter.

Armed and Ready's Second Amendment commitment bore fruit.
Courts responded to Jim's lawsuits by overturning all the gun restrictions
he challenged. Meanwhile, Lindsey Satterwhite's announcement put the
other manufacturers on the hot seat. Barney turned up the heat, compil-
ing data from gunfire crimes all over the nation, publishing the names of
victims, the weapons that killed them, and the manufacturers' names. He
produced statistics comparing deaths and injuries to sales profits. None
of the figures were new; none of the stories were unique. But coming
from America's leading gun rights organization, they packed a wallop of
bad publicity. "Armed and Ready announced today that it has paid $1.3
million in medical bills, burial costs and financial aid to victims of the
Tupelo massacre," a TV newscaster said. "CEO Jim Axelrod called on
firearms businesses to do their part to prevent such tragedies."

The hold-out manufacturers fought back, withdrawing their A&R
advertising, cancelling their corporate donations, and funneling their
support to smaller firearms lobbyists.

"You're going to drive us out of business!" Calvin Butcher wailed at an
A&R board meeting.

"Be patient," Jim responded. "Remember the basketball story." Firearms dealers suffered increasing embarrassment from news stories and
on-line popups announcing where the murderers bought their weapons.
"Armed and Ready announced today that it has paid $250,000 to victims
of an AR-15 attack that took seven lives here in Des Moines last September," a newscaster said. "The gun dealer, Thorne's Hunting Supply,
declined to comment." The public backlash against guns grew with each
new attack, and with each news video showing A&R members around
the nation working on behalf of victims. Over a six-month period, NICS
reported a fifty-eight per cent increase in background checks. Gun shops
began to impose waiting periods on all gun customers. By the end of
the year, semiautomatics had almost completely disappeared from retail
outlets and gun shows.

Jim didn't forget his base of support. A&R continued its national
target competitions and free gun safety clinics. The A&R magazine
and website ran positive articles about game hunting, target shooting and home defense weapons. The website offered videos of people

pursuing legitimate hunting and shooting activities. Other stories praised gun sellers whose background checks caught convicted criminals attempting to buy firearms. A special A&R publication honored Vern Saginaw and other Americans who devoted their lives to preserving the Second Amendment.

As the Garden of Remorse added new memorials, the TV networks broadcast heart-rending stories about them. *The New York Times* ran a lengthy series on American families torn apart by gun violence.

The results were mixed. By the end of that year, gun deaths nationwide had dropped twenty-three percent. But A&R membership suffered a similar decline as hardline gun owners abandoned the organization. The A&R directors called an emergency meeting, sparking rumors that Jim was on his way out. But he was ahead of everyone.

"I'm pleased to announce that we have some new friends," he told the board. "The Committee for School Safety wants to form a partnership with A&R. And five anti-gun groups are interested in working with us."

"That's all very warm and fuzzy," Harvey Wexler said, "but won't this prove we've gone over to the enemy?"

"All these institutions have promised to join our campaign against legalized gun control. Their support makes the Second Amendment safer than ever. In other words, gentlemen, that particular battle is over."

Jim kept his job. A&R's new alliances prompted Congress to approve an amendment to the tax code allowing deductions for corporations that helped gun violence victims. Congressmen, no longer caught in the middle of the gun issue, endorsed A&R's campaign and hosted fund-raising events on its behalf. Smaller gun rights organizations joined the bandwagon. Eventually, even some of the rebellious donors and advertisers returned to A&R.

A few of the manufacturers surrendered partially, agreeing to the ten-day waiting period. Lambert & Moore stopped selling semiautomatics to retail outlets, since most weren't stocking them anyway. However, it continued selling them online.

Despite all Jim's victories, the killing went on. There were two more school shootings the following year, with semiautomatics as the weapons of choice. But when several congressmen introduced legislation to ban them, A&R's lawyers fought for the Second Amendment.

"Rome wasn't built in a day," Jim said at the annual A&R convention.

"But look how much we've done in just one year. Our Constitution is still intact. Our organization has new respect. Gun fatalities are down. Our country is in a mood of compromise. And we did it all without a single new law."

CHAPTER 30

A substitute for somebody else

Shaker kept his word to Alvin and attended every symphony concert the season after LaRonda's death. He sat glumly in the audience, the music reviving memories of their final date, their intimate chat in the coffee shop, their first kiss, and his marriage proposal. "This is a waste of time and money," he muttered, driving home after one performance. "I'll never be able to let her go this way."

He took a day off from work and drove to Livingston, where his police badge got him past the guard towers and razor wire into the Polunsky Unit, Texas' Death Row. A guard led him along the gloomy corridor. "The warden said take all the time you want, but I gotta stay here and watch you." Unlocking the cell door, the guard left it open and leaned against the wall.

Short as he was, Dixie Prince seemed shrunken since his conviction. Reclining on a cot, he eyed Shaker apathetically. "Who are you?"

"I'm Officer Patterson, Sandstone Police. I want to ask you something about LaRonda Cage."

"Get lost." Prince turned away and closed his eyes.

"It'll only take – "

"I don't gotta answer no more cop questions! Beat it!"

Shaker sat on the cot at Prince's feet. He waited silently. And waited. "You ain't goin' away, are you?"

"Nope."

"All right. What?"

"Right before you shot Officer Cage, she said something to you. What was it?"

"Why?"

"A witness in her patrol car said you rolled down the window and she spoke to you. What did she say?"

"What difference does it make? She's dead. So am I, once they reject my appeal."

"LaRonda Cage was my girl."

The man sat up and regarded Shaker for a moment. "If you're trying to make me feel guilty, you're wasting your time, lover boy."

Shaker had left his service pistol at the security gate. He figured he had about ten seconds to grab Prince by the throat and strangle the life out of him before the guard could stop him. Prince seemed to read his mind. "Go ahead," he smirked. "Nothing to do in this place anyway, and the food's lousy."

Shaker closed his eyes, counted to ten and thought of Alvin. "Just tell me what she said. Please. It can't matter to you."

"I get it. You want to know what her last words were." Prince walked over to the bars, his back to Shaker. "It's not too late."

"Too late for what?"

"That's what she said. She tapped on the window. I rolled it down while I reached for the gun with my other hand. I figured to climb out, make her lie down and cuff her with her own handcuffs." Prince's eyes focused on a corner of the cell, as though seeking an answer. "But she didn't order me to get out. She just said, 'It's not too late.'"

"And that's all?"

"It threw me off. I didn't know what to do. She was looking at me with those deep brown eyes, waiting for me to ... I don't know what. Anyhow, the next thing I knew, there was a bang and she disappeared. It was like watching a movie. Then I was *in* the movie, cranking the engine and hitting the gas." He turned to Shaker, his eyes burning. "Why did she say that? What kinda cop pulls you over and says, 'It's not too late'?"

Shaker realized he'd been holding his breath. "And that's all she said?"

Prince returned to his cot. "I didn't wanna kill her. I just didn't wanna get caught." He lay down. He stared at the ceiling. "Satisfied?"

Shaker rose and exited the cell. The guard locked the door.

"Hey, boyfriend. You gonna tell me what it means? You're the one who knew her."

"If you haven't figured that out by now, it is too late." He turned to the guard. "Let me out of here."

The spring concert featured Brahms' D Minor Piano Concerto. Shaker slouched in his seat as the orchestra warmed up, resigned to another melancholy evening. But when the guest soloist walked onstage, he sat up. Her radiant smile and poise as she bowed and settled herself at the piano took his breath away. Shaker had never heard of Marianne Silva. Her face was a stranger's. But everything else about her was LaRonda.

He sat mesmerized as the orchestra launched into Brahms' stormy first movement. The woman's intense focus, her facial expressions and her ecstatic keyboarding brought out qualities in the piece he'd never noticed before. Or maybe she was playing it as LaRonda might have done if she'd been a musician instead of a cop.

Shaker couldn't take his eyes off Marianne Silva for the entire performance. After the applause, he followed the audience to the reception room, where he found her autographing programs and chatting with admirers. Shaker stood apart, absorbing her beauty, smile and gentle voice.

As the crowd diminished, her LaRonda eyes cast a curious glance his way. Shaker stepped forward to offer his program. "Do I know you?" she asked, signing and returning it to him. "I get the feeling you think you know me."

"Sorry, I guess I was staring. It's just that you remind me of someone."

"Now there's a stale pickup line."

He laughed. "I didn't mean it that way. My name is Shaker Patterson. I'm a police officer."

Her eyebrows rose. "Am I under arrest? I played the best I could."

"You were terrific."

"So, I look familiar to you. Maybe you saw my picture somewhere. I'm not famous, though. This is my professional debut."

"Well, it's not your face. It's..." He looked around. Others were waiting to chat with the soloist. "Could we talk some more when you're finished here? Maybe I could buy you a drink."

"Show me your badge." Shaker drew it from his pocket. "Well, I couldn't be in safer company, could I Sergeant Patterson? If you don't mind waiting a few minutes, I'd love to accept your offer."

Marianne revealed that as a teenager she had qualified for the Juilliard School. Unable to afford its extravagant tuition, she supported herself by giving private piano lessons while earning a performance degree at Sandstone University. Pursuing her dream of a concert career, she lived like a pauper, saving every penny for traveling and appearing in some of the top piano competitions around the world. It was an uphill battle against the younger talents who tended to charm audiences and judges. However, she did win second place often enough to get noticed. So tonight, at age twenty-nine, Marianne Silva had played professionally for the first time.

"Enough about me," she said. "Who is it I remind you of?" She listened as Shaker unburdened himself. "So I seem a lot like LaRonda to you?"

"Well ... you don't look anything alike. But you have a way about you that ... Did you ever just *know* something?"

"Like intuition? Yes, in a way. I've always known I was meant to play the piano."

"Then you know what I mean. So I just had to come backstage and talk to you."

"I'm glad you did," she smiled coyly. "This night has turned out even better than I'd hoped."

It was only a week later that Shaker introduced Marianne to Alvin, whose jaw dropped the moment she walked through the door. "Welcome to my home," he managed to croak, his eyes moistening as he took her hand.

Shaker courted Marianne aggressively as the weeks passed. "I never go anywhere, I'm so busy with music," she told him. "You're the first date I've had in about six years."

"That's another way you remind me of LaRonda." He juggled his work schedule to follow her to concert bookings in other cities, leaving his mother to stay overnight with Alvin. The depth of Marianne's repertoire amazed Shaker. She played chamber music in trios and quartets. She played Chopin scherzos and Mozart sonatas. Wherever she went, audiences loved her.

But at every performance, Shaker couldn't help imagining that it was LaRonda at the keyboard. During visits with Alvin, Marianne noticed Shaker's eyes wandering to her picture on the wall. Alvin kept forgetting himself and calling her LaRonda. Both of them looked at Marianne as though she were someone else. Rehearsing in her apartment, Marianne would glance up from her piano, catch the trance in Shaker's eyes, and turn grimly back to her sheet music.

One night after a performance in Houston, she became quiet as they dined in a restaurant, picking at her meal and avoiding his gaze. "Are you okay?" he asked. "You look like you got a bad review or something."

"Shaker, this isn't some movie like 'Sleepless in Seattle,' or 'Vertigo.' I'm not LaRonda. I'm me."

"Yes, you are. And you're everything I loved about her."

"But I'm *not* her! And this romance isn't going anywhere unless you make up your mind which one of us you want."

"I want both of you."

"You can't *have* both of us! She's *dead!*" Marianne fled. He paid the bill and hurried outside to find her crying in the parking lot. "Shaker, I'm tired of coming in second. And I won't be also-ran to a ghost!"

Shaker felt like a heel. He tried to convince Marianne that he loved her for herself. But at home, LaRonda's pictures and invisible presence stalked him from room to room. "I want to marry her," he told Shelley. "But I'm in the same spot LaRonda was in. I have to look after Alvin. If Marianne and I live there, LaRonda will always be between us."

"Then you have to find a place of your own."

"How? Alvin needs me."

"Maybe we can figure out a way to pay for round-the-clock care."

He shook his head. "Celeste's only available weekdays, and we can't afford more people from her agency the rest of the time. Besides, he deserves friends, not sitters."

"Let me think about this."

"Absolutely not!" Alvin declared. He wheeled himself away from Shelley, who followed him into the kitchen.

"Alvin, I'm going to have to sell my house anyway. I can't afford it much longer on what I make with Senior Outreach."

"No! Shelley, this is far beyond the call of friendship. You and Bruce have your own lives and your own problems."

"Well, moving in with you would solve one problem. And it would free Shaker and Marianne to build a life of their own."

Alvin sagged. "God, why did you do this? I've lost my wife. I've lost my daughter. Half my body. My career. I'm like Job, a thing to be tended, like a wilted shrubbery in somebody's yard! What did I do to deserve this?"

Shelley kneeled. "Alvin, God's not done with you yet. If He was, you wouldn't be here." She cupped his chin and raised his eyes to hers. "I have to find a cheaper place for Bruce and me anyway. You'd be doing us a favor. Besides, I love you. I love anybody who likes my cooking."

He laughed through his tears. "What about your mother? I've only got one extra bedroom."

"She wants to move in with Abigail Morton across the street from me. They're both widows and they've become close friends. Bruce could take over your extra room. I could use LaRonda's. With your permission, of course."

Alvin embraced her. "Shelley, I don't know what to say."

"Yes is good enough for me."

Marianne still had doubts. "Shaker, even if you do love me for myself, Alvin's your friend. And I can tell he thinks of me as LaRonda. He's counting on me to take her place."

"How do you feel about that?"

"Alvin's sweet. But I've struggled my whole life to become what I am. I can't be two people. Maybe this isn't going to work."

Shaker skipped her next road trip and spent the weekend thinking things over. "What's your favorite concert city in America?" he asked when she returned.

"New York or Boston, I suppose. Why?"

"What if we moved to one of those places? With my background, I can probably get on with either police force. Then we wouldn't be around Alvin so much, and it would help me forget LaRonda."

"You're willing to give up your life here? Your job, your friends, everything?"

"Anything to prove I love you for yourself."

They were sitting in her apartment. Marianne moved to the piano and picked aimlessly at the keys.

"Shake, you fell in love with me because I reminded you of LaRonda.

No matter where we went, I could never run away from that. If we got married, I'd always know I was a substitute for somebody else."

"Does that mean you won't marry me?"

"It means I have to give you up or accept things as they are." She raised her tearful eyes to him. "And I know I can't give you up. You're the man I play this piano for."

Shelley put her house on the market. By the time she found a buyer, Shaker and Marianne were married, with Shelley as matron of honor and Alvin as best man. Shaker moved into his bride's apartment, while Marianne continued teaching music and building her performance résumé.

Shaker kept courting her even after the wedding. He sent her flowers and texted love notes when she was on the road. He studied piano with her and learned some simple tunes. He took a cooking class and prepared her favorite meals, which she dutifully consumed even when he botched them.

One evening, Marianne walked onto the Civic Center stage and found the first seven rows full of uniformed cops, applauding her entrance. Shaker grinned at her from a front row seat. Stunned, she turned to see the conductor and musicians grinning too. As the noise diminished, she turned back to Shaker. "How in the world did you pull this off?"

"Shut up and play, lady!" he replied. The audience laughed.

She took her seat and looked up at the conductor. "How does this thing go again?" More laughter. Marianne smiled gratefully at Shaker as the orchestra struck up Mozart's C-Major Concerto.

At the reception, Marianne met Captain Vanderbilt. "Did you have anything to do with this?"

"Shaker and I thought it was about time these guys got some culture."

"What about the people who had season tickets for those front rows?"

"The symphony staff contacted everyone and told them what was up. They moved to other seats to get in on the fun."

"How sweet! I hope all those cops liked the music."

"Whether they did or not, they came because they were Shaker and LaRonda's friends. And now they're yours."

Shelley and Bruce sold their excess furniture and settled in with Alvin. Celeste continued as his daytime companion. In her new home, Shelley found herself surrounded by LaRonda wherever she turned. It gave her a wistful kind of peace. "I wish Hank and LaRonda had known each other," she told Alvin. "I wish we'd all known each other. If only the guns hadn't gotten in the way."

Soon afterward, Marianne invited Alvin, Shelley and Bruce to dinner and played a little jazz piano for them.

"That's wonderful," Alvin applauded. "Now let's hear something classical."

"I thought you didn't like that kind of music."

"LaRonda did."

Marianne's eyes met Shaker's. She patted Alvin's hand and introduced him to Beethoven's Moonlight Sonata.

One day, Alvin got a call from Captain Vanderbilt. "I've got a rookie officer who was shot in a drug raid last week. Looks like he's going to end up like you, Alvin. Would you be willing to work with him and his family?"

"Doing what?"

"The emotional and practical adjustments they'll have to make. This guy's only twenty-three. He's got a wife and two small children. After what you and LaRonda went through, I thought you might be able to help them."

"Don, I'd be glad to." Alvin hung up the phone and wept. It was the first time in thirteen years that he'd felt needed. Shelley chauffeured him to the young family's home, where he shared his own experiences with the demoralized couple. He showed them his spoon dolls and puppets. "If you can't do what you want anymore, you just do what you can," he told the man. Over a period of weeks, Alvin helped pull the cop out of his depression and convince him he was still valuable as a husband and father.

The experience got Alvin to thinking. He went on line and applied for a volunteer counseling job with the Veterans Administration. After he completed the training program, the agency was delighted to have him. "I wish I'd thought of this a long time ago," he told Shelley after a day with disabled soldiers home from combat.

"See?" she replied. "I told you God wasn't done with you."

Sometimes Shelley felt guilty about letting Bruce grow up without a father. Still, she kept her promise to herself and never remarried. Bruce got his male nurturing from Matt, Shaker and Alvin. "I always wanted

LaRonda to give me a grandchild," Alvin told Shelley. "In a tragic way, she did." When Bruce turned twelve, he graduated from Cub Scout to Boy Scout. The three men helped him celebrate with a camping trip that included Macy and other members of his troop. When school was out, Bruce swam regular races with Alvin in the therapy pool, each pretending to let the other win.

Matt was still the football coach by the time Bruce reached high school. He played wide receiver and defensive back. Macy became Mason, a hard-hitting ballcarrier and linebacker. Matt showed no favoritism. He yelled at both of them.

Soon after Bruce's sixteenth birthday, Shelley received a call from the manager of a nursing home. The man had heard about Shelley's outreach work and offered her a job as a caseworker, at higher pay than the church could afford. Health insurance and a 401(k) plan came with the job.

"What do you think?" she asked Bruce. "Should I take it?"

"You've earned it, Mom. Grab it before they ask somebody else."

"Don't worry about Senior Outreach," John Daniels told her. "The volunteer base you've built up is bound to have somebody qualified to replace you."

The offer was tempting. Shelley's income was smaller than Shaker's, so she and Alvin had to watch their money carefully. But Shelley loved Senior Outreach. She had emotional ties to the people she served and to her volunteer staff. It was Hank's letter that helped her decide. If he could be brave enough to walk away from A&R, she could be brave enough to stay put. Shelley's faith bore fruit over the years as several of her clients died and left parts of their estates to the church. The elders used the windfalls to raise her salary. Eventually, she paid off Alvin's mortgage, greatly easing their monthly burden.

Bruce and Mason graduated from high school, both with honors. Their proud parents were surprised when they announced they were postponing college to work with the Afghanistan Relief Organization. "Afghanistan was a war zone before Dad was even born," Bruce explained. "It still is. I want to help those people. I think it would have meant a lot to Dad." The two young men spent the next five years teaching elementary school courses to children in war-ravaged villages.

A few months after the boys left, Shelley was at a nursing home, visiting a woman who'd undergone a knee replacement. As they chatted in the common room, she noticed an old man sitting alone in a far corner, watching TV. Something about him seemed familiar.

Wrapping up her visit with the patient, Shelley approached the man. Then it hit her. "Vern!" she whispered. "Vern Saginaw!"

He didn't seem to hear her. His eyes stared vacantly at the screen. The robust, self-assured champion of gun rights was gone.

She summoned an aide. "I know this man. Do you know what's wrong with him?"

"Yes, Mr. Saginaw actually belongs in our Alzheimer's unit. We bring some of them up to this floor once in a while to give them a change of scenery. Most of them are too unpredictable to be let outside."

"What about his family? Is he all alone?"

"He has a son who visits when he's in town. Mr. Saginaw's wife died a long time ago. I don't know about any other relatives. Are you a friend of his?"

"Well, yes I was, in a way." She recalled her bitter words at Hank's funeral. "So does he just sit in a chair all day? Nothing else?"

"Alzheimer's patients are all different. You never know what they might do. But yes, he's mostly quiet." The aide noticed the Bible in Shelley's hand. "If you're really interested, he does like to be read to. He seems to brighten up when he hears people speaking."

The aide moved away. Shelley turned back to Vern, who remained docile. She turned off the TV and pulled up a chair.

"Hello, Vern. It's Shelley Phillips. Hank's wife. Do you remember me?"

Vern turned slowly to face her. His expression remained blank.

"I understand you like stories and reading. May I read to you for a while?" She opened her Bible, searching for an appropriate place to begin. Then she thought of the perfect passage, from Isaiah. She cleared her throat and began.

Many peoples will come and say,
"Come, let us go up to the mountain of the Lord,
*   to the temple of the God of Jacob.*
He will teach us His ways,
*   so that we may walk in His paths."*

The law will go out from Zion,
the word of the Lord from Jerusalem.
He will judge between the nations
and will settle disputes for many peoples.
They will beat their swords into plowshares
and their spears into pruning hooks.
Nation will not take up sword against nation,
nor will they train for war anymore.

If you liked this book, please share it with a friend.
This book is also available through Kindle Publishing at
Amazon.com

Made in the USA
Columbia, SC
21 December 2024

50422652R00161